CAKED IN DUST

MEL A ROWE

COPYRIGHT

***Caveat: As a courtesy, there may be some sparse language choices in this story that may represent an obstacle for the reader and I am offering this warning. Please note this language is purely for fictional purposes only and not designed to offend any individual persons, culture, or religions implied.*

*The Following Is Written in Australian English

I consider the ELSIE CREEK SERIES a love letter to the unique individuals that continue to shape the Northern Territory into a truly amazing part of Australia.
My dad would've loved it.

ONE

Chasing down a water buffalo before breakfast was not how Lucy had pictured the start of her day. Sipping a coffee to watch the stunning sunrise would've been better than this.

'Come on, Cecil, you can't pluck the weeds today.' She kicked at a stone, stepping over the metal railway line that sliced through the outback's centre and disappeared into the never-wherever of Northern Australia.

She patted the large rump of the pygmy buffalo as he sniffed at a bunch of limp lotus flowers lying before a pair of white-painted crosses. A slight breeze carried the scents of dust, cattle, the warmth of summer, and the echo of children singing.

Cecil raised his big head as goose bumps squirrelled along Lucy's spine and they both stopped to search for the childlike singing floating in the darkness.

Her eye caught the train station's kitchen lights streaming through the open doorway where music played inside. Music her boss would never approve of.

'Look, Cecil, I've got a beautiful bunch of flowers with your name on it, smuggled fresh from the pub's kitchen, just for you. Don't tell them or I might lose my other job.' She held out a posy of sad daisies that made the buffalo's eyes shine.

'Where's your crazy chook friend? Not awake yet?' Again, she peered into the shadows, this time searching for the menacing red-feathered fowl who had a habit of attacking people. No wonder their town's softball coach was threatening to turn it into a Sunday roast.

Wild birds stirred with their morning song, as the pink haze of dawn chased the violet night sky. It led the chorus of slow murmurs from hundreds of brahman cattle contained within the station's fenced yards. But no red hen.

And she had yet to coax its furry partner in crime off the tracks.

'If you care to follow me, good sir, I have your standard train day reservation of breakfast with a view.'

A white daisy hung from the lips of the beast as he chewed on the posy, while Lucy untangled the ribbons wrapped around his wide horns. Cecil's black coat was covered in a mash of coloured chalk. No doubt the kids at the small bush school had drawn all over him.

At the rear of the Tea House that made up part of the Elsie Creek train station, Lucy safely secured Cecil into his pen with fresh food and water.

She grabbed her two-wheeled trolley filled with milk crates, dragging it behind her. She passed the packed cattle yards, up to the back shed with its dim glowing globe covered in a swirl of bugs performing their strange tornado dance. It barely gave enough light for her to steer around the outstretched swags holding snoring stockmen spread across the veranda.

The nearby car park held four massive road trains, taller than houses, their empty trailers snaked behind them.

They overshadowed the assorted utes that held more sleeping stockmen in their back trays.

It was so typical for train days.

Lucy pushed on the small shed's sliding door. Its ear-splitting squeal made her flinch, stopping the chorus of snorers. 'Sorry,' she muttered in reply to the men's grumbles and groans.

Flicking on the light, she dragged her trolley inside as more stockmen stirred from their swags, sliding on their wide-brimmed Akubra's before slipping on their boots. They stretched, dusted themselves off, and with toothbrushes and towels they swaggered towards the rainwater tank.

Lucy checked on the urn resting beside the trays of mugs next to the tea and coffee jars. From her trolley, she pulled out the large plastic containers, removed their lids allowing the aromas to escape into the shed's air, still warm from the oven. She was proud she hadn't burned this morning's batch of hearty bacon and egg muffins, thick slices of buttery banana bread, and the crowd's favourite of Anzac biscuits to slip into their pockets for later. It wasn't much, but the men never complained.

'Morning, Miss,' said the stockman, tapping the brim of his sweat-stained hat.

'Morning.' He was handsome, yet familiar to her. Even though they all looked the same with their deep suntanned faces and collared shirts stiff with sweat and dust. Wide-brimmed hats shaded their eyes as they wiped away the sleep with work-hardened hands.

'How's your dad?' He asked, making himself a cuppa as the scuffle of many boots started a line behind him.

'Good.' Lucy shrugged, dishing out her food while wracking her brain over who this guy was.

'Where's you dad these days?'

'Out back of Mataranka.'

'Say G'day to him for me?'

'Sure.' *Whoever you are?* Why was he talking to her? No one talked to her—especially cute stockmen. 'Um, I'd better go open the kitchen.'

'Shame they won't let us mob eat in there, then you wouldn't have to cart this lot down here.'

'I don't mind. Besides, it's Nancy's place, Nancy's rules.' Nasty Nancy refused anything with dust, coffee, or cattle inside her traditional Tea House—which excluded all things male.

'If any of you care to donate to the cuppa cause…' She held her breath placing the empty coffee tin onto the bench. This honour system worked well so she didn't have to hang around. 'Please don't take the mugs with you or I'll cop an earful from Nancy complaining about stockmen stealing her crockery.'

'No worries, Miss. We wouldn't want the Station Hand's daughter getting into trouble.'

Again, she wracked her brain at how she knew the guy, but was too shy to ask.

'Your dad would skin us alive with his stock whips to make himself a new pair of boots for himself, if we mucked up your day, Miss,' said another stockman, sliding a bunch of gold coins into the tin before grabbing a mug.

'And then some,' mumbled the cute stockman, taking a bite of his muffin. 'But these are the best.' He pulled some bills from his dust-stained denim pockets and popped them into the tin. 'Please give Nancy our compliments on her cooking.'

'Erm, sure.' Unlike Lucy, Nancy had the sparkly reputation as the cake queen of scones and sponges in this town.

But Nancy never cooked for these men.

Dragging her trolley back to the kitchen, baking aromas lingered in the air. A new playlist from her housemate livened up the atmosphere as she entered the dining room.

One of the ancient ceiling fans groaned and rattled as it wound up like an unbalanced aeroplane propeller. She frowned at its irritating squeak with each rotation of its wide blades. Would it survive the day?

Lucy opened the glass bifold doors hoping to remove any scents of her baking business. They wouldn't be open for long before the heat, cattle dust, and flies would stir with the rising sun to drive everyone crazy.

Yet, with hints of frangipani and wild jasmine growing in the nearby local park, it disguised the corralled cattle, making it sweetest this time of the morning at the station. It matched the sky's pink hazy highlights in the lengthening clouds that stretched across an infinite horizon.

With a watering can in one hand, and a wrapped muffin and coffee mug in the other, she headed for the station's main platform.

The only bench seat, with a plaque for some long-forgotten reason, was now a part-time shelter for Homeless-Hank.

'Hank. Hank.' Lucy poked at his shoulder as he lay asleep across the bench.

'What?'

'Have some brekkie. Come on, you don't want the Station Master—or worse, Nancy, catching you.'

Hank sat up, his wild hair and beard as woolly as a bushman who'd been out scrub for far too long.

'Ta,' Hank croaked out. His shaky hands gripped the mug as he slurped his coffee. 'Train day, huh?'

'Yep.' She watered the thirsty potted palms, then grabbed the broom and swept what she could to at least last the morning rush.

Lucy brushed the fine layer of grit from her cheek as the humidity climbed higher, making her dress stick to clammy skin. Fine floating red dust particles fell over every uncovered surface. Sweat trickled along her hairline as she gazed at the tease of heavily pregnant clouds in the distance.

It hadn't rained in months. And like everyone else in the Northern Territory, she hoped today would be the day it rained. Really rained. Not some sprinkling shower—Lucy wanted walls of water!

'What time is the train due?' Hank asked between mouthfuls. His hand steadier as he sipped from the mug.

A light came on at the Station Master's house highlighting the Stock Inspector's vehicle parked out front, catching both their attentions.

'In an hour,' she said.

'They've got a lot of cattle out back.'

'I reckon it's the last big run of the musters, before the wet.'

'I know nothing about cattle, but all I smell is cattle.' He screwed up his nose.

'You get used to it. And the dust. And the heat. And the flies—no, you never get used to the flies.' It's what she hated the most about this time of year, the small sticky black flies.

A set of car lights flashed from the town's main street and crossed the train tracks, its squeaking suspension a dead giveaway.

'Hank, she's here.'

'Bugger. Where's Cecil?'

'In the pen.'

'Good.' Hank bundled up his tattered hessian sack that tinkled with tins and other metals. 'I'll leave your cup by the back door. Best batch of muffins you've made yet,' he said, screwing up the napkin and tossing it into the rubbish bin.

Her smile broke wide. 'I'll sneak you a refill later.'

'Coffee?' Hank asked, jumping down from the platform and onto the tracks to hide in the shadows.

'Sure, if Nancy doesn't see me.'

'Have you got anything stronger?'

'Not today.' She'd never hesitated to feed him, but never his addiction.

'Bugger,' Hank mumbled, lazily loping along the train tracks.

Lucy returned her watering can to its home by the Tea House's open doors. Thankfully, the fan had stopped squeaking and was doing its best to stir the soupy air in the dining room.

She cast a picky eye over the wooden tables and chairs set for the many regular bookings. Handmade lace doilies rested on the antique sideboards holding an assortment of fine bone china teacups with matching saucers. Silver cutlery glinted off the lights beside silver serving trays. It suited the black and white images of the many women that lined the walls made of corrugated iron and river stone.

It was quiet now, but soon it would be full of chattering customers.

A car door slammed behind her.

'Close them flamin' doors, will ya. We don't want the flies and heat in there,' hollered Nancy, waddling up the steps carrying her large cane basket. 'Gawd, the cattle are strong this morning.'

'I hadn't noticed,' replied Lucy, closing the bifold doors.

'Nah, you wouldn't.' Nancy stood in the centre of the room, her hands resting on generous hips. Her grey eyes sparkled amongst the many crinkles as she inspected the empty tables. 'Right, I've got flowers for the tables.' She pulled out a bunch of white orchids, ferns, and some pink honeycomb gingers, their heady aroma wove its way around the room. 'Where's that pesky water buffalo?'

'He's in the pen.'

'I should be charging Esther for babysitting that rogue beast of hers.'

Babysit? Nancy did nothing for Cecil. 'Isn't Esther your friend?'

'And that's the only reason I put up with it, or I'd have one of them ringers out back shoot him for tucker.'

'None of them would dare.'

'Why? Because you say so, missy?'

'Erm, no.' Lucy lowered her head, hiding her hands in her apron. She was a nobody.

'He's an oversized pain in the posterior, is what he is. Why Esther had to have a flamin' pet buffalo is beyond me. She could've had a dog, or a bird like the rest of 'em. But no. Typical Esther, she's always gotta be different.' Nancy grumbled as she scuffed her slippers across the floorboards towards the kitchen. She grabbed a starched apron and tied it around her waist, opened the large industrial oven door and sniffed at its barren cavity. 'Have you been baking again?'

'I was practising.'

'How come it doesn't smell burnt?'

'I didn't burn anything.'

'That'd be a first! And, it'd better not be meat? Not in my flamin' cake oven, you don't,' Nancy said, sifting flour into a large mixing bowl. 'Tell me why the flamin' heck you're here so early?' She shook her head causing floppy jowls to shift in unison. 'And why you stay in this town is beyond me. Your housemate is never home… You should do what she does and—'

'Become a bush-pilot?'

'Mmm…' Nancy took a pinch of salt and sprinkled it over her flour mix, then dusted her hands. 'It might be safer for you and everyone else if you stick to the ground. You know, it's not too late to hitch a ride on the next road train back to your dad. There's better places than this to call home, you know. There's an entire world out there.' Nancy cracked five eggs into a separate bowl, then lightly whisked them.

With a wooden spoon, she folded the rest of the ingredients within the large mixing bowl. 'Gawd, I hope none of them flamin' stinky stockmen think they can come in here today?'

'They'll be fine.' She watched Nancy scoop out a cup of sugar, hoping to guess the measurements of Nancy's secret sponge or scone recipes. Lucy had tried to replicate it, but she'd burned her batches. Every. Single. Time.

'Good. I'm glad that Station Master's got that coffee club in the back shed. It stops that mob from dragging their stench and dust in here.'

'They work hard.' Lucy's father was a stockman, and she was protective of them all.

'And what the heck am I payin' you for? To stand and gawk at me all flamin' day. Now, get a shimmy-on, missy, that dining room needs prepping before the train gets here.' Nancy then scowled at the ceiling. 'Turn that rap-crap off will ya, this isn't some cheap nightclub! This is a respectable Tea House and we'll have none of that.'

'Yes, Nancy.' The skirt on Lucy's dress swung as she swivelled on her boots to face an empty dining room that would soon be full. She loved train days.

* * *

The train shifted and Jax's head banged against the window. He winced, cracking open an eyelid to peer through the smeared glass. They'd been chasing the same storm cloud for most of the night. Not that there was much to look at, but now, as he sat up, it was dawn.

Outside was a flat, sprawling space of nothing. It was like he'd landed on the moon. The trees were spindly and sparsely scattered amongst an endless sprawl of red dirt.

Jax scratched at the bristles on his chin and checked his mobile phone but it was useless. Aeroplanes had better Wi-Fi than this train, where he'd lost signal less than ten minutes out of Alice Springs.

Still, he'd never trekked this far north, earning himself another tick off the brotherly bucket list.

Sipping his warm bottled water, he narrowed his focus on the tiny white lights in the distance that appeared to be floating just above the sea of red dirt.

Was that the fabled Min Min lights?

As the train sliced through the outback, buildings rose from the sunburnt soils to form the township of Elsie Creek.

Sitting taller, he searched for a decent vantage point amongst the smeared glass. The town appeared like a speck surrounded by a whole lot of nothing.

What the hell was he doing out here?

The dividing door opened, the roar of the engine competed with the rattle of the wheels spinning on the track, it filled the carriage as they hurtled closer to town. The train's engineer slammed the door shut behind him. 'Hey, Jax, we're coming up to Elsie Creek.'

'Thanks, Mike.' They'd shared coffee on the few platforms they'd stopped at overnight. Mike had even given Jax a tour of the train and the driver had allowed him to steer, making him feel like he was twelve-years-old again.

His brother would have loved this—and it was another tick off that list.

Mike wrestled with the windows to allow the morning's hot air to fill the cabin. 'We'll unload your gear and the town's freight first. Hopefully, there'll be enough room for your vehicle to park with their stockman's ute muster they've got going on.'

'The what?' Jax stretched out, stiff from sitting too long on the hard seats. He'd only slept out of boredom.

'The stockmen are here to load the cattle. They camp at the station, then when we leave, they'll cross the tracks to visit the pub. I swear their utes are like a mobile home to that lot.'

'Yeah, right?' Jax did own a decked-out ute, but he wouldn't call it home.

The train started to slow down as it approached the station. A smoke-machine-like fog curled over the empty wet highway that ran alongside them. 'What is that? Mist?'

'Steam. It's a sauna out there, mate. Reckon you'll get used to it?'

'That's a lot of steam.' Streams of white steam curled off the wet road like water sizzling in a frying pan. Jax's t-shirt and cargo pants stuck to his skin as perspiration built across his brow.

It was meant to be springtime, but there was nothing green or glossy out here. Just thickets of grey olive green that contrasted against the red dirt.

He could smell the rain and dust when a combined odour of wet dog and rotten eggs hit him. It was potent.

The source was a herd of large grey and white beasts waiting in railed yards. 'What kind of cattle are they?' They weren't typical milking cows that's for sure.

'Brahman.'

'Yeah, right.' He'd never seen so many, but he was more interested in learning about this place. 'So, is this it?' Jax asked Mike as they leaned out the window. Google didn't show much about the town or anything else in this tiny region surrounded by a whole lot of nothing.

'Guess so.? We try not to stay here long.'

'Why?'

'Because of those.' Mike sighed heavily as he pointed to the side of the track where two small white crosses stood in the red dirt, spotlighted by the rising sun. 'They reckon this place is haunted... or cursed. No one saw them. Sure, we'll hit the odd cow, donkey, or camel out here on the tracks—but kids? Mate, there's no how-to company policy to recover from that one.'

'That's tragic.' Jax could empathise, he'd witnessed first-hand the carnage caused by aircraft and assorted road vehicles, but never trains—and he didn't want to.

But he was keen to check out the place that was about to become his new hometown.

*　　*　　*

The dining room was buzzing with female voices as Lucy served litres of tea and pounds of fluffy scones. 'Here you go, ladies.' Lucy placed a steaming teapot on the table for the supermum Karen Kimble. Seated beside her was the ever-creative handy woman, Kat. Both fellow players of their outback softball team, the *Dusty Dingos*.

'Please tell me you smuggled in some coffee for me?' Kat whined.

'Not today, sorry. Nancy's at her—'

'Nastiest,' finished Karen with a grin.

Lucy squeezed her lips together to hide her grin, placing a three-tier cake stand onto their table, laden with the traditional Tea House three courses. Starting with dainty savoury sandwich fingers of thinly sliced cucumber, assorted cold meats, scotch eggs, and cheese flan wedges. For the second tier, plump, buttery scones were served with pots of local jams and clotted cream. Leading to the finale of petit fours, macaroons, sugared-jellied fruits, hand-made chocolates, and slices of Nancy's supreme sponge cake. All the trimmings of a high tea served, no matter what time the train arrived.

'What this town needs is some decent coffee,' said Kat, dropping a spoonful of sugar into her dainty teacup. 'We should go steal Doctor Stewart's coffee machine.'

'Why have you stopped calling him the Hot-doc? It's your nickname,' Karen asked Kat, pouring out their tea.

'I have a husband who'll get jealous, so I do my best to avoid Stewart.'

'Why? You kissed him, so what?' Karen said with a shrug.

'You did? When?' Lucy asked, peeking around to see if Nancy was busy with her guests and took a rare moment to sit in the spare seat at the table.

'That happened before I got back with Kyle,' said Kat as bluntly as always. 'Hello, this is a small town, so I had to tell him. Hey, talking about gossips, where's our walking billboard, Cecil?'

'Snacking in his pen out the back. Although, Esther should have collected him by now. You must try the sandwiches. Tell me what you think?' Lucy asked in a soft voice, fidgeting with her fingers. 'I-I did something new with the mayonnaise and it has to be my best horseradish crème ever. Just don't tell Nancy, huh?'

'You are such a great cook,' said Karen, closing her eyes dreamily as she bit into her sandwich.

'No, I'm not.' Lucy caught the supermum's cocked eyebrow. If it wasn't for Karen dragging Lucy to their softball games, she'd never play or do much of anything but hide in the kitchen. 'I'm getting better.'

'Glad to hear it, hon,' said Karen, patting Lucy on the hand in a motherly fashion. 'My six boys would eat nothing but spaghetti 24/7 if I let them. We should all be like Verily who can't cook but has her guy dishing up the most delish-of-dishes for her. Speaking of the coach, here's our queen of the road now.' Karen pointed toward the large road train pulling in.

Its massive wheels stopped with a hiss. The driver's door opened and Verily climbed down from the high cab, to stroll across the car park in her well-worn boots and jeans. Her sports gear was a rarity these days, kept purely for practises. She opened the Tea House's front door, scraped her boots on the mat and removed her Akubra before stepping inside.

A scowling Nancy moved to block Verily at the door.

'It's okay, Nancy,' hollered Karen as if on the softball field. 'That's not a jillaroo, it's our celebrity world champion. Hey, I can brag about it now, huh? We're on the wall of fame.'

Verily side-stepped Nancy, then smiled widely at her friends. 'Hey there, guys.' Lucy moved from her seat. 'No, stay.'

'I can't, sorry,' said Lucy, although she'd love to. 'I'll get you some water, and the usual tea?'

'Yes, please. Although today I'd love a coffee,' Verily said with a pronounced American twang to her accent. 'They have coffee in the stockman's shed, why can't we get it here?'

Lucy winced at Nancy swirling around as if to pounce on a palm rat.

'That isn't a shed!' Nancy screeched, with hands on hips, scowling at the youngest women in the dining room. 'If you want floor scrapings and coffee among the cattle, by all means, there's the door where the sign says *Traditional Tea House*. Not café. Not coffee shop. Tea. House. And we have a tradition in this town that this is and shall always remain a Tea House. If you want coffee, you can go—'

'They're customers, Nancy. W-w-women,' butted in Lucy. 'You can't kick them out, it's against t-t-tradition.'

Nancy's frown deepened at the wincing Lucy. 'Well, if they wanna stay, they eat and drink what's on the flamin' menu, or leave.' Nancy patted down her apron, pasted on a smile, then swivelled on her slippers to return to her guests.

'Bloody tea snob,' muttered Kat and the four of them sniggered like rebellious teenagers.

'Besides complaining about the tea, what brings you here then, Kat?' Lucy asked.

'I'm delivering my last case of candles, hoping the materials I need to make more are on this train. I sold out of everything at the Rosella Festival, including all of Aunty Bea's tutus.'

'Didn't you say you were going to do a candle making class, Kat?' Karen asked. 'I want to be ready before the storms start.'

'Why? What happens?' Verily asked. 'Remember, this is my first wet season in the Territory.'

'We get black-outs at the first crack of lightning,' replied Karen. 'The power gets zapped and we're all scrambling for candles while unplugging everything before it fries our circuits. Last year, our boat-shed got hit. Will you be sharing your candle recipe that keeps the midges and mozzies away?'

'Absolutely. That's the one Aunty Bea's been bothering me for the most,' said Kat, retrieving her phone from her backpack. 'We should set a date suitable for everyone.'

'I vote Tuesday night,' said supermum Karen, raising her hand as if in school. 'I can lock in my husband to watch the kids, and I'm sure Jenny has that night off from the hospital. What about you, Verily?'

'I'll be there. We're day-drivers only now, I enjoy going home at night,' said Verily with a wistful smile behind her teacup.

'What about you, Lucy?' Kat asked, scrolling through her phone's calendar. 'Aren't you working nights at the pub?'

'Only Friday night and the train day dinner rush in the dining room.' Lucy reached for the calendar kept by the sideboard. 'Here, use this. I've marked down the train days for the rest of the year.'

'What is this?' Kat crinkled up her nose as she flicked over the pages for various pictures of scones.

'All its missing is my aunt's rosella jam,' said Verily, giggling. 'I doubt they'd let us put Alex's rosella beer on there. It'd clash with the crockery.'

'It's the town's fundraising calendar,' said Lucy. 'They would have sold a lot more if they'd added some spicy fireman or something.'

'Are our local firemen hot?' Verily asked.

'God, no,' said Karen, screwing up her face. 'Maybe when he was younger, but we've only got the Chief Fire Warden, who's retiring.'

'Lucy didn't send him into early retirement, did she?' Teased Kat, winking at Lucy.

'I have burned nothing, in...' *two days*. 'It's not my fault, I blame the stove.'

The loud rumble of the train's arrival stopped all conversation in the room, filled with assorted perfume, baked goods, and tea varieties. Porcelain cups clinked as they rested on matching saucers, cutlery clanked on plates, and the chattery room was replaced by expectant stares.

Hot steam rose like a curtain of fog from the station's platform as the fresh teasing sprinkle of rain dissipated into the air. The train rolled to a stop and the carriage doors opened near the locomotive. A man stepped forward where the mists curled around his staunch figure.

Lucy gasped with hand to her throat. Her heart pounded in her chest.

He wore no Akubra. No RM Williams boots. No denim jeans, but sturdy steel-capped boots with cargo pants that hugged stocky thighs. His tight torso was gift-wrapped in a black t-shirt that accentuated his muscular, ink-covered arms. Dark sunglasses shielded his eyes. It was as if the sultry devil of sin had stepped free from hell's steam bath. She bit on her lower lip to stop sighing.

'Is that another miner?' Kat whispered.

'They're on shut down—my Hubby's home, giving me the gift of this rare child-free moment,' said Karen as they all watched him through the window. 'That guy is hot.'

'Is it me, or did it suddenly get warm in here?' Verily asked.

'Didn't I just say that?'

'Oh, my god, he's coming inside. Will the women fling their tea bags and scone crumbs at him?' Kat said as they burst into giggles.

'Where's Tess when you need her to slide over and cut him off for his own safety,' said Verily.

'Post office duties. Like I should be returning to mine.' Lucy didn't have Tess's long legs that made traffic stop in this town.

Returning to the kitchen, Lucy loaded the industrial dishwasher and shoved down the handle.

Nothing happened.

She re-opened the dishwasher door and slammed it down hard then thumped its side. 'Come on.' She did not want to handwash lipstick-stained teacups all day.

With a whirl and a whine, it chugged with a hiss as the water cycle began.

'Thank you,' she said, patting the machine as if it was a live beast.

'We need more sandwiches, Lucy,' ordered Nancy, dropping an empty platter on the sink. 'The girls are enjoying them today.'

Was that a compliment? 'Yes, Nancy.'

'Use the bread slicer, we want their sandwiches to be perfectly even.'

'Yes, Nancy.' Nancy was very particular about her presentation. It's what Lucy had enjoyed learning the most.

Now it bored her.

The same presentation styles, the same scones, the same tea, the same freaking crustless cucumber sandwiches. It was always the same.

Lucy flicked the chunky ceramic switch at the power board. Sparks shot from the frayed cord that led to the ancient bread slicer. She turned it off.

'No, not today.' Her bread cutting skills weren't good enough for Nancy's standard. Nancy would measure each bread slice with a ruler, berating Lucy for being millimetres out.

Tradition. It was all about tradition.

Bah! What about flatbreads, pinwheels, pitas, focaccias?

No, she had to use the same white bread Lucy could bake in her sleep.

For once, Lucy would love to make a menu of cupcakes and mini BLT's for fun and flavour. She had notebooks full of ideas.

Shoving a loaf into the oven to warm it, she returned her attention to the old-fashioned bread slicer, pulling it further away from any danger. Holding her breath, she flicked on the socket, praying it worked.

There was a pregnant pause before it rattled in time with the whine of the dishwasher. Soon the sparks again spilled from the socket dripping onto the hissing washer.

'Oh no.' The lights glowered then dimmed and the distinct smell of smoke rose in the air. 'Not again.'

✳   ✳   ✳

Jax stopped at the doorway, the air-conditioning's cool wave was a welcome reprieve from the steamy outdoors. He removed his sunglasses as the door closed behind him with a very distinctive *click*. 'Yeah, right…'

He was the only man standing in a room full of seated women.

Their perfume reeked as they gawked at him like he was some stripper at a hen's party. Thank god he wasn't wearing the uniform.

He searched for a counter, something, or someone that resembled a waitress.

A short woman with generous hips and slippers approached him, crevices of misery were etched deep across her face. 'Cattlemen go around the back,' she ordered.

'I'm not a cattleman. I'm here to collect some keys from Tobias Clare?'

'Tobias left ages ago.'

'And the keys?'

'LUCY!'

Jax winced at the humongous squawk that came from such a short woman. It was impressive.

Until he smelled… *smoke!*

Jax searched for the smoke's source as it curled across the ceiling. He frowned at the ceiling's fire alarms with their lids hanging open displaying empty battery cavities. *'Fire!'*

Nobody moved.

'Bloody hell, LUCY!' Hollered the short woman.

Jax brushed past her and did his best to dodge the women who'd remained seated, sipping their tea, carrying on with their business as normal.

Did he not say *fire* loud enough?

Into the kitchen, Jax found a young woman swatting at sparks showering from the wall socket.

Straight into action, he pulled the young woman free from the danger, kicked the machine away from the wall, then flicked off the ancient switch with a wooden spoon. He snatched up the fire extinguisher resting in the corner, and in seconds he'd stopped the fire scorching more of the wall.

On the other side of the small kitchen, thick black smoke continued to pour out of the oven. He turned it off and opened the door to discover the cause—a burnt loaf of bread. He stabbed at it with the wooden spoon and hurled it out the back-screen door where it smouldered like a lump of charcoal in the red dirt.

All while the two women just stared at him.

'Why haven't your fire alarms gone off?' Jax demanded, pointing to the silent alarms in the ceiling.

'We took the batteries out coz they kept going off every time flamin' Lucy burned something,' said the older woman.

'That's illegal.'

'Bah.' She scowled, waving her hand at him like he was a school kid, even though he towered over her.

'And this is rubbish,' he said, shaking the fire extinguisher in hand, 'it's outdated and empty. Where is your fire blanket? It should be next to the oven.' There were no extractors, no fire plan, nothing. 'This place is a fire hazard.'

'Hey! Who are you calling a fire hazard? It'd better not be me,' said the young woman in the apron. She glared at him with nothing but fire. Thick black lashes framed her large dark eyes that reflected the sunlight streaming through the door behind him. She was gorgeous.

'Who the hell are you to come into my flamin' kitchen,' barked out the elderly woman.

'Kitchen?' He shook his head. 'This is a death trap. Those power cords are frayed and those hazardous power points were banned back in the seventies. They should be shutting this kitchen down.'

'Why don't you just mind you own beeswax and leave, whoever the flamin' heck you are?'

'I will. As soon as I get the keys left for me from Tobias Clare.' It wasn't his job to interfere anymore.

'You're Jackson Turner?' asked the stunning lady in the apron, tall and slender with shapely lips and plump cheeks.

'Jax. Are you Lucy?' That's all he had was a name and this place to collect his keys.

'Of course, that's flamin' Lucy, and I'm Nancy, and this is my place.'

'It's okay, Nancy, Jax is the guy who bought Tobias Clare's farm.' Beside an old clothes rack drying some towels, stood a long deep bench containing plastic boxes and books. On a shelf that contained jars of jams and preservatives, Lucy pulled out a box and passed it to Jax. 'This is from Tobias and me.'

'What is it? Jax asked.

'It's a care package to say welcome to Elsie Creek.'

Inside the box was milk, vegemite, coffee, tinned soup and other food items, including batteries and things he'd take camping. 'Did Tobias do this?'

'No, but I helped Tobias clean out his cupboards so I know you have nothing,' Lucy replied, placing a loaf of bread and other baked goods into a bag on top of the box.

The aroma of fresh bread had his stomach rolling with hunger. These past few days he'd eaten nothing but vending machine food found at train stations. 'Um, thanks.' He wasn't used to this kind of hospitality. 'I don't suppose you'd have a map?'

'There's a mud map in the box. Sorry, my drawing's not that good.'

Jax pulled out a piece of paper that had a childlike scrawl to it, but it was legible. 'This'll work. Thanks.'

Lucy smiled the sweetest smile at him. Damn, she was pretty.

'Is Lucy burning the food again?' Some cowboy said through the back-door's fly screen.

Lucy went bright red, dropping her head she stepped away from Jax, mumbling, 'It wasn't my fault.'

'No, this place should be condemned for the public's safety,' said Jax, hitching the box higher to his chest.

'You're absolutely right, whoever-the-heck-you-are,' said Nancy, again waving that finger of hers. 'And that's why I'm shutting this place down.'

'You're what?' Lucy cried out.

'That's it, I've made up my flamin' mind,' said Nancy, flinging her hands in the air. 'I'm closing down the Tea House, effective as of today.'

'You can't,' barked out Lucy.

'I can, and I will.'

'But what about tradition? What about my job?'

Oh, hell no. The look on Lucy's face said it all, and it hit Jax like a kick to the guts. He searched for the nearest exit.

'This fella's right,' said Nancy, now waving her hands at Jax.

'Hey, don't drag me into this.'

'You started this,' Lucy snapped back to Jax.

'You were the one in danger.'

'I was not.' Lucy scowled at him fiercely.

'There was smoke, and smoke means something's burning.'

'Lucy's always burning stuff,' said the cowboy at the rear door.

'What do you want, Rigsy?' Lucy snapped at the cowboy.

'I've got the keys to this really fancy ute, and I was told it belonged to the only guy game enough to step inside the Tea House.'

'Do you mean me?' Jax almost ran for the freedom of the back door.

Rigsy grinned at Jax as the sounds of shouting women followed them. 'Helluva first impression there, mate.'

'What is that place?'

'Women only.'

'I noticed.'

'And they're gonna hate you forever if Nancy shuts down their Tea House coz of you.'

'I didn't say to close it down.'

'Nah, mate, you said it should be condemned,' said Rigsy, giving a cheesy grin as he adjusted his cowboy hat and ambled towards the car park with his no-rush-swagger. 'It won't be long before the women in this town will be gunnin' for you. Best you bolt in that fancy ute of yours, eh?'

'I was just trying to prevent a fire.'

'It's the Tea House, and it's just the kitchenhand, Lucy, who's always burning stuff. Hey, why were you in there, anyway? Have you got a death wish or somethin'?'

Jax frowned at the cowboy having fun at his expense. 'Tobias Clare told me he'd given the keys to Lucy.'

'Tobias should've told you to go to the back-door coz they don't allow men in there.'

'It said Tea House, not women only.'

'Everyone knows that's secret women's business in there, mate, and they'll be talkin' about you long after this load of cattle's been shipped off to Darwin.'

'Yeah, right.' *Welcome to Elsie Creek, brother.*

TWO

'That'll do for today,' Nancy said, folding up her apron. She slid it into her cane basket, then dug around for her car keys.

'So, you're not closing down the Tea House?' Lucy asked as she washed the last of the delicate, tiered cake dishes at the kitchen sink.

'I am.'

'But—but—not because of what that stranger said? He's nobody, and the place still works fine.' *Most of the time.* 'What about your friends, where will they go for their meetings? What about all those bookings? All those people who wait to collect their freight? All those women who've driven hours from surrounding cattle stations just for one of your servings of tea and scones?'

'Someone else can take up the lease, coz I'm done.'

Lucy stepped back with eyes widening. 'The Tea House is leased?'

'I've run this Tea House for over thirty years and I don't wanna do it anymore. Not when that fella condemned this place.' Nancy scooped up her basket and left a few keys on the counter. 'Lock up when you leave.'

'But—but—'

The front door banged shut.

The tap in the sink dripped. Again. And again.

Nancy will come back. Maybe?

Lucy grabbed her trolley and headed for the back shed. The train was long gone. The car park was empty, and there were no swags holding sleeping bodies across the shed's veranda. Cecil had been set free and the breeze whistled through the barren cattle yards.

Inside the empty shed, the men had only left crumbs in the containers, but the money-tin was almost full. Bench cleaned, lights off, she pulled the shed's screeching roller door shut then dragged her trolley back to the kitchen. Just like she did every train day.

The train had its set schedule, and in another week, it'd stop here, and by then Nancy would've changed her mind.

Although Nancy was known to be a very stubborn woman.

Hank and his bag of recyclable tins clattered and clanged as he wandered over from the deserted car park.

'I've saved you some cans, they're in the kitchen.'

'Bewdy,' Hank said, stepping alongside. 'So, is it true they're shutting down the Tea House coz of your latest fire?'

'I just burned a loaf of bread, that's all. It was this idiot who told Nancy they should condemn the place.' She scowled, parking her trolley by the back door next to her bike. 'Just who does this Jax think he is? Not even here less than five minutes and he's putting the place down like that. The wanker.'

'That's not like you to speak badly of anyone, Miss Lucy,' Hank said. 'I heard he's got this fancy ute full of gadgets. All black and shiny like it'd never seen dirt, them blokes were all over it.'

'It won't stay shiny for long out here,' she said, carrying a crate of crockery into the kitchen.

Hank followed, hauling in the last crate as she loaded the cups into the dishwasher.

'Come on, you silly thing, it's the last load.' She slammed on the door then thumped its side and was relieved to hear the wash cycle begin. Was this her last time in this kitchen?

'Was that your doing?' Hank pointed to the black scorch marks spread above the electrical outlet.

She felt like a broken record, saying, 'It's not my fault the bread slicer caught fire. Do you want it?'

'Heck, yeah.'

'Great, you can help me take it outside.' They carted the small machine out where Hank made quick work of pulling it apart.

'Hey, Lucy, this slicer is stuffed,' he said through the open window. 'It's not your fault it caught on fire, the wiring's all worn.'

'I wish you'd share your prognosis with the world.' Who only saw her as the kitchen hand who burned everything.

She dropped a bag of tins by Hank's sack of recyclables. 'What are you going to make with the slicer?'

'Dunno?' Hank shoved the blades and bulk of the machinery into his duffel bag. 'Shame you haven't got a ute to drop this around.'

'I have a bike with a brilliant trailer that this nice man made me.'

'I'm not nice,' said Hank with a frown.

'You are to me.' She grinned as he turned to hide his smile.

She loaded the cans into the tiny trailer, a converted wheelbarrow that hooked onto the back of her bicycle. It was as good as any car boot for carting groceries.

Hank dumped the bread slicer's engine into the trailer, then made quick work of dismantling its frame. 'What are you going to do with no café, Miss Lucy?'

'Tea House.'

'Whatever. The town needs a café with coffee. Not just tea.'

'It's tradition.'

'Says who?'

'Nancy. And I only found out today, she leases the place.'

'From who?'

'No idea. All I know is that Nancy isn't going to renew it because of…' She frowned at the thought of Jax, the man who'd taken her breath away, and the cause of losing her job. 'The idiot.'

'Do you want me to rough him up a bit?'

'Can you fight, Hank?' The guy was tall, tanned, hairy, and lanky. He was all bone from his liquid diet.

'Nah. I just mumble my way out of blues.'

'You're never in trouble. Except with Nancy when you hang around her kitchen.' Even the town's police would let Hank snore off his belly-full-of-booze in the cells and give him coffee and breakfast whenever they found him stumbling along the road.

She shoved a paper bag in his hand. 'Here's some pastries for you. '

'You don't have to keep feeding me.'

'Unfortunately, you have the job as my chief taster-tester, so I can't have you go hungry.' She locked the kitchen's door and stared at her keys. Was this her last shift in this place?

'Why don't you apply for the lease?' Hank said between mouthfuls as pastry crumbs scattered through his beard.

'Me—are you kidding?' She shook her head as she started to push her loaded bike. It was heavy.

'Nah, I'm serious. Here, let me.' Hank took the handlebars from her.

'I'm just the kitchen hand.'

'You're a cook—if you don't burn stuff. You cook for them mob out the back sheds, and I've seen you sneaking your snacks into them men that play cards in the hardware store—'

'Kat calls them the outback mafia, the knights of the round card-table.'

Hank chuckled. 'Suits 'em.'

'You know, there's always a shower and plenty of couch space at the unofficial Elsie Creek Inn. Monet says you can stay, even in the stables if you want.'

'Where is your high-flying landlady these days?'

'Roper river.'

'Have you been there?'

'Yep. You?'

'Me, no. I go nowhere.' Hank kicked at a stone as they left the empty car park and onto the road heading out of town.

She wanted to ask, but knew Hank would clam up if she did. He didn't ask much about her past and she reciprocated, which worked in their weird friendship.

Clip-clop. Clip-clop. Clip-clop. From the other direction strolled the water buffalo, Cecil, with a red hen squatting on his broad black shoulders like a stout squinty-eyed-general.

'I see you've found your hen, Cecil,' said Lucy, giggling. 'Don't go near Agnes, she wants a roast chicken for Sunday.'

'That chook's a bloody menace.'

'She's just lonely and lost all her friends to the dingoes. She might be homeless, but she's lucky to be alive.'

Hank scowled at the road.

She could've kicked herself for saying homeless. But Hank wasn't homeless, he was a squatter who lived in a great place.

Cecil strolled past them with his black coat shining and his red hen balancing on his back. Bright new yellow ribbons fluttered from Cecil's horns and tail. On his cleaned sides written in yellow chalk was: *Entries now open for the Billabong Barbie Bake-Off.*

'Is it that time of year again?' Hank asked, pointing at Cecil the ribbon-wearing water buffalo strolling past them, heading towards town.

'Must be.'

'Have you ever entered?'

'Are you kidding me? That's Nancy's crowning moment of glory.' Lucy plucked a few branches from the thriving shrub on the side of the road, tucking them into her bike's front basket. Snatching a leaf, she rubbed it between her fingers then inhaled the rich and enlivening lemon myrtle aroma. 'Kat's brother-in-law, Jimmy, is the barbecue king and Nancy's the bake-off queen.'

'You should enter,' said Hank, giving the bike a hard push where the bitumen road ended and the dirt track began.

'So everyone can make fun of me when I burn stuff?'

'Nah. You'll win it, then they'll know how good you are and then they'll come to the Tea House.'

'What?' She stopped and stared at him. 'I can't.'

'You can,' Hank said, strolling past her with the bike and trailer leaving track marks in the dirt. 'You could, you know.'

'I'm not good with tests, and I'm not used to being in front of a crowd. I enjoy being behind the scenes.'

'Well, hide behind a barbecue then.'

'But to cook in front of everyone.'

'Isn't it your dream?'

She faltered, kicking up a small dust cloud. It was true. She'd always wanted to run her own kitchen. Be her own boss.

'Do you think I could do it?' Lucy asked, scurrying after him.

Hank shrugged. 'I guess you'd need to get over your shyness first. When is the Barbie Bake-off?'

'Not sure? Soon, before the wet season hits or we'll never get near Mankie's billabong. They usually give six weeks' notice. I remember that from Nancy practising all the time.'

'How would that woman practise?'

'Ugh, it was hell.' Lucy rolled her eyes, plucking a group of seed pods from an overhanging wattle, putting them alongside the lemon myrtle. 'Six weeks of daily dishes, timing Nancy as she cooked against the clock.

'Which gives you plenty of time to practice. We'll use the billabong at my place to re-enact the scene, so you can get used to it. I suppose I'll have to clean the barbie, and someone would have to get some gas for it. Or we could use wood?' Hank shook his head. 'Nah, might be best we keep away from all fires.'

Lucy frowned at him. 'Hey, it's not my fault I burn stuff.'

'Not you… that.' He pointed to the big metal sign with a half-circular chart showing the National Fire Rating system, warning of bushfire dangers. Its needle hadn't moved in months, pointing to a total fire ban.

'We haven't had enough rain for it to shift yet.' Thanks to the dry season's burning-off regime, everything was black. From the scorched ground to the black bark on the trees where heat waves shimmered above the red dirt road.

Yet from the mere sprinkling of rain that they'd had, life was returning. Soft green shoots of red-stemmed eucalypts stood among a fine spread of matt rush. Lucy plucked a few lush stems for her bike's basket.

'I reckon you'll give Nancy a run for her money in this comp thingy.'

'Oh, sure. I'll steal a tiara from one of the town's tutu-loving princesses to play queen in my apron, with a wooden spoon as my magic wand.'

Hank chuckled. 'How will you know if you don't try?'

'But—but—I'm not qualified.'

'I heard Nancy's not a qualified chef either, and she's been training you, hasn't she?' He poked at the air between them, saying, 'You need to practise, that's all. And while you're at it, you can find out about the Tea House's lease and use this cook-off as your way to prove to the town you can do it.'

'No one would come.' It'd be her worst nightmare.

'If only you'd tell that mob of men it's you who feeds them on train days and not Nancy, they'd come.'

'Nancy doesn't allow stockmen in her Tea House.'

'But it wouldn't be Nancy's Tea House, it'd be Lucy's.'

'Oh…' She stopped and stared at the infinite blue sky. The fear of failure and the hope of her dream job mixed inside her chest. Her own place.

Lucy's Tea House.

'What would I need to do to get a lease?' Again, she skipped to catch up to Hank as the ideas and questions made her giddy with excitement.

'First, you'd need to find out who owns the property. Then when you win the crown at the Barbie Bake-off, you can announce the Tea House will be re-opening under new management.'

'Hey, hold on a second, what about my stage-fright?'

'Yeah, that might be a problem, huh?'

Their footsteps created tiny cloud puffs of red dust as they strolled along, deep in thought, with the trailer rattling behind them.

'Stage-fright is the same as being camera-shy, isn't it?' Hank asked.

'Guess so. I don't enjoy being in front of a camera either.'

'Well, 'bout time you did.'

'Excuse me?'

'You practise cooking on the barbecue while I eat and do the filming. I'll time it like you did with Nancy, then we'll put it out there on the internet to help with this shy thingy of yours.'

Her face screwed up in horror.

'Yep, we'll make you a channel thingy on that YouTube.'

'I don't think so—'

'Do you know anyone who does YouTube?'

'Kat does. She gives online tutorials on repurposing pieces of furniture, then auctions them off in her digital store she manages from her website. Her interior decorating is amazing on what she does to her properties she leases in the city.'

'You should ask this Kat about YouTube and what you'd need for a lease.'

Could she do it? 'I can't do that.'

'Do what?'

'Enter the bake-off.'

'Why not?'

'Because it's part scavenger-hunt for food.'

'You're scavenging bush tucker all the time.'

'That's different.'

'How? I've seen you cook with those herbs you're always collecting,' Hank said, pointing to the gathered foliage in her bike's basket.

'Part of the Barbie Bake-off is the scavenger hunt for food *before* you get to the billabong. I don't have a car to drive, and it'd take me forever to get there on my bike.'

'Borrow one.'

'I can't, I've only got a learner's permit.'

'How come you've never gone for your driver's licence?'

Lucy shrugged. She sucked when it came to doing tests; she failed every time. 'I've been busy.'

'Annoying me,' Hank mumbled. 'Are you going to check on Tobias's farmhouse today?'

'Oh, I forgot,' she said, screwing her nose up. 'I'm no longer farm-sitting, because *he's* arrived.'

'Who did?'

'That guy who told Nancy to shut down the Tea House.'

'What has that got to do with Tobias Clare's farm.'

'He owns it. It's him, Jackson, or Jax,' —*the arsehole*— 'He's your new landlord.'

The bike and trailer skidded to a stop as Hank stared at her. 'If that bloke in his fancy ute reacted like that at the Tea House, what's he gonna say about me?'

'Mr Clare must've told him about you.'

'Tobias didn't bother about lots of things before he left.' Hank grunted, pushing the bike off the road and down the simple wallaby track that disappeared into the scrub. Pink flowering turkey bush created a corridor beneath the banksia's abundant blooms of orange honeysuckles flavouring the air.

'Who else knows you live here, Hank?'

'Well, Tobias would visit with his brandy. And you, with your tucker of torture.'

'Hey!' She'd found Hank when she'd been hunting for herbs and stumbled across his amazing home beside the billabong.

Hank chuckled as he pushed through towering long-grass that opened into a wide clearing surrounded by bushlands. In the centre, a sea of white waterlilies stretched to follow the sun's path. Long-legged black storks and spoon-billed herons waded along the water's edge as pygmy geese floated on the shimmering surface of the spring-fed billabong.

'Well, I'm not telling the idiot anything,' said Lucy. 'It's his farm. He can find you, not me.'

'Nah, you never say anything to anyone, Miss Lucy.'

'I don't like attracting attention or causing trouble.'

'Me neither. I like living life under the radar.' He grinned, parking her bike under the shade of the khaki-coloured tarp that stretched over the top of a locomotive. An entire train engine connected to a railway carriage served as Hank's bedroom. It was a massive hunk of silent machinery in the middle of the wilderness with the perfect view of the flourishing billabong.

On the train's far side, metallic sculptures stood in various stages of development. On the edge of the wilderness, dry weeds poked through a pile of tin scraps, aluminium frames and odd metals, where he added the bulk of the disused bread slicer.

This was Hank's home.

Few people could say they lived in a vintage freight train engine.

Lucy wasn't going to spoil it for Hank. Jax had caused her to lose her job and he had the power to make Hank homeless—she never wanted to see Jax again.

THREE

Jax woke up in a pool of sweat, with a fly jab-jab-jabbing in his face. He wiped at the rivulets of perspiration and stared at the ceiling fan full of cobwebs.

It had stopped working. Again.

Stumbling into the kitchen he turned the tap. Hot water dribbled into the kettle. Flicking it on, nothing happened.

'Yeah, right?'

Last night the power went out as soon as the sky came alive with the best electrical storm he'd ever seen. Lightning flashes were blinding and the thunder so loud it vibrated through his chest. He'd almost slept on the front porch to take advantage of the cooling winds—except for the surge of kamikaze bugs that slammed into the lights and windows.

Again, he swatted at that pesky fly and frowned at the silent kettle.

A scuffling clod shifted outside and a large shadow approached the screen door. A big, black shiny animal nose pushed it open.

'What the hell?' Jax stepped back from the beast. Its wide horns, wrapped in green ribbons, prevented it from poking its whole head inside.

'GET OUT.' He shouted.

Startled, the black beast raised its eyebrows, stumbling backwards in a panic off the veranda.

Jax followed, only to suddenly duck and catch a screeching monstrosity flapping red feathers in his face. 'What are you?'

The hen's squawks were ear-piercing.

The buffalo huffed and puffed, slamming his front hoof into the dirt, drawing a cloud of dust. It then lowered its horned head at Jax as if to charge.

'Okay big fella, let's all calm down.' Jax dropped the squawking chicken to the floorboards. It shook its wide mass of red feathers and flew to the shoulders of the snorting, ribbon-wearing beast with chalk smeared down its sides.

Jax stepped back inside the house, closed the door, and watched the odd pair stroll down the driveway towards the rising sun.

All this action and he hadn't even had his coffee yet!

Jax dug around in the cupboards for a saucepan, jumping back as the doors fell off like a house of cards, dropping to the floor one by one all around the kitchen.

'Yeah, right.' At least he could see what he owned, which wasn't much. But he wouldn't need much to cook with, right?

Stacking the cupboard doors against the wall, he added *door screws* to the shopping list resting on the table, all while the water trickled into the pot.

Finally, he had enough, and lit the stove's gas flame. Within seconds thumping noises and tiny squeals came from the oven. He opened the oven door and three sets of black eyes stared at him. One of them hissed with a mouthful of sharp little teeth. 'What the hell?'

Possums were nesting in his oven.

'Right, that's it!'

Dressed only in his Calvin Klein cotton boxers, he slid into his steel-cap boots and kicked open the front door. He dug around in the back of his ute, grabbed the torch, his safety helmet, thick industrial gloves, and his trusty halligan hammer. He slipped on the long gloves, tapped down the clear visor on his hardhat and headed back into the house.

Screeches soon echoed from the kitchen until a big possum and two small ones bounded out the back door.

Satisfied, Jax rested his halligan by the doorway then set about making his coffee.

He sniffed at the oven, his eyes instantly watering at the reek of animal faeces.

Disconnecting it, he dragged it outside, and with his steel-caps he gave it a hearty kick. It rolled off the veranda's steps as a handful of mice scattered from its base and scurried off in various directions across the red dirt.

'Well, that's just great.'

What a morning. A buffalo threatening to charge him. Scratched at by a hen. Snarled at by possums and a bunch of mice fleeing from him.

'Anything else living in here?' He said back at the house.

If he had snakes, he was moving back to Melbourne.

He stared up at the stupid house he'd bought with its wide verandas and corrugated roof covered in an overkill of solar panels. Why so many for a hot water system in this climate?

He flicked the sweat from his brow.

Who was he kidding? He wasn't a farmer.

At least he had skills in making a fire.

At the fire pit that hid last night's attempted dinner of tinned soup, he stoked fresh flames in a matter of moments. He put the old charred billy on the coals, then sat at the nearby table in the cooling shade of the veranda. Grateful he had a landline that hooked him up for wi-fi. It was the first and only thing he'd unpacked.

And that was his housewarming. Downing a bottle of bourbon while checking out the houses and half of the sheds. After many days of travel, broken sleep, and the stress of the move, exhausted, he crashed where he fell.

Today he would at least try and make a plan. Otherwise the days would mould into one another and he'd get nothing done.

Jax ate the last of the cereal from Lucy's care package. He shook out the final drops of milk into his coffee, then settled in to watch YouTube tutorials on house renovations.

He'd started to do an inventory on the place that had sheds scattered in various directions. One held a tractor that appeared to be in a better condition than this house. At least he'd brought his own tools, courtesy of the old owner warning him he'd need to do repairs.

Jax just wasn't prepared for the level of repairs needed.

The structure of the house seemed solid, but it had… issues.

The water only worked when the power came on. The toilet bowl was home to a green tree frog that croaked at all hours of the night. Tiny geckos would run along the interior walls, dropping their tails in fierce fights for wall space.

Sadly, they were the only things that kept him company, where the silence of the place was ear-crushing. Even the music blaring from his car's stereo couldn't stop the loneliness weighing heavily across his shoulders.

But he'd made a pact to be here.

It just sucked he had to do it alone.

He rubbed the pain in his chest, then picked up a pen and continued adding to his shopping list. *Mouse traps, dishwashing detergent*—but no food.

Jax didn't cook. His microwave wasn't working and he was used to shops being available 24/7 offering endless choices and door-to-door delivery service. But who'd deliver out here?

The surrounding scrublands topped with a monster skyline only made him feel small. Layers of loneliness and the heat's humidity seemed to want to smother whatever happiness he had left inside.

He sighed, wiping a hand over his face, feeling the red dirt's grit mix with sweat on his skin. It was everywhere.

But he'd made a promise and thrown everything into this.

What an idiot he'd been. He'd never get his money back.

But Jax had never been a quitter. It only made him hunker down to push through the worst that life had thrown at him. So there was no way he was going to let the local wildlife and a house get to him.

This was meant to be his home.

His castle.

And he would learn how to manage this farm—even if it killed him.

But who could he ask for advice on farming? He'd get laughed at by the burly cowboys who'd wrestled with the huge cattle at the train station. Their sun-leathered skins and wary eyes showed how tough they were. And he wasn't part of that club.

First, he needed to learn to cook to survive. He typed the word *cooking* onto his tablet. Google's response was a mountain of over 48 billion posts. All about stovetop cooking … yet his stove rested face-down in the dirt.

Barbecue, was added to the shopping list. He then typed *simple barbecue cooking in the bush*, and that narrowed down the field of millions to one page.

Barbecue bush cooking by the billabong, caught his attention. It was made in the Northern Territory, his new home state.

He sipped his coffee and pressed play, only to blink as he leaned in closer to the screen.

'H-h-hi, um, w-w-welcome,' said the nervous young woman. Tall, slender, wearing an apron, a summer dress and sandals, standing beside a simple hot plate. But the backdrop showcased a stunning billabong dotted with white flowers and clear skies. It was almost a mirror image of his own sky.

She held up a snow globe and smiled.

Jax recognised that sweet smile.

'My name is Lucy, and today I'll be cooking three dishes that have something to do with these snow globes.'

'Why the snow globes?' called a gruff male voice from behind the shaky camera. It was the same question Jax was asking himself.

'Hey, you can't talk while filming,' Lucy said.

'No one's watching,' scoffed the voice behind the camera.

Jax chuckled, sipping his coffee. He was probably the only fool who was, but he couldn't stop watching the way the sun shone on the loose black curls that framed her light, caramel skin. It was a stunning combination that only highlighted her sweet smile.

'Um…' Lucy cleared her throat and held up her snow globe that caught the sunlight. It reflected in her big dark eyes as if showing a world within a world. 'Because my housemate said we needed a gimmick, and this is the only way we'll get snow in the outback.'

'Good gimmick,' Jax said to the screen, leaning back in his chair to watch a cooking show. He would've never bothered doing this in the city, chasing the clock, doing up reports and schedules—now he had nothing to do.

With all this nothing, you'd think the heaviness of stress would have left his shoulders and loosened the knot of dread in his guts. It was torturing him enough to want to snatch up another bottle of bourbon and drink with the rising sun. Instead, he reached for his coffee mug to watch her show.

Lucy placed the snow globe on the corner of the small table laden with mixing bowls and other utensils, the same items he had in his crappy kitchen. He was hopeful he could follow this.

Until she picked up a tattered soft-covered book and explained, 'This is the outback cook's bible, the gospel of many country towns, it's the CWA—'

'The what?' Jax and the gruff-voiced cameraman asked together.

'Sorry,' she said, shyly shrugging.

It was cute. She was cute. Her vulnerability was reaching him in ways he'd never experienced.

'Country Women's Association. They release a cookbook of tried and tested recipes from around Australia. It may be an old copy I got from my mother, but it's perfect for cooking with the few ingredients you have in any kitchen. Out here when the wet season hits and we're flooded in and can't get anywhere...'

'Yeah, right?' Jax eyed the desert of dust that surrounded him. What else would he need to be prepared for this wet season, besides candles when the power went out? He'd come from a place of four seasons, but the Territory only had two—a wet and dry season. Whatever season this was, it was hot.

'With this show,' Lucy said on the small screen, 'I'll be using some local foods and what's found in any simple kitchen pantry. I'll then cook it on this barbecue because no one wants to heat up a hot house in summer.'

'Good girl,' he murmured, sipping from his empty coffee cup. He reached for the billy making himself a black coffee, playing his part as a rugged bushman learning how to cook.

'So, these snow globes,' said Lucy, pointing to the one resting on the corner of her table, 'represent a town. I'll use that town as inspiration for the entrée, a main course and a dessert from this cookbook with a time limit of two hours.'

A stopwatch filled the entire screen making Jax sit back.

'I'm ready, Lucy, go,' said the gruff-voiced cameraman.

'I haven't said what I'm cooking.'

'Talk while you cook, I'm hungry.'

Jax nodded in agreement with her cameraman, who was hopeless. The filming was shocking. It was either out of focus, shaky, or at times dropped with muffled swearing. Jax laughed so much he was brushing away happy tears from the corners of his eyes.

Lucy knocked over bowls, dropped tongs and spoons, batted at flies with a whisk, and slapped at mozzies with an egg-flip. She mimicked the honks from the overhead magpie geese squadrons, then did a bobbing dance with a tall jabiru on the edge of the billabong—but the results of her cooking were mouth-watering.

She'd cooked massive steaks and char-grilled vegetables. Harvesting ingredients directly from her surrounds, she'd wash and slap them straight onto the hotplate. She made it look so easy.

Jax watched Lucy catch freshwater prawns and yabbies she called red claw and cherabin. Plucking them from a mesh pot floating in the billabong that was a major part of the spectacular scenery behind her. With skirts hitched high, showing off slender legs, she waded along the billabong's edge to gather water-weeds to use as herbs and vegetables.

As he munched on stale vegemite sandwiches, Lucy sautéed freshwater prawns with wild garlic and bush tomatoes. She unwrapped a crusty lemon myrtle damper baked in tinfoil on the hotplate. She then whipped up a gooey chocolate dessert using some local berries she'd plucked straight from a tree and tossed into her saucepan. All caught, cleaned, cooked and presented in less than two hours, then condensed into fifteen minutes.

The basic dry ingredients Lucy had used on her show were in Jax's welcome box of goodies she'd given him at the Tea House. From his spot on the veranda he recognised some of the trees she'd used, but he wasn't confident enough to go bush-tuckering just yet.

So he sat and devoured all of her shows, with promises of more.

Even with all of her mishaps and mumblings, Lucy had shared the names and uses of the bush plants she had cooked with. She'd talked about the weather she called *Mango season* and gave handy tips on surviving the mozzies and the heat.

It was as if she'd created the show just for him. Talking directly to him while she made a masterpiece of food on a simple barbecue. It made Jax hungry.

If only she didn't burn stuff, he'd be well and truly hooked.

Sure, she'd created culinary masterpieces, but she'd set tea towels alight. With flames leaping, she'd tossed them straight into the billabong, sending the waterbirds screeching for cover.

He'd winced when the barbecue's fat sparks caused a fire among the dried twigs and leaves at her feet, which she stopped by dousing them with her soup.

In the next video, they'd raked the area free from debris with water buckets at the ready. But she still managed to burn the base of her cupcakes.

In every video she had managed to burn something.

Lucy may not understand fire safety, but she shared her knowledge of the outback, and for that he was grateful.

Jax sipped the last of his coffee and placed his pen beside his finished shopping list. Thanks to Lucy, he now had a plan. She had unknowingly become his mentor of sorts, without having asked a single question, but he had plenty more he wanted to ask.

It was a pity Lucy was such a walking fire hazard.

And Jax was well-trained to avoid risky firetraps at all times—no matter how cute they were.

FOUR

Showered, shaved, and almost human again, Jax drove to town leading a huge plume of red dust on the wide dirt road. Weird assorted sculptures created from sticks and tins stood on the verge. Were they waiting for the rubbish truck, as an outback-style of bin day?

He hit the asphalt with the sign warning him to slow down for trains and a buffalo. On the right, he passed the deserted railway station. Its barren yards that had once been filled with cattle, and the death-trap for a Tea House, were closed.

Over the train line, and onto the main road, Jax made his maiden journey into Elsie Creek.

He cruised past the large pub on the corner towering over the row of shops. There was a post office, a craft shop, and a small supermarket. Further along stood a hairdresser and a few other shops, along with a large hardware store boasting about a drive-thru for animal foods.

But there was no café. No takeaway stores. No popups or coffee vans. Nothing and nowhere to buy a coffee and a quick bite.

He frowned at the big-butted buffalo, this time orange ribbons waved off his horns with the words: *Barbie-Battlers wanted!* The feral chook sat square between the buffalo's shoulders as it strolled past people, as if it was completely normal.

'This place is crazy.'

On the edge of town, he followed the sign pointing to a small bush hospital with a helipad out front. There was a volunteer ambulance centre nearby, and an airstrip to the right with a few fixed-winged aeroplanes parked near the aircraft hangar.

The police station was next. Within its compound stood several four-wheeled drive police vans, a police boat, and a slick-looking highway pursuit car. It was a great set up.

'You have got to be kidding.' Jax stopped in front of what looked like a doll's house toy dropped in the middle of the red dirt. It was the smallest firehouse he'd ever seen. It had red painted corrugated walls and white doors with lace curtains in the windows. All that was missing was a white picket fence, a big brass bell, and a dalmatian to add to the cliché!

'Not my place.' He'd hung up his helmet and left that part of himself behind.

With his shopping list attached to his ute's dash, his first stop was the hardware store.

The temperature dropped as he entered the wide-open double doors. He nodded at the two men behind the counter. Were they twins?

They wore matching leather aprons, but that's where the similarities ended.

One of them had a perfectly straight hair part and was dressed in a starchy shirt with the top button done up leaving room for a missing bow tie.

The other guy had his glasses caught sideways in a tangled mop of hair, wearing a stained shirt, and a pair of odd footy socks that fell to his boots. What made it even more amusing was he was standing before an entire shelf of matching pairs.

He sniffed at the cigar smoke and frowned. *Who's smoking inside a public space?* Although technically this was a shed with ceiling fans—that worked—and kept the place cool on this humid day.

To his left was a large round table where four elderly men sat playing cards, with coffee mugs before him.

They've got coffee! Dare he ask if they sold coffee?

'Morning, mate,' called out a man with grey clipped hair, suspenders and a friendly enough grin. The other three narrowed their eyes at him in suspicion.

'Morning,' Jax replied with a curt nod.

'Can I help you?' Asked the guy with the odd socks.

'Do you sell barbecues?'

'We do. Are you practising for the Billabong Barbie Bash?'

'The what?'

'Obviously not. So, what type of barbecue are you after?'

'One that cooks and boils water,' replied Jax. It's what Lucy recommended on her show.

'We'll sort you out, mate, don't you worry none,' said the odd-sock guy, escorting Jax down the aisle.

Barbecue chosen and carted to the counter, the store owner went to fill Jax's new gas bottle, leaving Jax to finish his list.

'Morning, gentlemen,' called out a bright female voice entering the store.

Jax recognised it and peeked out from behind the shelf.

It was Lucy, with her hair in a pony tail leaving a few loose curls to frame her face, highlighting her sweet smile. The sunlight streamed in behind her, silhouetting her curves through her summer dress. She was even better looking in real life, carrying a platter to the men's round table.

'Well, if it isn't the lovely Station Hand's daughter,' said the man with suspenders as they shifted coffee mugs and ashtrays aside for her. 'What have we got today?'

Lucy removed the foil unleashing a steamy aroma into the shed. 'There's a variety of mini quiches with bush spinach, bacon and other goodies to keep your figures fabulous.'

Watching her show had made Jax hungry. Smelling her food for real had him starving.

'Give our compliments to Nancy on keeping the peace,' said one of the men reaching for a delicacy.

'Thanks, I will.' Lucy collected an empty dish from under the shelf and shook another container that rattled of coins.

'Is it true, Nancy's shutting the Tea House?'

'I believe Nancy's friends are trying to talk her into staying open.' She sighed and her shoulders drooped.

Lucy's expression was like a kick in the guts for Jax, so he slipped back down the aisle to finish his list.

'She's gonna miss train day, you know,' said a man at the card table.

'Good on her, I say,' said another.

'But she'll miss train day.'

'So what? It's just train day.'

'You don't have to put up with my wife carrying on about no tea on train day and how they're breaking a tradition.'

'Talk some sense into her, will ya, Lucy,' said the first man at the large table.

'I'm the last person Nancy will listen to,' said Lucy so quietly, it was a strain to hear. 'Anyway, I'd better get back to it.'

'Tell Nancy, thanks from us mob. We've put a few bob in there to keep the cook happy.'

'Thank you, gentlemen, it's much appreciated. Hopefully, we'll see you in a few days.'

With Lucy gone, the men picked from the platter as their voices carried through the building.

'I heard this new fella, in his spaceman's super-ute, told Nancy her shop was illegal,' said one of the old men. It was as loud and clear as the food's aromas filtering through the shelf space making Jax's stomach rumble, while he checked out door hinges and screws.

'What's illegal in that Tea House? It's tea. Nancy's not the type to slip the odd herb in her tea,' said another man at the table.

'Maybe she should, then she wouldn't be so nasty,' one of the men declared and the others chuckled in agreement.

Jax shifted to the paint section, determined to fix one room at a time. The bedroom was the easiest of rooms to start with, according to his new plan.

With his shopping basket filled with brushes, sandpaper, a tin of primer, carrying a roll of fly screen mesh over his shoulder, he headed for the counter the long way around. Jax did not want to go near that table of food that was making his mouth water.

'Fire hazard that fella said. He reckoned they should condemn the Tea House,' added one of the men from the round card table.

'Well, little Miss Lucy does cook there—'

'Burns there, you mean. Poor girl can't cook without burning everything,' reported one man with a chuckle.

'Doesn't our Fire Chief inspect the Tea House?'

Jax doubted any respectable fireman had visited that kitchen for a very long time.

'Nah, he'd get chased out by Nancy and her broom,' said one man, slurping his coffee.

'It'd be nice if Nancy flew away on that broom and let us lot in there.'

'Why? We'd get henpecked for playing cards and smoking cigars. That's their place, this is ours. Nancy supplies us with tucker so we don't go poking into her business. It's the deal, gentlemen, for keeping the peace.'

'Besides,' said another card player, brushing the crumbs from his chin and hands. 'Isn't Fletcher going into early retirement?'

'He is. They'll be advertising the Chief Fire Warden's job soon.'

'Who's applying for it? Any of the volunteers?'

'We want a local this time, not some dog's body who's never been out bush.'

'It'd better not be some blinkin' air force wahoo.'

'You're an ex-air force wahoo, what's your problem?'

'Nah, I'm talking about that lot who poisoned the water system outside of Katherine playing with foam at the airbase. If we had one of those fella's working here, there'd be an angry mob stoning our firehouse.'

'What's the latest on their class action?'

'It'll be years before they get a verdict. But I do know truckies are still delivering drinking water to those affected properties. There's mango farmers letting the fruit die on the trees coz they can't sell crops livin' in that red zone. Their bore water is contaminated. Property values have nose-dived. Tobias Clare got out at the right time.'

'So, who's the mug that bought Tobias's place?'

'Someone reckoned it was the same fella who shut down the Tea House, driving that space ute.'

At the counter, with his back to the cardplayers, Jax watched odd-sock guy ring through his purchases on the outdated cash register. He wanted to ask if the water on his property was contaminated? He sure as hell was going to test it when he got back.

'I'll help you carry it out,' said the cashier.

'Thanks, I appreciate it.' Jax hoisted the barbecue over his shoulder, carrying the paint and assorted bags in the other.

'You're a strong fella. What do you do?'

'I'm trying to restore a house at the moment.'

'Which is your car?' Asked the odd-sock guy, struggling with the roll of flywire.

'That black one people are calling a space ute.' Jax nodded at the men seated at the table with food frozen halfway to their mouths.

'Gawd, did you get a gander at all them tatts on the fella? Is he a drug dealer?' Blabbed one of the seated old men.

'Or a drug grower,' said another. 'Crikey, that's a lotta ink.'

'So that's the bugger who bought Tobias Clare's place, eh? Well, good luck to him, I say.'

Jax frowned at their voices. They were right, he needed all the luck he could get to steer clear from mobs threatening to stone people, tea-drinking women, and cranky red-hens carried by ribbon-waving water buffalos.

Boy, didn't he pick the wrong town to call home.

FIVE

Shimmying up the tree, Lucy slid along the branch as she eyed the last plump, flawless piece of fruit. For weeks she'd been watching it grow and ripen whenever she rode past.

Miraculously, the birds had missed these spindly roadside trees with their beautiful but stringy mangoes. They were perfect for cooking and Lucy had a pork dish dying for some fresh mango.

She reached out with her fingertips, but only brushed the side of the plump fruit that swung away from her. 'Bugger.'

She shunted further along the branch with her legs dangling on either side of the limb that bent and creaked beneath her.

The sound of an approaching car caught her attention.

If it was a ute, they might let her climb onto the back tray to pluck the fruit. She leaned down, hoping to recognise the driver.

'Oh no.' She frowned. *It's him… Jax!*

Nope, she wasn't going to waste her breath talking to the guy. Ever.

She swatted away a pesky fly and reached for the dangling fruit. With the tip of her fingertips she pushed it, forcing it to swing backwards and forwards, stretching for the soft warm flesh.

'Gotcha.'

Jax drove past in his black ute blinding her in a cloud of red dust. '*Arsehole*. You slow down when passing people on dirt.' She coughed, shooing away the dust cloud swamping her.

The branch cracked beneath her. It happened so fast, all she could do was scream as it gave way and she was left with nothing but empty air.

Falling hard, she landed on her back with a thud on the dry bed of native grasses.

She couldn't breathe.

Wheels skidded in the dirt then reversed to stop nearby and a car door slammed.

'Are you okay?' Jax asked, hovering above her.

She clutched his shirt, gasping for air, as tears squeezed from her eyes. 'Can't. Breathe.'

'Right, I think you've winded yourself,' he said, checking her over. 'I'm going to sit you up to help you breathe, okay?' Crouching beside her, he slid his arm around her shoulders and helped her upright. 'It's okay, Lucy, calm down and take a little breath. Inhale, exhale, you can do it.'

Her eyes were going to pop right out of her skull as her lungs squeezed in pain, but Jax held her two hands in one if his, rubbing her back with the other. He showed her how to breathe and she followed.

He'd be good in a labour ward, helping his wife breathe— which was a random thought out of nowhere. Was that going to be her final thought on this earth? What happened to her life flashing before her eyes?

'Breathe, Lucy, you can do it.'

She inhaled and exhaled in shallow pants as the squeeze on her ribcage eased.

'Good, let's inhale a little deeper,' Jax said in soothing tones.

Her pulse pounded in her ears and her heart threatened to burst out of her chest as she focused on his eyes and his words.

'Breathe in. Breathe out… There, you're doing fine, Lucy.'

She inhaled enough to give a slight sigh of relief.

'Well done. I'll get you some water.' Jax dashed to the truck and soon returned with a water bottle. 'What were you doing in that tree?'

Her hands trembled so much it was hard to hold the bottle. 'Mmm-mmm-mango.'

'Here, let me.' He opened the lid and held it to her mouth.

Parched, and fuzzy in the head, Lucy clutched onto his big hand as she went to take a sip but somehow misjudged the distance where the bottle's lip hit her teeth.

'Slowly, Lucy.'

'What's wrong with me?' With the back of her hand she wiped her mouth, discovering tears slickening her face.

'You fell out of a tree.'

'Not my first tree. But this…' She hugged her ribs.

'You got winded. It's a scary thing.'

Not being able to breathe was terrifying, she couldn't stop crying.

'Is anything broken? Are you in pain anywhere else?'

'My head, my ego, my lungs—did I say my ego?'

It was amazing the way his eyes crinkled and shone as he smiled, it made her a different kind of breathless. She had to look away.

Cupping some water, she splashed it over her face.

'I've got a towel for that.' Again, he jumped to his fancy boots and rummaged around the back of his fancy ute.

She tried to get to her feet, realising she was in the dirt, covered in sweat and dust, with the planet's most handsomest man coming to her aid. This wasn't right.

The world shifted, and she slumped back to her knees.

'Hey, okay Lucy, I've got you.' He gripped her shoulders before she fell back into the grass.

'I'm fine, I was getting this.' She reached for the stupid mango, when what she really wanted to do was crawl away into the tall grass and hide in shame—if only she could see straight. 'It's not my fault.'

'It was. You shouldn't have been up there in the first place.'

'I just wanted this mango.'

'I think you may have a concussion? Look at me.'

'No.' She hung her head low as the heat rose to her cheeks.

His fingertips lifted her chin and she winced up at him.

'Where does it hurt?'

'My head.' She whimpered, grasping her scalp that unleashed a blinding headache.

'Right, come on.' He scooped her up in his arms and against his chest.

'What are you doing?'

'I'm taking you to the hospital.'

'I'm fine, I know where it is.'

'I do too.'

'Do a tour of the town, did we?'

'Yeah.'

'That would've taken you all of three minutes, huh? Unless you stopped for snacks and took photos.'

'I stopped in front of the fire station, it's tiny.'

'It's cute.'

'It's silly.'

'What is? You carrying me? Or this whole tree-falling thing where you get to play the hero?'

His laugh carried through his chest. She would have smiled with him—if she didn't hate the guy. 'Hey, put me down or I'll ruin my perfectly good mango by throwing it at you.'

'Let's not waste the mango you risked life and limb for, on me.'

'I'll be fine and can ride myself back.'

'I saw your bike on the side of the road,' he said, putting her down to open the passenger door.

'I'm not getting in there?'

'Why not?'

'It looks brand new and I'm dirty.' Brushing at her filthy dress she caught her reflexion in the glossy polish of the ute, twigs and leaves were entangled in her hair. *How embarrassing!*

Jax picked up her bicycle like it weighed nothing and put it into the back tray next to some paint tins, a roll of fly wire and some boxes.

'New barbecue?'

'Yes. Do you think it's any good?'

She shrugged. 'Looks shouldn't matter as long as it cooks—'

'And boils water.'

'Um, yeah.' She frowned at him for daring to finish her sentence and went to walk away, but her world tilted on its axis.

'Oh no, you don't.' Jax caught her in one strong arm. His cologne was divine and she was itching to trace the ink swirls on his arm and follow the trail to—

'Erm, what?' She looked up at the guy she was meant to hate. She'd lost her job because of this man.

'Come on, in you get.'

'I'm okay.'

'Sure you are, but I'll let the hospital decide.'

'No, really, I'm fine.' She went to grab the door frame but missed it, falling into the plush leather seats.

Before she could climb out, Jax closed the door and ran around to the driver's seat.

'This has to be the nicest car seat on the planet.' She wriggled back into the leather, cocooned in a new car smell. 'It's like a lounge-chair. One of those fancy recliners, huh?'

'You could say that, but you need to put on your seatbelt.' He helped her clip the seatbelt into place, then turned the ute around heading back into town.

'I smell chicken?'

'It's roast chicken.'

'Did you get that from the supermarket?'

'Yep, I was doing some shopping.'

'Okay…' As if the sexy Demi-god of sin wanted to talk about shopping with her.

Her head, shoulders and back ached. No matter how soothing the chair was, she couldn't stare out the window without getting dizzy. Clutching the mango in her lap, she peeked up at the guy who was all muscle. 'Are you rich?'

'No.'

'Must be if you've got this fancy car and bought the Clare farm.'

'I invested in the place.'

'Bet it wasn't what you thought it would be.' She almost felt sorry for the guy, catching his frown.

'I had no expectations.'

'Didn't your wife want to see it first, before moving in?' She searched for his wedding ring.

'It's just me out there,' he said, gripping the steering wheel tighter as a frown creased his brow. 'The place was well below my budget. Cheap enough to spend my money on other things.'

'Like this fancy ute. There's so many buttons and doodads on this dashboard, do you use them all?'

'My brother and I used to go four wheel driving a lot down south.'

'You're not one of those part-time suburban warriors, are you?'

'What? No. It's just got some rock-crushers and deflector plates—'

'Are you going to war in this thing like one of those survivalists?'

'No.'

'But you are military, aren't you?'

'The haircut a giveaway, huh?'

'Yeah.' She grinned at him, almost punch-drunk on his aroma. 'You should introduce yourself to the outback mafia—

'

'The what?'

'The knights of the round-card-table at the hardware store.'

Again, he frowned. 'Why should I bother those old guys?'

'They're ex-military, sitting on their service pensions. Is that what you're doing? You're not that old.' He was definitely older than her. And so serious.

'I'm not. Anyway, why the interest in my finances?'

'I'm not. Sorry for prying.' She sat back and stared at the stupid mango in her lap, embarrassed for speaking. Normally she didn't talk at all. What was wrong with her?

They drove in silence until they hit the tarred road and skimmed over the train tracks. She frowned at the dark and deserted Tea House. 'You can drop me off here.' She went to unclip her seatbelt, but he held her in place.

'Stop, Lucy, we're almost there.'

'F-f-fine.'

'You did not just say *fine*?'

'What?'

'*Fine*—when it's not *fine*. It's anything but *fine*.'

'It's just a word.'

'A word women throw around all the time, when we all know it's not *fine*.'

'Well, I am *fine*.'

'Sure, you are! So, why are you arguing with me?'

'Why am I even talking to you?'

'Because you fell out of a tree and winded yourself.'

'Huh… you came to my rescue. Um, thank you,' she mumbled into her lap as the heat inflamed her cheeks—again.

'You're welcome. It's been a while since I've saved a damsel in distress.'

She gave a snort-laugh, now long past being embarrassed. It had to be the first time anyone had called her that. 'Full-time profession, was it?'

'Why? Do women regularly fall out of trees in this area?'

'Oh yeah, it's like drop bears, mate, the outback's lousy with them.'

'Drop bears?' He arched his eyebrow at her.

She giggled. She couldn't believe she'd blurted out that overused cliché the ringers used in the pub to bait overseas tourists with as a sport. Was he playing with her? 'Are you really a tourist?'

'I guess I am until I'm called a local,' he said with a grin that made her toes curl.

He parked at the hospital's main entrance and was standing by her door before she climbed out.

'I can do it,' she said, trying to push him away.

Jax stepped back, raising his hands in surrender. 'I only want to help, Lucy.'

'I've had enough of your help, thank you.' She went to grab her bike, but the headache was blinding.

'Come on, let them check you over first and I'll drop you home after.' The hand he placed on her shoulder was soothing.

His grand gesture and the sorry tone to his deep voice, destroyed what fight she had left. She had no choice but to take her enemy's arm and allow Jax to escort her inside.

*   *   *

'What happened to you?' The nurse asked, approaching Lucy and Jax as they walked through the sliding doors. Cooling air greeted them while heat pressed against their backs.

'Hi, Jenny, I'm fine thank you, how are you?'

'Lucy is not fine,' said Jax, shaking his head at the tough little nut. Jax explained to the nurse, 'Lucy fell out of a tree and winded herself. I suspect she may have a concussion. Her speech is slurred, she's dizzy and uncoordinated on her feet.'

'Take her to the first bed in the examination room, I'll text the doctor,' Jenny said, directing them to the small ward, with phone in hand.

'Not the Hot-Doc too?' Lucy whined, leaning against Jax's arm.

Jenny giggled as she tapped on her phone. 'Well, with this one at your side, it's your lucky day, Lucy.'

'Yeah, right, hooking up with enemy number one has always been on my dream-list—*not*.'

'Hey, I was only trying to help you.' It should have offended him, but she was too damned cute to stay angry at. 'You were the one who fell out of a tree, not me.'

She stood taller, lifting that dainty chin of hers.

He wanted to pinch it between his fingers.

'It was you who covered me in dust when you sped past,' she said. 'Don't you know it's impolite not to slow down when passing pedestrians on dirt roads. Most drivers do to either offer a lift, or so they don't cover people in a dust cloud—like you did.'

'Now I've been told, I'll know for future reference.' And told him she did. 'I honestly didn't see your bike until I drove past. But I saw you fall in my rear-view mirror.' He was so glad he did.

'Who's your friend?' Jenny asked.

'Not my friend,' Lucy mumbled.

He couldn't blame her for hating him.

'This is Jax,' Lucy said to the nurse, 'he's just a lost tourist.'

'I'm not a tourist, I've moved into town.'

'Welcome. I'm Jenny, Head nursing sister,' she said, with a warm smile.

'Thank you, Jenny. Nice to meet you too.' Finally, someone was being nicer to him than little miss sulky pants.

'He's single, Jenny,' mumbled Lucy, trying not to lean against him.

Jax wasn't game enough to let her go in case she fell. 'You're not going to broadcast it on some outback dating service, are you?' She grinned up at him. Almost chest to chest, he had to grin back.

'You said you didn't have a wife.'

'That doesn't mean I'm looking for one.'

'Yep, I'm in that club of singledom too,' said Lucy, pushing away from him and stumbling to the chair.

'The bed, young lady,' Jenny ordered.

'I've got her.' Jax hoisted Lucy to feet. 'Want me to carry you?'

'No, I'll stagger there myself, thank you very muchly, Mr Muscle Man.'

'This is the chattiest I've ever seen you, Lucy,' Jenny said. 'You really must've hit your head, or are you drunk?'

'I've only drunk tea and water. It's all Ironman and his Tonka Truck's fault,' she said, scooting onto the bed.

'Who's Ironman?' Called out the male voice entering the room behind them with a stethoscope hanging out of his white doctor's coat. He stopped and nodded at Jax. 'Oh, I see.'

Jax crossed his arms over his chest and stared at the young doctor with the blonde hair swept back like a lion's mane. 'Not that I know much about men, but I'm guessing you must be the hot-doc.'

'We don't say it to his face,' said Lucy, laughing with Jenny.

'My name is Stewart, and you are?' The Doctor asked, holding out his hand.

'Jax. I've just moved into town.' He shook hands with Stewart, but directed his frown at Lucy. 'I'm hoping the Ironman nickname doesn't stick.'

The women giggled and Stewart shrugged, saying, 'In this town, who knows. What brings you here?'

'Another woman fell out of a tree,' Jenny explained to the doctor.

'Another one? Is it really a common thing for the local women?' Jax asked the medical team.

'Trees, treehouses, although wine is usually involved. Were you drinking?' Stewart asked Lucy as he began his examination.

'No. I was trying to pick a mango.' Lucy winced at the light and went to lean back but Jax swiftly moved in behind her so she didn't fall off the bed.

'I've got you,' he murmured, holding her against his chest. Even with twigs and dirt, her hair smelled of warm florals, still soft and shiny. She had the thickest eye lashes and wore no make-up. With her large, dark eyes and clear skin, she didn't need it.

Surprisingly, she let him stay as the doctor conducted his examination, then he waited in the foyer while they did the x-rays. He should've gone home, but Lucy's fragility made him stay. He wanted to make sure she was okay, even if she hated him.

She'd smile at him all playful, then she'd remember they weren't friends and frowned at him, all in the blink of an eye.

Women.

At the sound of female voices, he recognised Lucy's and rose to his feet. Jenny was pushing her down the corridor in a wheelchair.

Had he overstepped his boundaries by hanging around?

Well, he did have her bike and precious mango in his ute.

'So, any broken bones?' Jax asked, eager for good news.

Lucy shrugged at him. 'I feel fine.'

'You look better.' He grinned at her blush.

The automatic sliding doors opened, letting in a wave of humid heat as another nurse strolled inside, carrying a small box. 'Another parcel came today, Jenny.'

'Another one?'

'I found it on the back step, it's creepy if you ask me.' She passed the box to Jenny and headed down the hallway.

'I don't think it's creepy.'

'What's not creepy?' Lucy asked as she slid into the seat beside Jax.

'I've been getting these gifts that just show up with no name, nothing, but they're adorable.' Jenny opened the box and pulled out a metal statue of bent tin and nails that sat in the middle of her palm. 'Oh look, he's made a statue of Cecil.'

'What's a Cecil?' Jax asked.

'Water buffalo,' replied Lucy. 'You'll see him wandering the streets, wearing ribbons on his horns and chalk on his sides.'

'With that red chicken on its back?'

'Yeah, that's him.'

'Watch that hen, she's scratched a few people,' said Jenny.

'There's nothing wrong with her. I like her, she's feisty,' Lucy said. 'That chook likes your washing machine, Jax.'

'My what? How does a hen like a washing machine? And, aren't water buffalos feral?' Jax had so many questions for her.

Was he that starved for conversation?

'Cecil isn't feral. He belongs to Esther. He's also the town's mobile noticeboard, if the kids aren't spoiling him at the school,' replied Lucy, staring at the statue Jenny held in her hand.

'Is that made of nails and a beer can?' Jax asked Jenny. He'd seen nothing like it.

'Yes, and screws and washers all welded together. It's clever.' Jenny passed it to Jax.

'Heavy. And intricate. The guy knows his way around a welder.'

'Can I see it?' Lucy asked.

Jax passed the small water buffalo sculpture to Lucy, spotting the recognition in her crystal-clear eyes. No longer hazy and dazed, she was back to normal. If he knew her normal. Whatever it was, it was gorgeous. 'Do you know who made that, Lucy?'

Lucy passed it back to Jenny. 'Do you know, Jenny?'

'No. I just call him the Tin Man.'

'Is he related to you, Ironman?' Lucy said, giving him a cheeky grin.

Jax could only shake his head, grateful she seemed okay.

'Why do you call him the Tin Man?' Lucy asked Jenny.

'A few months ago, I started getting these wild orchids. Not just the flower but the entire plant cut from the tree itself, all ready to hang. They fill my small balcony,' said Jenny, staring at the metal buffalo sculpture cupped in her hands. 'The first sculpture was this flower, then birds and a camel. I'm getting quite the collection in my office.'

'You have a secret admirer,' gushed Lucy, with hands on knees and that dainty chin raised. Her smile was so wide it shone all the way to her eyes.

It was a hundred times better than what he'd seen on the small screen.

'I guess I do. I'll go find Stewart to see if you can go home. Take good care of her, Jax,' Jenny said over her shoulder, pushing the empty wheelchair down the corridor.

'I'm fine.' Lucy waved her hand in the air like Nancy from the Tea House.

A woman he'd met once, and would never forget.

'You don't have to hang around, Jax,' Lucy said.

'I've got nowhere I need to be in a hurry.' He had no schedules to keep, not anymore.

'Don't you have shopping in the car?'

'I do.'

'It'll bake in this heat.'

'Most of it's in eskies and I've got a decent car fridge.' She'd taught him that while chatting as she cooked on her YouTube channel. It was like he knew her without knowing her. It was weird. Did that make him some strange fan of hers?

'You would in that fancy car.'

'I've seen fancier.'

'I haven't.' She dropped her head as if ashamed.

How could she get embarrassed over his ute? There were plenty like his everywhere in the city.

He glanced through the main doors to the small car park. All of the locally owned utes were the standard square-bodied styles with sturdy bull bars across the front. Aerials came in various lengths and widths, but they all wore the same red dust, ingrained into the off-white paintwork. They were work vehicles, while his black ute shone like a toy. 'I see now why you've called it a Tonka Truck.'

She giggled and he was glad to hear it, even if it was accompanied by a shy smile.

'Okay, Lucy, all clear on the x-rays,' said Stewart, approaching them. 'Jax can take you home to get some rest. Take two of these after you've eaten, then bed.' He held out a plastic bottle containing some pills. 'These will cover the headaches for tonight.'

'I'll be fine,' she said, tucking her hands behind her back.

'Thanks, Stewart. Any other instructions.' Jax took the pills and read the label as Lucy scowled at him.

'She can use paracetamol tomorrow. After that, if the headaches persist, bring her back in to see me.' Stewart scribbled on his pad, then ripped off a page and held up to Lucy's face, she had to take it.

'What's this?'

'A medical certificate. You can't go to work for the next twenty-four hours with concussion, and I hear its train day tomorrow.'

'But—but—' Her shoulders dropped and the happiness leeched right out of her.

It dragged Jax down with her. What was wrong with him? He'd never been like this. 'Come on, let's get you home.'

'I can ride.'

'I've got the ute.' With an arm around her shoulders, he led her back to the car. 'I've also got this roast chicken we can share for dinner.'

'Why? You don't know me.'

'I owe you, Lucy.'

'For what?'

'It's my fault the Tea House is closing. It's your job, isn't it?'

'Aww, man!' She whined at him with a frown as he held open the passenger door.

'What did I do wrong now?'

'You're being nice.'

'That's the plan.'

'Well, it's hard to hate you when you're being nice.'

He chuckled at her grim expression.

'I'm being serious.'

He laughed harder. 'Get in and tell me where you live or I'll ask some stranger on the street.'

'You're not giving me a choice, are you?

'Nope.' With his hand on her elbow, he helped her into her seat. His day was working out better than planned, and their conversation was the most he'd had with anyone in a week. He didn't want it to stop.

Lucy wanted to jump out of the cab filled with the pure masculinity of Jax. Not only was the guy gorgeous, she'd been close enough to feel his strength. His stomach was a washboard of pure hot muscle. She wanted to see it, touch it, and lick him all over.

Which sucked.

She was supposed to hate him, or at least be mad at him. What made it worse is that he was nice too.

'I live there.' She pointed to their driveway where Rigsy's ute was parked near the stables.

'Your car?'

'No, it's Rigsy's.'

'Is that your boyfriend?'

She snorted another laugh. 'Rigsy is our resident couch-surfing cowboy.'

'Housemate then?'

'Only when he's in town. He's my housemate's cousin. Well, thanks for the lift.' She jumped out, desperate to get away from his divine cologne.

'Did you forget about your bike, Lucy?'

'Oops.' She swivelled around only to do a stumbling side-step. Jax caught her by the arm before she kissed the wall.

'Hey, take it easy. No pirouettes until tomorrow.'

This sucked. 'We save that for our softball cheerleaders and their tutus.'

'Huh?'

'Long story.'

'I've got time,' he said.

'Um…' She lost all thought, biting her lip at the way the tribal ink shifted along his bulky arms as he hoisted her bike out of his ute. It was sexy as hell.

It was then she realised the guy knew nobody and lived alone. 'Did you say you had food?'

'I did.' He smiled at her.

How could she hate the guy when he smiled like that?

'Come on in, but don't judge us. We're not fancy people...' *in fancy cars.*

'What did you say?'

'Welcome to the *unofficial Elsie Creek Inn*,' she said, waving at the large yard with its one tree and patchy lawn that stretched to the large holding pen and stables.

'Big tree. Have you fallen out of that one?'

She chuckled at the cheeky man rolling her bike over the cracked concrete path. 'I've never climbed that tree.' But she'd cooked many a Sunday roast under it with Monet and her barbecue.

It was their Sunday ritual after the guests had all gone. Monet would drag out her kid's wading pool and fill it up under the tree's expansive shade. They'd then kick back listening to Monet's latest playlist, making up names for clouds, sipping on nameless cocktails while waiting for dinner to cook. Lucy missed her high-flying friend.

'Do you own this place?' Jax asked, following her through the creaky back door, and into their simple, outdated kitchen.

'No. I'm the unofficial caretaker while Monet's away.' Lucy peeked around the old, slightly elevated, blended colonial style house, making sure it was tidy. It's bank of louvres and shutters allowed for the breeze to keep the place cool.

'How many snow globes have you got?' He pointed to her snow globe collection lining the tops of the cupboards, all the way around the large open kitchen.

She shrugged. 'It's been a while since I've counted them. I like them.'

'Obviously.' Jax put his shopping bags onto their well-worn dining table with mismatched chairs. 'Salad okay?'

'Absolutely. Although, I haven't met many men who eat salads, let alone buy it by the tub.'

'I believe in eating healthy.'

'I can see that.' The guy was a walking advertisement for perfect health.

'So why is this place called the unofficial Elsie Creek Inn?'

'Not sure? Monet would know. I always assumed it was because of the swags taking up floor space on train day, paydays, and weekends.'

'You're speaking a foreign language.'

'Sorry, I forgot there's a tourist in the house.' She grinned, grabbing some odd plates and mismatched cutlery. Everything was second hand in this place. It was pitiful compared to the impeccable table settings in the Tea House.

'The stockmen will stay at the train station watching over their cattle until they're safely onboard the train,' she said. 'When the train leaves, their job is done, so they cross the tracks to the pub for their knock-off sessions.' Which was on Lucy's side of the train tracks, the wrong side of the tracks, Nancy would say. 'Most of the men crash in their swags in their utes, but if it's raining and the pub's rooms are full, they'll crash in our lounge room while their horses hang out in the stables. Take a seat.' *Let's hope the chair doesn't break on the guy.*

'So, anyone can crash here?' Jax pulled out a chair, removed the lids from the plastic takeaway salad tubs then passed them to Lucy.

'Don't wait for me.' The man had table manners that would've impressed Nancy.

'So, there's no rooms? Just floor space?' Jax asked, pointing to the lounge area of outdated couches, odd chairs, and lots of bare floorboards.

'Sure, we've got rooms. And stables. But everyone knows its cooler to crash in the lounge with all the louvres open and fans going. Most of the men have their own swags to stretch out on the floor. Some mornings you can't see the floor through the bodies. They even spread into the kitchen area where the snoring is horrendous.' How must that look to someone like Jax, who was politely eating white meat with a knife and fork, not tearing at the chicken's legs like most men? He was too fancy for this place.

'So, no bookings?'

'You do realise this is a small community,' she said. 'We all know each other in some way. Most of the guests leave a few beers in the fridge, or food from their farms. And they all leave a few dollars in the cookie jar by the kettle for a hot shower and a cuppa before they head back home. It's an honour system that's been here long before I arrived.' Was Jax judging their simple way of life, in a kitchen where nothing matched?

'What happened to the stove?' He pointed the hole in the wall.

'It broke—it wasn't my fault. It broke long before I moved in.'

'Did I say it was your fault?'

Everyone else would have. 'We cook on the barbecue out the back.' Oh god, they were red-necked ferals! Bush bumpkins. Hillbilly hicks. Compared to the slick Jax who oozed sex appeal in his fancy ute and fancy boots—why was he still here?

'These salads are good, for a supermarket.'

'The girls do a good job. It's almost homemade, except they use jar mayonnaise.'

'You don't?'

'No, I make my own.' She reached for the rattly fridge next to the old tuckerbox freezer and pulled out an assortment of sauces. 'Dead horse, I presume.'

'What?'

'Tomato sauce, and I've still got some mayo left.'

'Did you make those?'

'I did, and that mango chutney and chilli sauce too. Careful, that chilli's mega hot.'

'Is this that chilli sauce you used for your mud crab?'

She gasped and fell back into her chair.

He'd been saying things all day, like he'd known her long before they'd ever met.

'I'll try this.' He took her sauces and added them to the side of his plate. 'Don't be embarrassed, Lucy.'

'But—but—' No, he didn't watch her on YouTube, did he? Shouldn't he be watching kickboxing or car chases or babes in bikinis? 'Tell me you didn't... watch?'

'Yes, I've seen your show.'

'Nooo.' She wanted to slide under the table and die in shame.

'It's good, you've taught me a lot. Hey, is the water at my place contaminated, or in some red zone?'

'What? No. That's Tindal. The Clare property has great water.'

'That's a relief.' He took a bite of his food with some of her sauce. 'This chilli sauce is amazing. You made it look easy when you cooked it.'

'You—'*Mr freaking Ironman* '—watched. Why?' She hoarsely whispered, horrified. 'Hank said no one would watch.'

'I did.'

'Which one?'

'All of them.'

'Oh, no. I can't believe you watched me cook,' she mumbled into her hot palms.

'I did. Now eat something, please, so you can take these pills and get some rest.'

'Whose giving who pills?' called out Rigsy, coming in from the lounge. 'Hey, it's the dude with the space-ute.'

'Tonka Truck,' said Lucy, fanning her face as Jax squinted his sexy eyes at her.

'Tonka Trucks are cool. I had them when I was a kid,' said Rigsy, turning the chair around to sit on it like he was riding a horse. 'Why are you covered in dirt, Miss Lucy?' He pulled a leaf from her hair.

'I fell over and I'm fine,' she said, taking a mouthful of her dinner. She was amazed how fast Jax had cleared his plate. The man must have been starving waiting on her at the hospital.

'Lucy fell out of a tree and has a slight concussion,' said Jax.

'Hey, blabbermouth much.' She did not just bark that out to Ironman? She never spoke to people like this. Jax just hid his grin and ate his food.

'No freaking way? Is this your fault?' Rigsy said to Jax.

'Excuse me?' Fork down, Jax frowned. It made Lucy do the same.

'Rigsy, stop it.' Lucy put a hand on her housemate's shoulder, which was stringy and shapeless compared to the well-defined strength in Jax's build. Rigsy was a boy compared to the manly Jax. 'Jax saw it happen and took me to the hospital. He insisted.' Jax was her hero.

'Well, okay then,' Rigsy said, pinching a piece of chicken from Lucy's plate. 'Your dad would kill us if anything happened to you.'

'Knock-knock, yell out if you're good-looking,' said a guy at the door.

'Well, that'll be me.' Rigsy jumped to his boots and opened the back-screen door.

'Not you, I'm talking about the female kind,' said the guy wearing a wide Akubra at the back door.

'G'day, Scotty,' said Rigsy. 'What brings you into town?'

'I was hoping for some floor space as a swap for a special delivery for the Station Hand's daughter and a slab of steak.'

'I'll chuck the steak in the fridge.' Rigsy dumped the bag into the rattly fridge, booting it shut. 'Now all we've got to do is catch that rogue red hen on Cecil's back and we can have steak and eggs for brekkie.'

'We've heard about that hen. Hey there, Miss Lucy.'

'Hi, Scotty. Welcome back to town.' She stood to greet him.

Scotty stopped mid-step, thumbing back his hat's brim to nod at Jax. 'It might be best if I stop asking for a cuddle, Miss Lucy, with your fella at the table.'

Lucy screwed up her nose at Jax. 'He's not—he's just a…friend.' So much for being enemies, with his smug expression as he scooped his meal onto a fork and chewed. Could they be frenemies?

'So, I've graduated from public enemy number one to friend, have I?' Jax asked her.

'Did I say that out loud?'

'You did bump your head.'

'I felt drunk.' She touched the tender lump on the back of her head. Was she still drunk to be so talkative?

'Who did what?' Scotty asked, turning to Rigsy for answers.

Rigsy pointed at Jax, saying, 'You told me Lucy only had a concussion.'

'Settle down you two. I'm fiiiine,' said Lucy, catching the slight frown from Jax. What was the big deal over one word? 'Did you say you had something for me, Scotty?'

'From your mum.' Scotty put an old biscuit tin on the table.

'Are you working out of Mataranka?' Lucy took her seat and opened the lid, inhaling the assorted earthy herbs and hearty smoked beef aromas.

'I am. I'm helping with the load for train day.'

'What's that?' Jax asked, frowning at the small plastic bags.

'Only the best beef jerky in the Territory,' said Scotty, with Rigsy's hand hovering over the tin.

'Go on.' She held the tin up for the boys to grab a piece each, then to Jax who only shook his head. 'The rest are bush herbs my mother collects, they're great for cooking.' She pulled out the envelope, looking forward to reading it. Her parents didn't Skype, they didn't even own an email and phone calls were rare. But the postal service, no matter how slow, worked for them.

'Your parents run a station?' Jax asked.

'Puh-lease,' Scotty said with a bulging cheek full of jerky, 'you're sitting at the table with the Station Hand's daughter.'

'Is that like some cattlemen's royalty or something?' Jax asked with a slight chuckle.

'We're no-one.' Again, the heat rolled up her neck.

'Get out of it,' said Rigsy, shovelling more jerky into his mouth. 'Lucy's dad is the greatest head-stockman in the Territory.'

'He's the best overseer in the North,' reiterated Scotty. 'I'm damned lucky to be working for the man who's legendary in running cattle. If you want someone to fix your station, he's the man for the job.'

'He's like a fancy city consultant saving businesses from going broke, except the man does it with beef,' explained Rigsy. 'He should be calling himself the overseer but only calls himself *the Station Hand*, but everyone knows he's bigger and better at the job than the bosses themselves.'

'Too true. He's the toughest, meanest man you'd ever meet,' said Scotty. 'If you're dating his daughter, you'll wanna be careful.'

'We're just friends,' butted in Lucy. 'And Dad's not that bad?'

'Your father would skin any man alive with his stock whips,' said Scotty. 'Then he'd make 'em dance by shooting the heels out of their boots while your mum shoots flaming arrows at them.'

'Mum does not shoot flaming arrows!'

'She's got all sorts of arrows, I've seen 'em. She even gave me lessons,' said Scotty.

'My mother enjoys archery as a sport,' she explained to Jax.

'She's also got the meanest crossbow and a dead eye, her mum has,' said Scotty to Jax. 'She's brilliant in goose hunting season. You'll never go hungry with the Station Hand's wife and daughter on the job.'

'Oh brother! Here, you jerks take some more jerky and shut up,' said Lucy, holding out the tin to the boys. What must Jax think of her? Why should she care!

'You can take these, now you've had something to eat,' said Jax, passing the bottle to her.

'Oi, what's with the pills, mate?' Scotty asked, stepping in closer. 'Rumour has it you're a dealer?'

Jax frowned so hard it was scary.

Lucy wanted to die of humiliation. 'Are you for real, Scotty! Those pills are from the doctor. Jax was only helping me,' she snapped out in Jax's defence.

'I'd better go.' Jax stood to full height making both boys crane back their necks to look at him, stepping back from his swinging distance.

'Thanks for your help, Jax,' Lucy said, also getting to her feet. 'I'm sorry to be a pain and ruin your plans.'

'It's okay. At least I got a tour of the hospital, and met a few of the locals.' He side-glanced the denim-clad lads chomping on dried meat, staring at his ink work.

'Do you ride a Harley, mate?' Scotty asked.

'Nah, he drives the Tonka Truck. It's a sweet ride,' said Rigsy. 'Hey, what do you do?'

'I'm trying to fix a house at the moment,' Jax said at the door. 'Please stay out of trees if you can help it, Lucy.'

'No worries,' *the cheeky thing,* '...thanks again.' On the back doorstep, she waved at the world's most handsomest man. She couldn't take her eyes off the way those cargo pants hugged his thick thighs and great arse.

'Are you perving, Miss Lucy?' Rigsy said close to her ear.

She jumped, slamming the screen door shut. 'No.'

'I reckon she was,' said Scotty, 'almost drooling she was.'

'Nick off, and go to the pub you pair of drongos.'

'Come with us?' Scotty begged her.

'Thanks for the invite, but I'm going to bed.' Her head was pounding. Placing the empty plates into the sink, she scooped up her tin and tablets.

'No sweat. You've got an early start for train day.'

'Mate, don't,' Rigsy said, elbowing Scotty.

'What?'

'They've shut down the Tea House.'

'Since when, Miss Lucy?'

'I'm sure Rigsy will explain all. Good night, boys.' She closed her bedroom door and sat on her bed, staring at the unopened letter from her mother.

Her mum will be expecting Scotty to take a letter back with him, but what should she write?

She'd moved out to find her own place, to be her own boss and have her own kitchen. She wanted to get out from under her father's shadow, to create her own reputation — and she had. Not the one she wanted, known as the kitchen hand who kept burning things.

Scotty would tell her parents everything. Then her dad, with his hot temper, would demand she move back in with them. Back to their rusty old utes and horse floats with their horses and dogs. It was a circus. More like run-down carnies who shifted from station to station, following the musters.

They weren't royalty. They were nomads.

She wasn't ready to go back to that way of life.

SIX

Lucy pedalled through the residential part of town. She passed the brick houses that kept patches of dry grass for front gardens or enviable native-styled cottage scenes.

And then there was one house that stood separate from the rest.

The last one on the street, with its rock garden of cycads like a scene from the stone age—except for its plague of garden gnomes.

They were everywhere. Sun faded, creepy, smiling, paint-chipped garden gnomes. In assorted scenes scattered among the rocks beneath the feathery cycad fronds.

Lucy could feel their little black beady eyes on her as she stopped her bike at the front gate.

She'd never been here.

She'd never dared until now.

'Come to steal a flamin' garden gnome, did you, missy?'

'Nancy?' Shading her eyes with her hand, Lucy peered past the rockery and sun-baking gnomes to where Nancy sat under the veranda's deep shade.

'Well, don't stand there lookin' like a lootin' loiterer. I'm not yelling across my yard and tellin' the neighbours my bloomin' business.'

Lucy leaned her bike against the small fence. The wire gate screeched then clanged behind her with a shudder. She paused for a moment, expecting all those scary gnomes to turn and frown at her.

'What do you flamin' well want? Money, I suppose.'

Lucy was owed a wage, but it wasn't her only reason for visiting. 'You didn't do the train day.'

'You didn't show up either. I heard you had a headache, falling from trees into the arms of handsome strangers. How long were you waiting for him to drive past to time your fall, all part of your plan, eh missy?'

'It was an accident. And, I was picking a mango.' She'd forgotten all about that mango.

Lucy stepped onto the decking with its cool misting fans. A teacup and saucer rested on the small ceramic table beside a notepad and pen where Nancy sat, glaring at the view of the rockery that blended into the scenery of the vast countryside.

'Nice view,' Lucy said.

'It hasn't changed for thirty years.' Nancy sipped on her tea.

There was no offering of a drink, or a chair, nothing.

Lucy swallowed hard and wiped her clammy hands down her dress. 'So, that's it? You're done with the Tea House.'

'I am,' said Nancy, crossing her arms over her chest. 'And don't even bother trying to talk me out of it.'

'What about your cooking gear?'

'It belongs to the shop.'

'Don't you own any of it?'

'Nope. The landlady does.'

Nancy had always made out she owned everything inside the Tea House. 'Who is the landlady?'

'Think you can run the place, do you?'

'I might.'

'Bah! With your reputation of burning everything, you'll poison the patrons.' Nancy's cackle echoed off the smiling garden gnomes as if they were in an amphitheatre of frozen miniature clowns. 'What about you feeding that mob out of the back shed on train days?'

Lucy's knees trembled. 'I-I-I did what you said. I kept them out of your hair and stopped them coming into the Tea House. You were always complaining about them, chasing them away, so I was doing you a favour.'

'By telling them I did all the cooking too, eh?'

'I didn't say anything, they just assumed it was you. Did you—'

'I told 'em nothing.'

It was so typical of Nancy to claim all the glory. 'They won't eat my cooking. Even though, technically they have.'

'Pft!' Nancy waved her hand in the air. 'Just coz you've fed a bunch of mongrel mud-eating drovers, you think you're good enough to manage the Tea House.'

Jax had said her cooking was good—but Jax had never tasted her cooking. Hank liked it—but she was feeding a man who rummaged through rubbish bins. She'd fed all the stockmen, ringers, drovers, stock inspectors, jackeroos, jillaroos, overseers, and truck drivers—but they never knew it was her cooking.

Yet, it was the women of this town she needed to convince the most that she could cook. And she'd fed none of them. *Oh no*. Her shoulders slunk at the realisation.

'Those men would eat flamin' charcoal if you gave 'em enough tomato sauce to disguise the flavour. They wouldn't care,' said Nancy with a scowl.

Hank had said the same thing, and her parents. So why was she setting herself up to fail?

'You taught me,' Lucy said. Nancy didn't have any formal qualifications, but she had decades of experience. 'I've been doing everything you said—'

'You've never mastered my sponges without them being soggy in the centre and burnt on their bums. Go back to your daddy—'

'Why can't I try!'

Nancy gave a smart sniff, as her grey eyes narrowed at Lucy. 'Why are you here then?'

'For you to tell me who owns the Tea House.'

'I'm surprised you didn't know already, little Miss Smarty Pants.'

'The Station Master said it's not part of the train company's lease.'

'Yeah, that smart cookie had a plan. Have you got a plan?'

'I'm working on it.' If writing a detailed letter outlining all her hopes to her mother counted as a business plan, Lucy had one. Now safe in Scotty's hands on its way to Mataranka.

Nancy rummaged around in the shelf filled with magazines and half-finished crochet work. She pulled out an envelope and dropped it in front of Lucy. 'Here, I knew you'd come sniffin' around.'

'What's this?'

'Your final pay. You were only casual so I don't owe you any holiday pay, nothing. I also deducted the costs of that burned bread, the scones and cake.'

'I paid for those ingredients myself.'

'You didn't pay me for the power you used to feed that coffee club mob, did you? I should take more.'

'I was practising to improve.'

'Just coz you fed a bunch of blokes who bathe under a water tank, you think you can flamin' cook for the Tea House.'

'I've been cooking with you for three years.'

'*For* me. Not *with* me. I'm the boss! And you're the simple kitchenhand who never perfected my scone recipe. Lord knows what you'd do to my pavlova!'

'You never showed me, you kept saying it was a secret.' No matter how much Lucy had asked, or tried to watch and guess the measurements in Nancy's recipe for scones, it never worked.

Scones. Simple scones. Baked in thousands of kitchens, Australia wide, and Lucy had never been able to bake one unburnt batch in three years!

'I'll take that recipe with me to my grave, I will.'

Fine! 'What are you going to do now?'

Lucy ducked from the swinging *For-Sale* sign Nancy dumped onto the table.

'I'm selling everything and I'm gone,' Nancy said.

'When? Where?'

'Right after I've kept my crown as the Queen of the Billabong Barbie Bake-off.'

'Won't you be too busy packing to enter?'

'Why? Have you got any money to buy this place?'

'No.'

'So how are you gonna afford to run the Tea House, eh?'

'You did.'

'I—unlike you, missy—had a husband, who made sure I was taken care of long after he left. May he rest in peace,' Nancy said to the misting fan that blew at her grey curls.

'Where will you go?'

'My daughter's in Queensland near the beach, where I'm going to make sandcastles and collect shells with my grandbabies.'

'That sounds lovely.'

'Stop sucking up and tell me what you want?'

'Who owns the Tea House and when does the lease expire?' Lucy wasn't going to leave until she had her answers, no matter how much Nancy bullied her.

'How much did you make from that mob in the back shed?'

'Enough to cover costs.' And to put money into her savings account. 'You still have plenty of train day bookings. You could still operate until you leave.'

'I've folded up my apron and I'm not going back.'

'Don't you have any sentimental attachment to that place? What about tradition?'

'I'm flamin' tired, don't you get it, missy. I don't wanna serve anymore, putting up with people's bulldust. I wanna be the guest and have someone fetch me more lemon for *my* tea. More ice for *my* water, a fresh plate, another napkin, and a fresh bloody pot of tea. For thirty years I have managed that place, and I don't care if it never opens again.'

'If you hated it so much why did you stay there for so long.' *No! Where did that come from?*

'I had to.'

'No, you didn't.' Why couldn't she shut up? Did she do some brain damage when she knocked herself on the head?

'I...' Nancy sighed with such deep sorrow.

Lucy could feel the grief emanating from the older woman in waves.

It didn't last long.

Nancy sat upright wearing that fierce familiar scowl. 'None of your beeswax. Now, what the flamin' heck do you want?'

'Is there any chance you'll go back to the Tea House? For anything?'

'Nope. Nothing.'

'No special cup? No favourite wooden spoon? No bowl?'

'I'm about to hold a lawn sale of all this excess crap, coz I'm downsizing to a one-bedroom unit. Why would I wanna cart all that flamin' crap with me?'

'When is your lawn sale?'

'In a few weeks, bring your cash then. I must tell Esther to advertise it on Cecil.' Nancy reached for her pen and jotted it down on her list.

'Who owns the Tea House, Nancy? Why the big secret?'

Nancy tightened her lips, deepening the lines around her mouth.

'I'm not leaving until you tell me.' Lucy stood firm, crossed her arms over her chest, and kept her eye steady—just like her dad would when dealing with a cheeky jackeroo.

'A pain in the posterior is what you are,' Nancy said, waving her arms in the air. 'It's the publican.'

'The publican owns the Tea House?'

'And all that land the Elsie Creek Station sits on. Including the Station Master's house, the cattle yards, and sheds, she's leased it all to the train company.' Nancy then plonked her elbow on the table and pointed her pen at Lucy. 'She's not gonna be impressed with you making shifty deals, selling stuff to stockmen in *her* shed without *her* permission?'

'How come the publican owns it?'

'Her great grandmother was the original Elsie.'

'The one who grew watermelons and sold it to the people on the train?'

'The Station Master's house was where they used to live before she built the pub.'

'She must've sold a lot of watermelons.' Lucy then grinned and stood straighter.

'What's with you?'

'I work Friday's in the pub's kitchen.'

'You don't cook, you're just the kitchen hand.'

'Their chef has been teaching me stuff. And as my father always says, there's no harm in asking, is there?' Lucy grinned wider as an excited energy bubbled inside her.

'It won't be that easy, missy.'

'Why not? You made it look easy.'

'Only coz I've been doin' it for thirty years. And, I'm having the power cut off *today*.' Nancy stood, waving her notepad at Lucy like she was a fly. 'Now, nick off, I've got to go practise to keep my title as Queen of the Billabong Barbie Bake-off.' Nancy slammed the door shut behind her. Conversation over.

Lucy stared at the shut door. 'Bitch.'

But she had a name.

Pedalling down the road, she nearly jumped off her seat at the car horn followed by the rumble of the beefy v8 engine.

'Sorry, I didn't mean to scare you,' called out Kat through the passenger window of her vintage ute.

'My fault, I was daydreaming.' Dreaming of a better future, in her own kitchen.

'Nice day for it. I'll give you a lift if you're going into town?'

'I am. Thanks.' Lucy hoisted her heavy bike into the back, remembering Jax throwing it like it weighed nothing. She hadn't seen Jax or anyone since she'd fallen, suffering with a groggy head and a full body ache to go with it. Her tree-climbing days were over.

Determined to catch up on lost time, she climbed into the cab. 'Thanks for this.'

'No sweat. Why don't you own a car?' Kat asked, as she drove the them into town. 'I mean, I didn't need one in the city, but out here everyone has one.'

'I've never needed one and I don't have my full driver's licence yet.' Another reminder of the many things she needed to achieve on her impossibly long list. 'So, where are you headed?'

'I'm dropping off some pamphlets for the candle-making workshop. Mrs Sternston wants to include it as part of her craft store's Christmas workshops. What do you think?'

'They're brilliant.' Advertising was way beyond Lucy's skill levels.

'I'd love you to do the catering.'

'You would?

'Sure, it'll be a Saturday, and I'd checked that there will be no train day clashes. Hey, is it true, you did my trick and fell out of a tree? Although, I fell out of a treehouse with Wendy. My daughter wouldn't talk to me for a week after that,' Kat said, giggling as she steered. 'So, fill me in on the gossip?'

'Well...' Lucy explained to Kat about Nancy leaving and hoping to take on the Tea House lease. 'Kat, you run a small business, is the Tea House worth it? You lease properties, what do you look for in a tenant?'

'References from past landlords,' said Kat as she slowed down to turn onto the main street. 'Good credit history to pay rent, which also means they need a job. Lucy, how can I put this when I suck at tact...'

'Just say it. Please?'

'The Tea House is only open one day a week. Will that be enough to survive on?'

Lucy shrugged. 'It used to be open for four days.'

'What happened?'

'We weren't getting the people. Nancy cut it to three days, then just train day where it's guaranteed to be full. I've saved up to buy this amazing coffee machine for the place.'

'That's a lot of coffee to make. What are your overheads for the shop?'

'Um, I get all the furniture and stuff, I think?' If the original Elsie made her fortune selling watermelons, why couldn't Lucy do it by making coffee and cakes?

'What about the power, phone, and other business expenses?'

'Like what?'

'Business registration fees, insurance, bookkeeping systems—I hate bookwork.'

'My housemate does bookwork for the stations. Monet could teach me,' said Lucy. 'You're starting to scare me, Kat. I didn't think it'd be that technical to just cook.'

'It's basic business,' Kat said, pulling to a stop in front of the craft store. The rumble of the vintage ute's deep engine echoed off the shop windows. 'Hey, if you get the Tea House lease would you be open for date nights? I'd love to have dinner with Kyle somewhere other than the pub.'

'I don't have a boyfriend, so I wouldn't know where anyone goes for dates around here, besides the pub?' Where she hid in the kitchen doing the dishes.

Besides, most of the men were too scared to go near her because of her dad.

Once she'd been crushing on this guy so badly, she followed him around like a puppy. He was nice to her, sharing her first kiss—until her father chased him off the station with his stock whips. Even now, hundreds of kilometres away from her father, his reputation still surrounded her. Maybe she should move to another state?

'Kyle and I take a picnic basket with some wine and do a lazy hike somewhere to watch the sunset,' said Kat with a dreamy smile. 'This town could do with something nice. You wouldn't have to do it all the time, maybe just once a month. Hey, what about catering for the Flynn Brothers' movie night?'

'Everyone knows the Flynn Brothers' movie night will never happen.'

'But it may be a future possibility.'

'True. You're full of ideas, Kat.'

'If I think of any more, I'll email them to you. Hey, do you make birthday cakes?'

'That's Nancy's thing.'

'The town's going to need someone to replace her when she goes.'

'But no one eats my cooking, and I burn stuff—' Why was she hesitating over birthday cakes when she wanted to run a food business? She could do this. She loved making cakes, especially children's cakes that were so much fun.

'What you do with the local bush herbs is amazing, it's your unique food signature.'

'I have a food signature?' Lucy blinked. Then blinked again. *What did that mean?* How hopeless a foodie was she if she didn't even know the city lingo for chefs?

'Oh, I've got to drop these flyers off,' said Kat, hoisting her day pack over her shoulder and scooping up the pamphlets. 'I'm running late. I promised to meet with Wendy and my sister-in-law this morning, we're doing a make-over on the caveman's boudoir.'

'How did Nora convince Jimmy to say yes?'

'As king of this Billabong Barbie thing, Jimmy's gone barbie mad. Practising daily, annoying Nora and his kids yelling out, *is it time? Is it time*? Nora has to play timekeeper and mystery shopper for his menu, she's demanded a room makeover as her fee.'

'Jimmy's practising?'

'Twice a day. Lunches at the workshop and then dinner at home. Kyle and JT are loving it. Not only are they eating like kings, all of the other tradies from neighbouring workshops supply the meat that Jimmy barbecues for smoko. It's like a carnivorous lucky dip. What is it with men and barbecues?'

'Who knows?' But Lucy now knew she had stiff competition, who were confident and talented. Her tree fall had put her behind schedule. Would she be able to catch up and find her self-belief to win?

SEVEN

Jax stood before a row of paint swatches within the hardware store. With so many choices, he was actually in need of a female's opinion.

He glanced along the aisle to the main street just as Lucy pedalled past, waving at people.

'There goes Miss Lucy, it must be her shift at the pub,' said one of the regulars at the round card table.

'Nah, Lucy works on Friday nights or train-nights,' said the man with suspenders and an old fashioned felt hat. 'She missed the last run on account she had a concussion.'

'Is the girl all right?' Asked his neighbour, pushing up his coke-bottle glasses.

'She looks fine to me,' said another as he pointed to the open door facing the main street.

'Bounced back I'd say. That young Rigsy and his mate Scotty said Miss Lucy didn't look too good. They said that drug dealer took her to the hospital in his space ute, or are they callin' it a Tonka Truck now?'

Jax frowned from his hideaway in the shelves. He'd avoided them by coming through the feedstore entrance, but their nattering still carried through the gaps in the shelves.

'Drug dealers wouldn't bother helping Lucy, would they?'

'What makes you say he's a drug dealer?'

'Well, he's no farmer, is he? And he's got all them tatts and short hair.'

'He looks military to me, with those boots.'

'They're not a miner's style of boots.'

'Nah, they're different boots, like the copper wears.'

'He doesn't look like a copper—more like a drug dealer.'

'How many drug dealers do you know?'

Unfortunately, Jax knew too many, but that didn't make him one—even if he was only in this town because of a deal he'd made.

He rubbed at the tight ache in his chest, feeling the weight of loneliness press down on him.

'It's just bloody walls.' He closed his eyes, reached out and plucked a colour swatch.

The winner of his lucky dip… *Eggshell white.*

'Figures.' The rogue red hen was now hanging around his place. Thankfully there'd been no further water buffalo sightings before his morning coffee. Only the silly chook watching him while perched on his washing machine on the back veranda. Then it'd fluff around in the dust, clucking to the music.

Taking his colour swatch, sandpaper, and brushes to the counter, the other twin brother in his starched shirt and leather apron served him. 'Good choice. Eggshell goes with everything, it's timeless.'

'Yeah, right.' Jax didn't have a clue. 'I'll take twenty-five litres. And, um, what do you have to feed a hen?'

'How many?'

'Just one.'

'Okay, I'll get you a small bag. We've got a good mush-mix.'

'Sure, whatever.' Jax leaned his hip against the counter and gazed out to the main street.

The men at the round card table were silent. He could feel their eyes on him.

A chair scraped along the cement and one of the card players approached. Thumbing back the brim of his old-fashioned felt hat that matched his snappy suspenders, he held out his hand. 'G'day mate, I'm Billy,' he said with a warm smile and a trickster's shine to his eyes. 'I believe you've bought ol' Tobias Clare's place.'

'I have. I'm Jax.' He shook the old man's hand.

'I just wanted to say what you did by helping Miss Lucy, by taking her to the hospital was a good thing. She's a sweet kid, that one.'

'You know Lucy?'

'She helps at the pub as a kitchen hand. Can I ask…'

Jax braced himself for it as the rest of the men at that table squinted at him through the cigar smoke.

'Did Lucy really fall out of a tree?' Billy asked.

'The branch broke, and Lucy fell with it, I saw it through my mirrors driving past.'

'What was she doing in a tree?' Called out the guy with coke-bottle glasses.

'She was picking a mango.' The same mango that was now on his ute's passenger seat filling the cab with its fragrance. Maybe he should drop it off at Lucy's considering the effort she put into plucking the thing?

'She's like her mother, always foraging she was,' said Billy, as the men at the table nodded and murmured. 'You wouldn't know where Lucy's dad is these days?'

'Mataranka.' How did he get into this crap, knowing the local gossip? 'You all play cards?' *Duh!*

'We don't play, we cheat,' said Billy with a grin and a wink, hooking his thumbs into his snappy suspenders. 'I'm the yardie at the pub. That eagle-eyed old fool with the bottle-coke-glasses, that's Jeffrey. James, then Johnny on the other side.'

'All J's.'

'Triple J's some kid called them, after that radio station. You heard of it?'

'Yes.'

'We don't get it.'

'What, the music?'

'No, the station. There's limited frequency out here. Although, Monet and Luke, the bloke in the bottle shop, they both know all about music and stuff.'

'Here we are, one bag of prime chook mush and a tin of egg-shell paint,' said the man missing a bow tie.

'That's Michael Flynn. Him and his brother Paul run this place,' explained Billy. 'Everyone knows them as the Flynn Brothers.'

'Oh, how rude of me, considering you've moved into the Clare's place. Welcome to town,' said Michael Flynn, extending his hand to Jax. 'It's a nice thing what you did, rescuing Lucy. We were told you were a thorough gentleman.'

'It was nothing.' *What did Lucy say?*

'Shame about the Tea House shutting down,' said one of the Triple J's at the table.

Crap. 'I'll see you around.' Jax grabbed his gear, hightailing it out of there before they bombarded him with more questions. He was used to walking into a shop in total anonymity.

Yet, what he'd done for Lucy seemed to have won over the locals. She was still helping him without even realising it.

And how did he repay her? By causing her to lose her job.

The guilt outweighed his need for conversation and headed for home. The thing was, it didn't feel like much of a home—just a big empty house in the middle of nowhere.

EIGHT

At the back of the large two-storey pub, Lucy wheeled her bike to the staff entrance where she found Lenny, the chef.

'Hey there, luv, how's the head?' Lenny asked with a cigarette hanging out of his mouth as he hosed out a bucket. 'We missed you on train-night.'

'I'm sorry, I couldn't make it.'

'Hey, no sweat. Scotty and Rigsy said you didn't look too good. Are you feeling okay?'

'Much better, thank you. Is the boss in?'

'She's in the office between shifts. What are you going to do now the Tea House has closed?'

'Do you have any extra hours in the kitchen?'

'Only what we've got now, luv. If you keep up the practise, I'd love you take over when I go on holiday.'

'When are you going on holiday?'

'Never. I live the eternal dream, right here.' He laughed, tipping his bucket against the fence line. 'Go on, in you go,' he said, opening the door.

She headed through the kitchen with its stainless-steel benches. A cold room stood near the pantry. A large dishwasher sat by two deep sinks, and a long serving bench with heat lights that ran down the centre of the room. Along the far wall stood the deep fryer, the industrial ovens, a row of gas burners, a large hot plate and grill. She'd burned nothing in this kitchen and thankfully, Lenny didn't mind teaching her on quieter nights.

Unfortunately, quiet nights were rare on train day and miner's payday. She was usually up to her elbows in dishes, making salads and desserts on the fly. It was hectic.

Even when the rare tourist bus stopped by from Kakadu National Park, it would be a crazy few hours making sandwiches and burgers, working alongside the publican herself.

Lucy hovered in the corridor, by the open office doorway. Inside, at her desk, the publican tapped away on her PC's keyboard.

The publican. A woman with beer in her blood. Born in this pub and rumoured to have been bottle fed on the amber liquid. A publican long before she could legally drink.

The locals called her God.

Her name, Samantha Myers.

Lucy tapped on the doorframe and waited.

Samantha swivelled around in her chair and gave a warm smile. 'Hey, Lucy, how are you feeling?'

'I'm okay. I'm not disturbing you, am I?'

'No. I could do with a break. Coffee?' Samantha motioned to the small coffee pot percolating on the side bench.

'Thanks.' Lucy took a seat in the guest chair and looked at the mountain of paperwork on the desk. Lucy didn't understand paperwork, she'd never finished school. She was a bush kid, not a businesswoman—who was she kidding!

Then she took notice of Samantha, blonde, pretty, determined. A year younger than herself, the woman had already accomplished so much and carried a tonne of responsibility.

'What brings you here?' Samantha asked, putting the mug in front of Lucy and returning to her office chair.

'Um, well, with Nancy closing the Tea House, do you have any more hours for me in the kitchen?'

'Only what Lenny wants, and I'm well trained to never upset the chef.'

'Good move.' Lenny was a man's cook with a no-frills traditional pub menu, known for his juicy steaks and gravy-rich-soupy sauces.

'I can put your name down for bar work when the next vacancy comes up? You get on with the staff, I'm sure the bar manager will play nice.'

'Umm…' The bar manager was scarier than Nancy on a bad day. 'Thank you for the offer, but I don't like working front of house, I prefer kitchens,' Lucy replied shyly, squeezing her hands in her lap.

'It's not for everyone, but the offer's there is you want it.'

'Thank you.'

'Don't thank me. You've got a great work ethic, always showing up on time for your shift. We like that. Do you know how hard it is to get backpacking barmaids to do that?'

'Why do you hire backpackers all the time?'

'Because every time I get a new barmaid, Lenny has to call in his kitchenhand to help because the pub is full of single cattlemen looking for love.'

Lucy giggled. 'Don't forget the miners.'

'How could I? Shh, don't tell the backpackers that.'

'I won't. Most don't talk to me.'

'And this is the most conversation we've had in a while. So, what else is new?'

'It's the Tea House lease. I—I—' Lucy wiped her hands on her skirt, biting her bottom lip she glanced at the ceiling fan trying to find her courage.

'Go on,' prodded Samantha gently. 'You can ask me. I won't bite.'

Lucy lifted her shoulders and whispered, 'I want to take on the Tea House lease.' There, she'd said it. And now, she held her breath waiting.

Samantha was expressionless, but she was famous — and feared—for her poker face. As the only legally licensed liquor distributor within a five-hundred-kilometre radius, the Elsie Creek Pub was the oasis in the outback desert. As the publican, no man would dare go against her for fear of getting banned from their beer.

Samantha was tough.

Until she smiled. 'We've been hoping you'd ask.'

'You have?' *Who's we?*

'I know you've been cooking for the stockmen in the train station's back shed.'

'Nancy said you'd be mad at that?'

'Are you kidding? I love it. Those guys needed the service, and you supplied it. You showed initiative.'

'I don't tell them I do the cooking, but I don't lie either, they just assume it's Nancy.'

'Do you cook for those card players in the hardware store, too?'

Lucy nodded. 'Nancy was only giving them stale biscuits, and I needed the practise.'

'Do you know why Nancy has to feed those guys?'

'To keep the peace, they tell me.'

'It's true. It happened before your time, but it was war.'

'No way.'

'Oh yeah, it was brutal too,' Samantha said, giggling behind her coffee mug.

'What happened?'

'As town tradition, the retired men would play cards and drink coffee in the main bar, smoking their cigars. My grandad used to play with them too. We never charged them for anything, but they'd always make sure there was money in the tin for the coffee, the use of space, and to ensure the ceiling fan kept spinning.'

'Why did they move to the hardware store?'

'The smoking laws. They couldn't smoke their cigars inside or anywhere near the pub. This was before we built the beer garden, so they took up veranda space at the train station.'

'Nancy would have hated that.'

'She did.' Samantha chuckled, sipped on her coffee and then said, 'Those stubborn old fools wouldn't budge. They kept saying they were paying customers, and they were. So we gave them that round card table, the kettle, and offered to hook in a ceiling fan for them.'

'So, what happened?'

'Well, Nancy tried to shoo them off with her straw broom and locked them out. One of the men tried to get in through the window to get some water for their kettle, and the entire front wall fell away. It was full of termites. People were jumping out of their seats, tables were knocked over, cups smashed, swatting at lots of angry termites. It was a massive mess.'

'Is that why there's new bi-fold doors?'

'Yep. By then it was an outright war between the cardplayers and the women of the Tea House. Johnny and Nancy were the worst at stirring that storm in a teacup. By then, with the Tea House under renovations, we all wanted peace.'

'Who came up with the solution to use the Flynn Brother's shed space?'

Samantha just sipped from her coffee.

'It was you who got the outback mafia to move to the Flynn brother's hardware store.'

'Where those retired men can offer their amazing practical advice to anyone who wants it,' Samantha said. 'The Flynn brothers tell me those men actually help sell stock in their store, making them feel useful and still a part of this town.'

'So, you negotiated a peace treaty?'

'An agreement. The men agreed that they'd stay away from the Tea House, as long as Nancy supplied morning tea on the days she opened. They'd still put their money in the tin for the privilege of the coffee and use of a ceiling fan. Then you took over feeding them, huh?'

'Do you think they noticed?'

'Billy did. That man misses nothing.'

Lucy adored Billy in his suspenders and vintage felt hat. Everyone did.

Samantha then patted Lucy's hand. 'Billy won't say anything until you're ready. We understand you have a tricky reputation.'

Was there anybody left in the Territory who didn't know she burned things? 'So, why risk giving me the lease?' Lucy blurted out.

'No one else has asked,' Samantha said bluntly, leaning back in her seat.

Probably because no one knew it was under a lease.

Lucy tugged at her dress's collar, feeling the heat burn her ears as she shuffled her feet under her seat while Samantha waited patiently, watching. 'So, um, what would I have to do to get the lease? I've never had one.' Why did she say that? It just made her sound dumb.

Samantha put her cup down and leaned forward in her chair. 'I'll tell you what, how about you do a trial run first? This way you'll know for certain before committing. Let's say on the next train day, you open up the Tea House and run the place like normal.'

'I can do that,' Lucy said, sitting up straighter—only to sigh in a heap. 'Nancy's cutting off the power.'

Samantha arched an eyebrow at her. 'I'd like to see her try when the power is in my name for the entire station, including the Station Master's house.'

Another one of Nancy's lies.

'I'll take readings and only charge you for the power you use on the day,' said Samantha. 'You can use that as an estimate for your overheads.'

'Deal. Hey, um, what was your deal with Nancy?'

'She's had the same deal she'd made with my grandmother. It never changed.'

'How come?'

'Nancy swore to have the Tea House open whenever a train arrived, no matter what the time. Even when it arrived in the middle of the night.'

'I'll do it.'

'You already do it now. Which reminds me, we're way overdue a stocktake for the accountant,' Samantha said, scribbling on a post it, 'so don't throw out any of the crockery, some of them are vintage.'

'I won't, I've always treated them as priceless. Do you own the pictures that line dining room walls too?' They were black and white images of the women with the train station in the background. A setting that hadn't changed much over the years. Her softball team's photo was also on the wall where supermum Karen bragged about it to anyone who'd listen.

'I do. If you don't want them, I'll get Billy to collect them.'

'I like them. They give the place character.'

'I agree,' said Samantha, taking another sip of her coffee. 'Now, if you want cheap rent, you'll need to be responsible for any maintenance and repairs to the equipment inside the building. That was the deal my grandmother had with Nancy.'

'That explains why nothing got fixed.'

'So I've heard.' Samantha sat back with the hint of a frown that would make any beer-loving man sweat with fear.

'Is that why you never visited the Tea House?' Not once had Lucy seen the publican cross the threshold into Nany's former domain. Samantha would wave when visiting the train station's platform, greeting guests, or they'd stop and talk when passing each other riding bikes on the tracks around town. Lucy pedalled like it was Sunday on her simple lady's bike with her basket and trailer on the back. The publican rode her flash mountain bike with speed, to keep fit.

'I don't drink tea. Coffee only for me and, well…'

'Beer.' Come on, the woman owned a pub! 'I'm getting a coffee machine,' Lucy announced.

'Great. If I'm not rostered on shift I'll go to your grand opening.'

'Wow, so, you'll let me have the lease?'

'I'll do some number crunching with the accountant, but I suggest you try it first before committing yourself. What do you say?' Samantha held out her hand.

'Yes, please. Thank you.' She smiled wide and shook the offered hand. The deal was done. 'So, do you have any business advice?' Lucy pointed to the piles of paper on Samantha's desk.

'If your housemate stayed in town more often, I'd hire her to do my bookwork for me—and that's who you should be talking to.'

'I will. Thank you, Samantha.' Lucy leaned over and hugged her boss. 'You'll be my guest of honour when I get the coffee machine—but isn't coffee against the Tea House tradition?' Lucy asked, sipping on her own coffee, although she felt like popping some champagne.

'The only tradition is that the Tea House is to stay open when the train is in town. That's it. Nancy broke tradition by not opening the other day.'

'Nancy's selling everything to move to Queensland.'

'She's been saying that ever since her husband ran off, and whenever she renews the lease.'

'She told me her husband died?' *Not another Nancy lie?*

'Her second husband did. Nancy was married to him for less than a year before he had a heart attack.'

'What happened to her first husband?'

'It's a sad story, that one,' said Samantha, shaking her head. 'He left with the kids. Nancy is the grandmother of one of those children that got runover by the train. I'm sure you've seen the crosses by the track.'

Lucy nodded. She saw them every train day, when she was chasing Cecil away from the tracks. 'I don't know much about the accident. No one talks about it.'

'Nancy was babysitting her granddaughter and a boy from another family. They snuck out of the Tea House —' Samantha sighed, staring at her hands in her lap, and said in a whisper, 'It was a terrible day for everyone in town. It was the worst.'

'Are any of the boy's family still living in town?'

'Johnny. He plays cards with the rest of the outback mafia. He was the boy's grandfather. He never forgave Nancy for not watching them properly.'

'Johnny told me his son is in Esperance.'

'Both sets of parents left, only Johnny and his wife stayed and Nancy had her Tea House. We put in a fence to stop any kids from wandering onto the tracks, but it's a huge area to cover.'

'Is that why Nancy won't allow any children in the Tea House?'

Samantha nodded. 'Did Nancy tell you what she's planning?'

'To go make sandcastles with her grand babies on the beach?'

'They must have forgiven her then?'

'Guess so.' All this time, Lucy didn't know this sad piece of Nancy's history. It'd be good for Nancy to be with her family.

'And Lucy—'

'Yeah?'

'If you have any problems over the Tea House, talk to me. We can always work something out.'

'I will.'

'Good. I'm glad you're doing this. Not for me, but for this town.'

'Elsie Creek is my home now,' Lucy said as a vibrant energy fuelled the excitement inside her. She was ready to start today.

NINE

Lucy, with a basket full of goodies strapped to the front of her bike, rode down the skinny dirt track hemmed in by the scrublands echoing a cacophony of desperately screeching cicadas. The din fell away as the track opened into the wide clearing of grey skies, teasing of rain. The billabong spread out in front of her, its elegant reeds waving in the breeze as it weaved toward Hank's massive train.

'Hank?' She rang her bike's bell, getting a chorusing reply from the flock of whispering ducks and scattered pairs of green pygmy geese. They'd gathered on the far swampy edge that led to the paperbark forest, shrieking with the echoes of nocturnal fruit bats.

Grasses brushed her knees as she pushed her bike into the shade of the train. 'Hank?'

A stack of cans spilled on the far side.

'I'm sssorry,' Hank said with loud sobs. 'Leave me alone.'

'Hank?'

She climbed the metal steps into the locomotive engine, peeking into the carriage he'd turned into a one-roomed style apartment, but he wasn't there. She then climbed down to the other side that was Hank's workshop area.

With his back to her, clutching a near-empty whiskey bottle, he pointed at the long spear grasses surrounding this section of the billabong. Their stems were taller than a man and were the colour of a dingo's pelt. 'I'm sorry.'

'Who are you talking to, Hank?'

'That cheeky pair. They won't leave me alone.'

'Who?' She peered into the tall grass whispering in the wind.

A chill crept up her spine at the sound of children's laughter. Lucy swallowed hard.

'They're right there.' Hank pointed with a shaky hand. Tears streamed down his sunburnt cheeks and were lost in his woolly beard.

A flock of magpie geese flapped their wings as if arguing on the water's edge. They sounded just like women in the tea house all talking at once.

'It's okay, Hank.' Was he hallucinating?

He whirled around, stumbling in his steps as his voice dropped to a growl. 'And where the bloody hell have you been?'

She stepped back warily. 'I had an accident and bumped my head.' She couldn't call him when he didn't have a phone. She certainly couldn't get Jax to tell his secret tenant either. 'I'm sorry I didn't tell you sooner? It happened on my way here—'

'You think I've got nothing better to do than sit around waiting for you to show up and trash my barbecue?'

'I'm sorry, Hank, it wasn't planned. I've got more food—'

'I'm not your slave. You don't own me. I work for no one and none of your company policies. You can't tell me what to do? It wasn't MY FAULT.'

Those were her words she'd said countless times—*it wasn't my fault.*

Every time she'd burned something, it wasn't her fault. Always blaming the equipment.

The only one who'd said it had been her fault was Jax, when she'd fallen from the tree while doing a risky and foolish thing. This was her fault and needed to fix this, to help Hank.

'Jenny says hi. She calls you the Tin Man.'

'The what?' He muttered, swaying in his boots as he took another swig from his bottle.

'The Tin Man. She adores your sculptures.' She'd recognise his artwork anywhere.

'You didn't tell her about me, did you?'

'No, never.' Hank didn't like attention. It's what they had in common.

'Why does she call me the Tin Man?'

Lucy shrugged. 'Because your sculptures are made of tin? I liked the water buffalo you'd made for her, the detailing is superb. Jenny said it reminded her of Cecil.'

'Tin Man, from the Wizard of Oz? Wasn't the Tin Man the wimp?'

'The lion was, for courage,' she replied, surprised she remembered the story.

'The Tin Man had no heart.' He whirled around with wide eyes. 'Am I a heartless bastard? I am, aren't I?'

'No Hank, you're a nice man.'

'I am not.'

'You haven't got a mean bone—'

'You don't know me,' he said, waving the bottle at her. 'Stay away from me. In fact, go. Now. You get. I don't want you coming around anymore. GET.' He stalked towards her with the bottle raised, threatening to throw it.

Leaving her no other choice, she ran to her bike and tore down the track.

A huge crashing clang sent flocks of birds squawking into the sky.

She stopped on the edge of the grasslands where the track disappeared into the corridor of trees that led to the road.

Hank staggered into the pile of cans he kept in sacks. Cans spilled everywhere, twinkling in the sunlight that peeked through the gaps in the grey clouds.

Did she dare stop to help him?

'GET! And don't come back,' he hollered at her.

She'd never seen him like this. It worried her.

Sure, she'd seen him on a binge now and again, but this was different. What had triggered this when he'd been semi-sober for so long? Would he be sober tomorrow, or would this binge last longer than a week?

She rode to the end of the track and hit the dirt road. The right led back to town, the left to Jax's house.

What now?

With no billabong, no barbecue, and no cameraman, Lucy was already behind. She needed the practise if she dared to compete against such experienced contestants who had the confidence to cook in front of a crowd.

None of the skills Lucy possessed.

Had Hank lost his confidence in her too?

TEN

'That's just great.' With a bundle of dirty clothes in hand, Jax frowned at the red hen nesting on the lid of his washing machine. Was this what Lucy had meant?

He peered around for the ribbon-wearing water buffalo, but didn't see it anywhere.

'Shoo.'

But the feathered felon just cooed at him.

Dropping his clothes in the laundry sink, he gently grabbed the hen and put her on the ground. He brushed away the feathers, turned on the machine, but the water trickled slower than the kitchen tap.

There had to be a trick to this?

Then the hen brushed its silky feathers against his bare legs.

'What are you doing?' He pushed it away with his unlaced boot, only for it to fly onto the machine and face him at chest height.

'Are you in love with laundry or something? And I'm talking to a chicken!'

He needed to get out.

Did he dare go into town for a lousy milk run and get more bourbon, or would the townspeople charge him with their pitchforks?

'Off.' He grabbed the hen but somehow it had tucked itself under his arm and cooed at him the way a cat purrs.

'I see you've made friends.'

'What the—?' He turned to find Lucy in her summer dress, leaning against her push bike. She was stunning. 'Come back for your mango, did you?'

'I forgot about that,' Lucy said with a shrug, parking her bike in the shade.

'How could you forget?'

'Priorities change.'

Priorities made his entire world change to land out here. 'Why are you here?'

'Most people say, *hello* to be polite when visitor's rock up.'

'Most people ring before they visit.'

'I didn't have your number, but I baked you some food as a thank you for what you did the other day. You know you have to turn the water on for it to work?' She jumped onto the veranda, reached under the sink and in the far corner she turned a lever. Water was soon rushing through the pipes filling his washing machine.

'How—' He thumbed to his machine suddenly alive.

'The tap to your washing machine started to leak, so to save water we turned them off. I'd say you'd be due to run the bore pump to refill your tank, the pressures a little slow.'

'Bore, pump, what?'

'That tank.' She pointed to the towering tank stand near the row of sheds. 'That tank's gravity feed gives great water pressure.' She grabbed a plastic container from the basket on the front of her bike and put it on his outdoor table.

'This place has water pressure?' He could hear it in the pipes.

'Yeah,' she replied, peering into his kitchen through the screen door. 'You're on solar power so you never have to turn your fans off.'

'I am? I thought they were broken?' Or was his head still fuzzy from his private bourbon party for one?

'I'll show you…' She crossed her arms over her chest, her eyes scanning over him from head to toe. 'If you want to get dressed and put down your chook.'

'It's not my chook.' He put the hen down, but it only rushed at him. 'What's wrong with my Calvin's—and this bird?'

'Did you just name drop over your underwear?' She asked, pointing at his boxers.

'It's hot.'

'Ah-huh…' She nodded as her widening eyes again walked all over him. 'Hot is one way to describe it.'

Jax felt naked. But he was also a man who didn't mind walking around naked. 'They're Calvin Klein classics.'

'Jeez,' she said, rolling her eyes, 'he's got the bloody jocks to match the fancy ute and boots.'

'They're comfortable and they're cotton. And I'll go put some clothes on if it makes you uncomfortable.' Jax clopped around in his unlaced boots to the back door.

'Don't you own any thongs?'

'They're on my shopping list.'

'Here.' She pulled out a plastic bag from her bike's basket and tossed a pair onto the veranda.

'Carry those around, do you? What else is in that magic basket of yours?'

'I bought them for a friend.'

'Me? Or am I still your number one enemy?'

'Frenemy maybe. My friend is preoccupied, so you'll do.'

'Whatever. I don't care if I'm second place, I'll take it.' He kicked off his boots and slid on a pair of board shorts, a t-shirt and his new thongs.

'Bore's this way, I'll give you a quick tour.'

'Yes, please. What is wrong with this silly bird?' He asked as the red hen waddled behind him like a dog, following Lucy to the shed.

'Have you been feeding her?'

'I got some mush-stuff down by the veranda. I haven't researched the intricacies of hen-keeping yet, it's not on my list of priorities.'

'She's lonely, and now that you live here, you're a part of her flock. You've inherited the chook. Congratulations, she's all yours.'

'Yeah, right?' He'd never even owned a house plant. What was he going to do with this fowl that shadowed him as they approached a shed he hadn't visited yet? The place came with a lot of sheds, each full of junk.

Wiping at the low hanging cobwebs, his eyes adjusted to the cool shade as the strong smell of diesel and other oils greeted him. Lucy turned large valves to a set of pipes and realised what she was doing. 'I feel like an idiot.' *Bloody bourbon!*

'Common thing for you, is it?'

'Oi.'

'Sorry, it's my mood, not you, I shouldn't have said that.'

He had to admire her honesty. 'I know what that is, that's the bore pump.'

'It is, all with one switch of a button.' At the power board, she flicked open the plastic casing and pressed a button. An engine started with a low rumble and rushing water ran along the pipe that disappeared underground. A few moments later, pop-up sprinklers burst into life, watering the dead lawn around his house.

'Why aren't you filling the tank?' Jax asked.

'It's best to flush the water for ten minutes through the irrigation system to your lawn. It acts as a firebreak to your house and helps clear the lines for clean water for the tank.'

'Makes sense.' *Idiot!* He was well-trained when it came to flushing hoses and pipes, the ins and outs of firebreaks, and green belts as fire barriers. How brain-fried was he from the bourbon?

'Do you know about generators?' Lucy asked.

'I do.' She didn't look at him like he was an idiot, but he felt like one.

'Good.'

Her one simple word made him feel so much better.

'There's two of them.' She led him deeper into the shed's shade and pulled back the tarps. 'This is your pump shed, where the generators live. This is your diesel beast known as the Thumper.'

'She thumps?'

'Loudly, but she's economical. It got rebuilt this dry season, so never sell her if you can help it. You'll need it for the wet season, to run the air-conditioner.' She then pointed to the barrels lining the wall. 'You've still got a few full drums, but you might want to top them up for the wet.'

'Do they deliver?'

'You've got a perfectly good loading ramp there that'll be easy enough to load and unload your fancy ute.'

'My ute's not fancy.' But he was starting to see the potential of the place. 'What did you say about solar?' Jax asked, peering back to the house where the roof glinted with solar panels. 'I thought those were an overkill for the hot water system.'

'Why would you want hot water in this weather?'

'I agree, but is there a hot water system?'

'Yes, with a gas booster for the dry season. The solar is for your basic power; fans and lights etcetera.' She pointed to the house roof as she walked and talked like a tour guide, and he was willing to follow and learn. 'Oh, and your gutters will need a clean before the storm hits. They fill your rainwater tanks.'

'How many tanks are there?'

'Six. They run direct to the house to the kitchen and bathroom. The rest runs on bore.'

'So, I don't have any contaminated water?'

'No, and we're not under drought conditions either. Tobias Clare put in new underground water tanks around the house last wet season, to be prepared. He was big on climate change prevention.'

'Good man.'

Then, with hands on hips, she gazed out over his property like she knew it a thousand times better than him. She looked pretty damned comfortable.

'What else can you tell me about this property? I know it's got a few bores.' It's what made him buy the place—the water. Coming from a drought restricted area, water was gold to him.

'This property has ten bores, three spring-fed billabongs, and out the back is Elsie Creek, it's a great spot for fishing—'

'And for catching red claw?'

She grinned at him shyly, sharing a half shoulder shrug. 'Those too, but its swampy and floods in the wet. You also have an Overseer's house on the far side of the sheds, and a few stockmen's rooms in another shed near the stables. They're a little run down, but they'll scrub up easily enough.' Continuing her tour, her sandals kicked up small dust clouds, as the tick-tick-tick of the sprinklers watered his dead lawn, cooling the place. 'Your chook has made a mess of your vegie patch.'

Jax glanced down at the silly red hen waddling beside him like a short dumpy shadow. 'Vegie patch? I don't know how to garden.'

Lucy pointed to a fenced area filled with dry weeds, where a fine mist of water sprayed over dry dirt and sunburnt grey hay. 'It's best you learn, because you need to run the irrigation for a reason, besides lawn. Tobias used to grow the best cucumbers. They were brilliant for cucumber sandwiches for the Tea House, and he was famous for his pickled cucumbers too. They go well with beer. You drink beer, don't you?'

'Sure. And bourbon.' Maybe too much bourbon lately.

Lucy headed around the back of the house, with Jax and the little red hen following her to a small shed on the edge of the brown lawn. 'Is that the garden shed?'

'The solar shed,' she replied, sliding back the bolt on the sturdy wooden door. 'This holds the battery banks to keep your house running. It's perfect until the monsoon storms hit where you don't see the sun for a week, that's when you use the generator as a backup. I disconnected them because no one was here, and just let them charge.'

From the corrugated shed's wall, she pulled out a wrench and started connecting batteries that stood on racks.

'That's a lot of batteries.' There were rows of them.

'Enough to be self-sufficient, so you only have to leave once every six months for fuel.'

'That's why you asked if I was one of those survivalists?'

She shrugged. 'What do you do? Don't say house repairs because tongues are wagging in town over what you do?'

'Like what?'

'A drug dealer, or a bouncer on witness protection programme —'

He made the sound of a game show buzzer. 'Wrong answer. Try again.'

'What's the big deal?'

'You're the only one who asked.'

'And normally, I ask nothing of no one.' She put the wrench back to the side groove where a battery tester rested. 'These tools stay here, don't remove them because you'll need them. And now, you're all set,' she said, dusting her hands.

The woman was an outback encyclopedia.

'Tell me more, please,' Jax said, following her into the sunlight

'Well they're your fruit trees too.' She pointed to the chook scrounging beneath a set of trees that were spread out along the edge of the dead lawn that held an old Hills Hoist clothesline.

'Yeah, right, that's gardening, huh?'

Lucy gave a slight smile, shaking her head. 'Diesel you can get from Kyle's yard, it's cheaper than the roadhouse.'

'Whose Kyle?'

'Kat's husband and owner of the only mechanic shop in town. It's just off the main street. Did you get a town map?'

'I only got a mud map from this amazing person helping a stranger. Although she'll only call me her frenemy.' And there it was, her first real smile. 'Now I've got power, and this new barbecue that boils water, I can offer you a coffee. Sorry, no tea.'

'Coffee's fine. It'll go well with the finger lime and poppy seed loaf I've made. I also got some mini sausage rolls, and I tried baking these savoury cheese scones but burnt their bums a little.'

'I'll try it.' Hell yeah, he was sick of his cooking. 'Why did you bring me food?'

'You shared your food with me after our tour of town and the hospital. I thought it was only fair to return the favour. I'm just being neighbourly.'

'Bit far to be a neighbour,' he said, putting his new kettle onto the gas plate of his new barbecue.

She didn't once ask about his stove lying face down in the dirt.

Mind you, Lucy didn't have a stove either in that inn she lived in. He liked it how she didn't turn her nose up at it, as if nothing phased her.

'It's just country hospitality,' she said, washing her hands at the laundry sink. 'Don't worry, I'm sure the few single women will introduce themselves shortly.'

'You're single.'

'I'm not here like that and I know you aren't, either.' She flopped down into the chair at the table like she owned it. The chair that faced the yard. Not the house—but the yard, wearing a faraway expression, like this was her second home.

'I don't care how it looks, because right now, Lucy, you're my freaking hero,' he said, taking a seat opposite.

'Behave.'

'It's true, and I'll be brutally honest like you've been…I have no idea what do with this place.'

He expected his confession to come back and bite him, but when she gazed up at him with those big brown eyes and thick eyelashes, all he saw was empathy.

'I don't know how to run a property this size,' he said, 'and my only resource for learning is on YouTube.'

'Is that how you found my channel?'

'Yes.' He grinned at his online mentor as she hid her face in her hands and groaned.

'No one was meant to see that,' she complained through her fingers.

'Why do it if you're so camera shy?'

'Because—because—'

Jax had all the time in the world to wait for an answer. How much his life had changed in a few short months.

'Please don't tell anyone.'

'I don't know anyone to tell.' And again, the weight of loneliness smothered him heavily, like the humidity that blanketed the heat of the day.

'Hmm?' Her eyes roamed over his face as if sizing him up. 'Why are you here?'

'You tell me first and I'll answer your questions.'

'Question for a question?'

'Sure.'

'Okay, that sounds fair.' She pried open one of her plastic containers and passed him a pastry on a napkin.

'I'll eat, you talk.' The savoury aromas had him taking a huge mouthful of buttery bacon cheesy heaven.

'Hank said the same thing.'

'Who's Hank?'

'Um...' She hesitated, picking off a piece of scone tossing it to the red hen hovering nearby.

'Is Hank your cameraman?'

'He is—or was. He quit,' she may have said it with a single shoulder shrug, but her eyes showed her sorrow.

Her emotions were so open, so unguarded, her innocence only drew him in, but her experience and knowledge of this place made her shine. It was a potent combination.

'He's funny, and he asks the same questions I want to ask,' Jax said, 'but he's shaky with his filming.' *And sucked at it.*

'Hank suffers from the shakes.'

'From Parkinson's?'

'Alcoholism.'

'You have a drunk filming you?'

'It's not like that.'

'I didn't say—'

'It was all Hank's idea. I only went along with it so he'd eat at least one decent meal a day and to help me get over being camera shy. But now he's on a grog-binge, who knows how long before he'll be sober enough to film again.' She gasped with her eyes widening. 'Damn, that came out of nowhere.'

'Is that who those thongs were for?'

'Yeah.'

'So, no more filming?'

'Not for a week, I guess. Or until Hank runs out of money.'

'I could do it.'

'Do what?'

'The filming.'

She choked on a laugh. 'What for?'

'Well, if you're feeding Hank, you can feed me instead and I'll be learning how to cook at the same time. I watch your show now, to learn how to use this barbecue. I made damper the other night. It worked too.'

'Well done… So, you can't cook. Don't garden. Can you farm?'

'Nope.'

'It's obvious you've never lived rural.'

'City boy through and through.'

'So why did you move to one of the remotest places in the country?'

The kettle boiled and Jax jumped from his seat. Inside the kitchen he scrounged around for another coffee mug and called out through the window. 'Do you have sugar with your coffee?'

'No.'

'Me neither, not since the ants got into it.'

'You keep sugar in the fridge this time of the year, and your flour and cereals, the humidity makes them cakey and weevily.'

'Is that why there are two fridges?'

'Yep. Beer fridge and dry goods out here, fresher stuff inside. They run on dual power.

'Power and gas?'

'Comes in handy for the wet season blackouts.'

Jax put the cups, coffee plunger, and milk on the table, returning to his seat. He loved the rich coffee aroma mixed with the fresh air. It was even better with the cooling tick-tick of the sprinklers. No smog, no traffic, just open air. His brother would've loved it.

But this time, the silence wasn't bothering him, he actually had company to share it with. 'How come you know so much about this place?'

'I've been farm-sitting for a while now. Tobias's grandson had leukaemia, and he left to support the family. It's why he sold this place, as is.'

'Walk in walk out. It was a sweet deal I just didn't think the house was so bad.'

'It's not that bad. I've seen worse. You don't have termites and she's a solid brick house with a great roof and new water tanks.'

'You'd know.'

She shrugged and faced the open countryside. 'Tobias told me that because of you, he's paid off his son's mortgage and they've built him a granny flat out the back. He's loving his retirement and sends a postcard now and again.'

'What did Tobias farm out here?'

'Cattle and cotton. But when his daughter wasn't interested in farming, he focussed on the slashing contracts for all of the council's firebreaks.'

'That's what the tractor is for?'

'Have you ever used one?'

'Hey, I am licenced to drive trucks,' he said, trying to save some form of masculinity.

Lucy just shrugged it off. 'Most blokes are in the bush. What are you going to do out here?'

'I'm focusing on the house first, and again, you've turned the conversation around to me.'

She grinned at him.

The clever little cupcake. 'Tell me why you've got a YouTube channel especially when you're camera shy?' Jax asked, pouring their coffee.

'Um…' She hesitated, blowing the steam across her mug before she sipped. 'Yum, this is good.'

'Thank you. So, the channel is for…'

'It's because of you.'

'Me? What did I do?'

'You told Nancy that the Tea House should be condemned.'

'I told you I'm sorry, but I still stand by what I said. That place isn't safe, but there's no harm in repairing it.'

'Nancy hasn't been back, and the lease is expiring.' She then took a deep breath and said softly, 'I'm going for it myself. Well, test it first to see if I want it to um…'

'To manage it?'

Hunching up her shoulders, she winced, nodding at him so timid-like. 'The landlady gave me the okay to do a trial run on train day. I'm petrified.'

He could see it, and again her open vulnerability sucked him right in, like the first time he'd seen her on her show. 'I've watched you cook, you know what you're doing when you're not—'

'Burning stuff,' she said, showing the bottom of her burnt scones. 'No one trusts my cooking because I'm the kitchen hand who's always burning stuff.'

And he'd seen her do it on every episode.

But once Lucy forgot she was on camera, all her inner confidence shone like a star.

'What has that got to do with your cooking show?'

She face-palmed herself. 'Ugh, I have a cooking show.'

'You do.'

'Huh.' She sipped on her coffee as if letting it sink in.

'You still haven't told me what the cooking show has to do with you and the tea shop?'

'Tea *House*.'

'Tea House. Picky thing you are, taking over—'

'I'm sorry.' She said, tucking her hands behind her back.

'I'm only teasing.'

She gave him a half-smile.

The sensitive thing.

'Please, go on,' he urged her, eating the scone, burnt bum and all. He didn't care. He was hungry.

'I need to prove to the town that I can cook, and not burn everything by winning the local Barbie Bake-off,' she said, slinking down into her seat. 'Which means getting used to cooking beside a billabong, in front of everyone for two entire hours.' She blew at a lock of hair, then sighed with slumped shoulders.

'That's why Hank's timing you on your show, to help you get over your shyness?'

Her reply was a slight nod, avoiding all eye contact.

'Tell me more about this Barbie Billabong thing?'

'Billabong Barbie Bake-off. It's two hours, three courses, using whatever you find as part of a scavenger hunt for food. The contestants' race around town gathering ingredients and no one knows what is on the menu because it depends on the food they find.'

'So, it's like a surprise hunt for food?'

'Yes. Last year they had to collect eggs from the hardware, or condiments from the craft store. It's loads of fun, although I've always been a spectator...' She hesitated with a frown, fidgeting with her fingers. 'I won't be able to enter now. Forget I said anything.'

'Why not?'

'I don't have a car.'

'Borrow one.'

'Or a driver's licence.'

'You're a grown woman, how can you not have a licence? Did you lose it—'

'I've never sat for the driving test. I suck at tests. I'm surprised I got my learner's permit at all. I mean, there I was hanging out with my housemate who had to drop some stuff off at the police station. And there's Monet saying, *here fill this practise form out*, while she had to do something for her pilot's licence. I didn't know it was a test, until she says, *congratulations, you've passed, now smile for the camera...* five years ago.'

'Five years for a learner's permit!' He stammered out. 'Can you drive?'

'Sure, on stations. Never in town.'

'So, you can use a four-wheel drive?'

She shrugged. 'Nothing as fancy as your—'

'Tonka Truck?' They shared a smile between them. 'So, with your background and your dad being who he is, growing up on stations...'

She frowned at her fingers she fidgeted with in her lap.

'Well, it's obvious you have experience with this place and I need help.'

'No, you don't.'

Yes, he did, and he was man enough to admit it. 'I'll make you a deal.'

'Oh, really?' She squinted at him with her head tilted, as if daring him with that small spark of mischief in her eyes.

'I'll help you film your shows.'

'Why?' Her face screwed up, horrified.

'Ah, hear me out,' he said, holding up his hand to stop her interrupting. 'You can feed me while teaching me to cook, then you can practise driving for the test in my ute while you show me around my property.'

'Erm, what did you say?'

'I said, I will help you get ready for the driving test. And, if you get your licence before this scavenger hunt, I may even let you use my truck.'

'No, it'd get dirty.'

'It's a drive to a billabong.'

'They throw flour bombs and stuff to sabotage the driver.'

He winced at his shiny new ute. 'How long before the race?'

'Over a month.'

'That's plenty of time to solve that issue, and for me to help you overcome your issues of fire safety.'

'Oh really. How?'

'I was a fireman.'

'You were?'

'Yes.'

'Where?'

'In the air force to start with, then I worked in civilian duty.'

'Were you any good? I mean, you know…' She pointed to the sprinklers and bore shed.

It was his turn to shrug and felt whatever manliness he had melt under the outback sun. 'I've been under a…' What could he say, a drunken binge-haze of bourbon? 'Focusing on—'

'The house,' she said, finishing his sentence.

'I was a Captain and made assistant Fire Chief for our firehouse.' He knew she would ask the next question, but he wasn't ready to answer it. Not yet. 'We have a month, so consider this a partnership where we'll be helping each other. You teach me, I'll teach you.' He held out his hand, hoping she'd shake on it. 'Do we have a deal, Miss Lucy?'

She paused staring at his hand, then faced him with such clarity in her eyes it reflected the world. 'We do, Mr Jax,' she said, shaking his hand.

Jax was surprised he could breathe easier because she'd said yes.

The chook jumped up onto the chair beside Jax and eyed off his pastry.

'What am I meant to do with this hen?' He frowned at the feathered pest.

'Whatever you want, you're the rooster of this hen house.' Lucy shared that sweet smile of hers, hand-feeding the crazy red hen at the table.

He leaned back and sipped his coffee as tiny rainbows flashed under the sprinklers watering his dead lawn. He had a farm, a rogue chicken, and perhaps a newfound friend.

ELEVEN

'What about this spot?' Jax asked Lucy as he drove them up a rocky crescent that exposed a small lake. 'That's not a billabong, is it?'

'No, it's one of your dams. Can you drive around and check for crocodiles?'

'Forgot about them.' He drove around the wall of the dam as shimmers of water reflected on the stones between the cracked, red soil.

'Stop-stop-*stop*.' She grabbed his arm while pointing through the front windows.

'Is that a log?'

'That log will kill you.'

Jax removed his sunglasses. 'Is that a crocodile? It's well camouflaged in the mud.'

'They do that, the sneaky buggers. He must have crawled in from the creek or you've got a whopping big hole in your fence?'

'Can we agree that whenever you speak you explain things to me like I'm a tourist? It'll save us both a tonne of time if you just give me the brutal black and white truth.'

'If you'll do the same for me?'

'Deal. So, I have a crocodile —'

'In your backyard.'

'No one told me that came with the property.' He grabbed his camera and zoomed in. 'Care to explain how he got here?'

'They walk across land in search of water, or if they're made to leave due to territorial rights, which might be the case with this guy. He's big, meaning he's old and he's missing a front claw. Pity, this dam had some good yabbies too.'

'Not anymore?'

She shrugged. 'Sorry, I didn't bring my underwater snorkelling gear to do a deep dive to count the fish. Oh wait, I'll blow up my inflatable glass-bottom boat and give you a proper tour, shall I?'

He chuckled as he filmed the crocodile. 'You do make the best tour guide, even with the sass. So, no-go on this place to cook dinner, then?'

Lucy shook her head.

The beast lay in the mud with mouth ajar giving a guttural growl.

'I think she's singing to you,' she whispered, her soft floral perfume floating in the air.

'How do you know it's a girl?'

'I don't. But if it is and you have a nest here, you'll be in trouble.'

'Why?'

'Duh, a nest means babies and if it's a good wet, they'll rock up to your back doorstep.'

'Bull?'

'Oi, you said black and white brutal honesty, and it happens. I must warn Hank to check his billabong too before the wet hits.'

'So, how do I get rid of a crocodile?'

'We'll call the ranger and they'll put in a trap. Or, we can call my dad and he can come over and make you a nice pair of boots.'

'Now, I know you're making that up.'

'Are you sure?'

'You get that tell-tale shine in your eyes and you can't stop smiling.' He wanted to see her smile more. 'So, where do we go from here? What about the ridge over there? We could get the sunset behind you and —'

'Your crocodile?'

'Come on. You've got to admit, it's pretty cool.'

'And deadly. I thought you were all about safety first.' She sat forward, weighing up her options.

The woman wasn't simple, she was shy with a whole load of bush smarts.

'He's old, injured,' she said, pausing, 'I'll only do it if you swear to keep an eye on him?'

'We wouldn't want the star of the show getting eaten now, would we?'

She rolled her eyes at him. 'I'm no star.'

He grinned at the way the blush darkened her skin. It was pretty.

With his new barbecue unloaded and table set for cooking, Jax said, 'Okay, let's talk about fire safety —'

'Says the man who wants to film a crocodile.'

'Don't worry, I'm keeping an eye on him… now, we want no leaves near the area or any other potential fuels that are recognisable fire hazards.' He said, kicking away at any sticks near the barbecue plate as Lucy did the same with the leaves. 'Now, we check the hoses on the barbecue and gas bottle for leakages… Have your water buckets at the ready, there's my small wet-pack handy, and a pump and water hose connected to my water tank on the ute. The hose is long enough to throw into the dam to drain that, if needed. I've also got a fire blanket for any fat spills, and here, hold this.'

'Why?' She grabbed the small fire extinguisher. 'It's heavy.'

'It should be, it's full. Now, pull the pin, grasp the handles like the brakes on your bike, aim and squeeze.'

She aimed the extinguisher, squeezed the handle and it hissed loudly, spewing a shot of foam. The crocodile scurried into the murky water with an almighty splash, bigger than any belly-flop at Bondi beach.

'I didn't realise something that big moved that fast.' It was quick.

'Told you so,' she murmured, staring at the fire extinguisher. 'Will this poison your dam water, like the Katherine thing?'

'No. And before you ask, I don't know their situation, Miss Lucy, because I was never stationed at Tindal.'

'Did you like that lifestyle, following orders?'

'I only joined to get away from my family and become part of a crew who enjoyed watching planes land.'

'Did you see any plane crashes?'

'A few. The pilot's ejected, so there were no casualties. I saw more carnage working for the state.'

'How?'

'Road accidents were the worst. You never knew what you'd find.'

'You wouldn't miss that.'

'I don't.'

'Do you miss the job?'

'I don't miss the stress of clock-punching and the paperwork, but I haven't been gone long enough to miss it, not with all of this happening.'

'Did you quit?'

He frowned at her.

'Question for question, remember,' she said, jutting out that little chin of hers he wanted to pinch between his fingers.

'All right, my turn. Tell me why the snow globes?' He pointed to the one she'd put on the corner of her cooking table. 'And what makes that one so special out of your huge collection?'

'How did you—?'

'You've been carrying it like it's some precious golden egg.'

She sighed, polishing the glass dome that shone in the low afternoon sun. 'My dad gave me this when I was four. It was the first of my collection, and a collector's item.'

'Are they all collectors' items?'

'Some.'

'So why snow globes?'

'You won't laugh at me?'

'No. I may poke fun at you in jest like you do with me, but not this,' he said, gently plucking the globe from her hands. He turned it upside down, then upright to watch the snow sprinkle over a man on a horse, frozen in mid-gallop. 'Is that the Man from Snowy River?'

'Banjo Paterson is my dad's favourite poet. When I was a kid—and if he wasn't scaring us with stories about the billabong bunyip—Dad would recite all these bush poems as we sat around the campfire, while I'd watch the last of the snowfall.' She gave a soft smile watching the snow swirl within the glass dome. 'It reminds me of the grey snow we get in the Territory.'

'Grey snow?'

'When they're doing the annual dry season burn offs, grey ash falls everywhere. It's the closest thing we have to snow, and my globes.'

'I've never heard of ash called grey snow. Go on...' He urged her. She was a natural at storytelling, he should be taping this.

Lucy assembled her basic cooking utensils and bowls on the table, putting everything in their place. Just like on all the shows he'd watched. The only thing missing was the snow globe.

'Living so remote, following Dad working on the musters from station to station, we didn't have a television,' she said. 'Somehow the snow globes became part my routine. No matter where we were, it was like home.' With her hand covering his, she made him shake the globe so the snow once-again swirled inside. 'For me, we didn't have the same house. It was always changing like the people, the bosses, the stations, or the lost boys my dad would train. Yet, if you took away the four walls and kept certain items, it all became a home.' She pointed to the sky where heavy grey clouds hovered on the horizon framing the sun. 'It's the same stars in the sky. The same sunrise and sunset shifting over the trees that grow on the same soil. It's the same country. Home. All of it. The days may change and the weather with the seasons but it's the same incoming flocks of magpie geese, the corellas, and the crocodiles. All of it is home.'

He swallowed hard at how she described the country, truly showing a connection she carried within. It was beautiful.

He may own the land that stretched further than the eye could see, but he didn't have the ties to it like Lucy. She carried an inner peace, a tranquil calm he would love to possess.

'My way of life must be so different from yours,' Lucy said shyly, tucking a stray lock behind her ear.

'Thank you for sharing with me.'

'Question for a question, right?'

'Ah, yes, my turn.' Standing taller, he cleared his throat and shook her snow globe that had captured the frozen scene of a rider on a horse. 'I hardly remember this story. Can you recite it for me?'

'One day, maybe. Stop changing the subject.' She took back her globe and put it on the corner spot of her table. Ready to cook.

He raised his camera and began taping her. 'How about you cook or we'll miss your two-hour deadline? Or do you want to cook with that prehistoric beast after dark?'

'Um…' She froze on the spot.

'I've got a timer on my watch, so we'll start now.' He pressed the button then grinned at Lucy. 'You did not just get camera shy, did you?'

She gave him the tiniest shrug.

Jax chuckled. He now understood why Hank asked so many questions. 'Why don't you tell me what you're cooking?'

'Um…' She cleared her throat, wiping her hands down her apron, focussing on the table. 'I'll be making a wild goose terrine for entrée, buffalo meatloaf, then a bush apple strudel.' She talked as she cooked, while he taped and asked questions. She shared childhood tales and names and uses of the ingredients she'd foraged from nearby native bushes.

'Time.' He called out at the two-hour mark, and again checked on the crocodile laying on the edge of the water on the far side of the large dam. A good safe distance away.

Lucy dished up their plates on the small table and stood back like a contestant in her own cooking competition. 'Are you one of those Hollywood movie makers?'

'No.' He chuckled, taking the camera from the tripod to zoom in on the meals' vibrant colours, with his stomach grumbling. 'This food looks amazing. Where do we eat this? I didn't bring any chairs.'

'We have a couch behind you.' She carried the plates to the back of his ute and climbed on board to sit on the roof. 'It's a great view from up here. We can watch the croc safely.'

'Good point. That thing hasn't moved for the last hour and the way your food smells, I'm sure he'll want some.' Jax sat next to her, eager to tuck in. 'How far does my land go?'

'A fair way. It takes a full day to drive around. You should do a boundary ride to check your fences and fire breaks. I did the ride a few months back, but if that croc's here…'

'Is crocodile catching a normal part of the ranger's duties out here?'

'I don't know if the new ranger does it, but I'm sure she'll know someone, or my dad will.'

Cutlery scraped on their plates as he devoured the extraordinarily flavoursome meatloaf with her exotic assortment of vegetables. 'What will they do? Remember, crocodile catching isn't part of my resume.'

'Usually they drop a big cage with meat inside, you then keep an eye on it to see if the croc takes the bait. But when it comes to getting it out of the cage that's when the fun begins. Let me know when that happens, I'd love to come and watch.'

'Sure. You can cook the barbecue and I'll eat and film the adventures of my big backyard. And, Miss Lucy, this food is amazing. My compliments to the cook.'

'Thank you,' she whispered, the colour darkening her cheeks as she looked away to hide her smile.

What could he do or say to help build up her confidence?

'We didn't have a backyard,' said Jax quietly, placing his cutlery onto the empty plate, resting it on his ute's roof. His appetite satiated.

'Pardon?'

'Growing up, we never had a backyard. We lived in city apartments that faced fences or brick walls. Nothing like this.' He waved at the endless sea of olive-green trees, that stretched beyond forever, where land became sky and sky became land. It would be terrifyingly easy to get lost out here forever.

Is that what he hoped for, to get lost? To lose his past? To lose himself.

'So, how, why…?' She hesitated.

'From the city to this?'

She nodded.

From a city of ear-screeching sirens, blinding flashing lights, regimented orders, with a constant shifting chaos of traffic and people to this… how indeed.

'Don't laugh,' he said. 'As kids, my brother and I liked to pretend we were these explorers having adventures in these far-off lands. Mum and Dad would be busy doing what they did, and we'd watch these four-wheel-drive shows on tv. In between cartoons, wrestling and stuff.'

'Figures,' she said, giving him a playful nudge. It helped lighten his mood.

'We only had this crappy TV. It wasn't anything upmarket otherwise Dad would've hocked it to score.'

'Score?'

Jax inhaled deep with this need to let go. They'd promised question for question in black and white truth, and the truth of his world was brutal.

In this new world, hopefully his words would get lost forever.

'My parents were drug addicts.' He'd finally given voice to his secret—one he'd never shared with anyone but family. And now, Lucy. 'My dad was a small-time dealer that paid for their habits, which left me and my brother to our own defences.'

'I'm so sorry.'

'It wasn't all bad. There were some good times too. We had this crappy car…' He grinned at the memory, patting the roof of his new ute. 'That car was a shocker, made of spare wheels pinched from other cars, with smashed locks from being broken into so many times. But as kids we thought that car was the best thing growing up. Especially when Dad took us for drives on Mother's Day. It's what Mum wanted. She'd make Vegemite sandwiches to save money for fuel to go have some scrappy picnic somewhere in the country.' Nothing like the food Lucy cooked, or the view he had now, but it jogged his memory. 'Mum used to tell us stories of her time in the outback, making daisy chains from weeds, while we sat eating our lunch on this old blanket.'

'Did your mother work out here?'

'Yeah. Mum had done a short stint as a jillaroo. She said it was a tough lifestyle, yet one of the best times of her life.'

Birds rose like they were bouncing above the tree tops, only to dive and disappear in the foliage, like dolphins skimming across ocean waves.

'Mum would've loved this,' he said waving at the scenery.

Then he frowned. 'As kids, when Mum got sick, we'd tell her we'd take her away to this place so she'd get clean.' He examined his palm that used to get swallowed into his mum's whenever she held his hand. Like the countless times he'd clumsily tried to wipe at the beads of sweat from her forehead, as it saturated her shirt with her body curled around the toilet bowl in their old bathroom. You had to jiggle the toilet handle to make it work. Plaster chips would crumble from the ceiling if you closed the door too hard, powdering her hair that stuck to her pale skin. Through tears, she'd begged them to help her get some medicine. Yet even as a boy, Jax knew the type of medicine his mother wanted would only make her sicker.

'My brother and I would tell our mother we'd buy a family farm for her to manage and teach us what she knew. To keep her clean. When she was in rehab, we'd draw pictures of this place we'd never been to. It became our happy place. A place we all wished for.' And here he was, sitting in a world without any family nearby.

His stomach lumped into ice, and he swallowed down the desire to reach for his bourbon. Instead, he drank thirstily from the water bottle.

Jax needed to change this conversation.

'My brother did the best drawings. He became a tattoo artist and did all of my ink work.' Jax shoved up his t-shirt's sleeve to proudly show off his brother's creations

'Did he always want to do tattooing?'

'No. He learned that in prison.'

Her eyes widened.

'Black and white brutal truth, Miss Lucy. I don't mean to scare you,' he said. 'The reason I'm saying this is, I can tell you're worried about your own background.' She seemed ashamed of it. 'Mine wasn't that perfect either, cupcake.'

'Cupcake?' She arched her eyebrow at him.

'I owe you for nicknaming my ute a *Tonka Truck*.' He shrugged, trying to make light of the heaviness still bearing down on his shoulders. He took another mouthful of his water. What he really wanted was a decent shot of bourbon to forget.

He frowned at the rocky dirt that formed the dam's wall.

Was he an addict like his family?

He'd done nothing but drink too much until Lucy showed up.

'My mother died,' he whispered to the treetops as they waved with the breeze. A flock of pink and grey galahs settled among the branches as if to sit and listen in. 'She'd overdosed. It was Dad who'd loaded her up.'

Her gasp rattled him some.

Should he stop?

Yet, his mouth kept dribbling out his dirty secret. His past. 'My father got charged with murdering my mother and he pleaded guilty straight away. Even though it doesn't exist, Dad pleaded for the death penalty. Instead, they reduced it to accidental manslaughter because he was just as high at the time and almost died himself.'

'Oh, my god.'

Jax wanted to stop, to not scare her anymore, but the words kept spilling as he spoke them aloud for the very first time. 'My brother swears my parents were doing some death pact. He took it badly and ended up in prison for assault. That's where he got clean and discovered his artistic passion through ink work.' He stared at his arms full of swirls and patterns, waiting for Lucy to ask questions about the ink he wore and their meanings. Most people did.

Surprisingly, she just grabbed his hand and held it, not saying a word.

But it spoke volumes to him.

It wasn't judgement, it was friendship, and right now he needed a friend.

'I was in the RAAF firefighters' unit. I loved watching the freedom and the power of those jets coming and going. It was impressive. I've got thousands of photos. The way they'd glide as if balancing on air.' A curve of a smile crept across his lips at the memory.

A group of honking magpie geese glided in to land clumsily in the treetops, which then swayed under their weight. They were big birds, grappling to balance on such small limbs with their webbed feet. Why didn't they find somewhere easier to land?

Why didn't they choose a more solid position instead of suffering a night of light sleep tossing and turning with an ever-present fear of falling?

Was it a practised habit from many nights of light sleep? Like the countless nights he'd endured as a kid, in their crappy apartment, whenever the front door banged in the middle of the night, while his brother soundly slept in the bed opposite.

His eyes and ears would be on full alert to the floorboards creaking outside their bedroom door, while he felt for the familiar lump on the edge of his mattress—the handle of the broken cricket bat.

Were they the footsteps of his parents?

Were they sober short steps or the shuffling slide of a stupor? One set? Two sets?

He'd listen for the whispering murmurs of his parents. Were they slurring, talking gibberish, or making more of their many secrets? How long before they too became laced with anger to feel the sting of their words?

All he could do was huddle under his sheets and wait.

Wait for the door to open for his parents to check on them, or for the creak of his parent's bed springs…that finally led to silence. Leaving him to balance on the fine ledge of sleep, still gripping that bat's handle.

'I couldn't wait to leave my family,' he said. 'Not because I didn't love them, but because I could see it happening. The drugs were going to kill them sooner or later.' The worry kept him up at night, eating away at him — until he walked away.

He had to. The worry he carried for his parents would eventually kill him too.

'I'm so sorry,' she whispered.

'It's not your fault, or anyone else's, it was theirs.' It was all about choice. Jax could only give so much. In the end he had to selfishly choose himself.

Did that make him a heartless bastard?

'It came as no surprise when my brother rang to tell me about our parents.' His voice was brittle and cold. He fingered the scar that ran down the centre of his palm, a reminder of his first fire. Caused by his passed-out parents leaving their midnight snack simmering on the stove.

Jax cleared his throat. The dam walls of denial had opened and his voice crackled, revealing his greatest fear. 'What scared me more was that I only had my brother left… My old man was a lost cause. In solitary, on the prison's suicide watch after what happened to Mum.' He sighed heavily, trying to blow-off the burden from his shoulders, to loosen the constricting ties around his ribs.

But those ties never allowed him to fully let go.

'I tried to be there for my brother,' he said. 'I left the RAAF for a job with the state and got us a house, as part of his parole. He was getting a great reputation at the local tattoo studio with bookings weeks in advance. On days off, we'd go and film our adventures on these insane four-wheeled drive tracks, along with every other man and their four-wheel drives. It was chaos.' He pointed to his ute. 'You think this is fancy, those guys had more.'

'I can only imagine,' she said, sharing a slight smile with him.

The smile soon left his face when he said, 'Last Mother's Day, we got a call from the prison saying Dad had hung himself.'

This time her gasp was barely audible.

'My brother went on a binge, and no matter what I did for him, he wouldn't listen.' He took a deep, shaky breath and said, 'I was on shift, fighting a deserted factory blaze. I'd just spent two solid weeks fighting bushfires and it was my first shift back with the city crew and it was a hell-fight. We were pulling out these homeless kids who'd gotten trapped in the smoke. When I got the call, to tell me my brother was in hospital, I found I couldn't leave my men.'

'Why not?'

'I couldn't do it, not until we had it under control. I kept thinking those kids were like my brother, I had to help them.

I was just putting off the inevitable because I knew what I was going to find at that hospital.'

The walk down the hospital corridor had been the longest in his life. Concrete had filled his boots that were chained to the fire truck pulling him away from the door that led to his brother's room.

He stood staring at the door for ages, summoning all of his willpower to push it open.

When he did, he found his brother on the bed, tucked in with white starchy sheets as machines beeped and hissed. All ashen in the face with sunken cheekbones, his spirit was gone leaving only a machine to help the body breathe.

'I'd made it to say goodbye,' Jax said as grief's cold fingers cupped his heart in a cocoon of pure ice. It burned. 'I was there when they flicked off his life support.' And he'd stayed there until the very end. Just him, holding his brother's cold hand, in an empty room, listening to the vents kick in stale air as shadows from the sun stretched into starlight, reflecting off the floor's tiles.

'I'm so sorry.'

'Me too. My brother used to rant we had some gene that poisoned us, making us addicts.'

'You don't believe that, do you?'

'I won't be like them. I've never touched drugs. I've never even smoked cigarettes when it was there all around me.' He'd always been determined to break the cycle.

'Do you drink?'

'Oh yeah.' With the bottles of bourbon he had lying around, this conversation was the wake-up call he needed. 'I'm not like my parents with their cheap wine.' But was he?

'Like Hank now?'

'Who?'

She wrung her hands together and surveyed to the dam. 'Hank is the town's rubbish warrior. I've been trying to help him.'

The cameraman she'd been feeding, who'd been on a binge. 'Trust me on this, Lucy. If someone is in that position, you can only offer them help—but they have to want to take it. You can't force them to change. My parents knew how to play the courts and rehab systems—we shouldn't have been in their custody half the time.'

'Surely welfare would have noticed.'

'Our parents were functioning addicts, they always made sure we went to school. Dad was big on breakfasts, giving us an endless supply of cereal that we'd eat morning, lunch, and dinner. When we got some new teacher or do-gooder looking at us a little too closely, we lied our little arses off.'

'You did?'

'We had our faults, but we were family and didn't want to be split up. My brother and I kept saying it's all *fine*. We were all *fine*. Everything was *fine*. When it wasn't.'

'Oh,' she said, sitting straighter with a wince. 'Now I understand why that word annoys you so much.'

'You don't have to change for me, Miss Lucy.'

'I'm not. I'll be warier, that's all.' She collected their plates and started to climb down. 'You know what I reckon?'

'What?' He replied, jumping down from the back tray and helping her pack.

'You're so different from any other man I've met out here.'

'Because I don't do cows?' Had he said too much?

'What I mean is, that we come from such different worlds but they're both tough and they've both had good times in them too. My dad would say to his lost boys, *the past is what made you who you are—but who you want to be tomorrow is made by what you choose to do today.*'

Lucy was right.

Except Jax didn't know what his tomorrows would be—except to fix a damned house.

TWELVE

'**M**iss Lucy, you drive better on dirt roads than me,' Jax said, from the passenger's seat of his ute with laptop open.

'Coming from you, Mr Jax, that might mean something to someone one day,' said Lucy, trying to keep a straight face as she steered them into town.

'How come you've survived so long in a place with no public transport and no licence?'

'I grew up on cattle stations, there's no need for licences out there.'

'When did you learn to drive?'

'As soon as I could touch the pedals.'

'And in town?'

'Dad drove.'

'Does your mother have a licence?'

'No. I never needed one until I moved into town.'

'How did you end up here?'

'Monet.'

'The bush pilot?'

'Housemate and best friend. She'll be coming back soon.' Lucy couldn't wait. 'Monet flew in to the station we were on, said she had a spare room and knew of some jobs available to keep me out of trouble. So I packed up my snow globes and off I went.'

'Ever regret it?'

'No. Don't get me wrong, I love my parents, they're the best, Dad is overprotective…'

'I hear he's got stock whips and a shotgun.'

'You're safe.'

'Why?'

'We're frenemies, remember.'

'Never had a frenemy like it, one that cooks for me, while I film her and then get to eat her amazing food.' Jax pointed to the screen on his laptop. 'You've had over seven hundred views on your last video with almost a thousand followers.'

'I do?' She peered through her rear-view mirror.

Jax laughed, pointing to his laptop. 'I'm talking about your YouTube channel.'

'Oh.' *Ugh!* The heat rose up to her ears.

'They have a lot of questions about your bush herbs.'

'Like what?'

'Where they can get some?'

'They just pick it. It grows wild all over your property.'

'Lucy, this woman is in Canada.'

'Oh, Canada? Why would she want some there?'

'To cook with. That's what you do with it, isn't it?'

'I don't smoke it.' *And I'm not dumb—if I didn't act so dumb.* 'Hey, we should try making smoked fish on the barbecue tomorrow. There's a great fishing spot out the back of your block, we can check some fences on that side while we're at it.'

'Sounds good,' he said, glancing back to his laptop screen. 'I've downloaded today's edited episodes from lunch and last night's dinner. I've even spread out your schedule so we've got episodes running now for the next six weeks.'

'Six weeks?' *No way!* This was only meant to be for practise, a short-term project until the competition.

'Twice a week on Monday and Thursday,' Jax explained. 'I've got an idea for an opening segment, like a proper cooking show using your snow globes. I'll match it with your new website I've made you, it's got the capabilities for an online store.'

'A store?'

'Which snow globe will you use tomorrow?'

'I'm not sure.' *About any of this!* 'I play lucky dip with them the same way you pick your paint colours for your walls.'

'Works for me,' he said with a chuckle. The way it softened his features whenever he smiled, she had to smile with him.

'Thank you for volunteering to be the cameraman, director, and website publicist.' The quality of his work was amazing.

'I don't mind.'

'You seem to know what you're doing. I wouldn't have a clue, living down the track and being out of range so often, it wasn't worth it. Monet keeps saying I should do Instagram for my food.'

'Good idea. I'll set you one up tomorrow; we can cross-post between them.'

'Are you some secret social media guru?'

'Me? No. I used to help my brother. We'd make movies of our road trips, or I'd tape him doing his ink work. We created his online portfolio and I managed his Instagram for a bit. It killed time during shifts at the station when I was avoiding paperwork. He scored a lot of new customers that way.' Jax sighed as the shine in his eyes dulled to that same dead-eyed, flat expression she'd seen in Hank. Only it saddened her more to see it in Jax.

'I'm so sorry,' she said, patting his shoulder.

'I'm all right,' he said, shrugging her off. 'Two hands on the wheel at all times.'

Frenemies. Just frenemies.

'Indicate, Miss Lucy.'

'Sorry, forgot.' She flicked on the indicators and turned into town.

'You're always forgetting. You'll lose points in the test for that, or someone will ram up your arse.'

'I know, I know. I should write it on my hand, or we could make a buzzer thing to zap me to remember.'

He laughed. 'As tempting at that sounds, I'm not into torturing cooks. If you remember to indicate and watch your mirrors more, you'll pass your driving test easily. How do they do driver's tests out here?'

'You book with the local police station and they make you drive somewhere.'

'Would dodging water buffalos count towards your score?' He pointed to Cecil without the red hen on his shoulders, cruising down the sidewalk past the pub. The purple ribbons wrapped around his horns flapped in the breeze and his coat was full of childlike scribblings.

'Has Cecil knocked at your back door, yet?' Lucy asked.

'Once. I swear he was going to charge me when I caught that hen.'

'*Your* hen.'

'I'm putting chicken house repairs on my list to do after I've finished the house.'

'There's always work to do on a property,' she said, but the man focused on the house first, not the farm. Whereas most farmers worked their land first because that's where they made their money. 'Have you thought about what you'll farm, yet?'

'Nope. House first. So, where do you want to go now, Miss Lucy?'

'Home. It's a big day tomorrow,' she said, steering toward the unofficial Elsie Creek Inn.

'Are you ready for it?'

'I hope so.'

'Think you'll get any sleep?'

'Probably not.' She was excited about her first day as boss.

'Have you got many bookings?'

'It's a full house of the regular women's meetings.' The thought of all those women coming to eat and drink had her excited, yet terrified at the same time. It had to be perfect.

'What time will you start cooking in the morning?'

'Early. Most of the prep is done and I've cleaned the place so much I swear I don't have any fingerprints left.' She'd revisited every nook and cranny, every piece of china, every face inside the wall of framed photos until the dining room sparkled.

'Cleaning won't help with the bigger issue, like the power points, the fire alarms—'

'I put the batteries back in them this morning.'

'You did?'

'Had to. There's this pesky fireman who has been giving me fire safety lessons, I thought I'd better do it or he'd never shut up.' His smile made all that effort worth it.

'Good girl.'

She smiled wider with pride warming her chest as she turned into her driveway.

'Indicate.'

'Sorry, I forgot.' She turned the engine off, put the seat back for Jax and stepped out into the muggy air. Still no walls of water, but some rain had tried to dampen down the dust.

'When will I expect you?' Jax asked, hoisting her bike from the back of his ute with ease.

'After lunch?' She needed to practise cooking on an impromptu menu with only a few weeks left for the Billabong Bake-off. Yet, if tomorrow was a success at the Tea House, she wouldn't need to continue taping her practice sessions...but then she wouldn't see Jax every day.

'Perfect. The second coat of paint should be dry then, you can help me shift my bed back into my room. Take this with you for the Tea House.' He slid a heavy red bag and box into her bike's front basket.

'What is it?'

'A fire blanket for the stove, and a new fire extinguisher. Let's hope you never have to use them.'

Aww. She could just hug the man. 'With your training, I won't. Thank you.'

'Good luck tomorrow,' he said from the driver's door.

'Thanks for everything.' She waved until his Tonka Truck drove away, sad to see him leave. They'd been having so much fun together. Fishing lessons, driving lessons, cooking lessons, fire safety lessons. Both learning from each other.

Not once did Jax put her down or make her feel silly.

He did ask lots of questions, which must be hard for a man like Jax. It showed how desperate he must be, to be her friend—*frenemy.*

Even so, it was hard to hate the guy, trying so hard to make amends for what he'd done.

But if Jax hadn't told Nancy off about the place, Nancy wouldn't have quit, then Lucy wouldn't be opening tomorrow as the boss. He'd done so much good for her, even refusing to set foot in the Tea House to not judge. She truly respected him for that.

She'd never had a man give her a fire extinguisher as a gift. It wasn't romantic, but it was a gift. Did he care? Or was Jax doing what he did so well, play fireman?

Which he was brilliant at. His eyes would shine whenever he talked about his time on the job. He'd taught her so much.

She couldn't hate the man when underneath, she adored him. Deeply. She wasn't getting her hopes up, because Jax wasn't interested in her like that. After all, she was just a stupid country girl who never finished school. The silly Station Hand's daughter who didn't know about city stores, click and collect, or hotspots, and all of the other things he talked about.

Yet with her life-long experience of living on the land, she recognised this much about Jax—the man wasn't cattleman material. He wasn't a farmer. Jax would get bored and eventually resent the place—if he hadn't already.

How long would it take, after Jax had renovated the house and believed the life debt to his family was over, before he put the place on the market and left?

The thought of Jax leaving hurt. Her stomach plummeted with the dread of loss. If she was like this now, how would she go when he did leave?

She'd miss his smile that made her grin back at him like a goofball. She'd miss his intense steely, sexy-as-hell stare when he talked about something serious—it was impossible to concentrate. She'd miss his coffee and comments as they stood side by side washing dishes or when re-loading his ute for the next day's cooking adventures. She'd miss his divine cologne that filled his ute's cab. She'd miss watching the way his tribal inkwork shifted and shimmered as he moved his body of pure muscle from fishing, to painting his walls, to hanging his clothes on the backline. She'd miss their endless conversations...and those comfortable silences while they shared their meals, staring at the open country, sitting on the back of his ute.

She missed him already and he'd only just left her driveway.

Should she prepare for his permanent departure now?

After all, they were only meant to be frenemies.

THIRTEEN

'I haven't got time for this, Cecil,' Lucy cried out, walking along the train tracks at dawn. She scrambled down the rocks, petals falling from the daisies in her hand, to where Cecil was sniffing around the two crosses. The smell of fresh paint mingled with the morning dew. The water jar had been cleaned with fresh wildflowers added, and the area around the crosses had been weeded.

Did the children's grandparents, Nancy or Johnny do this?

A shiver squirrelled up her spine at the sound of children singing nearby. It carried closer on the breeze like a whisper. *'Come play, Cecil…'* they sang.

It was right behind her.

The words brushed across her shoulders like a dry ice vapour, making her scalp prickle. Lucy didn't dare look.

Her eye caught the light of the kitchen ahead where the stereo played inside. *Just the stereo. It's just the stereo.*

'Come on, Cecil, leave those flowers there, they're not for you.' She held the daisies under his nose and he followed.

She was jittery with nerves, like a jar of fluttering Christmas beetles. 'I should've booked with your owner to advertise that the Tea House is under new management.

What d'ya reckon, Cecil, do you think I'll make a good manager? You eat my food, don't you?' She led the buffalo into the pen where water and hay were waiting and locked him safely inside. 'Please, don't shout out your compliments too loudly. I'll get you to sign my guest book later, when I get one.'

With a nervous laugh, she grasped her small trolley loaded with plastic milk crates and dragged it towards the back shed. Only a few bodies in swags stretched across the veranda as the stars began to fade the higher the dusky pinks crept across the horizon. A low line of clouds rumbled in their race across the parched land, heavy with humidity. When would she get her walls of water?

Steering around the snoring bodies, she unclipped the padlock, slid back the bolt and rolled the door open, careful to not make it squeal.

Even though she'd done this a gazillion times, her body started to tremble.

Trying to breathe through her nerves, it took three shots at the panel to flick on the light. 'Come on, I do this all the time.' She shook her hands to kill her nerves.

She then flicked on the urn, put out the cups, then opened the plastic containers unleashing the fresh aromas of her baked goods.

The last thing she put on the bench table was her coffee tin for money collection.

Again, her hands shook and perspiration trickled down her spine making her dress clingy.

She still hadn't put a price on her cooking. But there was no more hiding behind Nancy's reputation—it terrified her. Her heart pounded loudly and she was tempted to run though the doorway to never return.

'Morning, Miss Lucy,' said Rigsy, strolling through the doorway. Freshly showered and shaved, her housemate winked at her as he grabbed a cup and muffin, then slipped some money into the tin. 'Brekkie looks good as always.'

'Thank you, Rigsy.' She sighed with some relief at the resident couch-surfing-cowboy.

'Are you ready for that lot inside?'

'I am. I hope. I think?' Where had all her confidence gone?

A few of the stockmen wandered in and grabbed their cups, mumbled their good mornings and went about their day. Nothing had changed.

'Is it true, Nancy's not cooking anymore?' A stockman asked Rigsy.

'Who's cooking now?' Asked another guy, sniffing suspiciously at the pastry in hand.

'Erm...' Lucy lost her voice and grasped her trolley's handle, ready to bolt.

'The Station Hand's daughter is the new cook,' Rigsy said to the men, thumbing up the rim of his Akubra. 'Has anyone got a problem with that?'

None of the men spoke, but Lucy felt all eyes on her. She wanted to peel back the concrete and hide like a burrowing bettong on sunrise.

'Listen fellas, it's the same tucker coz Miss Lucy has *always* been cooking for us. She was just too shy to tell you, that's all. Nothing's changed. It's still a decent spread for brekkie.' He took a bite of his food and again winked at Lucy.

'I told you, you don't have to worry about this mob, Miss Lucy.'

'Thank you, Rigsy.'

The men lined up as normal, filling their coffee cups and eating her food, putting extra money into her tin.

'Good luck with the ladies,' said Rigsy, tapping his hat's brim in a one fingered salute.

She needed it.

Through the Tea House's warm kitchen, her stereo rang out from the playlist Monet had made for the occasion. Lucy flicked on the dining room's lights, the squeaky fan spun like an unbalanced aeroplane propeller as she opened the bifold doors.

She grabbed her watering can, and with plate and cup in the other, she approached the one and only bench on the platform.

'Hank. Hank.' She poked his shoulder as he stirred.

'What?'

'Breakfast.'

'I told you, you don't need to feed me anymore.'

'Don't care, it's there. Eat it or throw it in the bin.' *The stubborn fool.* She put the plate and cup on the bench next to him and walked away. She had lots to do before sunrise. 'Leave the cup at the back door when you're done.'

She'd seen little of Hank, being busy with Jax, practising for her driving test, the bake-off, and her cooking show. In turn, she helped Jax with his place as a fair trade. But even if she didn't see him, she still dropped off food for Hank daily, on her way to Jax's.

Lucy paused to check over her shoulder, expecting Nancy's car with its squeaky suspension to cross the tracks any second now.

But there would be no car coming.

Cattle began to stir out the back. The light at the Station Master's house came on, highlighting the Stock Inspector's ute parked in the small driveway. Stockmen clambered out of their utes to make a line by the rainwater tank. It was business as usual.

Lucy caught herself closing the doors and stopped, deciding to keep them open just that little bit longer today.

She smiled wide as her heart opened, warming her chest. She almost floated. Her dream was coming true.

She always loved train days, but today was extra special.

This was it. It was opening day.

FOURTEEN

Jax steadily paced his veranda as another earthy rumble rolled from the thunderheads thickening on the horizon. Lightning crackled with skeletal fingers that crawled in an extended flash across the weighty clouds, dragging shadows over the scrublands. A percussion of meaty thunder tumbled with a warning of its ferocity contained within this concentrated cell. It was a brutish storm blackening a monstrous skyline.

All the wet season preparations he'd done with Lucy were about to be tested.

Again, he checked his watch, paced the veranda, while the red hen watched him from her perch on his washing machine.

'Lucy should be here by now, she said lunchtime.' It was almost two and he was dying to know how her first day went at the Tea House. He wanted to text her, but Lucy wasn't technically attuned to texting, or social media DMs.

He'd been teaching her, enjoying the way her eyes lit up when he showed her emojis. They'd pulled faces trying to do selfies that he would use for her new Instagram account. He had lots of photos of her food, and even more of her sweet smile.

So many fun memories.

Lucy had taken photos of Jax with his first barramundi. The time he'd pulled in his first catch of freshwater prawns while keeping an eye out for crocodiles in what Lucy called a small creek—that was a tidal river at the back of his property. Crossing dried rocky river beds, she'd made him walk upon soft river sands that shifted underfoot, shovelling its secrets deeper. She showed him how to read the tracks of wallabies, goannas, and snakes. He'd seen long-neck turtles float among the duck weeds' green carpet in the billabong, shared by a herd of wild buffalo, as she told her tale of the bunyip. She'd even made him chase wild boar in his ute through the savannahs and onto dried floodplains, that she foretold would be under water in a matter of weeks.

His place was a full-on wilderness adventure safari.

All those things his brother would've loved.

All those things he'd meant to share with his brother, he'd been sharing with Lucy.

Most of all, Jax had discovered he'd been able to breathe freely without the burden of grief whenever she was near. Somehow her presence filled a void that had set him free from the sorrow and stresses of the outside world. There was something about her. That shine in her eyes, her sweet smile, even the way she carried herself with an inner calmness that spoke louder than words ever could.

She was the sunlight to his dark rain.

He wanted her, but there was no way he'd wreck the only friendship he had in this place.

'Where is she?' He asked the red hen, as he continued to pace.

A crack of thunder detonated. Windows rattled. The rumble rolled through the soles of his thongs, followed by a blinding thwack of lightning. The hen squawked, cowering lower onto the washing machine as the house lights brightened then dimmed.

'Right. That's it.' With forceful steps inside, he swiped the ute keys off the kitchen counter, grabbed a t-shirt and headed for his ute. He did not want Lucy pedalling in this weather.

At the door of his cab he glanced back and there she was, on her bike coming down his long dirt driveway. 'I was about to search for you… Lucy?'

She rolled to a stop. Her face reddened and sweaty, her watery eyes were bloodshot and puffy.

'What's wrong?'

'They didn't come,' she said with a quivering bottom lip, red and raw as if she'd chewed on it.

'What?'

'They didn't come.' She let out a sob as fat tears rolled off her cheeks.

His heart that wasn't meant to feel—cracked like an ice shelf breaking off the Antarctic, sending a wave of icicles tingling to his scalp. 'Those bitches.' Her tears were widening the crevice within his heart. Were they too close already?

Another deafening rumble of thunder rolled as the wind picked up and the lightning crackled in stereo. The storm blocked out the sun and the temperature plummeted to match the cool spike in his chest.

'I forgot to tell you, we need to unplug everything with all this lightning,' Lucy said, wiping viciously at her tears as she pushed her bike towards the house. 'I'll do the veranda and pump shed, you do the house and we'll meet in the middle.

'Yeah, right, onto it.' Jax bounded up the steps, through the front door as more lightning crackled. He unplugged the television, the stereo, his PC and charging mobile. Then ran to the bedroom to unplug the air-conditioner. He did a sweep of the bathroom he'd been renovating, unplugging the tools recharging in the hallway, that by the time he'd hit the kitchen Lucy was in there disconnecting his new microwave and electric kettle.

That's when the lights went out.

A crackle of blue lightning flashed over the entire house. The hairs on his arms rose from the static electricity. Thunder dropped like a bomb overhead. Lucy squealed. Instinctively, he pulled her into his chest, checking his surrounds. They were on a concrete slab, in a safe space. Windows rattled, and the building groaned, but the house stood stolid.

'That one was close,' he said, holding her against his chest.

'We're in the heart of it now.'

The wind howled, pitching dust sideways at the windows. Trees bent like feathers.

'Will this house handle a cyclone?'

'Oh yeah, hands down,' she said, opening the kitchen's back door.

Did he dare pull her back for another hug?

'It's a good thing I brought wine for me and a bottle of bourbon for you. Come on, let's go drink and watch the rain fall and your grass grow.'

Now that sounded like a plan. 'Why did you bring me bourbon, not that I'm complaining?' He hadn't touched it, not since their conversation by the dam that housed his crocodile. Which reminded him to find a ranger.

'I bought it as a thank you and a supposed victory drink,' she said, putting the bottle onto his outdoor table. 'But now it's just a…' She stopped and again her eyes watered.

'I'll get the cups and ice.' It hurt to see her like that, he hated any woman crying.

'Here, put this in the freezer.' She handed him plastic bags of food she had tied to her bike.

'What's all this?'

'Wild warrigal quiche, bacon tartlets, mini macadamia and mango strudels, sour cream banana bread, watercress and crab pikelets, dainty devilled eggs, coffee meringue kisses—no, I ate those… but there's loads of other stuff to eat for the next week. Or feed it to your chook and make her obese. Have you got a name for her yet?'

'No. I don't do pets or houseplants.' He didn't think he'd do country either, but here he was.

Jax inhaled the amazing baking aromas from the food she'd brought with her, there was tonnes of stuff, still warm. *Oh no, it's the food from the Tea House.*

Didn't that kill his appetite.

He put the food away, grabbed their coffee mugs and sat in his chair by the outdoor table. It had the best view of his property. The ferocity of the wind had died down but the rolling wall of clouds reminded him of frozen waves just before they crashed onto a beach.

'This is for you too.' She pulled out a large manila envelope from her bike's magic basket.

'What's this?'

'Our local Fire Chief's, sorry the official title is,' as she read from the envelope, 'Senior Chief Fire Warden's job is being advertised, that's the boss's job.'

'At the doll's house? No thanks.' He dropped the unopened envelope onto the table.

'But—but—don't you want to be a Fire Chief?'

He couldn't bring himself to tell her that part of the job would mean shutting down the Tea House. It's why he avoided the place, knowing he had a duty to report it. The Tea House meant a lot to her and he did not want Lucy to hate him, not again—it'd kill him if she did.

Besides, it was a doll's house of a fire station. He'd get bored being in command of something that small. 'Didn't I tell you? I'm like Peter Pan, the boy who never grew up.'

'Bit of a drop from Ironman, don't you think, or are you a lost boy, too?'

She'd said that a few times now, *lost boys*.

He splashed a decent shot of bourbon over the ice in the coffee mug and passed it to Lucy. She looked like she needed it. 'Enough about me, what happened at the Tea House?' He sat back, blinking to himself. Did they sound like a married couple asking, *how was your day at the office, dear*?

'Nothing much.'

'You rode up here in tears, two hours late. Don't you dare say you're *fine*, or I'll toss you out into the storm.'

He poured himself a cup, rested the bourbon bottle on top of the envelope, then settled in to watch the storm. 'Question for question, Miss Lucy,' he said, raising his mug to her.

She hung her head for a moment, inhaled deep as if to find her strength, then clinked her mug against his. 'Question for question.'

'The black and white brutal truth.'

She swallowed deeply from her mug and stared at the storm.

'Did the cattlemen give you any grief this morning? They'd better not.' *No way*—the protectiveness he had for her was a heatwave surging from his chest.

'No. They were normal, and so were the knights of the round card-table.'

Get a grip, mate. This is Lucy. A mate. A friend.

Jax drank his bourbon to cool himself down, inhaling the crisp wind carried by the storm. 'Didn't you have all those bookings for the Tea House?'

'The place was fully booked.'

'And…'

Her lower lip quivered and her eyes watered.

He had to know. 'Who showed up, Lucy?'

'Only three.'

'Three groups, three tables—'

'Three people.'

'You're kidding?'

'Only Kat, Karen and Verily showed up. My friends. That's it.' Lucy took another deep swig of her bourbon, then slammed down her mug like a thirsty drover at the pub.

'What about that floral society meeting thing—'

'They didn't come. No book club. No orchid club. No bridge club. Nothing.'

'Did they ring and cancel or did they think it was still closed?'

'They knew it was open and being managed by me. Everyone did.'

Oh no.

She gulped another mouthful, wiping her mouth with the back of her hand like a pirate on the rum. 'That bitch boycotted my first day out.'

He pinched himself to not laugh. 'Over a Tea House?'

'It's not just a Tea House.' She glared at him over the rim of her cup and downed another mouthful. She was power drinking.

'Okay, Lucy, calm down.' He reached into his beer fridge and pulled out a water bottle. 'Drink this before you drink anymore bourbon.'

She drank the bottle dry.

'So, please explain to me how you boycott a Tea House?' This whole topic was so foreign.

'Nancy rang all of her friends telling them I'd stolen her lease and would poison everyone with my cooking.'

'You wouldn't know how to poison anyone, it's not in your nature. Do you want to go over there and smash all her garden gnomes with my halligan? I'll drive, and we can say it was storm damage,' he said, pointing to the ferocious weather.

'Tempting.'

It was a relief to hear her tinkling laughter, but it wasn't enough. Jax wanted that sweet smile of hers to shine. 'Or we could breach the walls of her gnome-front to rescue all her gnomes as part of the secret gnome liberation group?' *Where did that come from?* Stealing gnomes is something his brother would do, while Jax always played Mr Responsible.

'Then we could smuggle them out to cattle stations with instructions to take a photo of those gnomes returned to the wild,' she said.

'There's my girl,' he said, admiring the glimmering reflection of the storm in her eyes. It was a damned site better than those tears still dampening her cheeks. 'So, I'd say the old duck is jealous of you.'

'Behave,' she scoffed.

'She must be, to go to all that trouble to ruin your first day. You're a threat to her, cupcake, and she knows it.'

'Cupcake?'

'You make cupcakes, it suits you.'

She laughed and he had to smile with her.

'Thank you,' she said.

'For the nickname?'

'No, for cheering me up.'

'You're not giving up, are you?'

She shrugged, facing the incoming storm.

'Oh no you don't.' Putting his elbow on the table, he pointed at her. 'It's just a setback, Lucy. Remember, you've got this whole online campaign running in the background —'

'What online campaign?'

'Your cooking show.'

'I only did that to practise for the competition.'

'You're still doing that, right?'

'Why? When Nancy's done this.'

'Then prove her wrong. Steal her crown, by outcooking the cranky cow. Don't let the woman win, not like this. She's expecting you to do that, isn't she?' He could see it. Nancy knew exactly which nasty button to push on Lucy.

This was Lucy's worst fear realised.

No wonder she was so upset. It made his blood boil.

Jax reached for his laptop, flicked it open and turned it around to show Lucy her site. 'Tell that to the three thousand fans you have and all these other people who like your show.'

'When did this happen?'

'Some micro-influencer on Instagram recommended your site.'

'Listen to yourself.'

'I finished your intro and I've re-edited all your past shows to give them consistency, like a brand.'

'You've branded it?'

'I got creative.'

'How bored were you?'

'I've been waiting for you so we can go cook somewhere.' Every meal was an adventure of spontaneity. With the barbecue in the back of his truck and a container of dry goods and utensils, they'd explore his property to find something to eat.

It was takeaway meals in a whole new way.

No zip down to the shop, it was let's check out the pots by the billabong while digging for wild sweet-potatoes. Picking spices off the pantry shelf was replaced by plucking a leaf off that tree, and seed pods from that bush over there. Jax ate like a king and had never tasted food so good. 'You've got a lot of queries, you should answer them.'

'I don't know those people.'

'Lucy, they want to know you and all about those bush herbs you use. You're the source of knowledge. You know this stuff, not me.' She was his outback encyclopedia.

'But—but—'

'Okay, you answer the questions, I'll type in your reply while we sit here.'

'How come you can type so fast?'

'From wasting hours doing reports and memos and paperwork crap—'

She leaned across and closed his laptop on him.

'Hey?'

'You're missing the show.' She pointed to a thick line of dark grey clouds, highlighted with flashes of lightning. Taking away his laptop, she put the camera into his hand. 'Come on, grab your drink, I'll carry the bottle and we'll go play storm chasers.'

With a bottle in one hand, cup in the other and her face into the wind, her hair whipped around her and her eyes reflected the storm. 'I'll teach you the rain dance later.'

'Is there any special technique to it?'

'Yeah, you dance like no one's watching.'

In that split-second moment, Jax felt a white light of warmth hit the centre of his chest. It spread all over as he filmed Lucy twirling in the storm, as wild and free as the weather. He followed, drawn to her.

Jax was not going to let Lucy quit, not on his watch.

* * *

Lucy heard music coming from the clouds. A red plane skimmed above the roof of the house with a straw broom painted on it's under carriage. 'The wild witch of the westerly winds is here.'

'Who?' Jax asked, aiming his camera to follow the plane's flight path.

'It's Monet.'

'Where is she going to land?'

'On your airstrip. Tobias told me this place used to be part of the Air Force camp for World War II, and that's the old airstrip.' She pointed to the long wide strip of red dirt, with sheds on the right and scrublands to the left. 'He'd mow it in the wet and use it as a fairway for golf.'

'I don't mind a hit of golf now and again. That also explains all the sheds I've got scattered everywhere. Hey, where was the main base camp?'

Bugger. That's where Hank lived in his train by the billabong. 'You should look it up in your research.'

'I will.'

Oh, no. 'How do you feel about people crashing over and playing squatters?'

'Like your friends?' Jax pointed to the small red plane landing in his yard. 'How loud…' Rock music bellowed out of the plane competing with the howling wind.

'I'm sure you'll like her music. Monet's single, you know.'

He frowned at her from behind his camera.

'Sorry, I forgot. You enjoy being solo, Peter Pan.' She giggled, tipsy from the bourbon and the day's high emotions.

The plane's door opened and out jumped Rigsy waving his Akubra at her, carrying a box of beer.

'Are you okay with this?' She asked Jax. 'They're house-trained, and you haven't had a house warming yet, have you?'

'No. And I've never had a plane land in my yard, either.'

'You should ask Monet for a tour of your property.'

'That'd be cool.'

Monet jumped from her plane in Blundstone boots, cut-off denim shorts and singlet. Her blonde, pixie cut hair ruffled in the wind as she gave them her mischievous wide smile. 'I heard you were hiding out here.'

'Hello to you too.' If there was ever a time Lucy needed a friend, this was it. She hugged her best friend. 'I missed you.'

'Me too. I'm sorry I missed your opening, I tried to make it earlier but I've been dodging storms all morning, doing the mail run from Gove.'

'It's okay, you didn't miss much.' She bit her lip, forcing down a lump in her throat, along with the desire to collapse onto the ground and throw a toddler's tantrum, punching at the dirt. The ride over here had taken her forever, wobbling on the bike as tears blurred her vision, heaving for air in between sobs. She almost didn't come.

Lucy had managed to keep up a strong facade, escorting her friends out of the Tea House. She'd locked the bi-fold glass doors, turned the lights off in the spotless dining room, leaving the wall of photos in shadows. With heavy feet, she dragged herself into the kitchen and huddled into the corner where the tiled walls and floor only amplified her whimpers.

She'd never felt so alone and defeated in her entire life.

She'd put everything into this, and for what?

Failure.

That one word weighed heavier than a fully loaded cattle truck.

It hurt to lift her head, stumbling out of the kitchen and onto her bike.

She didn't want to waste all that food she'd put her heart and soul into. Most of all, she didn't want to disappoint Jax, who was the joy to her day. She needed him. Especially when today had been the biggest of life's disappointments.

She'd failed.

Every test. Every time. She failed.

The weight of failure only dragged down her shoulders.

Monet slung her arm around Lucy, giving her friend a squeeze. 'Rigsy told me what that stupid rotten….' The storm clouds crackled, drowning out Monet's colourful explosion of swearwords.

'Oi?' Rigsy said. 'It was bad enough being stuck in the cockpit with you complaining your head off on the way over here. If you're gonna ear-bash all night, me and ol' mate here are gonna go drink in the shed.'

'Who are you calling old?' Jax asked.

'It's just a term, Jax,' said Lucy, forcing a grin. 'You know Rigsy, and this is my mate, Monet.'

Monet shook Jax's hand. 'Wicked ink work.'

'Jax's brother was a tattoo artist,' said Lucy proudly. The detailed tribal work on Jax's body was more than just a part of him, it moved with him. Very few showed or honoured their commitment to family like Jax. His commitment to family was for life. It was nothing you'd shrug off lightly, only to remember at Christmas time. For Jax it was soul deep, in the strength of his solid stance and his square shoulders. The man who seemed so surly, like unbent steel on the outside, cared deeper than most for family. He literally wore his heart on his sleeve, represented by his brother's ink work. It was a badge of honour to his family.

Sadly, it was also a heart-wrenching reminder that he had no one left.

'Was?' Monet asked.

Jax took a mouthful of his drink, frowning at the storm as it rumbled overhead. 'Is your plane going to be okay there, with this storm?'

'Sure, it's insured. We can chain it to the shed so she doesn't fly away, if that'll make you feel any better?' Monet said, giving her mischievous smile that Lucy's dad dubbed *trouble*. As the wind whipped her blonde hair, Monet reached under the plane's hatch and pulled out a boat anchor. Then, with a small backpack over her shoulder and esky in the other hand, she dragged the anchor attached to a thick chain, toward the house.

'What is she going to do with that?' Jax asked Rigsy who shrugged and followed.

Monet dropped the anchor at the end of the chain's length and pushed it down into the dirt with her boots. 'Just in case… See you in the morning, Gertrude.' She saluted the plane then hooked her arm through Lucy's. 'Now, let's get this rain dance started, shall we?'

Lucy caught Jax's questioning look. 'Don't worry, Jax, I know where the spare towels are.'

'We heard you've got a tonne of food. Monet's got the tunes and this is the first storm of the season,' said Rigsy, hoisting the box of beer over his shoulder. 'I'll put this beer in the fridge first. Good to see it's in the same place, Jax.'

'Obviously, you've been here before?'

'Relax, Jax, it'll be fun. You'll see,' said Lucy, hooking her arm through his. With Monet on her other side, the first big fat drop of rain hit her shoulder with a splat. More fat drops hit the leaves of nearby bushes making them move the way a cow flicks their ears. 'It's coming.'

Back at the house, drinks were poured, music got sorted, and they sat around the table on the veranda, waiting for the rain to arrive.

'I like her music,' Jax said, pouring them another bourbon.

'I knew you would. Your tastes are similar.' She was glad to see him finally relaxing, instead of working all the time. He worked on the house, or on her stuff, tapping away on the keyboard. The only time Jax stopped was when he had the camera in hand filming her, or when they were exploring the property. He never scrutinized the land like a farmer, checking fences or bores, he viewed it like a tourist.

Maybe this storm, the company and party atmosphere might make him settle in more?

Hold on a second, why was she worrying about Jax like this? The guy was his own entity, who'd probably only stay a year before he got bored and left.

But right now, she could see he liked this storm and party atmosphere, it made those dull eyes of his come alive. They were as sexy as his smile.

And watching him made her forget her own troubles.

'Here it comes.' She pointed, feeling the energy from the storm system approaching them with a roar.

'I've never…' His voice was lost to the wind, followed by the solid sound of pouring rain.

Finally, Lucy got her walls of water.

She stood beneath it, letting it wash away the sweat, tears, shame and disappointment of her day. It drowned out any and all of her thoughts. Craning her neck back, mouth open, arms wide, it was like a baptism, washing away all her sins. It was freeing.

Laughter bubbled inside her, the music a distant din in the thick refreshing rain. She dragged Jax out to dance in the warm summer storm, splashing in puddles like they were kids.

She'd never felt more alive.

Jax stood beside her with his face to the heavens.

'You okay?' Lucy asked him, wiping the rainwater and wet hair from her face. Her dress clung to her. Mud splattered her legs and covered her bare feet, but she didn't care. She was raw with emotions, from the lowest of lows to this cleansing high. She had nothing left to hide. She needed to climb out of this rock-bottom day. If she sank any lower, she doubted she'd have the strength to survive.

'Yeah,' he said with a nod. 'Thanks to you, I know I'm going to be okay.' Jax cupped her face, leaned down and kissed her. Lips to lips.

She stood still, stunned by his swiftness. She twitched with surprise, then softened, accepting him, kissing him back. The heat and the power of their connection was like the spark of a match. A small flickering light that burst into flame powering into a brushfire that swirled inside her chest. Mingled with the taste of rain and Jax, a wave of fiery desire engulfed her she swayed on her feet, gripping onto him. It was Jax who stood as the solid centre of her storm.

Lightning crackled and the ground rumbled beneath their feet. She jumped back from him, stunned at her reaction to their kiss.

His eyes were as dark as the storm, with a body gift wrapped in ink, that wove a spell around his strong shoulders and solid chest. The wind battered at her and she swayed towards his heat. She pushed against his stomach, a wall. Of pure. Hot. Muscle.

Did she dare kiss the Demi-god of sin harder? Longer. Deeper.

Did she dare run her hands over the contours, following the ink swirls over his chest and down the ridges of his stomach?

She licked her lips as a sizzle of lustful heat zipped through her bones. Was that from the storm, or Jax?

Either way, it felt amazing.

She let her smile free, allowing the emotions to burst without restraint, and she danced in the rain splashing around in the muddy puddles. Determined to forget—to live within this single purest moment. She now understood what Jax meant. She felt it too—she was drunk on life.

*   *   *

The night continued, the storm passed, his guests partied and Jax was having a great time. He laughed and danced in the rain, it was something he'd never done.

He learned the gossip from Monet, who was funny, and loud, but she did nothing for him. Not like Lucy.

He'd kissed Lucy.

She'd kissed him back, then kept dancing.

He didn't mean to kiss her, but now he couldn't stop thinking about kissing her again. He'd enjoyed the surprise of her lips, the twitch of her tongue, the colour that deepened her cheeks when he kissed her. He wanted to do it again.

Why would he risk ruining this perfect friendship?

With Monet passed out on the couch and Rigsy snoring on the floor nearby, Jax turned off the music. He found Lucy in the kitchen, washing dishes after their feast of amazing leftovers.

Jax surveyed his kitchen benches, filled with assorted foods and drinks and that gaping cavity waiting for a new stove. The old oven still lived in the dirt in the rain, now beneath other rubbish as he continued his renovations.

He'd had his first party. An impromptu housewarming that even his brother would have loved. Hell, his brother would have debated with Monet over music choices, then wrestled in the mud with Rigsy.

Jax missed the guy who wasn't just a brother, they were best friends.

He gazed at his newest friend, following the curves under her dress. Her hair was up, exposing the soft spot where her hairline met her slender neck. He wanted to run his fingers across the back of her neck, to cup that spot on her nape, to curl that one dark ringlet that always fell loose from her pony tail.

In bare feet, she washed the dishes at the kitchen sink while the rain thrummed on the roof and the green tree frogs croaked their bad opera. It was the kind of domestic bliss seen only in the movies, never in his reality. Past girlfriends had tried to play house with him before, but he'd never felt like this about them.

What would Lucy do if he pushed her up against that sink and kissed her? Hard.

'Here, I'll take that, you go crash,' said Lucy, taking the plates from his hands.

'So, um…' He cleared his throat, pushing the need inside *waaay* down. He did not want to mess up a good thing. 'Are you and Monet going to do an aerial bombing of Nancy's later?'

'Nah, we're thinking of letting Rigsy strip for her and give her a heart attack.'

'Are you sure she won't jump him?' He wouldn't mind if Lucy jumped on him.

'Probably.' She laughed, returning to the dishes.

'Hey, you don't have to play kitchenhand here, so step away from the sink or I'll throw you over my shoulder—'

'In a fireman's hold. Isn't that what firemen do?'

'I think I need practise, it's been a while.' He leaned down, picked her up over his shoulder and patted her cute behind.

'Hey, put me down.'

'Say please.'

'Please.'

He put her down. Helped to wipe her hair away, exposing her flushed face and sweet smile that shone in her eyes. 'I'm glad to see you smiling again.'

'But where's yours gone?' She poked at the corner of his mouth.

'Here, see if you can find it.' He didn't hesitate, leaning in to kiss her again. His hand cupped that spot at the back of her neck, his fingers twined through her soft hair, pressing his lips to hers. He kissed her deeper, bringing her closer to his chest. Her mouth was sweet, her skin warm, soft and sensuous.

He stopped, almost gasping for air, close to breaking. She needed gentle—but Jax didn't do gentle. He did primal and had an overwhelming animal-like instinct to grab onto her cute arse-cheeks and wrap her legs around his body.

But the way she looked up him, his sweet Lucy with her swollen lips, there was a fire in those eyes, and baby, he wanted to stroke those flames into an inferno.

'Miss Lucy?'

'Yes, Mr Jax.'

'Are we okay?' Dry in the mouth, his voice was like gravel. 'You're not going to hate me in the morning, are you?' Would he hate himself?

'We're just frenemies.' She grabbed the side of his face and kissed him with such ferocity it stunned him. 'Shut up or we'll be fighting any second now.'

He wouldn't argue with that.

He'd expected gentle, not the hungry tenacity she had in the skill and power of her mouth. Passion had never tasted so sweet.

His skin tremored under her palms as they skimmed over his shoulders and down his back. Her body was pliant against his. Her thighs were smooth like silk as his hands followed them up her dress. She raised her leg, wrapping it around him. She pushed at the hollow at the base of his spine, her fingernails scraping under the edge of his jeans that were suddenly too damned tight. A deep hungry growl from his chest responded to the tiniest squeak from her throat and he lifted her, pressing himself into her body as he backed her up against the wall.

The rain poured, setting the frogs off on another rousing chorus, competing with the loud buzz of Rigsy's snoring coming down the hallway. He wanted more, hell she did too, he could taste it. Without stopping, lips meshed against hers he carried his prize into his room and kicked the door shut behind him.

For one night only, he would make this rain dance run between them until dawn — after all, they were only meant to be frenemies.

FIFTEEN

A dog howled nearby. Jax jumped out of bed at the foreign sound and rushed through the glass doors to the veranda. The night was still cool and crisp from the rain. Stars twinkled through the gaps in the clouds along with the pink glow of the approaching dawn.

'It's okay, just a dingo,' said Lucy, seated at the outdoor table.

'Where's the chook?' He searched for the feathery shape that lived on his washing machine.

'I've got her, she's asleep.' Lucy pointed to the hen tucked safely into her lap.

'You're wearing my shirt?' He didn't care that he was naked, he liked how her eyes slowly checked him out.

'I couldn't find my dress in the dark.'

'Yeah, right…' He grinned, taking a seat next to her at the table. *Let's hope the houseguests don't wake up.*

Without thought, he rubbed the sweet spot at the base of her neck where that lock beckoned to be twisted around his finger. 'Were you going to do a runner on me?'

'Is that what normally happens?'

'Yeah,' he said, clearing his throat and removed his arm. 'Although it's usually me doing the running. I never take them back to my place.' He was a callous bastard with women, they'd never mattered to him.

'I gathered that.'

Lucy saw the good in people, but she was also adept at reading him well. Too well. Was she going to give him some speech on what they'd done?

He rubbed his hand over his face and bristly chin, still fighting off sleep. The aroma of fresh rain and coffee greeting him.

'Coffee's there, Ironman.'

Well, didn't that make him smile. 'Thank you, coffee and a compliment on sunrise.' He poured himself a cup from the plunger on the tray. It's obvious she'd been up a while. 'What is the time?'

'Five.'

'Are you normally awake this time of the morning?'

'I am, and I wasn't sure where I was when I woke up.'

'Was I snoring?'

Her sweet smile shone with no form of embarrassment. She'd said they would be okay—she was right. There was no awkwardness over what they'd done last night, and done very well together. It was a whole new side to her and he liked it.

'No, but I heard the dingoes howling,' she said.

'How close are they?'

'Close. You need a dog. Trigger used to live here, he kept them away.'

'I'm assuming Trigger was some kind of cattle dog who went with his owner?'

'Oh yeah, he's retired to body surfing on WA beaches that I hear are crocodile-free.'

'They are. With a swell you can surf in. Can you surf?'

'No. I've always been too scared to swim, unless it's in a pool.'

'Yeah. I imagine living with crocodiles, you'd fear all kinds of water.' He sipped his coffee and leaned back, brushing shoulders with hers to watch the sunrise.

'Why are you here?'

'Huh?'

'I mean, why here?' She asked. 'Why this town? You could have gone anywhere and kept working in the fire department. Why did you quit the job you love, that you're so good at, to come here?'

Defenceless against those questioning eyes of hers, he muttered, 'My brother.'

'Oh.'

He rubbed the pain in his chest with the heel of his palm, drawing deep from the coffee, trying to find the strength. He gazed at the faint light of a new day, all washed free from dust, as if reborn. Free from pains of the past.

'We were meant to do this together,' he said, spotting wallabies grazing on the far edges of his once-dead lawn. 'We both said as soon as we could afford to, we'd do it. We were saving up for it as one of those things you say, we'll do it one day. Some day. But for him, that day never came.'

She reached out and put her warm hand on his arm. He grabbed it and toyed with her fingers, so soft in his. Never saying a word.

The woman had the gift of silence down to an art. It spoke louder than words ever could.

Somehow, it made his words spill more.

'I'd forgotten about it until my brother's will,' he said. 'We'd both done it as a pact, years ago, when I made him work on our wills. He would only do it if we wrote out the *brotherly bucket list*.'

'You do like lists.'

'We liked this one most of all, because for weeks that list sat on the kitchen table. We'd add to it constantly, all those things we wanted to do, not just as adults, but what we'd missed out as kids too. My brother, who was always the big kid, had somehow turned the morbid exercise of writing our wills into a fun game. I was the one who always played the responsible grown up.' Yet Lucy had helped him find the fun side he didn't know he'd had.

'What was on that list?' Lucy asked.

Jax hadn't opened that list in weeks, not since he'd started renovating the house. 'Simple stuff, like take a train ride across the country. To find the outback, like how we used to describe it to our mum. To live where no one knew of our past, and that was the Northern Territory. Yet those guys at the hardware store saw through me in a minute calling me a druggie's hitman on…'

'Witness protection.'

'Yeah, right.' He sighed into his coffee mug then swallowed down the flavour.

'You should apply for the Fire Chief's job.' She tapped on the manila envelope, still in a pristine condition under the near-empty bottle of bourbon. 'The locals will understand about the Airforce thingy. Your aviation experience will be perfect—'

'It's not just that, Miss Lucy,' he said, tenderly caressing her soft curls. 'I've got a house to fix, and this cooking show to film and edit.'

She screwed her nose up and whined, 'Are we still doing that?'

'Hell yeah. You're not letting that woman beat you. It's one of your goals you're so close to—'

'What are your goals?'

'To live in a place where I could have an adventure in my backyard, and I have.' He grinned at the dawn creeping higher, outlining the sheds and Monet's plane in the middle of his new-found fairway. 'I've had a water buffalo at my back door, a crocodile lurking in my dam, a plane land on my front lawn and we cook what you find on my property. I am living the dream my brother and I talked about. It's like an adult's summer camp full of fun and wonder.'

'So, you're not here to farm?'

'I haven't thought that far. I'm focusing on the house first.'

'Don't you miss being a fireman? You're good at it.'

'How do you know?'

'I googled you.'

He was impressed and glad she was branching out.

'I saw the awards and articles about you. How come you don't have them on display?'

He shrugged. 'Different life.'

Sipping his coffee, staring at the manila envelope holding the Senior Chief Fire Warden's application. Lucy had hand-delivered it to him from her magic basket on her bike. Even amidst all her own dramas, she'd still thought of him and he hadn't even read the list of duties for the job.

She nudged him softly with his elbow. 'Go on, admit it.'

'Yeah, all right, I do miss parts of it, but I don't miss the paperwork. And, yeah, I wanted to be a Fire Chief once.' He'd been working towards it, testing himself, always learning and improving for the job. His ambition used to drive him out of bed daily. 'But my brother's death made me realise there's more to life than working shifts and running after a clock, fighting traffic and people.'

'Are you saying you were ready to leave the city?' She studied him with searching eyes, holding her breath.

'Yeah, I think I was. Once I'd made up my mind, it didn't take me long and everything seemed to fall into place. The longest hold up was getting my bosses to let me go.'

'You resigned?'

'No. They wouldn't accept it. They made me take leave without pay for three years with the option to extend.'

'So, this is like a holiday? A test, to see if you can make a go of it?'

'Kind of.'

'I hate tests. I fail every time,' she mumbled, stroking the hen in her lap.

'This isn't a test.'

'How can you be so sure? You've left yourself options to go back.'

'I bought this property because it was well below my budget. I'll repair it and get the house in order, then I'll farm something. I don't know what, yet. Have you got any ideas?' The woman was his outback encyclopedia with extraordinary skills for making something from nothing.

'It's your property, not mine.' She'd said it so sadly, as if it bothered her.

'What are your long-term goals?' Jax asked, tucking her hair behind her ear.

She shrugged. 'Me? To pay bills.'

'Come on, question for question, Miss Lucy.' He grinned at her eye roll. 'Is the Tea House a part of your dreams?'

'No, that just happened.'

'Circumstances, sure.' With his big mouth playing a huge part. 'You jumped at the opportunity pretty quick. So, was it a part of your goals?'

'No, I mean yes,' she said, shuffling in her seat. 'I love cooking and I enjoy feeding people and trying new things.'

'You're very adventurous.' He liked that about her, she brought it out in him too.

'I couldn't work in an office, I know that much.' She hesitated and he dropped his head to meet her eyes, waiting for her reply. 'I want to be my own boss, run my own kitchen. I don't care where, or how, as long as it has a stove.'

'You do that now, with the barbecue.'

'I want something more than a barbecue hot plate. I want a chalkboard menu and a place with a proper oven, no matter how small. I live in a house with no stove, and you...' They grinned at his stove still lying face-down in the dirt. 'At the pub, I have an amazing view of the sunset over the sinks and I'd see the sunrise at the Tea House. But now, it's like your job with the fire department; it's had its run, it's time to try something new.'

He didn't believe that for a second. Lucy loved to cook, you could taste it in her food. 'Is that because of what Nancy did to you?'

She dropped her head to her chest, and he put his arm around her shoulders.

'Don't give in to that bitch, you hear me? You can beat her, you're a brilliant cook, and from what I gather, Nancy only cooks the same dishes.'

'But no one will eat my food.'

'Not true. Rigsy said the stockmen didn't complain and tipped you more than normal. Were the Triple J's at the hardware store nice to you too?'

'They were, and so were my friends.'

'So nothing changed, and Nancy got to live up to her reputation as being nasty. You know what I'd do?'

'What?'

'I'd hunker down and do my thing. Let her shoot herself in the foot with what she's saying. When the truth comes out, and it will, she'll not only embarrass herself, but all those other women siding with her too.'

She sat up with widening eyes. 'That's why you're not telling anyone about being a fireman and letting them make up their own minds.'

Jax grinned at her, admiring the way her eyes sparkled in the twilight.

'Clever.'

'You know what else I'm clever at?' He said, lifting the sleeping hen and placing it back on the washing machine.

'What?'

'I'll have to show you.' Sliding his hands under her legs, he picked her up and held her to his chest.

'Do you like carrying me?'

'It's what firemen do.' He smiled at her tinkling laughter. 'And, I am the rooster of this hen house.' And this rooster had better ways to greet the day, kicking the bedroom door shut behind him.

SIXTEEN

Lucy rode down her cracked concrete driveway and around to the back door that was never locked. The towering tree's shadow stretched over the patchy lawn and empty stables cooling the place down. She parked her bike, skipped up the steps and into the cool kitchen where loud music washed over her.

'Hey, do I know you?' Monet asked, turning down her music, seated at the kitchen table with paperwork and laptop before her. 'You look like this girl that used to live here.'

'Hello to you too, Monet,' Lucy said, taking a seat at the table.

'To what do we owe the honour of your visit to the unofficial Elsie Creek Inn?'

'I'm working at the pub tonight, so I'll be elbow deep in dishes for the fiftieth tonight.'

'It's Taylor's?'

'You're going, I assume.'

Monet's wide smile said it all. 'I will be. What about Jax? You should ask him to come and not be so dark and mysterious.'

'I think Jax is looking forward to a night off.'

'Or are you in desire of a night free from Jax? You two have been pretty cosy lately.'

'We've been busy.'

'I hope the sex is good?'

Lucy grinned behind her water bottle, scrunching her toes. *Good—the man is a god!*

'With that look it's obvious he knows what he's doing. And this is where, as your faithful friend,' Monet said, patting a palm over her heart, 'I need to do this whole be-careful-speech-thing. The guy's probably a skirt-chasing player who is not after anything serious.'

'We're just frenemies with benefits.'

'Huh?'

'Inside joke. Jax is helping me get my licence, and I'm helping him get settled onto his block of land. He has no idea what he wants to do on the farm, because he's always been a fireman. He's got a stack of bravery medals, too, but don't say anything.'

'Why not? The town still thinks he's a—' Monet paused. 'That tricky bugger. He's letting all those gossipers make fools of themselves.'

'It's what he's telling me to do about Nancy.'

'Smart move. If it was me, I'd be around there with my cricket bat to see how many boundaries I'd score with Nancy's garden gnomes.'

'You don't own a cricket bat.'

'Rigsy does. It was that or your softball bat. You know, we used to sneak into Nancy's yard at night and move them around on her.'

'Did you ever steal any?'

'No, never. The town's too small for that. We always wanted to put them on the side of the road with hitchhiking signs on them.'

'Like Hank's roadside sculptures.'

'Have you told Jax about Hank yet?' Monet asked.

'I've been trying to.'

'Aren't you showing Jax around his property?'

'Yeah.'

'Well, isn't that World War 2 Airforce dump part of his property too? I'd want to know if it was my place. Wouldn't you?'

'I don't want Hank homeless.'

'I've told Hank there's always room for him at the Inn,' Monet said.

'He knows that, but he likes the train.'

'A train he doesn't own. It's Jax's now, Tobias Clare sold it to him. What will Jax do when he discovers he's practically got a national treasure in his yard?'

'It's not treasure—it's the Airforce's old junk.'

'Kat would call it treasure when the woman does a good job of turning trash into cash. Can you imagine what she'd do with a whole train engine and carriage.'

Lucy scrubbed her palms over her face. 'You're right. I should've told Jax sooner, or Hank should have. He lives there, not me. Honestly, it's between the pair of them.'

'You're the one sleeping with the owner, who trusts you to tell him things. It's a pretty big secret not to tell a guy.'

Lucy sighed, slumping into her seat. 'I know. I know. You're right. I'll tell Hank he has to talk to Jax, and I'll take Jax around there to meet Hank tomorrow.'

'Good,' Monet said.

'You suck when you're serious.'

'It's a rare moment, so suck it up, buttercup,' Monet said, sipping from her coffee mug with the tea-tag fluttering on the side.

'Isn't it beer o'clock for you?'

'I want to finish these books. Then I'll take them to the pub, where I plan to drink my hard-earned money away and drag some poor male home to have my wicked way with him.'

'Only to kick them out at dawn.'

'Tough life for some. Hey, Jax isn't doing that with you, is he? I've seen how that man makes you smile—you're falling for him. Big. Time.'

'I am not,' said Lucy, jutting out her chin. 'I'm like you, just having fun.'

'Ah-huh,' said Monet as she shuffled higher in her seat, leaning closer to Lucy. 'As much as I love to hear that I am your supreme mentor of happiness and deviously wicked fun, you're not built like me, Lucy.'

'What makes you so different?'

'Because heartbreak and me go way back, leaving me with no heart left to hurt. You do—and it's a big and beautiful thing. Look, all I'm saying is, take it slow with Jax, that's all. No harm is there? Not when you're busy trying to start your own business. Which reminds me, have you got a name for it yet?'

'No.'

'We have time. But I do need some ID for the other paperwork. So, cough it up, let's see that learner's permit you've had forever,' Monet said with an open palm.

Lucy dug around in her bag for her purse.

'It'd help if you had your full licence, so be prepared if they ask for a copy of your birth certificate.

'It's a business account. Not a loan,' Lucy said. 'Do you think I'll have enough to live off if I run the Tea House?'

'One day a week, no.'

'Hey, you could have said that a little nicer,' said Lucy, frowning.

'People pay me for my brutal honesty.' Monet scanned the licence with her phone, then handed it back to Lucy. 'Coz you're my bestie, you get the el primo treatment, so buckle-up, babe,' Monet said, putting her hands over Lucy's. 'Here is the unsugared truth.'

Lucy held her breath. 'Hit me.'

'It will cost you more to open that place that you will *not* be making a profit, let alone a living. I did a cost estimate on the Tea House's trade and it's nothing but a money pit.'

'You're kidding?'

'Is this the face of a liar?' Monet drew her finger around her face. 'I've been called lots of names, mostly crazy, but never a liar—especially with my friends.'

'Sorry. I believe you, just…' Lucy leaned over to peek at Monet's screen of numbers.

'How Nancy managed it is a mystery,' said Monet, pointing to the screen.

'She told me she'd inherited some super and investments from her husband.'

'That makes sense.'

'What does? I sucked at maths in school, how am I going to do bookwork?'

'I told you, I'll teach you, or you'll be feeding me cake and coffee forever.' Monet sat back, chewing on her pen, her eyes narrowing at the small screen. 'I bet Nancy purposefully ran that place at a loss.'

'Why?'

'For the tax benefits. There is no way Nancy could've made a profit these past few years. She must've been earning money on her investments and used the place as a tax dodge. Companies do it all the time.'

'Are you saying that the Tea House won't make me *any* money?'

'No,' Monet said, shaking her head. 'One day a week is not an income to survive on. You've scored a few weekly shifts at the pub and you had the mango picking to get you through the dry season. The musters will be over soon and the pub's always quiet after New Year, so what are you going to do then?'

Lucy slumped into her chair. 'I'm so stupid.'

'Hey, don't give up, okay. You will always have a room at the Inn, free—'

'I don't want to be a charity.' It's why she cleaned and cared for the place. Monet charged no one rent, and her door was always open.

'Didn't you say Kat had some ideas?' Monet asked.

'She did, they were catering jobs, and I know Nancy made specialty cakes for people.'

'But that's still not enough to live off.' Monet sighed and shifted in her seat, saying, 'You lost money last week when no one showed and—'

'Only because Nancy told them to stay away. I bet they'll keep staying away because of Nancy,' said Lucy with an acidic taste of panic swirling inside her. 'What do I do? I don't want to go back to station work. I love it here, Elsie Creek is my home.'

'I don't want you to go either. I'm sure we'll come up with something. There's a group of us going tonight, we'll brainstorm ideas over beer and wine. If not, we can attack Nancy's garden gnomes one last time before she has her lawn sale. Are you going to check it out?'

'No. You?'

'I won't be here. I'm off to Kununurra for a bit, but I'll be back in time to watch you win your crown in the Billabong Barbie Bake-off. Rigsy and I have been working on something special.'

'Rigsy's not going to moon the world out of your plane window again, is he?'

'Not since his arse got stuck,' Monet said, laughing. 'You should have seen the landing crews' faces, waiting for their charter flight back to Darwin, with Rigsy's bum in the window. Boys, ha.'

They both chuckled when Lucy sobered up and asked, 'What do I tell the publican? I'm sure she's heard what happened last week with no one showing up.'

'You're still under trial and Samantha is a very patient person. She'd have to be, growing up in a pub. She wouldn't have given you this opportunity without having thought about it. If she wants the Tea House to stay open, you could negotiate cheaper rent.'

'I've never had to negotiate.'

'Well, see what Samantha offers first, then tell her you'll seek guidance from your crazy number crunching guru—me—and we'll work it out. What do you say?'

'This is all too hard,' Lucy said, again scrubbing her hands over her face. 'It was easier working for someone else.' Like her father did his whole life.

The man would have made enough money to buy ten cattle stations, if he'd wanted it, but he never did. Settling for the old ute towing the horse float, shifting from one station to the next. Her dad was always working for the bosses.

Lucy wanted to work for herself.

She wanted something in her name that was hers. That's why she wanted the Tea House, she wanted to be her own boss.

But it wasn't going to happen. Not now. Not ever. There was too much resistance.

Did she have the strength to fight it?

Lucy got up from her seat, mumbling, 'I'd better get to work.' After all, it's what she was trained to do her whole life, work for someone else.

Why would a fancy fireman like Jax bother with someone like her? If they passed each other in the city, Jax wouldn't even notice her.

It's best they remain frenemies before she got too attached. Especially when Jax was already well-trained at detaching himself from people, places, jobs, and women. The man admitted he was a player, dealing with grief and loneliness.

How stupid was she to think he'd want anything long term with her?

In fact, she was just like her father!

Oh no…

She'd been helping Jax sort out his property, the same way her dad had done for countless property owners all over the country.

Lucy was doing exactly what she didn't want to do.

What's worse—she wasn't getting paid for it!

The realisation swamped her chest, it was hard to breathe. She wanted to curl up in the corner and cry. Again.

Instead, she grabbed her apron from her bedroom and went to work for the man.

What a fool she'd been to dare dream of a bigger future.

SEVENTEEN

Jax drummed his fingers in time to the music on the steering wheel, heading into town. He hadn't slept well, not without Lucy. He missed her. Shouldn't, but he did.

On the passenger seat sat the large manila envelope with the application for Elsie Creek's Senior Chief Fire Warden's position. At Lucy's silent insistence, he'd filled out the paperwork she'd left under the coffee plunger as a reminder. Daily, she'd put the application in his way, finding it on his outdoor chair by the table, in front of the kettle, on the bathroom cabinet, even on his pillow. She didn't say anything, just left it there for him to find. He liked that about her. She was offering him a choice without making demands.

This morning, he'd filled it out over coffee as he hand-fed that red hen as the only company he had on the property.

He'd thought that by moving here, he'd be done with resumes and job applications. His last job application wasn't that long ago, for the Acting Fire Chief's position in Melbourne. A stepping stone to becoming a full Fire Chief of a busy fire station—not some sleepy outcrop in the middle of nowhere that was just a dollhouse. He'd get bored.

But he still filled out the application, going through his past experiences that was a revisit of his ladder-climbing career.

Lucy was right, Jax loved the job. He loved the smell of a fire house, the uniforms and the trucks. Everything about it. It didn't change from Airforce to State, it was just a change of uniform and truck colours. Underneath, it was still the same job.

Was he ready to face the job again when he'd willingly walked away for a family commitment? A family who weren't even here to share it with him?

The application brought up questions, and he was on his way into town to do some research. He needed to know if this job was suitable for a man like him.

Ahead on the dirt road, strange wooden sculptures stood on the verge like tee pees, topped with broken materials made from rubbish. He'd seen the council truck in town collecting them and guessed it was bin day soon.

He spotted a lone figure. Tall, lean with hunched shoulders, carrying an empty sack. Yet the way he carried it you'd swear he was lugging a load of concrete boulders.

Jax slowed down, as part of Lucy's outback protocols so he didn't shower anyone with dust.

Was this Hank? The one Lucy talked about.

'Do you need a lift?' Jax asked through the lowered passenger window.

The guy stopped and stared at him with his sun-leathered skin, wild woolly beard and hair. He was also clean, like he'd bathed. Not the typical homeless guy Jax used to see in the city.

'Wouldn't want to bother you, mate.'

'Are you Hank?'

'Ah, yeah. You're Jax.'

'Get in, Hank, or Lucy will give me grief if I leave you on the side of the road like this.'

'She would, she's persistent for someone so quiet.'

'Don't I know it.' But he liked her. A lot.

Hank hesitated at the door, wiping his hands on his trousers that were ten times too big for him. 'You sure, mate? This is a flash ute.'

Lucy had done the same thing. 'I wouldn't offer if I wasn't sure.' Jax shifted his paperwork, tucking it into his blanket of many pockets he and Lucy had used to sit on the ute's roof, she called it his couch.

Hank gingerly climbed into the passenger seat. 'This air-con is nice.'

'It's humid from the rain. 95% they said on the radio.' It was like walking around in a sauna that got worse the higher the sun climbed with clouds on the horizon teasing of more rain. 'Where are you headed?'

'Train station.'

'To see Lucy?' Jax wanted to go see her, but she might still be asleep, having worked last night in the pub's kitchen.

'Um, nah, it's not train day. Nasty thing what them women did to her, eh?'

'Were you there?'

'Yeah, it devastated Lucy. That Nancy was always chasing me and the other stockmen away with her broom.'

'I only met the woman once. That was enough,' said Jax, as the ute left the dirt and drove onto the bitumen. 'Lucy told me it was your idea for the cooking show on YouTube?'

'We did it to help her get over her stage fright for that Barbie Bake-off. She told me you're filming her now, doing a good job.'

'I'm having fun with it,' said Jax. It was a hobby, not his idea of a career to play cameraman, but he did enjoy it, watching Lucy smile. 'I'm eating like a king.'

'Me too.'

Jax realised Lucy was feeding both of them. 'Do you think Lucy will win this Barbie Bake-thing?'

'I hope so.'

'Do you know the competition?'

'Not really. There's the caveman—'

'The who?'

'Big Jimmy. He runs the mechanic's shop with his brother. They've got all the tradesmen in town backing him for the title of king. There's a few ringers and some fishermen who might toss their Akubras into the ring. Then there's Nancy.'

'Lucy was telling me that Nancy's practising to retain her title.'

'Only coz half her friends are the judges and none of them other women would dare to enter, only Nancy.'

'Really?' Jax said, as the roof of the town's pub came into view.

'Don't quote me on the intricacies of the thing, I've only seen 'em when they're driving past on their scavenger hunt,' said Hank. 'You can drop me off here, thanks.'

'No worries.' Jax pulled over to the side near the train tracks. The train station was deserted. There were no cattle in the yards and the Tea House was closed. 'Lucy told me she gives you breakfast on train days, is that true?'

Hank shrugged. 'I like to be here so she's not on her own so early.'

'The men wouldn't bother her, would they?' The protectiveness in his chest burred up over Lucy's wellbeing.

'Not in this town,' said Hank. 'Lucy's father would hand-feed them to the crocodiles, then he'd make himself a new pair of leather boots after the beast had digested the bastard.'

'That's a scary thought.' And a reminder to find the Ranger's Station for the crocodile living in his dam.

Hank gave a short nod, then hoisted his empty sack over his shoulder as if carrying the world. He didn't go to the platform, but walked along the train tracks, collecting trash.

Was Hank really homeless? Itinerants were known to cart all their worldly possessions with them. This guy carried an empty sack wearing old clothes, but they were clean.

Jax crossed the train tracks into town and turned right onto the main street. If this place had a café, he'd get two coffees then go visit Lucy.

Instead, he drove past the main shops, turned left at the sign for the Hospital and stopped in front of the Elsie Creek Fire Station.

It was tall, long, thin and red. The doors were white and matched the lace curtains covering the windows. The concrete driveway was spotless of any oil stains and the dead lawn was neatly clipped. It was still a dollhouse dropped in the red dirt.

He tried the door, it was locked. He knocked but there was no reply. The notice stuck in the window said to visit the police station next door, where a four-wheeled drive police wagon approached and reversed into the driveway.

'Can I help you?' The Senior Sargent asked, climbing out of the driver's seat. The guy had a set of shoulders on him that matched Jax's, and he was about the same age.

'I was hoping to chat with the Chief Fire Warden.'

'He's long gone,' said the cop, unlocking the wagon's back cage. Juggling another set of keys, he approached the roller door.

'Is it his day off?'

'No. Early retirement. His wife got diagnosed with Alzheimer's so he moved her close to their kids and their old hometown while she's still got her memories. Nice lady too, she was the town's seamstress.'

'Sorry to hear.' That explained the lace curtains—he felt horrible for making fun of them.

'Are you the guy who bought Tobias Clare's place?'

'Jax.'

'Marcus,' he said, shaking Jax's hand.

'Is that your watch-house?' Jax pointed to the station next door.

'Yeah, just me, a couple of connies, auxiliaries, and a few ACPOs.'

'ACPOS?'

'Aboriginal Community Police Officers. Can I help you with something?'

'I was hoping to check this place out. Lucy's given me an application for the job.'

'Tea House Lucy?'

'Yes.' He was surprised Marcus didn't call her the Station Hand's daughter, like everyone else.

'She's a sweet thing, that one.'

Did Jax have the right to be jealous when it came to Lucy?

'Lucy's always trying to set me up with her friends when she drops around food platters now and again,' said Marcus. 'Especially when we have ol' mate Hank sleeping off a hangover. I saw you giving her driving lessons.'

'Lucy doesn't need lessons, she can drive,' said Jax, confident of her skills.

'Lucy is like most bush kids, they've been driving as soon their feet could reach the pedals. I just wish she'd come in for her driving test.'

'Maybe I should book it in.' Although, Lucy shied away from tests.

'Anytime. So, if Lucy gave you the job application for this place, where were you stationed?'

'I was Acting Fire Chief, for the MFB, stationed in Southbank. My rank is Captain managing the Emergency Rescue Unit.' Jax retrieved his ID wallet to show his badge to the cop like it was an informal job interview.

'I know the place. I was a Detective stationed around the corner at City West Police Station,' said Marcus, returning the badge back to Jax.

'Tough crowd that one.'

'You too, one of the busiest fire stations.'

'So they say.'

'Come on in.' Marcus pushed up the roller door, exposing a beefy lime-yellow four-wheel drive. It looked brand new.

'Nice.'

'Yeah, they give you firies the best gadgets to play with.'

And Jax loved his gadgets.

This beast made his ute look like crap.

'I wasn't expecting this… or that.' Jax pointed to four beefed-up four-wheeled drive Landcruiser's with tanks and hoses that made up the swift Grass Fire Units (GFUs) and one large fire truck. But the Chief's truck made his mouth water. 'It looks like a dollhouse on the outside and they've got this in here?'

'We both get the toys. I've got a boat, a high-pursuit car and the four-wheel-drive vans, but not like this toy,' Marcus said, patting the bonnet. 'The old Chief drove it 24/7 being on call, not that much happens around here.'

Jax could handle driving the ultimate Tonka Truck around town. 'Can I take a look?'

'Knock yourself out.'

Jax opened panels and doors and checked out the Chief's truck. 'This is top of the range equipment.' All of it in excellent condition.

'They take care of us out here when it comes to equipment. They kind of have to, considering we're on our own.'

'You don't say?'

'Our jobs are a little different, there's no black and white standard operating procedures or a line on a map for jurisdictions. We have to rely on each other.'

'Yeah, right?' Jax understood that cops and firies had their tense moments, but as first responders they worked together.

'Our nearest backup is Katherine or Darwin and it takes six hours to get boots on the ground. We're lucky the locals help out a lot. We don't have a police plane, but there's a few bush pilots who volunteer.'

'So, no helicopters or water drops?'

'Nope, just those trucks.'

Jax breathed in the smell of the firehouse. It was still there, the itch under his skin, tingling at the fingertips, with that curl of excitement in his chest. A sensation he only got on the job—but this wasn't his job. 'Any idea about the size of this station's jurisdiction?'

'It's the same area as mine.' Marcus pointed to the map pinned to the sidewall. 'We cover all of this area.'

'That landmass is over a third of the size of Victoria.' His old home-state, where his old station's jurisdiction wasn't even a speck on this map.

'That's why we get all the toys. Like I said, we're all on our own out here. The bonus is, there are no bosses to bother us.'

'I like the sound of that. What about paperwork?'

'I try to avoid it if I can.'

'I hear you.' Jax chuckled, sharing another thing in common with Marcus. 'How many other staff do they have?'

'There's the Fire Chief, some Auxiliaries, and a tonne of volunteers. They used to have weekly training sessions out back with a barbecue afterwards, it was good for town morale.'

'I'm learning the art of barbecuing.' Thanks to Lucy. 'Anything else you might know about the job?'

'You've got a dual position, it's unique.'

'How?'

'We're too small a population to have a full-time fire service, but we're big enough an area to also have someone and his team do more than what's expected for his volunteers.'

'I get it, rural firies and townies with their lines on a map you don't cross. It's all about funding. So…'

'No lines. You make your own rules and they give you plenty of scope to do it, too. Lots of blokes are applying for the job.'

Jax had no idea it was like this. 'Go on, because the job description was vague.'

'Because they want someone who's flexible. One minute they could be issuing fire permits, then next helping with a car crash scene, then working on a backburning operation as part of the bushfire land management plans. The indigenous are brilliant with that. You'll pay visits to the local communities and schools, giving fire drills. You ever do that?'

Jax grinned. Yeah, he loved doing that with the primary school kids, teaching them the drop and roll routine to escape smoke. 'Highschool or—'

'Bush school. They're good kids. It's when they're adults they get into a bit of mischief?'

'Yeah, like what?'

'Crack of dawn I got my first screaming phone call about someone shifting a yard full of garden gnomes into some drunken orgy, there were beer bottles everywhere.'

'Garden gnomes?' *No, they didn't*? Instantly, thinking of Monet and her cousin, the couch-surfing cowboy, Rigsy.

'Oh yeah, real national emergency that one.' Both men laughed as Marcus raised the rear roller door.

The view made Jax stop.

It was an uninterrupted, expansive view of the outback that was a part of the town's airstrip.

He could just picture himself finding a recliner, with a coffee and his camera in hand to watch the planes come and go as part of his day job. Just like he did at the Airforce.

He'd only left that job to help care for his brother. Sacrifices were what you did for family, feeling that pull in the pit of his guts for being the last man standing.

'So, is this job part of the ARFS?' Jax asked.

'Sorry?'

'Aviation Rescue Firefighting Service,' Jax said, pointing to the airfield.

'Not sure,' Marcus replied with a shrug. 'They are hoping whoever applies for the position has experience with airports or the air force as well, so they'll get funding for it. The more skills the guy's got, the more they're willing to pay from three different types of fire services.'

And Jax had worked them all. Lucy had told him the job would be perfect for him, and now understood her persistence. Did he dare dream it could be true?

'We share the gym equipment,' said Marcus, tapping on the cage that contained a weight set, rowing machines and other assorted equipment. 'I see you work out?'

'I like to keep fit for the job.'

'Me too. You spar?'

'I do a combined Muay Thai and boxing. You?'

'Finally, someone who knows his way around a punching bag. We should spar some time, I could do with the practise. Don't suppose you'd give me a hand?' Marcus asked, unlocking the back cage where a group of folded metal barbecues waited. 'They want me to check out the barbecues for the Billabong Barbie Bake-off.'

'Don't the competitors bring their own barbecues?'

'No. They got donated a while back to make it an annual fundraising event.'

'Fundraiser for who?'

'For the local firies,' Marcus said, thumbing back to the small silent fleet.

'Yeah, right.' Jax instantly grabbed one end of the barbecue and helped Marcus carry it out. 'It'd be handy having the first responders all nearby like this.'

'It is. The Doc, Stewart, he lives at the back of the hospital.'

'The one they call *Hot-Doc*?'

'And I heard you were called *Ironman*.' Marcus laughed.

Jax dropped his head but the grin grew. Lucy still called him Ironman in the bedroom.

'Yeah, that's Stewart,' said Marcus. 'He's got a killer of a coffee machine if you're ever on night shift. Don't tell the rest of the town or they'll be lining up at his door.'

'I won't. Does he deliver?'

'Sometimes. He'll come to the station to watch the footy if I'm on shift. Stewart's meant to share shifts with his dad at our town hospital, but he lives at the place like he used to when he worked the ER at the Royal Melbourne.'

'I know the place.' That's where his brother died. 'Any idea where I'll find the Park Ranger? I've got this crocodile in my dam.'

'I think she's working in Kakadu, helping them out for a few weeks. How big is the croc?'

'Here, this is it.' Jax scrolled through his phone and showed Marcus his favourite image of the crocodile, with Lucy driving his ute to compare sizes. The beast was bigger.

'Woah! I'll make the call, but I doubt they'll have a cage big enough. Have you ever caught a croc?'

'Never. You?' In his world crocodiles were never a part of his conversation.

'If the opportunity was ever to arise, and while under the advisement of a croc-wrangler, I'd give it a go. You?'

'I'd certainly think about it,' said Jax, matching Marcus's grin as they carried another barbecue out of storage. 'Do you want me to test the gas lines on these? I saw the gas reader in the truck.'

'Could you?'

'If you don't mind sharing the pros and cons to this job?'

'Want the dirt, huh?'

'The black and white brutal truth would be good.'

'I'd say your first job would be...' Marcus faced Jax squarely and said, 'to introduce yourself while doing a fire inspection on the shops in town. That'll rattle some cages.'

Damn. Just like Jax had done at Lucy's Tea House.

Yet, the way Marcus studied Jax, it was obvious the cop knew all about Jax's first day in town. As a Detective, Marcus would've learned all there was to know about the newest resident. If he was in Marcus's position, Jax would have done the same.

'All part of the job,' said Jax, with a nod. There was no hiding his past now.

Marcus nodded back, then gave a wry grin. 'How would you go handling a flower-eating water buffalo, who likes to colour co-ordinate his ribbons?'

'I've inherited his chook.'

'Is that where it went? We thought Agnes the softball coach had caught it for her Sunday roast.'

'Nope, it lives on my washing machine. I can't believe I just said that.' Jax shook his head with a chuckle.

Marcus grinned, patting Jax on the back, and said, 'This town will do it to you, mate. Welcome to Elsie Creek.'

EIGHTEEN

Lucy forced her bike down the dirt track that might be wet on top but it was still dry, cakey red dust underneath. It made riding a challenge, leaving fresh tracks behind her.

Down the tree-lined corridor, it was like the rain had flipped on the flora switch for the native trees. Long, feathery pink and grey grevillea flowers covered its bushes. Overshadowing them were trees covered in bright orange bottlebrush flowers. The nectar so thick she could taste the native honey on her tongue.

Screeches rang out from the rainbow lorikeets feasting on the flowering grevillea. Drunk from the pollen, they competed with cicadas that were as loud as the people in the pub last night.

The bush fell away as the track opened to wide grey skies and the billabong in its grassy clearing. Snippets of sunlight peeked through the clouds, dancing on the train engine.

Was she going to make it to Jax's for practise today without getting wet?

With no breeze the sweat trickled down her back, the skirt of her dress stuck to her skin as she pushed the bike through the weeds towards the train. On muggy days like this she could handle cruising in an air-conditioned car.

Lucy parked her bike under the tarp's shade. She climbed the metal steps into the large engine bay that provided a great viewing platform of the area.

On the far side of the billabong that led to the paperbark swamp, waterbirds waded among the willowy reeds, while wallabies grazed on new grass shoots between the water and the woods.

She climbed down to the back workshop area where Hank was welding. 'Hank.'

'What?' He barked out, lifting the lid on his welding visor. 'Hey, Lucy.'

'I brought you some lunch.'

'You don't have to keep feeding me.'

She shrugged as she studied his latest sculpture. 'This is incredible. A horse, right?' Made from the broken bread-slicer and other metals he'd meshed and welded into the body of a steed.

'It's a work in progress.'

'What brought this on?'

'Brumbies are in.' He pointed to the far edge of the billabong.

'They'll be searching for water. I should tell Jax, he'd love to see them.'

'That Jax gave me a lift into town, this morning.'

'We need to tell him.'

'Tell him, what?' Hank asked, sizing up another piece of metal for the horse's mane and tail.

'About you and this place. Jax owns this train.'

'Shoot.' His skinny shoulders slumped in his sweat saturated shirt. 'What do you think he'll say?'

'I don't know, but I can't put it off any longer. Someone in this town will eventually tell him that he owns part of the Airforce dump—and Jax is ex-Airforce, he'll want to see it.'

'It never bothered Tobias Clare.'

'But it's Jax's place now. You know there's always room for you at the unofficial Elsie Creek Inn.'

'Monet would be a bit too much for me before brekkie,' he said, cheekily. 'Besides, I like it here.'

'I know you do, but we need to tell Jax. He's a reasonable guy, but he won't be too happy about this.' She pointed to his welding.

'My sculptures?'

'No, the weeds that are so close to where you're welding. Jax would call it a fire hazard. Even though we've had some rain, it's still dry underneath and that's fire fuel, if you're not careful.'

'That's rich, coming from the woman who burns everything.'

'Not nice, I haven't burned anything in a while.'

'Where have you been cooking?'

'Only on the barbecue.'

'Are you going to open the Tea House on the next train day?'

'Yes,' she said, with head held high.

'What changed your mind?'

'The publican. Samantha told me every business has a rough start, and this town doesn't like change.' And the publican had business smarts.

Last night, when Lucy had tried to hide in the pub's kitchen washing dishes, when Samantha strolled in. She slipped on an apron and helped with the party's dinner rush, not once mentioning anything about the Tea House until it was over.

Samantha then handed Lucy an icy cold top-shelf beer at the end of the shift where they chatted out the back door of the kitchen. The darkness of the outback stretched beyond the back fence line, the stars glowed above and the sounds of the partying pub behind them.

But it was just the two of them sitting on the back step sharing a beer.

Lucy had thought she'd failed, but Samantha didn't see it that way at all. She saw opportunities and lessons to be learned. Giving Lucy more encouragement in a five-minute blunt conversation that had Lucy excited once again.

'She's a clever lady, that one,' Hank said. 'Is she older or younger than you?'

'Younger. I told her I'll decide after the Billabong Barbie Bake-off.'

Hank nodded, even sharing a slight grin. 'So, you're still going for it then?'

'I have to. Like you said, there's only one way I'll be able prove to everyone that I can cook, and that's by beating Nancy.'

'Good.'

'Right now, I think we should tidy this area up a bit before you get a house inspection.'

'No! This is my stuff. You leave it alone. I'm not cleaning up for no one. I have squatter rights or something. You leave off and tell your boyfriend to shove off too. Leave me be,' he said, turning his back to her. Hank grabbed the flint, turned on the tank, and lit the flame of his welder's torch.

'Hank, you shouldn't be welding so close to those weeds.'

'Leave off.' He dropped the lid of his dark welder's mask. The breeze blew up, the sparks sprayed in an arc as he began to weld.

'Oh no.' She saw it right before her eyes. One spark hitched a ride on the breeze. It was only for the shortest of distances before it fell onto a bed of dry leaves and started smouldering. She jumped on it, stamping it out. 'Hank, stop it.'

Hank ignored her under his dark helmet, following the curve of the horse's tail, sending a spray of sparks into the grass.

Lucy was helpless to stop them.

It was time to test all those fire drills Jax had put her through these past few weeks, but she sucked at tests.

Think.

She spotted Hank's old sack and a bucket nearby.

Snatching them up, she rushed to the billabong, dumped the sack into the water, filled up the bucket, then ran back.

'Hank, stop it. STOP. HANK. FIRE!' She thumped his shoulder, hurling the bucket of water over the flames. They flared backwards with a hiss, catching onto the Gamba grass. It was like an explosion of fuel, crackling as the flames spread between the piles of twisted metal in a dance of flames, jumping so swiftly it was impossible to contain them. They were twice the height of Lucy. The radiating heat was ferocious, it was if she were standing in front of a thousand giant ovens.

Hank lifted his helmet back, turning off the welder, then froze. 'Jeez—'

'Stop staring at it and grab another sack and refill the bucket.' Lucy tossed the bucket at him, then started slamming at the flames with the wet sack. It was useless.

But she had to do something. Positioning herself between the fire and the train that was Hank's home.

'LUCY, the gas bottles!' Hank dove for her as the pressurised gas erupted into a massive fireball.

NINETEEN

Jax was heading back to the farm after Marcus's in-depth tour of the town's fire station. He'd learned a lot about the Chief's job. A job that was bigger than he'd imagined. *If* he took the job, and *if* he got the job, he'd be in a partnership with Marcus and his team.

Marcus seemed keen, even offering to hand-deliver Jax's application to the knights of the round card-table, who were somehow part of the interview committee before head office could accept it. How did that happen?

Jax did not like his chances with those card sharks.

A smoke plume rose high in the air as he headed out of town, getting bigger the closer he got to his property. The smoke was a light grey, signalling a scrub fire of sorts.

Jax slowed the ute down. Leaning over the steering wheel, he frowned at the smoke spewing higher. Even though they'd had some rain, they were still under a total fire ban. After fighting many horrendous bushfires down south, he slowed down to read the smoke.

The billowing cloud churned above the tree tops, turning black and thick, the colour of an industrial fire and burning rubber.

An almighty explosion erupted and a red, angry fire ball spewed high into the air.

'Shiiit.' That had to be a gas bottle.

He put his foot down and his ute kicked up a spray of soft dirt. Only one set of fresh tracks ran along the road in front of him, bicycle tracks. And there was only one bike he'd seen on this road—Lucy's.

His heartbeat quickened as his grip tightened on the steering wheel following the bike tracks down a skinny path. Tall grasses bent as he forced the ute through the brush that opened to a clearing with a wide billabong and a massive train engine on fire.

'What the—' *How the hell did a train end up out here?*

Then he saw her. 'LUCY!'

He bounded out of the cab to where she lay on the ground with Hank. 'Lucy…' He grabbed her arms. 'Are you okay?' Covered in black soot and dirt, her dress soiled, tears and sweat streamed down her face.

'Jax, Hank's been hurt. He was protecting me when the gas bottle exploded.'

He brushed back her hair, making her face him. 'Are you okay, Lucy?' He had to know.

'I'm okay.'

'Let's get you both out of danger.' He dragged Hank back to the safety of the ute. 'Hank, talk to me, mate?'

Hank could only groan.

Was he shell-shocked from the explosion with his back a bloody mess?

Jax cut away Hank's shirt, surveying the damage. Lucky the shrapnel was to the back region and nowhere near the head. But how deep did the shrapnel go? And with Hank not responding…

Lucy kept at the fire, hitting at it with the sack, but it was useless.

'Lucy get away from there.'

'But the fire—'

'Grab the hose from the back and we'll hook it up to the water pump.' Jax reached for the first aid kit in his cab and started bandaging Hank's back.

Lucy snatched the hose and dragged it behind her flattening the grasses as she bolted for the billabong.

'What about crocodiles?' Jax swallowed hard, searching the empty billabong. There weren't any birds floating on the surface, but he'd spotted the wildlife in the distance, sticking close to water.

'There's none here,' she shouted, running through the reeds and mud, throwing the hose ahead of her. She half swam in the water and mud, pushing the hose into the centre, free from reeds so they didn't block the pump. Just like they'd practised.

The water pump and hose were part of Lucy's fire-training drills whenever they did her outdoor barbecue. Then, as a welcome reprieve from the heat, they'd play with water like lovers on a summer holiday.

Now they were trying to stop a fire for real.

Jax flicked the switch on the pump and the water spewed through the hose. He aimed the water spray at the flames licking the side of a train engine. 'What is this place?' Jax asked Lucy as she ran back with the bottom half of her dress and legs covered in mud.

'It's the old Airforce dump from the war.' She grabbed the sack and again started hitting at the flames.

'This… Is this—'

'Yours. Yes. It's part of your property. It's your train.'

Why hadn't she told him?

He didn't have time to dwell on it, returning his attention to the fire. 'Take Hank to the hospital.'

'I can't leave you here.'

He could just hug her for that. 'Lucy, I'm trained for this.' Jax reached for his satellite phone and made the call. 'Marcus, I need help with a fire on my property. Yeah, hold on, Lucy will tell you where it is.' He didn't have a clue, only that it was on the road to his place on his freaking property. 'Give Marcus the details.'

Lucy took the phone and gave directions as he scouted the scene while battling the flames with one simple hose currently draining the billabong.

'They're coming,' she said, giving him back the phone. ''What do you want me to do?'

'I need to get rid of those gas bottles before they explode,' Jax said, passing the hose to Lucy. 'Aim the hose to keep them cool.' He grabbed his gloves and helmet from his ute. The last time he'd worn them was to chase out a family of possums and mice from his oven.

He dropped the visor, then ran for the gas bottles. They were almost full, so he threw them into the billabong. He then searched for other hazards among the grass and trees and a whole freaking train!

'Lucy, go. The fire crew are on their way.' He could hear the sirens.

He dragged the pump off the back tray of his ute and grabbed his water bottles. His skin remembering the all-too-familiar burn from the radiating heat as he slid on his old protective fire coat he'd kept as a souvenir. 'Take my ute and get out of here. Now!' He wasn't giving her a choice.

'I'm sorry, Jax.' Her tears carved tracks through the soot and mud on her face. 'It was an accident. I'm so sorry.'

He bundled Hank into the passenger seat, the pain visible across his pale face as blood seeped through the bandages.

Jax then dragged Lucy to the driver's seat. 'Get out of here, Lucy. Now. Help is on its way, and right now Hank needs you. Life is more precious than a property fire.' He closed the door in her face.

Picking up the hose, he watched his ute reverse out. Lucy's driving skills for off-road were much better than his.

He battled the blaze as best he could, but it took hold of the train and the grass around it. Flames caught the tarp, devouring its ropes, it fell like a sheet of paper, covering a table and chairs. And there was Lucy's bike, with its magic basket, melting in the flames.

Red and blue lights flashed across the wilderness reflecting off the train's broken windows and rusty paintwork. A police car led the two fire crews in their kitted-out grass fire units.

Jax's experience kicked into action. 'We attack from the back and push it to the billabong. It'll burn itself out,' he ordered the four men and two women.

They just gawked at him in their yellow Bushfire NT vollies' uniforms.

Of course, they didn't have a clue who he was, they all thought he was some drug dealer's hitman on witness protection.

From his back pocket, he pulled out the card folder. Flicking it open, he held it up. His badge caught the flickering flames as he shouted in a clear voice of authority. 'My name is Captain Jackson Turner with the Victorian Fire Rescue Service and this is my property.'

Marcus came up alongside him and said, 'Jax is the real deal, he outranks the lot of us, so you take orders from him.'

'Where do you want us, Chief?' Rigsy called out with a nod. He'd swapped his cowboy hat, boots, and jeans for a firefighter's uniform.

'Drivers, I want one GFU that side, the other unit on the other side. Crews on the back, aim your hoses high and we'll use the Cruiser's bull bars to push over the long grass. We'll force it to backburn into the billabong.'

The volunteers scrambled into position as Jax barked orders. With a combined effort, they soon contained the flames.

Finally, there was an almighty clap of thunder and the grey clouds burst at their seams, allowing the rain to pour.

Jax raised his head. Removing his helmet, he shut his eyes, allowing the rain to trickle over his hot skin as the crew cheered around him. It soon doused the flames into smoke and steam that surrounded a massive train sitting alongside a billabong in the middle of nowhere.

TWENTY

Lucy was in an absolute panic. The drive to the hospital had been a blur with Hank passed out in pain. Stewart and Jenny met them at the hospital's doors where they'd whisked Hank away on a gurney.

Now Lucy waited, huddled in Jax's multi-pocketed car blanket. She'd paced back and forth, inside the main entrance of the small bush hospital. The same place she'd playfully teased Jax when she'd fallen from a tree.

Bandages covered her lower legs, hands and upper arms. She hadn't noticed the burns or deep scratches while battling the blaze.

It was the scariest thing she'd ever done.

She'd also panicked, while Jax was calm under pressure.

But she'd seen the look in his eyes, disappointment and anger for lying to him.

The police cruiser pulled up, stopping by the glass sliding doors. Jax got out of the passenger seat. He was here for his ute and answers.

She dumped the blanket on the waiting chairs and scooped up his keys. Her body shook with nerves and the tears started as she met him just outside the doors. 'I'm so sorry, Jax. I'm so, so sorry.'

'Are you all right?' He hesitated to touch her as he looked her over.

'I'm okay.'

'You don't look it. What about Hank?'

'Still in surgery, they're removing the shrapnel. They've told me Hank will be okay,' she said, trying to hide her burns, they were nothing compared to the pain of guilt inside. 'I'm sorry this happened, and I'm sorry I didn't tell you sooner.'

'What were you doing there, Lucy?'

'I—ah…It's all my fault, I'm so sorry. I'll understand if you never speak to me again,' she said, holding out his keys.

'You lied to me.'

'I know.' She hung her head in shame. *Stupid girl.*

'You showed me around my property and not once told me I owned a train, why?'

She swiped viciously at her tears. She hated those tears, and what she'd done to Jax. 'I didn't want Hank to be homeless.' She didn't want to lose Jax either.

'Did you just choose that guy over me?'

She gasped at him, stepping back. 'He's a human being too. Just because he doesn't drive a fancy ute doesn't make him any less of a person.'

'I didn't say that.'

'I thought you'd understand, considering your background.'

'Then you'd also know how much I hate being lied to by the one person I care about most in the world.' He shouted so loudly his words echoed off the outside walls. 'You hid this from me. You didn't trust me enough to tell me that this guy was living on my property. With all that training I gave you, you still caused a bushfire. I thought I'd taught you better.'

'You did.'

'No, I didn't or you would've recognised the hazards to start with. How can I be expected to train volunteers in fire safety, when I can't teach you! All those volunteers who helped me fight that fire today kept saying you're always burning stuff.'

She wanted to say she didn't start it, but what would that mean for Hank? 'You're right, it was my fault.' She swallowed her pain, her feelings didn't matter. Not now. Inhaling deeply, she straightened her spine, squeezed her hands into fists, and raised her chin. 'The whole thing was my fault. I'm the one to blame.' If she hadn't distracted Hank, none of this would've happened.

It was obvious the town, including Jax, were already blaming her for it. Her reputation had made it so. She had to take the blame for Hank, she didn't want him in trouble. Especially causing a fire during a total fire ban, there had to be consequences for that. 'I'm sorry, I'll pay for the damages.'

'With what? You work as a kitchenhand.'

He made that sound like she was the lowest of the low. 'I don't know how, but I will. I'll come and help with the clean-up and—'

'Stay away from me and my property, Lucy. You've done enough damage.'

Her heart fell. It hurt to breathe.

Worse was the hurt she saw in his eyes.

She'd done this. She'd caused all of this pain. It was all her responsibility.

'You could've just told me,' said Jax. 'Not make me find out like this.'

Her anger lashed out. 'What would you have done? Poke around like a fire inspector and condemned the place? Just like you did with the Tea House you never go near.'

Jax stepped in closer with darkening eyes, anger was coming off him in waves of heat. 'I don't go near that place because if I did,' he said in a low tone, 'I'd have to report it and shut it down. It's the *only* reason why I'm *not* taking the Chief's job is because of you and that bloody Tea House you shouldn't even be cooking in for your own safety.'

'But—' She whimpered with trembling lips.

'Safety,' Jax said, jabbing his finger in the air between them. 'You get it. For YOUR OWN SAFETY.'

Every single word cut through her like a knife, wincing as they rang in her ears.

'Its obvious Hank took a dive to protect you when it could have easily been you in there getting surgery. Or worse.' Jax stepped back, heaving in the air. 'Wake up, Lucy. You live in this dream state that the world is always good with snow globes and stories, but it's full of danger at every turn.'

'This is the outback—'

'That has crocodiles and bushfires. We were lucky I live so close to town because that could've taken off and burnt the entire property down. So, guess what? Your mate is homeless now. There's nothing left.' Jax headed to his ute, then stopped and said to her over his shoulder in a tone filled with sadness. 'The thing is, Lucy, I would've let Hank stay and made sure he had a safe work area, because as the property owner, that train is my responsibility. I'm the one who's liable for allowing that man to be at risk. Not your property. Not his property. Mine,' he said, tapping his chest. 'I'm the one who is responsible in the eyes of the law. You should've told me, Lucy, not hide this from me, and you should have never, ever lied to me.'

'I'm sorry,' she whimpered. She'd never lied to Jax. Not really. Her only crime was keeping a secret. A secret that wasn't even hers. There's no way Jax would believe her now. 'I'm so sorry.'

'Me too. I should never have gone near you from the first time we'd met when you'd set fire to the Tea House kitchen. I knew then to stay away from the fire hazard you are.' He got into his ute and drove away without looking back.

The tears blurred her vision as she choked out a sob. Holding her stomach, her knees weakened. She wanted to crumble to the ground, run after him or something. Anything but this. This hurt was excruciating. Clutching her heart, she wanted to throw up but couldn't swallow—she'd never felt more alone.

She'd ruined it for Jax.

She'd ruined it for Hank.

Nancy was right. Lucy might not poison the food, but she was poison to everyone around her, ruining it for them all. It really was all her fault.

TWENTY-ONE

The gaggle of geese and the dance of the lean-legged brolgas weren't the only noise coming from the billabong. Buzzing insects skimmed across the surface, sending ripples that mirrored long-beaked white herons, stretching their wings as if frozen in flight as the sun's climb created a pink haze to grey clouds.

Jax's boots crunched on the charred earth as he filmed the scene around the massive train, blackened by fire. He poked around the coals, cool now from the rain, trying to find its ignition point. Unable to sleep, still angry at what Lucy had done and said and what she didn't say, he'd arrived as soon as it was light enough to see.

The woman kept secrets. Big secrets. The size of a freaking train!

Her bike's scorched skeleton leaned against the train. It was lost.

Like everything he'd once held for Lucy.

He'd rather run into a burning building with no chance of getting out than suffer this level of hurt.

How the hell did he allow this to happen?

He'd come to this place of nothingness to get away from people for a reason. Yet he'd let Lucy get under his skin and burrow so deep within his veins, that had once pumped light and warmth, were now clogged with soiled sludge.

A police cruiser rolled through the well-flattened track and parked beside Jax's ute.

'I bring coffee from the Doctor to keep us alert while we write up our reports,' Marcus said, holding out a large thermos and two mugs.

'I won't say no to a decent coffee.' He needed something to douse down his foul mood.

Marcus poured the steaming brew into the mug and passed it to Jax. 'So, did you talk to Lucy and Hank about what happened?'

'No.' Not since his shouting match with Lucy at the hospital, he'd spoken to no one. 'You?'

'No. I thought I'd wait for your findings first, to see what you wanted to do.'

'Did your doctor mate tell you how Hank is doing?'

'Hank's going to be fine, he's got a few stitches across the back. Lucy stayed by his side until Hank kicked her out.'

'He did?' Was Hank mad at Lucy for the fire too? After all, Hank had lost everything.

'Stewart told me they had to sedate Hank. He was a mess, and mad as hell at Lucy, shouting at her to leave him alone. Were you aware Hank was squatting here?'

'No,' Jax said. 'Did you?'

'No one did.'

'Lucy did. That's her bike.' He pointed at the skeleton. He was livid with Lucy, yet he missed her at the same time.

'I see…' Marcus adjusted his cap, peering up at the train. 'I'd heard rumours about an Airforce dump around here, from the war.'

'Really?'

'This whole area was a base camp for the military that was close enough to use the Elsie Creek train station. You'll find airstrips they used all along the Stuart highway from here to Darwin. They bombed Darwin, and those who died from the aerial attacks got buried in the cemetery out back. It hits home for many of us on ANZAC Day to know that diggers, right along with postal workers, died to save this place.'

'I'm still learning about this place.'

'You could live out here another ten lifetimes and only learn half of the secrets to the Northern Territory,' Marcus said. He sipped his coffee, with wary eyes searching the scene. 'Except you own an entire train.'

'How did it get here?'

Marcus shrugged, climbing into the locomotive. 'You've got to admit, it's a cool place to live with a view of the billabong, and carriage for a bedroom.' Marcus led them deeper into the charred cabin that had been Hank's home, with Jax filming behind him. 'You know who this guy is, don't you?'

'Lucy called him the town's rubbish warrior.' Jax now understood why.

'Just before you arrive at the town's train station, you'll find a couple of memorial crosses on the side of the tracks. Have you seen them?'

Jax nodded. 'The Conductor mentioned them briefly when I first arrived. Something to do with kids.' *And hauntings*, that Jax wasn't going to mention. 'Do you know the story?'

'Yeah. The old Sergeant told me about it after I dug up the report. I had Hank as a guest of the watch-house one night, drunk, mumbling all sorts of stuff, talking about those kids. It had me curious.'

'Was Hank there?'

'It was Hank who was driving the train!'

'What happened?'

'Hank was pulling into the station with the sun in his eyes, but a clear run ahead. The conductor and co-driver were with him and none of them saw anything standing on the tracks. You can see cattle, camels and buffalo for miles ahead the land's that flat.'

'Lucy says every train day she searches for Cecil to make sure he's not on the tracks.'

'Hank too.'

'I've seen him walk the train tracks, picking up rubbish.'

'It's his way of cleaning up the mess Hank reckons he made. He wasn't charged over the incident, it was purely accidental.'

'What happened?'

'Those two kids were stretched out across the middle of the tracks. You couldn't see them, no one did. When Hank was pulling into the station the Conductor called out, spotting them first, but it was too late.'

'What were they doing there?'

'Protesting, according to their grandfather,' replied Marcus. 'They snuck away from their grandmother, Nancy, and went down to the tracks. The little boy and his mother were supposed to take the train to Darwin then catch a plane to Sydney. But those kids believed if they stopped the train from getting to the station, they'd disrupt the time schedule and miss the plane so they'd never have to leave.'

Marcus paused to gaze out through the train carriage's broken windows to where the waterbirds waded along the billabong's edges, untouched by fire.

'They got what they'd hoped for,' said Marcus quietly, 'those two children got to stay, buried side by side. Except for Nancy, and their grandfather, Johnny, the rest of those families left—heartbroken.'

'And Hank? Did he have a family?'

'Divorced. Hank's from Adelaide, where the train company had cleared him of any form of negligence and offered him a desk job. Until he got up and walked away.'

'When?'

'Six years ago. That's when his sister filed a missing person's report on him. I've told Hank to call her using the station's phone, but he won't. Yet, the stubborn fool walked the train tracks right through the red centre of Australia all the way back here to Elsie Creek.'

'That's a tough hike.'

'You're telling me,' said Marcus, shaking his head. 'Ever since then, he's been collecting the rubbish, caring for those kid's crosses, and making sure nothing wanders onto the track on train days in this town again.'

'You'd think he'd want to be like the rest of the family and leave their tragic past behind.' It's what Jax had done.

The two men stood silently inside the train, sipping coffee while they stared out over the billabong. The honks of geese and other water birds broke the silence on the far edge that led to the paperbark forest.

Jax surveyed the area. It was obvious Hank had lived here for a while. 'The fire didn't start in here.' But it had burned everything, only leaving the metal skeleton of a carriage and a locomotive.

'Check that out. You have a metal museum.' Marcus pointed to the rear side of the train where assorted sculptures stood amongst the black ash. Hat racks made of horseshoes and firepits from old gas bottles. A large, metallic horse stood tall as the centrepiece.

They jumped out of the train and inspected the many pieces.

'He's good with the welder,' said Jax, examining an intricate scene of men mustering on horses, carved into the side of gas bottles and old drums that had been turned into a fire pit. There were many types of sculptures, all made from scrap metals. 'I bet it's Hank who's been leaving those tiny sculptures for Jenny, the head nursing sister.' Jax scooped up a small bird out of a pile of charred tin flowers made from bent cans and nails.

'Are you saying Hank is the Tin Man?' Marcus asked.

'Yep.' Another one of Lucy's unshared secrets. Didn't she trust him?

Jax frowned, squatting at the base of the horse sculpture. 'This is where the fire started...' He leaned close to the scorch marks. 'Sparks from the welder,' he said, following the trail, discovering a burnt hose and a welding gun lying in the sooty soil next to an indent from an exploded gas bottle. 'If Hank was welding with no shade, in the heat of the day, those bottles would've already been volatile.' Jax pointed to the muddy tracks that ran from the billabong, back to the metal horse.

He spotted another set of tracks that ran through the bent grass from where he'd originally parked his ute yesterday. The tracks went through the mud and grass when Lucy had dragged the pump's hose into the billabong.

When they'd gone fishing, Lucy had shown him how to tell the difference between animal prints, from dingoes to goannas and cattle to buffalo.

All of those tracks marks that ran to the billabong, besides the birds and wallabies, were from a human. Lucy.

Determined, Jax scrutinised the area, following all of her tracks. He found a burnt bucket and the sack she'd been using to bash back the flames. 'Lucy didn't start this — she was trying to extinguish it.'

'Did Lucy actually admit to causing this fire?' Marcus asked.

Jax stared hard at the ground as he went over their entire conversation.

The realisation swamped him. A lead weight pulled on his heart, twisting his guts into a tight knot. 'No. She kept saying sorry, that it was her fault.' He faced Marcus and said, 'Lucy is taking the blame for this because —'

'Of her reputation as the cook who's always burning stuff.'

Jax rubbed the back of his neck, now tight with tension. 'Lucy's blaming herself to protect Hank.'

'Why?'

'Because she cares about the guy. She's always feeding him. She'd check on Hank daily on her way to my place.' Jax pointed to Lucy's bike that was nothing but a molten mass of burnt rubber, and no more magic basket. The site only made his guts wring tighter. 'Lucy only sees the good in people and doesn't care where they stand in society's standards.' She'd accepted Jax, faults and all.

'You have the right to charge Hank for trespassing,' Marcus said.

'Do you think he'll return after this?' There was nothing left, just silent sculptures.

'No idea, but you might want to consider putting a fence out here. It won't be long before some of the locals will want to come and check it out,' said Marcus, pointing up to the train. 'Mate, you have a vintage train in your yard.'

'No one will claim it?'

'Nope. I did some digging around last night. The defence force leased this land from Tobias Clare's family back in the war. They've always owned it and no one has a claim to it but you.'

'What do I do with a train?' Jax scratched his head as a small whirly-whirly picked up speed, sending dust and ash swirling into the air. The ash floated back to earth slowly and softly, like snow. Grey snow.

Fine particles of ash landed in his outstretched palm. To Jax, it had always been ash — to Lucy, this was her outback snow.

'Are you going to charge Hank and Lucy for trespassing, property damage, and for causing a fire during a fire ban?' Marcus asked. 'I need to know if I'm heading back into town to arrest them?'

TWENTY-TWO

From her bed, Lucy peeked through the gap of the curtain to watch the train pull out of the Elsie Creek Station, heading to Alice Springs. For only the second time in three years, she'd missed it.

She wanted to cry, but she'd cried so much there were no more tears left. Defeated, Lucy collapsed back onto her bed. She didn't even remember coming back to her room. Still clothed, still wearing her bandages—she didn't care.

She'd lost Jax.

Sure, they were only meant to be frenemies, and to keep it simple, but he meant more to her than that. The ache in her chest made it hard to breathe, hugging her pillow. Miserable.

'*Yoo-hoo, Lucy?*' Sung out a female voice from inside the house.

'Kat?' Lucy sat up and stared at her closed bedroom door.

'*Hello, Lucy.* Where are you?' Another female voice called out with an American accent.

Was that Verily?

'Her room's down here,' said another female voice as footsteps carried down the corridor.

Not supermum Karen, too?

'Lucy, get up,' said Karen like a mother knocking on her bedroom door.

'I'm sick.' She hid under her pillow as her bedroom door opened. *Bugger*—she'd forgotten to lock it like she normally did. She didn't have to lock anything at Jax's place.

'There she is,' said Kat. 'Would you get a load of all these snow globes?'

'I didn't know you had so many,' said Verily, checking out the collection on her side cabinet. 'They're gorgeous.'

'You wouldn't want the tiara-less tutu-loving princesses near this place, they'd all be wanting one,' said Kat.

'I'd love one for my little girl,' said supermum Karen. 'Where do you get them, Lucy?'

'Around. Take them,' Lucy mumbled.

Suddenly, it hit her and she sat up with her hair everywhere. 'Wait! I'll sell them to you. I need money to pay back Jax and Hank for the damages.' Even if Hank and Jax hated her, she had to do something. 'Hank will need money for clothes and the things he lost in the fire, and Jax...' *Everything*.

'Are you sure?' Karen asked.

Lucy nodded. 'I have to do something.'

'What about the Tea House?' Verily asked. 'Kat might prefer to only drink coffee, but I like tea. And what about the Billabong Bake-off thingy, it'll be my first time to see it?'

'Visiting the Tea House is my excuse to be kid-free for a few hours on train days,' said Karen, sitting on the bed. 'But I'll buy a snow globe for my daughter. Which one do you recommend?'

'Take this one, it plays music and the horses move in the carousel,' said Lucy, picking up a soft pink one.

'Why are you selling them?'

'It's time I grew up.' Jax was right, she was living in a fantasy world. Jax wasn't Peter Pan—she was! She was the one who played with the lost boys, living in Never-never-where-ever-land with her childish snow globes in the searing outback.

It was time she grew up.

'I'm serious, I'm selling my snow globes. I have a stack in the kitchen to sell, too.' It was the only thing Lucy owned that had any value. 'I have a YouTube channel and a website, to advertise them. Kat, can you help me set up an online shop, like you have?'

'Sure…'

'How long will it take?' Because Jax took care of all of that for her. It wasn't fair to rely on him like that and she felt guiltier for using the guy. How could she ever repay him? He'd never forgive her now, but she had to do something.

'Not long,' said Kat. 'We can set up your digital store from my place, while we're working on your surprise.'

'What surprise?' Lucy asked.

'What YouTube channel?' Verily asked, scrolling through her smartphone. 'I'm surprised Alex hasn't found it, he's always on YouTube.'

'I have a cooking show,' Lucy announced. Then her shoulders lifted to her ears, realising she was sharing her secret with people. Her friends—who just blinked at her. 'As much as I am honoured by this visit, what are you ladies doing here?'

'I wanted to see what the unofficial Elsie Creek Inn looked like,' said Verily, poking her head out into the hallway. 'It's got character.'

'It does,' said Kat, tugging on Lucy's hand making her get out of bed. 'Come on, we have a surprise for you. Go have a shower and get changed, and I'll make coffee,' said Kat, heading for the kitchen. 'Why don't you have a stove?'

'It broke—and before you say it, that was before I moved in.' What did it matter, her cooking career was over.

'I'm not judging,' cried out Kat from the kitchen.

'I'll start polishing up the snow globes,' said Karen, collecting an arm full.

'Ditto on that one,' said Verily, reaching for more. 'Kat, come and get some globes.'

'But—but—' Lucy stood there, unsure.

'We're not letting you quit,' said Verily, walking out to the hallway with her arms full of snow globes as Kat walked in carrying a tray.

'Guess what? Hank is the Tin Man who's been leaving presents for Jenny,' Kat said, putting the snow globes onto the tray.

'How do you know?'

'Jenny told us at the hospital when we were searching for you. Jenny gave us some ointment and new bandages for your burns, so shower,' Kat said. 'You have to show me where this train is hiding in the middle of nowhere that everyone is talking about—'

'I can't. It's Jax's property and he told me to stay away.' Lucy slumped back onto her bed, pressing her hand to her crushed heart. 'Hank kicked me out yesterday and also told me to stay away.' Just like Jax. 'You should stay away from me too.'

'Oh, hell no,' said Kat, sitting next to Lucy, she slid her arm around Lucy's shoulders 'We're teammates and friends.'

'Ditto to that sista,' said Verily, returning to grab more globes. 'The whole team wishes they could be here, but they're going to meet up with us at Kat's place. We're having a shed party in Kat's man cave, or should we be calling it Kat's she-shed?'

'It's a party shed, that's for sure,' said supermum Karen, returning with an empty beer box.

'Why are you here so early?' Lucy asked the women packing up her snow globes. Her much-loved snow globe collection was being boxed and carried away. It hurt some… but how she'd hurt Jax devastated her more.

'It's not early. It's our normal time to bother you at the Tea House,' said Karen. 'Like everyone else in this town, we'd only just found out that Hank was the train driver who accidentally ran over those children. That poor man…But you knew who he was, didn't you, Lucy?'

Lucy sighed, fidgeting with her fingers in her lap. 'Hank swears they're haunting him.'

'There's heaps who've seen those kids, like ghosts walking along the tracks,' Karen said. 'Have you seen them?'

'No. I…' Lucy brushed her arms as the goose bumps pebbled across her skin. 'I've heard children singing when I'm walking Cecil back from their graves, I thought it was the stereo.'

'Why didn't you say something to us about Hank? We would have helped him,' said Karen. 'I remember when it happened, it was horrible. I couldn't stop hugging my oldest boys non-stop for weeks after that, every time I was in arm's reach. Just last night, my husband and I sat down and reminded all our boys about what happened and to never *ever* play near the train tracks.'

'Both Kyle and I kept hugging Katlyn as he told us the story,' said Kat.

'Alex told me,' said Verily. 'Poor Hank, to go through that… Now I understand why he drinks. How can we help him? I know my aunt Molly's on the job, gathering goods—'

'Hank didn't want anyone's help,' said Lucy. All she could do was feed the guy and let him know he wasn't alone. 'You can't help anyone unless they're ready to accept help.' Just like Jax had said about his own family fighting their personal demons.

Lucy had worked out who Hank was ages ago when she'd discovered the newspaper clippings of the accident that he kept in the train. She'd recognised the lilies and the grevillea he'd taken from his billabong to put on the small crosses. Hank did what he could while carrying the heavy burden of guilt over an accident that had never been his fault.

Lucy rummaged for her bag from the pile she'd carted home from the hospital, wrapped in the blanket from Jax's car. A large, folded manila envelope fell to the floor.

Scooping it up, she opened it and her eyes widened at the pages.

He filled it out!

'Ladies, I need your help.' This time Lucy was not going to be shy about it. It was time to speak out. Today.

TWENTY-THREE

'You shouldn't be making me drive,' Lucy said to Kat, seated in the passenger seat, with Karen and Verily taking the back seat, along with a car full of snow globes.

'To get your licence you need to practise. Aunty Bea won't mind, she put up with me bashing the Beast into things all those years. Now, off you go. We've got a lot to do.'

Lucy headed for the town's main street and through to the feedstore's drive-thru, then parked the small car. She wiped her hands on her dress nervously with her wrists wrapped in fresh bandages.

'Want us to come with you?' Verily asked, with Karen nodding beside her from the back seat.

'Thank you, but no. I won't be long. I can do this.' She needed to do it.

Lucy pushed open the driver's door of the air-conditioned car, only to be slapped by the outsides intense heat and humidity.

A series of car doors shut behind her, as her friends followed Lucy into the shed.

'Like I'm always telling my children,' said Karen, hooking her arm through Lucy's. 'You do the hard stuff first then the fun stuff as the reward.'

'Hey, there's Speedy, we'll fill her in on the plan too,' Verily said, wandering over to the counter where their softball team's pitcher was working.

Fun is what Lucy needed.

But this wasn't going to be fun.

She entered the rear of the hardware store and her eyes adjusted to the shade. She almost tiptoed down the aisles of stocked shelves. Cigar smoke greeted her as she waited on the shadowy edges for them to notice her.

But they didn't see her.

It was time they did!

She dropped the manila envelope onto the table, in the middle of their card game. 'Gentlemen.'

'Lucy,' the elderly men chorused.

'You all right, luv?' Billy asked, hoisting himself out of his chair, lifting one of his suspender straps higher onto his shoulder. 'We heard about the fire.'

'You start it?' Jeffrey asked.

'Leave the girl alone,' said Billy, frowning down at the men while patting Lucy's shoulder.

'I'm okay.' She wasn't going to let them think any different, for Hank's sake.

'What's that, Lucy?' Johnny asked, pointing to the envelope on the table.

'It's an application for the Fire Chief's position. It's Jax's.' Jax already hated her, so she had nothing to lose — she had to do this.

'Isn't he some drug dealer's hitman?' James asked.

'Thought he was military myself,' said Jeffrey, pushing up his coke-bottle glasses. 'Isn't he your boyfriend?'

'Jax is not a drug dealer,' said Lucy, proud of the man who despised her. My-my, hadn't the tables turned when she'd been the one to hate Jax when they had first met. 'Jax is a decorated fireman, and he's not my boyfriend. He's my frenemy.'

'Your what?' The Triple J's asked.

'Enemies who pretend to be friends.'

'Gawd, the hate-sex must be hot,' said Jeffrey as the other men chuckled.

'*Hey!*' Lucy glared at them and they sat back with raised eyebrows. She'd never spoken like this to anyone, most of all to the knights of the round card-table 'That is Jax's application and he's more than qualified for what this town needs. He was acting Fire Chief to one of the busiest stations in Victoria. He was a captain in the Air Force where he ran a team that manned the airstrips for fighter jets.'

The men frowned and she scowled back at them with hands on her hips.

Lucy was not done.

'Before you jump to any conclusions,' she said, 'Jax was never based at Tindal. He said those other servicemen would've only been following orders and doing what matters first, and that's saving lives. He saved my life and Hank's, in that fire yesterday. Jax also has the patience of a saint for trying to teach me all about fire safety, and I'm sorry to say, I failed that test! But until that train fire, I've burned nothing for almost a month, ever since Jax has been patiently teaching me about fire safety. And if Jax can teach me, he can teach anyone.'

'What about the Tea House, Miss Lucy?' Billy asked.

'I won't be taking on the lease because of Jax's recommendations, it's too much of a hazard. I'm sorry gentlemen…' She hesitated, choking down a sob. 'There will be no more morning tea on train days from me. It's over,' she croaked out, pinching herself to stop the tears. She wanted to go back to bed. 'I can't cook in the Tea House anymore.'

The men scowled.

'Don't you dare blame Jax for this either! Not when he is right about all those things that are wrong with the Tea House,' she said, wagging her finger at them. She was protective over Jax, more than anyone she'd ever cared for. 'Jax was doing it for my safety and for the safety of everyone who goes there. Because he cares.' She tapped on the application, saying, 'Jax is a man who is willing to put his own life at risk to save others. He's got the medals to prove it too. *And* he chose to live here of his own free will, *before* he even knew about the job. He chose to make Elsie Creek his home town *first*. That's what makes him the perfect Senior Chief Fire Warden for this town. You wanted someone with a local's recommendation, well I'm giving it to you. This town needs someone like Jax, and you'd be a bunch of fools if you let him get away from here without offering him the job.'

Her whole body trembled with adrenalin, holding fists at her sides. She'd never spoken out like this for anyone. Even if he hated her forever, she'd done this for Jax because it was the right thing to do.

'Thank you for your time, gentlemen,' she said, and scurried back to her teammates who were watching from the aisles.

She had lots to do and was not going to sit around moping about it. Her father would be telling her to roll up her sleeves and tackle the herd, head-on. After all, she was the Station Hand's daughter and her father never backed down from anything, or anyone. Neither would she.

TWENTY-FOUR

Back in the car, Lucy drove out onto the road. *Indicate.* Remembering to do so, as the other girls talked, with Speedy now joining them in the backseat. It was a full house in Aunty Bea's car. Carrying a load of assorted snow globes, they headed for Kat's place to start work on her online shop.

She waved at Marcus driving past in his fancy police car. Like a voice in her mind, she heard Jax saying to her: '*Two hands on the wheel, Miss Lucy.*'

She missed him so much.

Through her side-mirror, the police car squealed with a flurry of smoky tires and it spun around as its siren screamed with a flash of red and blue lights. In a matter of moments, it had sped up behind them.

'What did I do?' Lucy called out to the car full of women as she pulled over to the side of the deserted road.

'It's just Marcus,' said Karen.

'I don't know Marcus,' said Kat, twisting around to peek through the back window like the rest of the passengers.

'He's pretty cool. Marcus helped me transfer my overseas licences so I could drive our road train,' Verily explained.

'Is Marcus going to arrest me over that fire?' Lucy asked, stopping the car and they all sat quietly.

Marcus's police boots crunched on the gravel, louder and louder.

They stopped and he tapped on the driver's window. Lucy rolled it down. 'Ladies.'

'Hello, Marcus,' came the chorus.

'What's wrong?' Lucy asked. They had 'L' plates on the car, she had her licence…

'Step out of the car, Lucy. Bring your ID with you,' Marcus said firmly, opening the driver's door.

Lucy grabbed her purse and followed. 'I wasn't speeding and I remembered to indicate.' She followed him like a twelve-year-old schoolgirl being led to the Principal's office.

Her sandals scuffed on a stone that rolled across the asphalt. Heatwaves shimmered from its surface as the sun peeked through grey clouds scattered before a pale blue sky. A blue-winged kookaburra watched them from his perch on the fence post topped with barbed wire that ran alongside the road. In the paddock, a flock of galahs glided in to join the cattle lazily grazing on the fine carpet of green shoots, shining fresh from the rain.

But all Lucy saw was the high-speed highway patrol car and knew she was in trouble.

'Are you going to arrest me over that fire?' Lucy asked the officer.

Marcus was a big guy. His shoulders were as big and buffed as Jax's, with the chest of a bull. He opened his car, grabbed his clipboard, and turned to face her.

'I'm ready to pay for my crime,' Lucy said, holding out her hands in front of her. 'You can handcuff me, that's okay, I know you're only doing your job.'

'I should charge you,' he said with a stern face, raising his clipboard and taking notes.

'F-f-fine.' Even if Jax wasn't there to frown at her for over-using the word, she still felt guilty for saying it. She missed him, rubbing at the ache in her chest, as her shoulders stooped. 'Bring it, I'll take my medicine.' Lord knows she deserved a double dose for what she'd done.

'Lucy, I'm talking about your driving.'

'My what?'

'Yesterday, I spotted you driving into town in Jax's ute, displaying no Learner's plates and with an unlicensed driver.'

That was when she'd been forced to leave Jax alone with the train fire and had barrelled the Tonka Truck onto the main road to take Hank to the hospital. On the dirt road, she'd pulled up alongside the police car leading the convoy of fire trucks. She was the one who'd given Marcus the directions to help Jax. It was Marcus who'd radioed ahead to the hospital to tell them that Lucy was on the way with Hank and told her to go. 'That was an emergency.'

'The law is the law.'

'F-f-fine. You *were* on my Christmas cupcake list.'

'Now, this is how it's going to play out,' he said, pointing with his pen. 'You will get into that car, with me, and drive down this road. You'll do a three-point turn and a reverse park. If you pass, you get your licence. If you don't, I'll have no choice but to fine you.'

She gasped at him, horrified. 'You're making me do a driving test? But, I'm not ready.' She was never ready for tests. Not when she failed every freaking time.

'She's ready, Marcus,' called out Verily, hanging out of the car's back window as the other women clambered out of the car. 'Lucy has been driving us around all morning.'

'Go, now, before we do the rest of the stuff,' urged Kat, dragging Lucy to the driver's seat. I've got to get something from the boot. It's the perfect spot.'

'Perfect spot for what?'

'You'll see, but driving test for you first. Focus on passing that,' Kat said, pulling the lever to pop the boot, then she closed the door, trapping Lucy inside. 'Ladies, I need a hand.' Kat and the others gathered around the back of the open boot. Snow globes tinkled as excited laughter rang out.

Lucy wanted to play with her friends and not be trapped in the car with a cop. Even if he was a nice policeman.

'I've told you before, Lucy, you didn't need to make an appointment for this,' Marcus said, getting into the passenger seat. The small car dropped from his weight, the boot slammed shut and Kat tapped on the car with the girls waving at her.

Was Kat holding up a tutu?

'Now, drive straight down this road,' he said, slipping on his seat belt.

'It's a long road, this goes to Kakadu.' And he was a huge guy who filled the car.

'Drive until I tell you to stop.'

'Um…' She inhaled deeply, wiping sweaty palms on her dress. She glanced at her side-mirror where her friends were standing in front of the fancy police car, waving at her.

'Lucy, I know you can do this,' Marcus said gently. 'I've seen you driving around town, and look, if the uniform is bothering you, I can put on another shirt?'

'No, I can do this. I should be able to do this—I want to do this. I need to do this.' She put the car in gear. '*Indicate,*' she said under her breath. Again, she checked her mirrors and pulled out onto the road driving in absolute silence with the officer giving her instructions on where to go.

She did the three-point turn, a hill start on the closest thing they could find to a hill, then back to his police car where she did another U-turn and parked where they'd started.

Under the shade of a straggly ironbark tree Kat, with the help of the others, were busily dressing-up a small ant mound. They'd turned it into an oversized outback gnome wearing a fluorescent lime-green tutu and a tiara.

'That'll glow in the dark,' said Marcus, pointing out the passenger window to the dressed-up ant mound.

No wonder Kat was eager to go and play on the side of the road. Kat, being the creative soul, would have to be the only woman Lucy knew who carried spare spray paint, a tiara, and a tutu in the car.

'You can switch off the car, Lucy,' ordered Marcus, ticking and flicking on his clipboard.

'H-how did I go?' Lucy swallowed air, her body tense. Was the town cop going to charge Kat and her friends for dressing-up an ant mound?

'Congratulations, Lucy,' he said, ripping off a piece of paper from his clipboard and passing it to her, then climbed out of the small car. 'Come and see me later at the station and we'll take a photo for your provisional licence.'

'I passed?' She called out, following him.

Marcus opened the driver's door of his police car. 'Lucy, you would've passed the day you applied for your learner's permit, years ago. I've been a passenger of yours way back on the stations when I did a summer stint with your dad. Remember?'

'Oh, I forgot.' She shrugged, there'd been so many men who worked with her dad. Being home-schooled, there was no such thing as school holidays, not when her dad's lifestyle was one big holiday for Lucy.

Huh? It was a holiday, free from overwhelming responsibilities of a kid allowed to grow up on a cattle station. She could climb trees, ride horses, and drive trucks. She ran around barefoot, skipping with the wallabies or rode bareback on ponies. She played with a crossbow beside her mother while they foraged for fresh herbs and fruits as part of her schooling. It was just the same as the adventures she'd been sharing with Jax this past month.

Growing up, there was no such thing as peer pressure, or the need to wear the latest fashion, or to have the latest app for some photo filter. Few kids rowe as lucky as she was to have enjoyed such an amazing childhood. She had a sudden urge to call her parents and thank them.

Lucy smiled and rushed up to give Marcus a hug. 'You and the police station are still on my Christmas cupcake list,' If she ever found a stove to cook on.

'Thanks, Lucy. Have you seen Jax?'

'No.' Jax didn't want to see her again. It crushed her. 'Hey, my friend Monet is still single.'

'Stop setting me up with your friends.'

'No harm in everyone being happy.' She wanted to be happy too, even if she missed Jax.

She peered at the piece paper in hand and at the word written in bold letters: PASSED.

She'd passed.

Lucy wanted to tell Jax, but couldn't.

At least she had her friends, who'd supported her when she didn't want to get out of bed.

Unexpectedly, she giggled at the group of women busily taking selfies with a red dirt ant mound. She'd seen countless ant mounds dressed like outback garden gnomes, but this would have to be the first one wearing a tutu and a sparkly crown.

Lucy waved the piece of paper in her hand. 'I passed.' It was like she'd made a home run in the first softball game they'd won in a decade—except this was so much better!

After all these years, Lucy had her licence. She really was growing up.

TWENTY-FIVE

Jax stared at the small screen as if his heart had been ripped straight from his chest and crumbled into pure ash. He was watching Lucy on his laptop, piping icing onto a tray of cupcakes she'd baked on the barbecue. Jax had eaten those cakes with her. Some of them were still sitting in his fridge.

He should have turned it off.

He should have blocked her channel.

But he just couldn't stop watching.

Sitting there, patting the silly red hen, just like Lucy did.

They both missed her. Jax more.

He could smell her fragrance on his pillows. The mango scent in his car reminded him of her. The food in his fridges and freezer was all Lucy. Even the barbecue stood silently waiting for her. Whenever he heard the water pump turn on, he'd think of her. All these little things everywhere, all reminded him of Lucy.

She'd been such big part of his day-to-day world, now, she was a face on a screen, like she had been in the beginning, when he'd needed to learn to cook.

Back then, he'd never believed he'd end up taping Lucy cooking elaborate meals on a barbecue twice a day. The menu and the scenes changed as they explored his block of land. Every episode had a different snow globe sitting on the corner of her prep-table, catching the sunlight.

Yet it was her sweet smile he admired, the shine in her big eyes as she cooked in the outdoors. She'd cook, talking about what she used, what she'd found to cook with, shaking her snow globe while telling stories.

Lucy had become a small YouTube sensation. There were lots of queries on how and where to buy the bush-herbs she used—all wanting the stuff that grew on his block like a weed.

People were crazy.

This town was crazy.

And he was just as crazy, patting a crazier chook in his lap that used to attack him every time he stepped through his back door.

He then frowned at the screen as it notified him of a new post. Without thought, he pressed play to continue this playlist of torture.

On the small screen Lucy stood before a sea of shiny snow globes as if she was in a snow globe specialty store.

'Hi, um, sorry…' she said, wiping her hands down her dress with the bandages on her arms. He hated the sight of those bandages.

'Don't say sorry,' he said to the screen. He'd edit it out if he was in charge. But he wasn't doing the filming, that was Lucy at her most vulnerable, standing inside the Tea House dining room.

'This will be brief,' Lucy said to the camera, 'I'm selling my snow globes to raise money to help my friends who are recovering from an accidental incident. I won't go into details.

So, via my website are images of the snow globes. A few you can bid for, but the rest you can buy today and we'll post a snow globe from our little corner of the globe to you. Sounds corny, huh?' She shared her shy giggle that used to make him smile. But there was no shine in her eyes that made up her sweet smile. Lucy was hurting too.

Curious, he flicked to her website. There was an impressive new digital shop showing off every one of her snow globes. Each had a story she'd shared while filming—one, in particular, had no story, just a mention of it being a collector's item, but he knew the story…The man from Snowy River.

It was her favourite, and on sale with people bidding for it.

'What are you doing, Lucy?'

It was obvious she was raising money, but for who? For him? For Hank? For both men?

Jax put the red hen back onto its perch on the washing machine, where she shook herself into a puff of red feathers. The back door slammed as he fetched the keys to his ute. He would not accept anything from Lucy, especially money from her snow globes.

Muggy humid air hung heavy like a hot, wet blanket, blurring the daylight in a haze. It competed with the heatwaves rising from the dirt road into town. He passed the barbed wire fence Marcus had helped him build. They'd put up a *Trespassers Will Be Prosecuted* sign in the middle of the trampled track that disappeared toward the deserted train that rested beside a billabong. From the rain they'd had earlier, it was obvious no one had been out here.

There were none of the tell-tale marks of Lucy's bike tracks that he used to smile at.

There was nothing.

And no one.

Just him.

The silence in the cocoon of his ute's cab was heavier and colder when laced with loneliness, landing with a tension-filled thud across his shoulders. It had been a long time since he'd felt like this. Not since Lucy showed up.

Only this time it was heavier.

He shouldn't be feeling like this. He'd lost his family and had been ready to embrace being alone. He was done caring for others. They'd lied to him. Stole from him. Kept secrets from him. And they'd left him alone. Like an idiot he'd always been there to try and help them. For what?

All the same things Lucy had done to him.

He'd tried to smother his attraction to her before it burned out of control, but it'd been useless. It's the quiet ones you had to watch, sneaking up on you until it was too late—which is just what Lucy had done.

She'd lied to him. She may not have stolen from him physically, but she'd stolen and burned his heart. Most of all she hadn't trusted him. She'd kept secrets from him.

Stupidly, he'd told her all his secrets. Everything. He had nothing more to hide.

She'd broken their deal. Question for question, and to tell the black and white brutal truth.

Was anything she'd ever told him true?

Did he really know the woman at all?

How could he permanently extinguish those embers she'd stirred inside him?

He drove his ute onto the sealed road and turned right into the train station where a few cars were parked. The Tea House lights were on and the bi-fold doors were open.

Foolish girl, still working in that Tea House after all his warnings. If she wanted to hurt herself, that was her problem.

But he still couldn't bring himself to drive away.

Determined, he stalked through the heat and into the open doorway.

Inside he found Billy, wearing his felt hat, flicking his suspenders, walking around the dining room with the Triple J's from the hardware store. It was strange seeing those men away from their card table.

'G'day, Jax,' said Billy with a warm smile.

'Billy. I was looking for Lucy.'

'Not here,' answered one of the Triple J's.

'Thanks, I'll leave you to it.' Jax was relieved she wasn't. So where would she be?

'Jax, stay a moment, mate,' called out Billy. 'We'd like to have a word with you, if you wouldn't mind.'

'What about?'

'Miss Lucy dropped off your application for the Fire Chief's job.'

'She did what?' Jax peered back to his ute, but couldn't remember seeing the application. With so much going on, he'd forgotten all about it.

'Miss Lucy dropped it in front of us, demanded we give you the job and gave you one of the best references I've heard,' said Billy.

'It's the most we've ever heard Miss Lucy say,' said Jeffrey, with Johnny and James nodding beside him.

'She did what?'

'It's obvious you didn't know about it,' Billy said to Jax. 'It's fair to tell you that our town's top cop—

'Marcus?' Jax asked.

'Yeah, he's also given you a glowing reference,' said Billy with a nod. 'So too did them volunteers who helped put out your scrub fire under your leadership. Do you really own a train?'

'So it seems.'

'What are you going to do with a train?'

'No idea, but I can't take that Chief's job.'

'Why not?'

'Lucy wants the Tea House.'

'No, Jax,' Billy said, thumbing up the brim of his vintage felt hat, 'she gave it up, mate. Miss Lucy said she won't be taking the Tea House lease because your job as a Chief mattered more.'

'She didn't…' Jax wiped his mouth, turning away from the men to face the deserted kitchen.

Through the open screen door at the back of the kitchen, the shadow of a person riding a bicycle stretched across the gravel. It parked up, and the door opened.

Jax expected Lucy to step inside. But her bike and its magic basket was nothing more than a burnt relic beside the train.

Instead, it was another woman in jeans and runners. 'Hello, boys. You must be, Jax?' She approached him with a hand out. 'I'm Samantha.'

'That's God,' said Billy.

'Behave, Billy.'

'Close to it, Luv. Samantha owns the pub,' replied one of the J's to Jax.

'Australia's Youngest publican, she was,' said another one of the J's.

Samantha was not what Jax had expected for a publican, she was pretty and young. 'You're the owner of Tea House,' said Jax.

'I am.'

'You are?' The Triple J's said, looking to Billy.

'It's not my job to know what my boss does,' Billy replied, hooking his thumbs into his suspenders, giving Samantha a slight wink.

'So, you're the guy who said they should condemn the Tea House,' Samantha said to Jax.

It was no secret in this town. 'The dining room is okay.'

'What about the kitchen?'

'Are you thinking of repairing it?'

'Nancy had the offer of cheap rent if she maintained it, but, like the pub's liquor laws are always changing, it's the same for commercial kitchens. I was led to believe that Nancy had done the same in here. So, tell me, Jax, what would this kitchen need to get up to scratch?' Samantha held out her arm to lead them from the dining room.

Jax followed and surveyed the kitchen. There were no warm cooking aromas, no lights on or music playing. Most of all, there was no Lucy with her sweet smile to greet him, with her care parcel of food he'd lived on for almost a week when he'd first arrived in town.

It was just an empty, old, cold kitchen.

The shelf from where Lucy had pulled out his care package that held various jars of fruit preserves and homemade jams. There were large plastic boxes labelled women's, men's, boys' things, girls' things, toys, books, knick-knacks for gifts. A clothes hanger stood nearby with blankets and linen, with a row of assorted boots beneath it. This small area reminded him of a tiny second-hand thrift shop. Why would they have that in here?

This was meant to be a commercial kitchen.

'You'll need grease traps. Overhead extractions. Power points made within this century. A sparky to tag every power cord within the place, and that's just for starters.' Jax spotted the fire blanket and extinguisher he'd given Lucy, sitting on the bench. The fridges were barren, open, and switched off.

It would have devastated Lucy to see this place closed. Jax didn't feel much better either.

'What about the oven?' Samantha asked.

'It'll need a gas test,' said Jax, leaning down to check out the oven. It was spotlessly clean.

He frowned at the dials. 'What the—' He pulled out a chock of ceramic wedged in the back by the thermostat. 'Why would you have this on the thermostat, it'll only make the oven hotter?'

'Would it be enough to cause someone to burn food, unintentionally?' Samantha asked, peering over his shoulder.

Oh, hell no—Lucy. 'How long has Lucy had the reputation for burning things?' Jax asked the room, passing the ceramic piece to Samantha. Lucy burned nothing this month while cooking with Jax.

'Lucy cooks in the pub's kitchen with my chef, Lenny. He was the one who first suggested to me that Lucy should take this place's lease. She's never burned anything in his kitchen,' Samantha said to Jax, passing the ceramic piece to Billy.

'Why would Nancy do such a thing?' Billy asked, handing the ceramic chock to the Triple J's.

'To keep her place as queen,' said Johnny. 'Nasty Nancy wouldn't want someone like Lucy beating her.'

'Poppycock,' said James.

'It doesn't matter,' called out Samantha. 'The repair bill for this kitchen is pretty high. Wouldn't you agree, Jax?'

He nodded. Also, it'd be impossible to prove if Nancy had done this. Lucy didn't have the money for the repairs this kitchen needed, no matter how many snow globes she sold.

Why would Nancy do this to Lucy? His Lucy! The Lucy who would help a homeless guy like Hank. The woman who'd stuck up for Jax, a stranger in this town. Most of all, she'd given up her dream of being her own boss—for him.

No one had ever sacrificed their own happiness for Jax. His own family had sworn to stick together, but in the end, they'd all let him down.

But had Lucy truly let him down? Doing what she always did—putting others before her?

'Has Lucy given up her application for the lease on this place?' Jax asked Samantha.

'Yes.'

'Why?'

'For you,' said Samantha bluntly.

Her words hit him like a double-punch in the mouth.

Samantha continued, leading them back into the dining room. 'I tried to talk Lucy out of it, but she said this town needed a man with your skills more.'

Now copping a double whammy kick to the guts, he felt ill.

'That's the thing I've always admired about Lucy, she loves this town,' said Samantha, glancing around the room. 'Lucy calls Elsie Creek home. To Lucy home isn't a place of four walls—'

'It's the sky, the stars, the soils that surround her and the people,' Jax mumbled to himself. Lucy had a connection to country that was truly beautiful.

'Do you know who she is, Jax?'

He shrugged.

'She's the Station Hand's daughter,' said Billy.

'So? It doesn't define a person for who their parents are,' said Jax, firmly.

'Did Lucy ever tell you about her lifestyle growing up?' Samantha asked Jax.

'Some.' Those were private conversations he'd shared with Lucy, who'd seemed ashamed of her past. Telling her about his own past, it had helped lessen his struggle of shame. He had hoped it had done the same for Lucy. Yet, every time she was called Station Hand's daughter, she'd drop her head and the shyness slipped over her like a grey blanket, dulling the shine of her soul.

'Lucy told me, for as long as she could remember, her job was to get up and check on their horses and cattle dogs,' explained Samantha. 'Every morning, before sunrise, Lucy would have the billy on the boil before any of the stockmen got up to start their day. She was performing all of those station hand chores in this place,' Samantha said, pointing out towards the train platform. 'It still has cattle. It still has stockmen. It was Lucy who organised the coffee for the shed out back to give them that cuppa on sunrise, and this place is called a station. As the Station Hand's daughter, Lucy has been doing her job, looking after this train station, better than Nancy ever did.'

'Is that why you offered Lucy the lease and a free trial run?' Jax asked.

Samantha nodded. 'Nancy made a deal with my grandmother to have this Tea House open on train days. Nancy did that—sadly, in the end, she only did the barest minimum. From what Monet and I can gather, this was a tax dodge for Nancy.'

'It's what?' Billy asked.

'Nancy used this place to avoid paying taxes on her superannuation. It would have rolled over when she turned sixty-five, the other week and nobody gave that lady a cake,' said Samantha.

'How do you know it was her birthday?' James asked for the Triple J's.

'I was reviewing the paperwork on the lease application.'

'Are you saying,' Jax frowned, swallowing down the spark of flames in his guts, as he asked Samantha, 'that this Nancy was looking for an excuse?'

'Yep, and you and Lucy were it. Nancy's a cunning one, I'll give her that. Not only did she find the perfect excuse to point the blame on someone else to shut down this place,'

Samantha said, pointing at Jax. 'Nancy also scored the sympathy card from all her friends to be pity buyers for her lawn sale while boycotting Lucy's first day as the Tea House's new boss.'

'Cunning,' said Billy.

Jax had a hell of a lot more colourful words than cunning to describe Nasty Nancy.

'The only problem is,' continued Samantha, 'Nancy has created a wide rift among the women of this town.'

'That's just women,' said Johnny.

'Watch yourself, mate,' Billy said, 'God is in the room.'

Samantha rolled her eyes as she wandered around the main dining room. 'Do any of you know the history of this Tea House?'

'Women like stirring storms in their teacups and blabbin' over biscuits all day long,' replied James.

'*Excuse me.*' Hands on hips, Samantha glared at James with a frown emanating such ferocity, he took a step back.

'It was for the outback sisterhood,' Johnny mumbled with a shrug as the men looked at him. 'My wife comes here, remember.'

'What sisterhood?' Jeffrey asked. 'We all know they've got clubs for everything but—'

'Outback sisterhood,' said Samantha, taking a steady breath she stood before the wall full of framed pictures. 'This Tea House were the first rooms ever built in this town. My great grandparents lived in a tent out the back while they built the Station Master's house. According to Frank…,' she said with a sigh as the other men bowed their heads for a moment.

'Ol' mate Frank died, before your time,' Billy explained to Jax. 'He was a bloody good builder and an even better mate.'

'Frank had a chair at our table,' said Johnny, as James and Jeffrey nodded.

'Yeah, right.'

'Anyway,' Samantha continued, 'because of the history, Frank didn't want to change too much when he put in those bi-fold front doors. These stone walls are the closest thing we have to a town museum and the women preserve it here within this simple little Tea House.' She pointed to a large black and white image in the centre of the wall. 'That was the first Elsie. She grew watermelons that she'd sell by the slice to passengers who'd get off the train to stretch their legs while they loaded the cattle. Then the military made their base here for the War and this station got busy loading and unloading military equipment and men. The train only ran from Darwin to Katherine, and during the war over two hundred trains ran through this town, per week.' Samantha pointed at the photos on the wall showing the town's growth. 'By then the pub was built and the stables for the unofficial Elsie Creek Inn. Followed by the rest of the shops in town. But back then, society frowned upon women daring to drink in the front bar—which is ironic when a woman owned and built the pub.'

'It wasn't proper to have a lady in a bar,' said one of the J's.

'Boy, didn't my great grandmother love to bend those rules,' said Samantha, chuckling to herself. She tenderly patted an image of a woman standing before the pub. A pub that had nothing else around it except a big tree. Jax recognised it as the one out the back of the unofficial Elsie Creek Inn. The resemblance between the woman in the photo and Samantha was uncanny.

'My great grandfather named this station after Elsie, who created this town, but before the town's official birth, my great grandmother created this place just for the women. Here, they could sit in the shade, have their tea and spend quality time with other women. The male to female ratio out here is one woman to over a dozen men.'

'How come you're still single then, Samantha?' Johnny asked.

'Aren't you dating the mine manager?' James asked. 'I imagine you'd have plenty of fella's linin' up for the—'

'Oi, behave,' said Billy, snapping his suspenders with a thwack.

Lucy had tried so hard to keep this place running, was this the reason why? Jax searched for an answer in the many framed photos lining the walls. It was all women. Lots of women. In various dress styles through the ages into today, including a modern team of softballers. And there was Lucy, with the biggest smile, standing with her softball team that even had Cecil, the water buffalo, carrying that pesky red chook of his, in the framed photo hanging on the wall.

'So, you were saying?' Jax asked Samantha. He had to know more.

'Most of this town's customers travel hundreds of kilometres from cattle stations, droving their herds to meet the train. They'd stay in town to stock up on supplies then go back home. It's a trade that hasn't changed in this town for over a hundred years. The men would go to the pub, and even though the women can go there, most preferred coming here.'

'Why? The men too brash for 'em?' Jeffrey said and Samantha scowled at him.

'Those pioneering women, would be tougher than all of you men put together,' she said smartly to the Triple J's. 'Whenever any of those women would visit, they'd bring clothes their children had grown out of, or what they'd made or had spare in kid's toys, preserves, fruits, and vegetables. But most of all they'd share a laugh and a story over a cuppa. It was their network, a sisterhood. If any one of those women were ever in trouble, they'd all offer their support instantly and without question. No matter how strong some personalities were, that may have regularly clashed, they'd help. Out here in the Territory's outback, it can be a very lonely place with all this country and so few towns. It's even lonelier for the women.'

That explained the shelf of boxed clothes, the jars of food and the shoes and blankets kept in the kitchen. They were to help others, watched over and shared by Lucy with a smile. Just like she'd handed him his care package the day he'd met her.

Jax also understood the many levels of loneliness, and how happy he'd felt the day he had found a friend in Lucy — his sweet smiling, outback encyclopedia.

'Is that how Nancy boycotted this Tea House on Lucy's first day?' Jax asked Samantha, his anger simmering beneath the surface.

'Yep. Nancy's playing them. Except now we have our town's softball team and their friends all on Lucy's side and

Nancy's friends on the other,' said Samantha, tapping on the team photo with Lucy in it. 'For the first time, they're divided and it's only going to get worse, fellas.'

'How do you mean?' Jeffrey asked for the J's.

'I was expecting those women to come back to the Tea House once Nancy left, and they would have, one by one,' said Samantha. 'But with Lucy pulling out completely and with her friends rallying behind her, it's split the women down the centre. This town isn't big enough for that kind of feud.'

'Lucy wouldn't want that.' Jax knew that about Lucy and now understood why she worked so hard to keep this place. 'Lucy wanted this place more for the town, for the cattlemen, for you guys,' he said, pointing to the Triple J's. 'Lucy was working on menus to cater for everyone. From the stockmen's breakfast to future softball parties, including monthly date nights and the Flynn Brothers' movie night.'

'Everyone knows the movie night is never gonna happen,' Johnny said.

'Only because they can't make up their mind what movies to choose.' Billy moaned with a roll of his eyes like the others.

'What I'm trying to say,' said Jax, if they'd let him finish, 'is Lucy never thought about herself and profit margins when planning for this Tea House. Lucy was doing this because she knew what this place needed and what it meant to this town.' It was much more than a roof with four walls. It had a history. This place had soul.

And he was the heartless bastard who'd shut it all down.

'With no one to man the Tea House,' Samantha said, facing the elderly men, 'those retired women might mess with you lot in the hardware store, because I don't want them asking the staff to turn down the jukebox in my pub.'

'You should've seen what them women did while they renovated the front wall of this place after Jeffrey broke the window,' Billy said to Jax.

'It was white ants, not me.'

'Whatever,' said Samantha, holding her hand up to silence the older men's bickering. 'What we need here is a solution. Not an argument. We have a Tea House without a kitchen—'

'And a cook without a stove,' said Jax, holding the ceramic chock in hand.

'Does our town have a new Fire Chief too?' Samantha asked, and they looked to Jax for an answer.

TWENTY-SIX

Jax's boots echoed down the corridor of the tiny bush hospital. He tapped on the open doorway where Jenny stood at the end of Hank's bed.

'Good, Jax, you can talk some sense into this man. Hank is refusing to eat,' said Jenny, storming out in a huff, leaving Jax to stand in the doorway.

Gone was Homeless Hank's wild and woolly beard and hair, Jax had to look twice, and checked for a name on the chart to make sure it was the right guy.

'I hate hospitals,' Jax mumbled, clearing his throat as he entered the room.

'Not my favourite place,' said Hank, trying to sit up. Sweat beaded on his forehead and his naked upper lip. He winced in pain, clutching his bedsheet with shaky hands.

Jax recognised the signs. 'Are they giving you something for the withdrawals?'

'The what?'

Jax pointed at his hands. 'You're not eating because it makes you feel sick, right?'

Hank leaned back on his side. 'Lucy didn't do it.'

'Do what?'

'The fire.'

'What happened?' Jax took a seat in the guest chair and waited.

'I was welding and Lucy was telling me to stop. I was mad at her and didn't want to listen.'

'Why were you mad at Lucy?' Jax sat stone-still, controlling his anger, especially when the woman had done so much for this guy. She'd put Hank before Jax—that's what hurt him the most. She'd done all those things his family had done—she'd lied to him, kept secrets from him like his parents did. She'd broken that trust by not trusting him. It hurt.

So now he wanted answers.

'Lucy wanted to tell you about me and that place,' said Hank, swallowing hard. 'She'd been trying to tell you for a while, but I kept telling her not to. The day of the fire, Lucy didn't want to keep it a secret from you anymore. She was trying to tidy up for some inspection to bring you around that day.'

'Go on.'

Hank cleared his throat, wiping at his sweaty forehead with a shaky hand. 'I didn't see the sparks from under the helmet until Lucy thumped my shoulder. By then it was too late. Lucy was hurling water at the flames, trying to put it out with a sack, telling me what to do.'

'She was, was she?'

'She said you'd been training her.' Hank then sat higher. 'Lucy is a kind person. She's always willing to give and share everything she had, never asking me for anything. Rarely asking me about my past.'

'Did she know who you were? About the train driving?'

'Yeah. I never told her, she guessed. People think she's simple, but she's shy and smart, she can read people.'

'I know.'

'So, are you going to charge me?' Hank asked Jax.

'For property damage, trespassing, and for causing a fire during a fire ban.'

'Yeah,' Hank said, dropping his head to his skinny chest. 'I have nothing. But I'm not shy if there's a debt that needs paying. I'll do yard work or something for you until it's paid off.'

'Are you an alcoholic, Hank?'

'What?'

'Simple yes or no.'

Hank swallowed, tucking the white sheet high to his chest. The air conditioner kicked in as he fiddled with the hospital band on his wrist, and mumbled, 'Yeah, I reckon I am.'

'Do you know why you drink?'

'To forget.'

Jax sat forward with his forearms resting on his knees to look the man in the eye. 'What happened to you with those kids, was tragic. I get it.'

'You do?'

'I've seen it. Every time I've attended road accidents on the job, or the aftermath of a fire sweeping through a house. I've seen devastated fathers who'd turned to the backseat where his kids were arguing only to hit a tree and kill them all. A young woman, losing control from a blown-out tyre, only to smash into a house where a family who fell asleep in front of the tv—never woke again. I can tell you dozens of incidences I've attended, but what I'm trying to say is, tragedies, unfortunately happen. It's circumstances beyond anyone's control.'

'I didn't see them.'

'I believe you,' Jax said, sitting back in his chair, 'and so does Lucy.'

'Huh?'

'It's obvious Lucy believed in you enough to be there for you. She made sure you knew you had someone looking out for you.' Just like she'd done for Jax. 'Lucy made sure you were fed daily, giving you a coffee in the morning on train days. I'm also aware she's offered you the couch at the unofficial Elsie Creek Inn over the years.'

'I told Lucy I couldn't handle that Monet first thing in the mornings, she's a bit much.'

'I agree,' said Jax, both men sharing a slight grin. 'Can I ask you something?'

'Depends.'

'Before the accident, did you ever do any creative sculpture work?'

'No. I just did it one day, sitting beside the billabong. I made a bird, a jabiru like the ones you see out there and gave it to Lucy. I like it. Never thought I would, but I do.'

'Did Lucy ever tell you about my background?'

'No.'

'Like she didn't tell me about you.'

'She's good at keeping secrets.'

'I noticed,' said Jax.

'Hey, I told Lucy to keep me a secret, so I didn't end up homeless. We weren't doing anything bad, I was only living out there. I've lived there for almost five years.'

'It looked like a good setup.'

'I didn't mind it. Gets a bit boggy in the wet and the mozzies are ferocious.'

'How did you cope with that?'

'Lucy got me a mozzie net for me bunk and mozzie coils. She means well.' Hank then stared at his hands covered in blisters and burns. 'How bad was the fire?'

'Some bushlands got burnt. Lucy's bike is ruined. All that remains is the train and your sculptures. When are they releasing you from hospital?'

'In a few days. Jenny won't let me go until I've, um…'

'Gone through the rest of the withdrawals?'

Hank nodded, again staring at his hands in his lap.

'Are you ready to quit drinking?'

Hank shrugged.

'I come from a family of addicts,' Jax said, crossing his legs at the ankles and arms over his chest, inhaling deeply. 'Lucy knows the story.' A story he'd only shared with Lucy, and here he was about to tell a stranger. 'My parents were the functioning type of addict, making sure my brother and I had breakfast to go to school, before they did what they did. My brother headed that same way too. Did Lucy mention why I came out here?'

'No.'

'Of course, she didn't.' He had to respect her for that. 'I'd made this pact with my brother that we would escape the city and live on a farm. We're not farmers, we haven't got a clue, but we liked four-wheel-driving. His dream was, he'd do his artwork in his own studio. He did all my ink work.' Jax showed Hank his arms. 'My brother would sell his designs over the net, with the both of us learning about marketing on social media, while we pretended to be farmers.' Again, both men shared a chuckle. 'I bought that place with my brother in mind because out there he'd be away from any temptation, making it easier for him to stay clean.'

'I've gotta admit it's peaceful out there. Sunsets are nice. Some brumbies showed up the other day.'

'Is that what prompted the horse sculpture?'

Hank nodded. 'Lucy was hoping to show you the brumbies.'

The woman was his personal tour guide of his own property. 'Have you been to my farmhouse?' Why didn't he call it home?

'No. Tobias Clare used to come and see me a bit. He'd asked if I could do the caretaking of the place when his grandson got sick.'

'Did you?'

'I've got no idea about bore pumps, solar stations, and generators—and he's got that feral red hen out there, too. The one who used to ride with that water buffalo, Cecil.'

'She's all right,' said Jax. That crazy red hen was the only thing keeping him company, following him around like a dog. 'There's an apartment inside one of the rear sheds Lucy said was for a station hand. It's what sold me on the place more than the house. It was going to be a studio for my brother, where he'd do his art. Like you do with yours.'

'I'm not—'

'Talented? You could sell all that stuff today if you wanted to.'

'Really?'

Jax nodded. 'By the way, I want one of those firepits you've got stockpiled. It'd look good by the back veranda. '

'Sure. Take the lot, I owe you. What about the train?'

'You can't stay in that train anymore. '

'Knew it,' said Hank with deflated shoulders.

'The fire ruined it. But I am offering you that studio space at the back of the property. It's like a unit with a bedroom, kitchen, bathroom, with plenty of shed space for your welding equipment and materials. You'll get all that in exchange for helping me on the farm.'

'I don't know farming.'

'Me neither, that's why I need help. Apparently, I've got fences to fix, especially the ones around a dam with this crocodile—if they can catch it.'

'Lucy told me about that one, she reckons its huge.'

'It's scary,' admitted Jax. 'So, here's the deal… You get the studio space for helping me. It's a safe space, free from any hazards for your welding. You'll still have a view of the countryside and privacy,' Jax said, pointing out the window that had a great view compared to what he'd seen in the city. 'And I'm also willing to give you the same deal I offered my brother.'

'What's that?'

'To be your sober companion.'

'You'd what?'

'Not that my track record is any good, but I have been there many times for both my parents and my brother when they went through rehab. I understand the battle you're going through, and it's there if you want it.'

'You mean I can't drink out there?'

'Do you want to stop drinking is the question you need to be asking yourself?'

'You sound like Lucy, only tougher,' Hank said.

Jax knew how tough it was going to be for Hank in the near future. This first part was a freaking cakewalk for what was to come. 'The first step, and the hardest step for any addict, is admitting they have a problem. Like you just did. Don't worry, I won't preach or babysit you. I'll just be around to listen if you need help, especially on those days when that black dog raises its ugly head.' Jax would hate to imagine the nightmares Hank suffered.

Hank stared at the sheets, fiddling with his hospital band on his wrist. 'Jenny told me Lucy's selling all of her snow globes to pay for the damage to your place, and to buy stuff for me.'

'So I've heard. There's no way I'll accept any money from Lucy.'

'I won't either. That fire wasn't Lucy's fault.'

'Like the train accident wasn't yours,' said Jax bluntly. 'It's the guilt you're carrying now. It won't ever leave you, and I get that. But you need to try to move on from it, and if you're ready, I'll help you.'

'Why me? You don't know me?'

'Because Lucy believes in you. If you're looking for someone who forgives you, and believes in you, it's always been Lucy.' He sat back brushing fingers through his short hair. 'Jeez, she did it for me without me even realising it, because I've been carrying the same guilt for not saving my brother. Maybe there's a reason this happened, and I'm sure the shrinks will wrap it up in a ribbon and call it destiny or some other BS—but what I do know is, he left me.' That was Jax's black and white brutal truth. 'Which puts me in a position to offer you this deal. Maybe we can both share that burden between us because what happened to make us both feel like this, to carry this depth of hurt—wasn't our fault. Sometimes, we need to be told to remember that. To find it easier to breathe as we forgive ourselves for something that was never our fault.' Lucy used to do that for him, just with her presence alone. It's the quiet ones that sneak up on you who shout the loudest—he was still reeling in the aftershocks and the gaping abyss of silence.

He looked at the broken man in the bed. Would Hank choose to recover?

'That saying of someday you're going to do this, or that, or stop this habit to do that?' Jax said, and Hank stared up at him with hollow eyes. The eyes of a man who'd been through hell.

Jax knew that place well, having danced in the devil's world of flame. Too. Many. Times.

'Today is as good as any place to make that someday today. And they say to start something new you've got let go of something old to make room for you to grow. You just have to be willing to do it.' Jax pulled out a small phone from his pocket and dropped it on the bed in front of Hank. 'That's a rechargeable phone with fifty dollars' worth of credit on there. The first number is mine. Call me if you want to take the deal, and I'll come pick you up when you get discharged.

The choice is yours.' Jax pointed at the phone and said, 'The other number in that phone, I suggest you ring today.'

'Who am I calling?'

'Your sister.' Jax stopped at the open doorway to survey the sterile room. 'I remember how I felt when I got the phone call and found my brother in hospital after he'd disappeared on a binge. He died holding my hand. Don't do that to your sister. She's family. They care.'

'She loves you, you know that,' called out Hank.

Jax frowned at him. 'What?'

'Lucy loves you. I can see it. You make her smile and give her this inner confidence that helped her out of that shy shell of hers. She listens and learns from you.'

Jax frowned at Hank. What the hell was he supposed to say to that? Approve it? Deny it? Hate the woman who'd kept secrets from him?

'It's true,' said Hank, 'Lucy is in love with you.'

'Lucy only ever called us frenemies.' Enemies who only *pretended* to be friends.

Jax gave Hank a curt nod and left the room. At the front entrance, he slid on his sunglasses, bracing himself for the day's heat.

As the sliding doors opened, Hank's voice carried down the corridor. 'Hello, Trace? It's Hank...'

TWENTY-SEVEN

Inside the unofficial Elsie Creek Inn, Lucy fidgeted at the kitchen table where Rigsy put a coffee cup in front of her and said, 'You'll put a hole through Monet's floor if you keep tapping away like that.'

'I'm nervous,' Lucy replied.

'No kidding.' Rigsy chuckled, taking a seat opposite.

'I've never raced or cooked in front of everyone.' Today was the Billabong Barbie Bake-off. It terrified her. 'Are you sure you'll be safe being my co-pilot? You should drive.'

'Nope. You've got your licence now, you can do it,' said Rigsy, sipping his coffee, staring at the back garden. 'Ah, Lucy, you might wanna check this out.'

'What?'

'We've got visitors.' He grabbed his hat, and headed outside.

'Who?' She caught the screen door before it shut and peered out to the cracked concrete driveway. Covered in a thick layer of red dust was the large four-wheeled-drive ute stopping beside the house. Its thick aerials waved in the wind, with fishing rods in their holders and spotlights strapped across the solid bull bar. It towed a horse float, with cattle dogs barking in the cage on the back.

'Oh, my god, it's my parents.' Lucy covered her mouth as tears blurred her vision.

'There's my girl.' It was her dad, with his sweat-stained Akubra and his wide smile deepening the creases in his leathery, suntanned skin. Only a few flecks of greys started to show in his hair and five o'clock shadow on his chin. But he was still the biggest man in her world.

'Dad.' She hugged him so hard and couldn't stop crying. She was that little girl all over again, wishing he'd take away all her pain.

'Oi, where's my cuddle, chicken,' her mother said, coming up behind her.

'Double cuddle for you, Mum.' Lucy held her parents tight, feeling like the luckiest kid in the world. 'What are you doing here?'

'Your letter,' said her mother. 'You told us you were entering the Barbie Bake-off, so we're here to see you win.'

'I'm freaking right out,' she admitted.

'Told you she would be, luv.' Her dad nodded, then faced the young man. 'Rigsy, right?'

'Yes, sir.' Rigsy stepped forward with hand outstretched.

'Ron's the name,' Lucy's dad said, shaking Rigsy's hand, 'and that fine lady there is my wife, Queen Elizabeth.

'Just call me Lizzie, luv,' said Lucy's mother.

'Could you give us a hand with the horses, mate?' Ron asked Rigsy.

'You're staying?' Lucy asked.

'Muster's over for the wet. We've got nowhere we'd rather be at the moment and thought we'd give you a hand,' said her father, lowering the back of the horse float. It was the same horse float, and ute, with the cattle dogs on the back.

Like an ingrained habit, Lucy grabbed a bucket and hose as her mum unclipped the dogs from the ute. The stocky blue and red cattle dogs bounded off the back, sniffing around the big tree that overshadowed the yard.

'Chicken, your father and I are also here to help you with the Tea House,' said Lizzie, sorting out the dog's leads and bowls. 'Your father's always been good with the tools, and I don't mind washing dishes and serving customers.'

'It's not going to happen,' said Lucy quietly, dropping her head to her chest.

'Why the bloody hell not?' Ron demanded, with a pair of horses stopping behind him.

'I'll take care of the horses while you explain, Lucy,' volunteered Rigsy. He walked the horses to the holding yard near the stables, brushed them down, watered and fed them. The dogs rolled in the grass and played in the water trough, while Lucy explained all to her parents.

'A whole train, in the middle of the scrub?' Ron asked, thumbing up the brim of his Akubra and Lucy nodded. 'All of your snow globes—sold,'

'Sorry, Dad.' After all, her father had bought most of them for her. 'I had to do it.'

'I get why, I do.' Ron said, giving her shoulder a fatherly squeeze. 'How big is this croc in that fella's dam?'

'Big,' said Rigsy, joining them. 'I'll take your bags or swag inside, if you'd like, sir?'

Her dad arched his eyebrow at the lad. 'Are you the unofficial bellboy of this Inn, eh?'

'Dad, Rigsy is dying to work with you one day.' She'd never seen Rigsy suck up like this.

Rigsy removed his Akubra and held it to his chest and said, 'Only if you have the time, sir, it'd be an honour.'

How could her father refuse that look from Rigsy? Lucy too put on a pleading face for her friend. She'd never interfered with her father and his crew, that was his domain.

Ron eyeballed Rigsy then Lucy, asking, 'Is he all right, Lucy my luv? Not another lost boy, is he?'

'No, I'll vouch for him.' She bit her lower lip, just as nervous as Rigsy, because she'd never done that for anyone before. Well, Jax was the first man she'd ever recommended for a job. 'Dad, Rigsy's been there for me. He's made sure I never walked home alone whenever I worked late in the pub's kitchen. It was Rigsy who stood up for me when the stockmen found out I'd been doing the cooking.'

Rigsy's blush deepened as he shuffled his boots, concentrating hard at something on the ground.

'Aw, he's so cute,' said Lizzie, wrapping her arm around Lucy's. 'Go on, luv, give the lad a go, if Lucy's vouched for him.'

Her dad sighed, crossing his arms over his solid chest, with his steely blue eyes narrowed at Rigsy. It was the same look he'd wear when working cattle in the yards, sorting out the stock. Her dad could read cattle, and control a herd.

Most of all, the man could read men.

Her father was legendary for not only sorting out cattle, but he could sort out the men from the boys, creating efficient crews. It was his gift in finding the potential when the few could see it within themselves.

'All right, give your details to the secretary and when and if something comes up, we'll call you,' said Ron in a well-used speech.

Rigsy began to breathe again.

'Now, what the bloody hell is that jalopy?' Ron pointed to the car, where the wind had blown up a corner of the tarp. He pulled the covering back to reveal a tiny, two-door ute painted pink. It had eyelashes painted on the bonnet around the headlights for eyes, and a bright red lipstick smile stuck onto the bull bar. 'That's gotta be the smallest ute I've ever seen. Is the circus missing their clown's car?'

'It's a jumbuck,' said Lucy.

'Who does that belong to? It smells freshly painted.'

'It's Lucy's,' said Rigsy with a grin.

'It's on loan for the race,' said Lucy. It was the big surprise she'd been given from her teammates, painting it at Kat's she-shed, while working on today's game plan.

'Oh, hey, I finally got my driver's licence,' Lucy announced to her parents.

'Oh, you passed a test! Congratulations, chicken,' said Lizzie, hugging Lucy again.

'Took ya long enough,' Ron said, when Lizzie thumped him on the arm. 'What? It's just a piece of paper, when the girl's been driving since she was seven. Talking about fancy overpriced paperwork, is this thing registered?' He pointed to the tiny pink ute.

'It's got a permit for the race. Kat and her husband, Kyle organised it. Rigsy's volunteered to be my co-pilot, but I've been trying to talk him into driving.'

'Why, chicken? You're a good driver,' said Lizzie.

'She should be, I bloody well taught her.' Ron then asked Rigsy, 'So, you want to work for me, do ya, mate?'

'Yes, sir.'

'Do me a favour?'

'Anything, sir?'

'Let me be co-pilot for my little girl in the race.'

'Dad!'

'Thank you, sir,' said Rigsy, even more relieved than before.

'You're not scared of my driving, are you?' Lucy asked their resident couch-surfing cowboy.

'No. It's just that Monet and I've got stuff planned for the race.'

'You're not the young fella who got his bum stuck in the window of Monet's plane mooning the world, are you?' Lizzie asked.

Rigsy dropped his head, and his blush returned with a vengeance.

'Boys will be boys.' Ron chuckled, dropping his big hand on Rigsy's shoulder. 'Mate, I reckon we'll get along just fine.' He then rubbed his hands together. 'How about we have a cuppa and you tell us your plan for this race?'

'If your father's going, can I come too, chicken?'

'If you don't mind riding on the back, Mum?'

'Absolutely. So, where's the kettle, the same place I presume?' Lizzie asked, heading for the kitchen.

Rigsy opened the door for her. 'I'll give you a hand.'

'Thank you, Rigsy,' Lizzie said inside the kitchen. 'You still haven't replaced the oven in this place, yet?'

'We've never needed one,' Lucy called out. 'Might be safer for this household if we didn't.'

'Lucy-my-love, people have been burning biscuits for thousands of years. It happens,' said Ron, dropping his arm around his daughter's shoulders and giving her a tender squeeze. 'What your mum and I can't work out is why you're burning your food all the time, when you never did with us.'

Lucy shrugged. 'Bad luck, I guess. That's why I don't want to do this competition.'

'Listen, we're here to see you win.'

'And if I lose and fall into a screaming heap after I've set fire to the world —'

'I'll play fireman to help stamp out the fire.'

Her heart squeezed. She'd had a fireman, who was a really nice guy, and she'd ruined it.

'Then I'd buy you a beer and tell you there's always next year. I'm proud of you just for trying.'

'You are?'

'I've always been proud of you. To be your own boss. It's something I never did.'

'How come?'

'I like walking away, having holiday pay, and not worrying about the stresses owners have. We get to see the countryside. But you, you're happy here. Being your own boss, that's gutsy.'

'It didn't happen.'

'What's the first thing I tell them boys about breaking in horses?'

'It's not a race but a marathon.'

'That's what business is and we both know there are more ways than one to skin a scrub-hen. Listen, if it's what you want, you'll find a way. That's why this race is important for you.'

Great, here comes the life lesson, she'd heard him say to his lost boys. Although, it was rarely aimed at her.

Her dad lifted her chin to face him.

'Regardless if you win or don't win, do this for yourself. Not for the town, for you. And I'll back you up every step of the way.'

TWENTY-EIGHT

Lucy sat behind the steering wheel of the tiny pink ute, with her dad in the passenger seat. Her mother, with Kat, Karen, and Verily stood on the back in their softball uniforms and helmets, with the addition of tutus and war paint, cheering with the crowd. The rest of their softball team wore the same, along with their permanent mini cheersquad, their children, bashing their drums and blowing their whistles, with war paint, team shirts and tutus. They were as loud and proud as if they were on the softball field, except now they were lined up along the main street of town, ready for the race.

'You could have worn the tutu to be a part of the team, Dad?' Lucy said, wearing her Dusty Dingoes' softball uniform with a bright pink tutu.

'Nick off. It would've interfered with my aim,' he said, holding up a large water gun with two more cannons at his feet. 'I like that Rigsy lad and his stash.'

'You stole his seat.'

'He's got a better offer, hanging out with lil' Miss Trouble,' he said, pointing to the skies where Monet's red plane with the straw broom painted on its underbelly circled above. 'Now, let me get this right, we've got to drive around town as the first part of this bake-off barbie thing. The town isn't that big for a race,' he said, holding up a small-town map.

'It's a race to find enough food to cook a three-course meal in two hours. We have no clue as to what food they'll supply, but it's less at each stop to eliminate the competitors. It's like musical chairs, you take away the chair and the last one standing is out of the race, except it's done with the humble portable ice-cooling esky, not chairs.'

'Gotcha. So, what's with the pit crew?' He asked, thumbing back to the women in tutus, on the back of their ute. 'Your mother is loving this.' Both laughing at Lizzie, shouting with the rest of their passengers, wearing a tutu over her jeans.

'The reason we have friends with us is, it's their job to slow down the opposition so we can get to the food first. The better the supplies, the better the dishes, the more chances at winning the final taste test. But first, we need to win this part scavenging for food to cook with, then race to the barbecue at the billabong. They only have six barbecues, so if we're too slow, we miss out.'

'How did Nancy do this if she's an old woman?'

'Dad.'

'What? She's old. What else am I meant to call her?'

'Nancy's a speed demon behind the wheel. She hires kids to do the running for the smash-and-grabs at the designated stops while she drives.'

'Are you expecting me to run?'

'No. You're guarding the car, I'll run, but, according to Molly and her brolly, she's Verily's Aunt—'

'The Olympic pitcher,' he said, thumbing to the back window.

'Yes, and our batting coach, Agnes,' explained Lucy, pointing to Agnes standing with Aunty Bea and Molly shading them all with a large pink umbrella that matched Molly's dress. They stood behind supermum Karen's tutu-wearing tribe of boys cheering them from the side of the road. 'They told us that Nancy always knew what the key ingredients were before the race began to plan her menu. She knew exactly what post office box had the steak, and what water trough held the fish.'

'So this Nancy had inside information?'

'Yes. She cheated.'

'Want me to tell your mum to go bop her one.'

'No, Nancy's an old woman.'

Her dad chuckled at her. 'So, what's that lot of tutu-wearing-yahoos got planned for Nasty Nancy?'

'Agnes and Molly asked the judges for a secret drawer last night, which most agreed to. The judges did a lucky dip for the name of an ingredient and one secret spot to hide their food eskies, and they couldn't tell anyone else.'

'Which means?'

'None of the judges know what the other ingredients are or where the food is going to be hidden. Nancy can't cheat this time.'

'Still want me to mention it your mum to bop her one?'

'No. I want to beat Nancy fair and square—*if* I don't burn everything, and *if* we get the ingredients, and *if* we make it in time to score a barbecue.'

He patted her hand, which was resting on the gear stick. 'She'll be right, luv.'

A noisy police siren got everyone's attention in the centre of town, where Marcus stood with a megaphone that he passed to another man.

'Who's that fella?' Ron asked from the passenger seat.

'Our town mayor. He's the owner of our supermarket,' replied Lucy, gripping the steering wheel. This waiting to race was killing her.

'I'm talking about that beefy cop. He looks familiar.'

'That's Marcus, and you do know him. He told me he worked with you one summer.'

Ron wiped the tip of his nose as his eyes narrowed through the windscreen. 'Not another lost boy sent out to behave, was he? Must've done my job right, if he's a coppa.'

'Was I ever a lost boy, Dad, like in Peter Pan?' She felt lost.

'No way, you were their Wendy,' he said, patting her hand again. 'Those lost boys behaved around you.'

'Only because you scared the absolute living daylight out of them.'

'That's my job,' he said with a chuckle, raising his colossal water cannons.

'*Racers, in position,*' shouted the mayor.

'Get ready, Lucy-my-love. We're about to have the race of our lives.'

Lucy couldn't swallow, only gripped the steering wheel tighter. Could she really do this?

TWENTY-NINE

Over two dozen outdated 2WD cars, vans, and utes, stood in a row on the main street of town. They were spray-painted in various colours, with stickers, toys, and other wacky paraphernalia resembling cars in a comedy street parade. Their passengers were just as colourful in their various disguises to match.

Softballers wore their game day uniforms with pink tutus that matched the tiny pink ute. Reams of pink frills covered its wheel arches, making them look like tutus. It worked perfectly with the fake eyelashes around the headlights and the bull bar's painted on smile.

The stockmen's team were dressed like pub-crawling yobbos. Bright streaks of sunscreen were slashed across their noses, barely shaded by their terry-towelling bucket hats. In thongs, the original stubbie shorts, and blue singlets, they proudly showed off their pillow-padded beer bellies. Their old Holden Kingswood was adorned with twin Australian flags waving off the front bull bar. They had a surfboard strapped to the roof rack beside a beach umbrella and a manikin wearing a bikini seated in a fold up chair. It was like they were heading to the beach instead of a race.

Nancy wore an army general's dress uniform with her young runners dressed like toy soldiers. It suited her VW painted in Army camouflage colours. Along the roof was a row of smiling garden gnomes, repainted as mini-soldiers going to war. It was scary.

The footballers wore their team's uniforms and painted their old Toyota Corolla the same colour. The local bush school teachers wore old fashioned scholar's robes, their car covered in old books and pages glued onto its panels with a large paper-mâché' apple on the bonnet.

The fishermen's team chariot of choice was a minivan they'd painted like an underwater river scene, with crocodiles, turtles, and other aquatic creatures. Its passengers were dressed like ugly mermaids, with long blonde wigs and beards. Their bikini tops were made from halved coconut cups that matched their hairy chests. On the roof, they had a small punt, where two fishermen sat in life jackets with their fishing rods in hand, ready to race.

Big Jimmy, the caveman, stood a head taller than the crowd, leading his team of mechanics with his brother, Kyle, behind the steering wheel. Dressed like a cross between the Flintstones and Vikings, their black Valiant Charger looked like it had crawled out of a Mad Max movie. Welded to the car roof was a faux-fur covered couch as a throne for the caveman. A set of fibre glass dinosaur horns curled up from the bonnet, it matched the horns the men wore on their helmets. They even had Cecil, the water buffalo, as their ribbon-wearing mascot.

The rest of the town lined the main street, cheering on their favourite teams as they got into position and waited for the start.

'On your marks….' Called out the mayor over the megaphone. 'Get set…' He lifted the air pistol as a row of miners on either side of the road aimed long red sticks at the street.

'Hey, those miners have got monkey's powder,' said Lucy's father, Ron. He pointed to the crew in painted hard hats with beer cans attached on either side, which they drank through a straw.

'Not dynamite, or flares, or…' Lucy's hands were sweaty, and it was like the world froze as perspiration trickled down the side of her face. She could hear herself breathing. It competed with her heart beating even louder in her ears.

Was it too late to back out?

'GO!' The starter gun went off, and the miners popped the caps of their candles, igniting flares that unleashed blue, yellow, red, and green smoke onto the street. It was impossible to see as flour bombs, rainbow coloured chalk, and water balloons were thrown at the competing cars kangaroo-hopping down the main street.

It sucked that her driver's window wouldn't wind up fast enough!

Lucy just floored it, more to get away from the rain of chalky flour bombs and coloured smoke. She couldn't see the shops at all. But her floury lips were sticky with a claggy-glue like the kind she'd made as a pre-schooler. Thick, gluggy, and tasteless.

'What's the first step?' Ron called out over the noise as the car was bombarded with weighty thuds of exploding water balloons and flour bombs.

'We head for the town's sign on the way to Kakadu. It's where I did my driving test. Dad, shoot the windscreen, I can't see.' Would her tastebuds recover from the flour flavour in the back of her throat? Should she ask her dad to shoot at her mouth too?

Ron half-heaved himself out the passenger's window and aimed his water pistols at the windshield. The windscreen wipers smeared the flour and water into a pancake batter.

Lucy drove with her head out of the window allowing the warm humidity to blow dry the coloured flour from her skin.

Was she really doing this?

Driving. In a race?

With her dad?

They followed the crowd to the large *Welcome to Elsie Creek* sign where oversized envelopes hung from bright ribbons. Each car stopped and grabbed an envelope.

The fisherman cast their Barra lure from their boat on top of the minivan, snagging an envelope, reeling it in without even stopping.

'I like that mob,' said Ron, pointing to the fisho's van with its ugly mermaids waving out the windows, now in the lead.

Lucy didn't look at any of them, focusing only on the nearest prize swinging on the flimsiest of ribbons. She snatched up an envelope, ran back with heavy legs, tossing the letter at her dad as she followed the other cars. *Don't think, just do.* 'Read it, Dad. Where to next?'

'It says, go to a place where snails are never mailed — that'd be the post office, right?'

'Every year.' She slammed through the gears, chasing the racers ahead of her. They drove back into town where the spectators waited with coloured powder usually seen at city fun runs, along with reams of crazy string, and endless water balloons.

Lucy was drenched by the time she'd left the car and climbed the steps to the post office boxes, but her pink tutu kept its shape, even if they'd caked her in crap. Wiping thick muck from her eyes, spitting tasteless flour from her mouth. Her nostrils were blocked with her ears no better. She would never be able to look at a cake batter the same after this.

But she'd made it. So, where was her father?

Up the steps, her dad strolled through the pack without a single skerrick of coloured powder and not one drop of water touching him. Many of the men tipped their hats at him as he shook hands with long-lost friends.

'Daaaad.'

'Excuse me mate, I've got a race to win. We'll have a beer later,' said Ron, patting the cattleman he'd been talking to on the shoulder. 'God, you look a fright.'

How did he do that? Her dad was spotless, and they'd covered her in enough coloured powder to make her own rainbow to slide across to Sydney. 'We search the boxes until we find one that opens and has food.'

'I'll take the left. You take the right. We'll meet in the middle.' Along with everyone else, they shouldered their way through the crowd.

'Lucy, what's this?' Ron called out, holding out a brown paper parcel.

With desperate hands, she ripped open the package like a kid at Christmas. 'Yesss!' No toy soldier or doll—but much better. 'It's flour, salt, baking soda and other dry goods.' This was a great start. 'Now we need the next clue' With her nails, she tried to pull open the small doors of the individual post boxes. The miners used pocket knives, the fishermen used long-nosed pliers, and the Vikings used wire, while she only had her fingernails.

'Yeessss. We scored,' called out one of the bogan's holding up two envelopes. Then the Vikings held up their envelope and pounded their chests like cavemen. In the small area that housed the post boxes, the victory roars from the men were frightening.

'Two envelopes,' said a fisherman to the bogan. 'We'll buy it off you.'

'Nah, that'll go to the little lady,' said the bogan covered in so much rainbow powder, you couldn't tell what was skin or clothes. 'My money is on you for the queen's crown, Miss Lucy. Tell your dad, I said g'day.'

'I will.' It was that same stockman she'd seen most mornings at the stockman's shed when she provided breakfast on train days. *Who the hell was he?* 'Thank you.' She tapped her dad on the shoulder. 'Come on, Dad, let's go.'

She ran back to the pink ute and climbed in behind the wheel. 'Dad, that guy says g'day.' She pointed to him, and he saluted back as he clambered into the car full of bogans with their Aussie flag and surfboard.

Dad tapped the brim of his hat with a curt nod at the guy. 'I remember that fella.'

'I don't.' But she didn't have time to dwell on it right now. 'Can you read out the clue for where we're going next?'

As she drove through the water bombers, her teammates and her mother shot back with their water cannons as if they were an armed escort. They were having a ball. She had to smile as she watched them in her rear-view mirror.

Ron tore open the envelope and read from the letter. 'A tiny figure with a long shadow that gets guarded by the plovers in the place where the movie night will never happen. What?' Ron screwed his face up.

'The town statue. It's in the park where the Flynn brothers are always promising to hold their movie night, but everyone knows it'll never happen.'

'Who's the statue of?'

'No idea.' She drove down the street, the competition thinning out as many were still playing lucky dip at the mailboxes. Nancy was in the front, neck and neck with the caveman's crew.

Lucy parked on the side of the road near the town's park. Her tutu-wearing teammates and her mother cheered her on.

Lucy sprinted toward the statue where a group of eskies waited at its base. She opened the lid to find cheese, milk, and eggs on ice. 'It's the dairy goods.' She tried to lift it, but it was so heavy she had to drag it back to the car.

'Here, Miss Lucy, allow me,' said the caveman, Jimmy, who hoisted it effortlessly onto his shoulder while carrying the other esky on his hip like a handbag.

'But—but—' Lucy craned her neck to face big Jimmy, who was defending his title as king.

'Tell your dad, I said g'day.' Big Jimmy put the esky in the back of her tiny jumbuck. He saluted his sister-in-law, Kat, who kissed him on the cheek, and climbed onto his throne on the roof of his car. His brother, Kyle blew a kiss to his wife, Kat, as he drove their Dinosaur-Mad-Max-mobile away.

Nancy was already well ahead with the rest of the field catching up fast.

'Dad, there's an advantage to having you here,' Lucy said, clambering into her seat and passing him the next envelope as she chased the leading cars.

'Yeah, why's that,' he asked, ripping open the envelope.

'These men are helping me, and telling me to say hello to you.'

'Must've been another lost boy, eh?' He winked at her.

It was then she realised it.

And her car slowed down…

'The reason they're so scared of you,' she said to her father, 'was that those boys who came out, they weren't there to work, they were there for you to sort them out. You were like a prison warden.'

'There's no prison out there. I was just a contractor managing the musters.'

'But all those lost boys you'd trained over the years…' There were different boys, every season, from all over the country, arriving in a tiny bush plane that would leave them stranded on the simple dirt airstrip. Most of them were so angry to be there, stuck in the middle of nowhere, on a cattle station in a forgotten part of Australia. There they were told to wait.

With a sweat-stained Akubra shadowing his face, he was a daunting figure to meet alone, stranded under the haze of the noon day sun. Shouldering a stock whip, with shotguns holstered in his saddle, in command of two horses, his crocodile leather boots landed with a thud in the dust.

Big, and Territory tough, with skin like leather, he had a steely stare that stripped your soul's shields to expose all of your secrets, leaving you with nowhere to hide. He was a man who never backed down from man or beast. Wielding an unseen authority, he had the power to run fear along your spine with one simple question — *'Do you wanna live, or die out here?'* He'd say. *'If you wanna live, you listen to me.'*

Sure, they'd buck up and rebel, and her dad expected it, with a full arsenal of tricks to tame many wild beasts and boys. He'd work them hard, like men, from sunrise to sunset, training them to become part of a team that handled the outback's extreme elements to control cattle herds.

All those boys learned lots of harsh lessons on life, both internally and externally. They grew up and were so different when they left, promising to send her parents postcards now and again, telling them of their journeys in life. And they did. Every year, sacks of Christmas cards would arrive from all over. From parents telling them how much those boys had grown and what great things they were achieving in their lives.

The big man with the humble title of *the Station Hand* helped many families and many boys, who grew to become men.

It's how he became a legend.

'I'll admit, their parents paid me to put their heads on straight when their lads were going astray,' Ron said.

'That's why the scary reputation.'

'They're just boys who needed a bit of direction. Like some farmers needed a hand to work their lands. Those boys needed someone from the outside telling them how it is, with no bulldust. And boys being boys—'

'They needed someone willing to kick their arses.'

'And to teach them something as I handed them the reins of a wild horse or to help jump a crocodile.'

Which he did. The day those lost boys landed, their first lesson was to ride a horse, and his lessons were simple, *hold on tight and follow me back to camp.*

'You helped all of those lost boys.' Who were friends, brothers, husbands, fathers.

'Always. Just like you've helped people in this town, like that Hank. I'm proud of you.'

'Why? How—what?' She stopped the car.

'Because, you've been doing the same as I do, but in this town, watching over this train station, as the Station Hand's daughter.'

It was a title she used to be ashamed of, this shadow she'd been trying to escape from. Were those men calling her that out of respect?

They never teased her, it was just said, most with a slight nod of their Akubras. A nod of respect.

They respected her.

Like they respected her father.

She really was his daughter.

'Thanks, Dad.' She reached over and hugged him.

'So, are we going to the pub and calling it quits, or are we gonna win this thing?' Ron asked, holding up the next set of instructions as the women on the back of the ute tapped on the roof.

Could she really do this? 'Where to next?'

'Where the dingos dance in the winter dust and the rosellas jam the lands,' Ron read from the letter. 'I'm guessing we're talking about your softball team, the Dusty Dingoes?' He pointed to the back where Lucy's teammates, and her mother, were screaming at them to go.

'The home of the Rosella festival.' Lucy put the car into gear and yelled out the window. 'Hold on you lot, we're going country.'

'They're all going that way?' Ron pointed to the cars heading out of town, while Lucy steered around the back of the shops.

'And I know this town's bike tracks.' Lucy drove off the bitumen and down a dirt path near the school.

'Won't be a second.' She stopped and jumped out, pointing to the overhanging fruit from the leaning tree. 'Mum, do you think you can reach those Kakadu plums? Safely. I don't want anyone getting hurt climbing trees. Not today.' She grinned at Kat, both having shared that experience.

With the help of her teammates, and Ron, Lizzie climbed onto the ute's small roof and picked the overhanging Kakadu plums.

'I'll grab that pandanus heart.' Lucy pulled her knife from her bag behind the back seat that held all of her cooking utensils she'd need for today—if she made it in time. She ran for the bent pandanus and chopped at the stem of its pineapple nutty centre.

'Chicken, that's an early wild grape vine there, you've had some rain,' called out Lizzie.

Lucy spotted the vine. 'Not enough to fruit.'

'But you can still wrap your meat in the leaves for that unique flavour.'

'I forgot. Thanks, Mum.' Lucy tossed the spiky pandanus fruit into the rear of the ute, then dashed for the vine climbing the tree to pluck large green leaves.

'Now that you ladies have done your shopping, can we please go?' Ron said, from the passenger side of the ute.

'Everyone settled in?' Lucy passed the leaves to her mother to stash away their bush tucker, and they were soon tearing down the dirt track.

'You knew all this food was out here, didn't you?' Her father asked.

'I've been watching them for weeks as they ripened. I knew they were going to use the sports field eventually. It's practically the same spots every year, the hardware store, the post office, the sports grounds. I mean there's only so many places, right?' She talked calmly as the tiny pink car sped down the single bike track, kicking up a plume of red dust as it knocked down spear grass that stood taller than the car.

They passed towering ant mounds and fenced-in cattle. Wallabies bounded from either side of the bike track, but the tiny pink ute, with four women in tutus hanging off the back, squeezed through with ease.

It was just like she'd done countless times on the stations with her dad going spotlighting, doing a bore run, checking fences and firebreaks, she almost forgot they were racing.

Over the tiny hill, Lucy drove around a few spindly trees and they entered the dusty sports ground just as the competitors came in from the far side.

'The footy goals,' said Ron, pointing to the group of waiting eskies.

'I don't believe it' Lucy had now advanced to be among the top four cars.

'Floor it, kid.'

And she did. The tiny engine whined as the miniature ute lurched over the irrigation lip, bounced onto the oval, then skidded to a halt. She parked it as close as she could with the rest of the competitors coming in behind her. There were only nine eskies left. The elimination for supplies had begun.

'It's meat. Beef and kangaroo.' With the help of her dad, they put the second esky in the back. Their tiny ute was full. If she bounced it too hard, she'd lose her load and her tutu-loving support crew.

Adrenaline raced through her. Licking her dry lips, she dared to waste precious seconds to scout out the competition.

The crew of stockmen, dressed like yobbos, hollered in a victory dance as they held a roast over their heads like it was the crown jewels. The caveman responded, yodelling as he pounded his chest while standing on his throne on the chariot's roof, while the ugly mermaids hammered the side of their mini-van.

Her dad opened the letter for the next clue, climbing into the passenger seat. 'It says, it's where the coffee is brewed at dawn before the dust stirs for the day''

Lucy jumped in behind the steering wheel, thinking hard. The rest of the cars were also slowing down.

'Where do you get coffee in this town, there is no café,' Ron said.

'Oh yes, you can.' And she slammed the car in gear. 'Hold on you lot.' She tore out of the sports ground car park, crossed over the main highway and for the first time, Lucy was in the lead.

'Where are we going, Lucy, they're all following you? The stockmen and their surfboard are coming up fast.' Ron laughed, pointing at the umbrella on top of the yobbo's car that was turned inside out. Their bikini-wearing mannikin resembled a crash-test-dummy stuck in a wind tunnel as the flags fluttered at the front of their car.

'Of course, the stockmen would know where to go.' Her foot flat on the accelerator, the tiny engine whined louder as the speedometer's taco climbed. She glanced at her rear-view mirror, checking the crew in the back were wearing their helmets and harnesses, strapped to the rear tray, as the speed and shakes in the tiny pink ute intensified.

'Where are we going?' Ron asked.

'To the shed out back of the train station. It's where I had the coffee urn set up for the stockmen on train days.' The small pink ute with its lipstick smile on the front, rattled over the train line. It skipped across the gravel, then around to the dirt track, passing the deserted cattle pens. At the back shed, instead of men sleeping on their swags stretched across the veranda she saw eight eskies and a dozen envelopes taped to the roller door.

The stockmen, the cavemen, and the fishermen with their ugly mermaids, overtook Lucy's pink ute, with Nancy and her scary army of smiling gnomes right up her arse.

'No!' She was done being bullied. Done being pushed around. Lucy was not going to let Nancy win.

Lucy pulled on the handbrake and the ute's tiny wheels skidded to a stop, stirring up a plume of red dust. She dived out of her seat, leaving the driver's door open and engine running. She sprinted as if stealing softball bases, barely beating the group of miners to claim an esky, but she did it.

Lucy frowned when Nancy grinned at her from behind the wheel. It was the same creepy grin worn by the warpainted gnomes strapped to the roof of her car. Her runner, dressed like a toy soldier, was already dragging back his esky to Nancy's car as she gunned her engine.

Focus! Opening the esky's lid, Lucy discovered coffee, sugar, bush limes, rosellas and bananas. 'Desserts.'

She loaded up the ingredients into her tutu and, with the envelope clamped between her teeth, she ran back to the ute where her mother stored them safely. They didn't have much room left in their tiny pink jumbuck. They didn't have much time either. Her place in the lead was gone.

But she was still in the race and there was no way she'd quit now.

The ingredients she had on board weren't that unusual. The only edge Lucy had was the bush herbs she'd collected. Agnes, their rule-abiding softball coach, checked and triple checked the rule book over drinks in Kat's she-shed last night. Making sure it was okay to collect food found along the way. So how much food did the other competitors have stashed on the side of the road? How big was Nancy's stockpile?

Lucy had a chance to cheat, but she wasn't going to. Even if it meant losing, she'd do it with honour.

She still had a chance to win.

Back in the driver's seat, she handed her dad the envelope who read out the one sentence, 'What's faster than a fast-food joint?'

'Speedy! She's our team's pitcher who works at the drive-thru feedstore.' Lucy drove past the Tea House. Her foot decreased its pressure on the accelerator and her heart grew heavy at the sight of the darkened rooms. The potted palms were limp. A thick layer of red dust lay across the walkways and the front door mats. There were no lights on inside. No cars in the car park. The lawn that led to the main platform was a brittle grey, and the only bench seat on the platform was completely deserted.

Her dad plonked his callused working hand on hers as it rested on the gear stick. 'Lucy-my-love, there'll be other places to cook. Let's just focus on this race first. Come on, you're so close.'

'You're right, Dad,' she said, resuming her chase of the other competitors on the road ahead.

Over the train line, right at the pub and back down the main street. They turned left and barrelled through the wide-open shed doors at the rear of the hardware store. The Flynn Brothers waited to greet them in their leather aprons, and so were the knights of the round card-table.

The Triple J's called out to her, pointing to the wall of shelves, 'Miss Lucy, look.'

'Obvious much,' said Ron, chuckling from the passenger seat.

'At what?' Lucy faced an entire wall of shelves loaded with boxes and bags, wasting precious seconds on a treasure hunt.

Then she saw it and grinned. Dashing across the driveway, avoiding incoming cars, she climbed up the shelf and grabbed the box labelled *We love Lucy*. 'Eureka.'

'What is it?' Her father asked.

'Some herbs, lemon, garlic, seasonings, and breadcrumbs.' From the bottom, she pulled out a freezer bag, unzipped it and smiled. 'Red claw. We now have the entrée.' She passed the box to the party crew on the back of the ute and jumped into the car as Verily passed the envelope to Ron in the front.

'Let's go to the billabong, Dad.' She waved at the Triple J's who saluted her and she drove out of the shed.

'Have you got enough ingredients?' Ron asked, tearing open the envelope and unfolding the letter for the next clue.

'For what I want to cook, yes.'

'But the next clue says—'

'It doesn't matter, Dad. The rest is for the other competitors who've missed out. We have enough.' There was a snap and sizzle in her bones as an energy rose inside. Her hands began to tremble with anticipation as she gripped the steering wheel tighter.

'Are you sure?'

Was she sure?

Hell, yes! 'I've cooked with less going through Mum's old cookbook.' She reached under the seat to drag out her ragged edged, flour stained, CWA cookbook. 'For a month, twice a day, Jax made me do driving tests while searching for food on his property. We'd go through this book, trying to work out what to make from the fewest of ingredients we found on that day. It's how we trained for this, dragging Jax's barbecue around, while having fire safety lessons.' She missed Jax, the pain dulling her excitement. It sucked she'd hurt him. If she could roll back time and do it differently, she would. Sadly, it was too late now.

'Rigsy showed us your cooking show. You're like a little tv star.'

'No, I'm not. I only did it because of Hank. He suggested it, saying it'd help me get over my shyness. Then Jax helped me—' *do so much more.* Jax had given her the courage to do anything.

She hadn't gone near Jax, not since the day of the fire and the hurt she'd seen in his face at the hospital. It had crushed her she'd done that to him. She didn't blame Jax for hating her.

Nor had she seen Hank since he'd kicked her out of his hospital room that same day.

She sincerely hoped they were both okay, wishing she knew of a way to make it up to them. Would the money she'd earned from the sale of her snow globes be enough?

As her father would say, that was tomorrow's problem.

Right now, she had a race to finish and then the scariest part would begin — cooking in front of the entire town.

THIRTY

Only minutes from the town of Elsie Creek, shiny fire trucks stood beside police wagons and the highway patrol car in a flat open plain surrounded by the wilderness. Behind them was the wide billabong with various flowering wild lotus that led to a river bed of soft sand. There, scattered tents sold water, food and assorted beverages. In the middle of it all, stood six separate barbecues.

From the town's direction, a thick plume of red dust churned high into the air rose. Through the hazy heatwaves coming off the sunburnt land, a row of cars raced towards them.

'Here they come,' said Jax, standing beside Marcus. 'Hank, she's there.' He pointed to the tiniest pink ute tearing across the dried flood plain as if in its own land speed race. Four women hung off the back, wearing pink tutus the same colour as the ute wearing a lipstick smile.

Beside them was an old van with a boat on its roof carrying a load of cross-dressed mermen. A black car with dinosaur horns curling out from the bonnet, it carried a man seated on a throne on the roof. From the other side, an old Landcruiser covered in old tyres made a break for it.

'What are those guys driving?' Jax asked, pointing to the car with a ring of tyres wrapped around it's panels like you'd see on a tugboat in the harbour.

'It's a buffalo catcher,' said Marcus. 'Where is our flower-eating water buffalo?'

'Wallowing in the billabong. Did I sound like a local saying that?'

Marcus chuckled. 'Almost, mate. They're having a fat time.'

Monet's red plane, with the straw broom painted on its underbelly, zoomed low from above with Rigsy hanging out of the window. He opened a sack and it rained water balloons and coloured powder, showering the buffalo catchers' car. It completely swamped them.

'Damn, Monet would come in handy for bushfires,' said Marcus, pointing to the red plane circling back around. Loud rock music blared from the plane as she flew in low and Rigsy dumped another load on the group of cars tailing the leaders. All of them copped a dousing.

Meanwhile the leaders raced ahead.

A camouflage painted VW, overtook the fishermen, who threw coloured flour bombs. They were all at it, passengers throwing flour, water bombs, even eggs. It was a mess. All racing for the row of barbecues that stood on the edge of the billabong.

There were only six barbecues with eight cars racing for a position.

'It'll be close,' said Marcus as Jax filmed the race with others standing on the trucks and utes recording the event with their phones or cameras.

'Give it everything you've got, NOW YOU MOB,' called out a male's voice that carried across the dried flood plain.

'Oh no,' mumbled Marcus, removing his sunglasses to glare at the incoming cars.

'What?'

'I know that voice.'

'Yeah, so, it's a small town.'

'That is the voice of the Station Hand.' Marcus pointed to the tiny pink ute where the softballers in tutus threw large bags full of flour, water, and coloured powder.

They covered the yobbo's car with its Australian Flags still waving through the commotion. It was forced to slow down, giving the tiny jumbuck the edge to power through to claim the last remaining barbecue on the far end.

Marcus pointed to the pink ute where a man with a large Akubra got out of the passenger's seat. 'Mate, that's Lucy's old man.'

'Yeah, right.' Jax watched Lucy's father lift the women like they weighed nothing, easily hoisting the food eskies over his shoulder like they were empty. 'He's younger than I thought he'd be.' The man would be in his late forties with leathery suntanned skin, like all the other stockmen. In a pair of crocodile-leather boots, all those warnings about being chopped up and fed to crocodiles made him wonder. 'Is it true he has stock whips?' Jax asked Marcus.

'Yep, three of them, and that's Lucy's mum. She's got a couple of deadly sets of crossbows. Are you worried?'

'Me. Nah.'

'I would be,' Marcus said, chuckling as he headed toward Lucy's dad, shaking hands with the man. The guy was a celebrity surrounded by men, all with wide brimmed hats and boots.

Jax didn't own an Akubra, or the same boots as these guys. Neither did Hank, standing beside him. 'Are you ready to do this, Hank?'

'Yeah.' Tugging at his new shirt, Hank walked across the cracked flood plain where tiny dust clouds rose from each step of his new thongs.

The breeze whipped around them, pushing the heatwaves across the soil as more cars and the school bus arrived, stirring dust everywhere. Clouds on the distant horizon teased of rain. Some worried if it would hold until the cooking was over.

If it was Lucy cooking, she'd dance in the rain. Probably not in front of this crowd, though.

As other crews got themselves sorted out near the barbecues, allocated judges inspected their eskies to get ready for the next phase.

The townspeople dragged out assorted styles of eskies and ice boxes, fold-up chairs and umbrellas and set themselves up alongside the billabong as if spending a day at the beach. Women in ballgowns and gumboots chatted with softballers in tutus. Music rang out from a set of large speakers sitting on the back of a ute. Someone set up a cricket pitch and a volleyball net. Sunscreen was slathered, as kids threw water balloons, coloured powder, homemade flour bombs, and dust at each other, all of them were caked in dust.

The mood was high with lots of laughter shared.

Jax and Hank made their way through the crowds until he saw Lucy and stopped, unsure if to approach her at all, letting Hank go ahead.

*　　*　　*

'I'll get that for you, Miss Lucy,' Hank said, grabbing the esky from the back of her tiny ute.

Lucy whirled around recognising the voice, but there was no woolly beard and no wild hair. It was the same lanky frame and the eyes she recognised. 'Hank?'

'Hey, Lucy,' he said, putting down the esky by her small table.

'Should you be carrying that? You'd still have stitches.'

'I'm okay. I've got that Jenny monitoring me so I don't overdo it.'

'Really? Are you okay? Are you dating Jenny? Are those new clothes, and who gave you the haircut?' The questions spilled out of her.

'I'm not dating Jenny. We're just having a conversation, and taking it slow.'

'You look great.'

'Molly the hairdresser came and saw me, and well, her and Jenny gave me no choice. I even got kitted out with a whole new wardrobe from the women of this town.'

'They do that.' It was another reason she loved this town, proud they'd done this for Hank. 'I've got some money for you—'

'No, I won't take any money from you, not when I owe you so much. I don't know how I'll ever repay you.'

'I just want to see you happy. You look well.' *And sober.* 'Where are you staying?'

'Jax is letting me stay and help out at the farm until I figure out what I want to do.'

She double blinked, not expecting that. 'Where? In the house?'

'No, he's set me up in the shed.'

'Did you move into the studio?' Her smile grew at Hank's nod. That area was perfect for Hank.

Bless Jax. The man was a saint under all that black tribal ink and steely stare.

'We've moved my sculptures and cleaned out the train.'

'How do you feel about that?' It'd been Hank's home for years.

'Good,' said Hank with a smile. It was the smile of a man who'd had a decent night's sleep. The ghosts were still haunting him in the stature of his shoulders and the downturn of his eyes, but it was a huge improvement.

'There're no mozzies to worry about, or any crocs crashing the billabong,' Hank said. 'I even spoke with my sister.'

Tears formed as she hugged him, bursting with joy. 'I'm so happy for you.'

'I'm sorry for kicking you out of my room and what I said at the hospital, I was ashamed at what I'd done in not listening to you.'

'Hey, that's all in the past now, and I've got a barbecue to cook.'

'Good luck, we'll be watching you.'

'That's what makes this the scariest part.' How soon before they could start?

To kill her nerves and not watch the clock, she checked over her utensils and table again. She had tongs, whisk, knives, and chopping boards. A water container and buckets for washing her hands. Food eskies under the table. She slipped her apron on over her crusty clothes and tutu as the judges inspected her food supplies.

Yet something was missing from her table.

Knives were in place, recipe book, salt and pepper, fire extinguisher and fire blanket.

'I think you're missing something,' said Jax, putting a white box on the corner of the table.

'Jax?' Her stomach swirled, catching herself from reaching out to hug him, followed by a wave of sorrow for what she'd done. 'I—I—'

'Open it.'

She lifted back the lid and peeked inside. 'It's my snow globe.' Her favourite snow globe of the iconic Man from Snowy River. 'I'd sold this...'

'If I'd been quick enough, I might have gotten the rest.'

'But—I was raising money for you and Hank.'

'I will not accept any money from you, especially when you've done nothing wrong.'

'I lied to you. I saw how much it hurt you. I'm sorry.'

'Remember how I told you about my brother and I lied our skinny little butts off to the welfare officers about our parents?'

She could only nod as the tears blurred her vision.

'I get why you did it. You did it because you care. And, it's because of the extraordinary lengths you went to protect Hank, I asked him to stay with me. I know you didn't start that fire, Lucy. I also know you dropped in my application for the Fire Chief's position.'

He wasn't happy about it. 'Are you taking the job?'

'That depends on you.'

'I can picture you sitting out the back of the fire station watching planes land. That job is made for you and you're perfect for this town. You are what they need.'

'What do you need?'

She shrugged, holding her snow globe to her chest.

'I'm also sorry too.'

'For what?' Jax had nothing to be sorry for.

'Because I didn't listen to you. All those times you mentioned squatters and guests, you were talking about Hank. I was blind to it. I also didn't see the signs. Not only about Hank, but mostly about you and me. It scared me, no— it terrified me, losing someone I cared about. So, I'm sorry, for not telling you sooner how much you mean to—'

'This had better not be the fella Jax?' Ron said, poking up his Akubra's brim with a death look Lucy knew well.

'Dad, don't—' She jumped in front of Jax to shield him from her father.

'Aw, crap,' mumbled Jax behind her.

'MUUUUUMM!'

'Coming, chicken.'

'Chicken?' Jax chuckled behind her.

'Listen, here mate.'

'Dad, no.'

'I have every right. What is your intention with my daughter?'

'Stop it, Dad, that's none of your business.'

'Hey, hold on a second…' Ron stepped back, his eyes widening at Lucy. 'Jeez, your mother was right. You are in love with the fella.'

'Oh man,' she whined, covering her face as the heat radiated between her fingers.

'I'm in love with Lucy, too,' said Jax.

'You are?' She spun around to face Jax. 'But—but—we're frenemies, with benefits. Great benefits.'

'I do *not* need to hear this,' Ron grumbled.

'Come here.' Jax led Lucy away from the gathering crowd to the far edge of the billabong. In the middle of it wallowed Cecil with pink ribbons stuck to his horns.

'First, I will not accept any apologies because you have *nothing* to be sorry about,' Jax said. 'I also won't take any of that money you made from selling your snow globes.'

'But—but—'

'I want you to use that money on you. For your kitchen.'

'It's going to cost too much to repair the Tea House.'

'I'm not talking about the Tea House. I'm talking about you, owning your own kitchen in something this town needs that'll make everyone happy—especially you, and I want to take you to Melbourne to show you.'

'Me? In Melbourne. I'd freeze.'

'It's summer, I think you'll survive. I might even get you some surfing lessons.'

'Why?'

'I want to show you their food markets, for ideas. You said to Kat to think bigger. Well, I'm thinking the opposite in streamlining things, but first you need to win this competition to prove, not to the town you can do this, because I already know you can. You need to prove this to yourself,' Jax said, pointing to the row of barbecues where everyone had assembled.

'But—but—' Her dad had said the same thing.

'You can talk to me while you're cooking, we have time to plan. Hank can watch the place or Marcus will while we're away.'

'But—but—'

He stepped closer, cupping her face gently in his hands and said, 'I love you, Lucy.'

She gasped. 'You mean that?'

'I've told no one that before, except my family, and I want you to be a part of my family. You already feel like my family. You made me realise family isn't blood, it's a connection,' he said, with his thumb stroking her cheek. 'To me, there is no stronger bond than family. You are my family, and I want you to come home.'

'You do?' She blinked. Blinked again. Was she hearing right?

'I should warn you, I have this crazy chook who hogs my washing machine and a kitchen that doesn't have a stove. Yet, I'm hoping, on my trip to Melbourne I can buy this amazing cook the best oven I can find her.'

Sold! It burst from her chest, a glowing warmth that made the colours of the world so much brighter, bolder, and flashier, and Jax was at the centre of it all. Unable to contain herself she hugged her man and held him tight. No way was she ever letting him go.

Jax brought her in closer, chest to chest. Her arms around his strong shoulders, she breathed him in.

'So, do you think you're up for the challenge?' Jax asked her.

Oh, hell yeah, sign me up today. Instead, she cleared her throat and said, 'I might be, if you're willing to take your turn cooking.'

'Anytime you want a day off, I'll do it, but I'll always help as your kitchen hand, as long as you never lose that spark.'

'So you'll get to play fireman, huh?'

'Cupcake, it comes with the territory.' He leaned down, pressing his lips to hers, and kissed her, long and deliciously slow. 'I love you, Miss Lucy.'

'I love you more, Mr. Jax.' Settling in for another one of those knee trembling kisses.

A woman with a stopwatch in hand blew loud on her whistle. *'Five minutes before the cooking begins.'*

'Great, burst my bubble,' mumbled Lucy. 'I'd better get into position.'

'Oh, hey, have you seen this before?' Jax asked, pulling out a small piece of porcelain from his pocket and handing it to Lucy.

'No. What is it?'

'I found it inside the oven, wedged over the thermostat in the Tea House kitchen. Did you only burn your food when you cooked there?'

'All the time. I could never work out why. I'd follow the instructions and double-checked the temperature on the oven and everything. It cost me money.'

'How?'

'Nancy was always docking my wages every time I burned something.'

'That bitch,' Jax spat out with a ferocious scowl.

'What's going on? Why are you showing me this?'

'Did Nancy ever burn anything when she cooked?'

'No, it was perfect, every time.'

'Did you see Nancy cook with that oven? Those cakes and things?'

'Um, no. I'd tried to watch but I'd be busy getting the dining room sorted and Nancy kept her scone and her sponge recipes a secret.'

'Lucy, she was sabotaging the oven…' Jax explained all he'd learned from the publican, Billy and the Triple J's, and what the porcelain chock did to an oven.

'Nooo.' Lucy stormed across the sunburnt sands to Nancy's table. 'Oi, you!'

'Well look at little miss high and mighty—'

Lucy slammed down the white ceramic piece onto Nancy's spotless black barbecue plate. 'You boycotted my opening day at the Tea House under false pretences, but you also sabotaged the oven itself so I'd burn the food, docking my wages.'

'You burned things all the time.'

'Because you played with the thermostat making it ten degrees hotter, Jax explained to me what that thing does,' Lucy said, scowling at the woman as she pointed to the porcelain piece on the hotplate.

With an eggflip, Nancy flicked the chock into the dirt. 'Prove it.'

'You're a liar.'

'Prove it.'

'For years you told everyone you've been cooking for the stockmen in the back shed of the train station, when it's been me from the very beginning. You also took all the credit for the food for the police station. The hospital's staff parties. The Christmas cupcakes. Even the weekly morning tea for the Triple J's in the hardware store. That was all me!' said Lucy loud and clear. 'Why?'

'I don't have to flamin' answer to you, missy,' said Nancy, sticking out her chin.

'Why not? Is it because you used us for your tax dodge to run that place into the ground? Blaming me for everything that ever went wrong in that Tea House—when it was you who was too much of a tight arse to fix anything? It was your responsibility.'

'Well, ask yourself, once you get down off ya high and mighty horse, missy—how would you feel after you've worked the place for thirty years what the flamin' heck do you get to show for it? Nothing. Not even a birthday cake. I didn't want some upstart from some station stealing my shop from me.'

'You don't own it, the publican does. Another lie, like the ones you told to your friends telling them I'd poison them—which I'd never. I was using your menu. I was planning to carry on your legacy and your traditions. But there's no way in hell, I'll do anything that resembles you now.' Lucy snarled as she pointed at Nancy and said with lowered tone, 'This. Is. War. And I'm coming for your crown.'

Lucy was fuming. She forgot about the crowds. She forgot about the competition and stormed back to her barbecue space where Jax waited, grinning at her. 'What?'

'You look like you're ready to do this.'

'I'd rather go—'

'Places, everyone.' Hollered the mayor, raising the starter gun.

'Good luck, Lucy, I'll be right here, watching,' said Jax, holding up his camera.

'Oh, no…' She froze behind her barbecue staring at a sea of faces. It was the entire freaking town.

'Hey,' Jax said, grabbing her hands to face him. 'It's just like we practised. You, me, the barbecue and that manky looking billabong. I think the ones we've got at home are better.'

She looked up at Jax. Really looked at him, and at the way he looked at her—he believed in her. He cared for her, and said he loved her, just as much as she truly adored the man.

'You can do this, Lucy, so get busy while I tape this for your cooking show.'

'You're not, are you?' She touched her ratty hair, trying to dust away wet clumps of flour off her tutu.

'As long as it's only you in my lens, I'll never get tired of taping the view.'

'Aww, that was so corny.' They both laughed.

'Do you feel better? Have you got your focus back?'

'I have.'

'Good,' he said, kissing her temple and patting her on the bum. 'Now go get your crown.'

The starter gun went off and the cooking was underway.

* * *

Jax watched on in pride, taping the event, when a large shadow came up behind him. He guessed by the shape of the hat who it was.

Jax turned around and said, 'My name is Jax. I'm a fireman, a Captain, and have been offered the Chief's position here in Elsie Creek. Whether I accept the position will depend on Lucy.'

'Why? Lucy was the one who nominated you?' Ron asked.

'She also gave up her dream of the Tea House for me, and I'll only do what makes her happy.'

'I see.' Ron thumbed up the brim of his Akubra, exposing the grey flecks in his hair and the deep creases around his eyes.

Jax wasn't backing down, even if he'd never met a more formidable father. He'd raced into burning buildings for a living, yet this might be his biggest challenge ever. 'If there is anything you want to know, just ask?'

Ron stood tall, crossing strong arms over a broad chest. 'Okay then, what are you planning to do with that train by the billabong?'

'No idea.'

'I also hear you've got a big croc hanging around in your dam?'

'I do.'

'Do you need a hand to catch it?' Ron's grin grew as he pointed to the topless, sunburnt Landcruiser covered in old car tyres. 'We've got that ol' buff catcher there, and a whole mob of men who are willing to wrestle the bugger. Now, you see that bloke over there that Lucy can never remember, he's a professional croc wrangler and egg collector.'

'Yeah, right?' Jax was pretty sure they weren't talking about chicken eggs, but playing chicken with a crocodile.

'It's fair that I should warn you about that croc-catcher.'

'Why?'

'When he was younger, he was Lucy's first crush, and she followed him around like a puppy.'

'And now?'

'She doesn't recognise him because she's only got eyes for you,' Ron said, poking the air between them. 'That's how I know she loves you.'

'Heh-mmm.' Jax kept a straight face, when he wanted to shout it to the world. But he did have a crocodile problem. 'Do you want to catch that crocodile to make yourself a new set of boots?' Jax pointed to Ron's footwear.

'Lucy said it's missing a claw, it won't survive long in the wild, that's why it's in your dam. We can send it to the crocodile zoo in Darwin. Or, we can talk that smart little publican into keeping it at her pub as a tourist gimmick for the town. I'm sure we'll have enough men willing to donate their time and materials to build it a comfy pen to retire in. We'll just need to chase down the new ranger for a permit whenever she gets back from Kakadu.'

'Are you sure you're not setting me up to feed me to the thing?'

'Why? Lucy would kill me, not to mention what my wife would do. Come on, I'll shout you a beer while we watch my little girl win. I'll introduce you to the fellas.'

'Yeah, right.' Jax had a feeling this was going to be a baptism of fire.

'What are you going to farm out there?' Ron asked.

'No idea. Lucy says it has the potential for crop farming, cattle, or anything I wanted. You're welcome to come and check the place out, I'd value your opinion.'

'Why, when you've got my daughter who's better at the job than any of the blokes here.'

'Is that because she's the Station Hand's daughter?'

'Too right she is. But, if you ever need someone to keep an eye on the place we'll come and farm-sit for you and Lucy, anytime.'

'That'd be good.'

'Honeymoons are even better.'

'Erm, what—' Jax stumbled.

*　　*　　*

'Time,' cried the Mayor. 'Tongs down. Barbecues off. And step away from the hot plates.'

Lucy tucked her hands behind her back, biting her lip, staring at her served up dishes. *Were they good enough?*

Now it was up to the judges.

The group of six judges gathered around the first barbecue where the caveman, big Jimmy, stood a head taller.

He gave his spiel of his menu selection of roasted meats that had the men salivating.

The judges shifted to the next barbecue, tasting the food, asking questions of the chef. All while Cecil the water buffalo wallowed in the background, having a fat time in the billabong.

The judges moved toward Nancy who oozed extreme confidence presenting her usual dishes. Her perfect scones and roast beef rolls.

Lucy wanted to find fault in Nancy's food, but it was top class.

How dare Lucy think she could win against these contestants who'd produced amazing culinary masterpieces? She was so close to jumping into her little jumbuck and skipping town, but her parents, Monet, and her friends wouldn't let her. Especially Hank and Jax. They were all watching and waiting, supporting her like a family.

Her dad was right, it didn't matter if she won or not; it was the fact she was trying and had burned nothing. *Nothing.*

If anything, it had made Lucy mega-aware of her cooking processes, to never burn anything again. Nancy had taught her that, and how to whisk egg whites into a peak to fold into flour. How to slice bread perfectly for crustless cucumber sandwiches. She'd learned how to set a table with silverware polished so finely she'd smile at her own reflection. All the little things that went into serving the Tea House's version of a traditional high tea.

But it was a different kind of tradition Lucy fell in love with, not the rigidness of rules, it was the conversation with friends over a cup of tea and cakes, sharing stories.

She grew up sharing stories with strangers around campfires with her dad and the many lost boys who were now men.

The outback sisterhood was a highlight. Her friends who'd rallied around her to make this a wonderful adventure to get here. All who'd helped her and those who'd challenged her, they all had a part in her journey.

'Lucy,' said the first judge, approaching her.

Suddenly, a huge wave of nausea and fear washed over her. She froze on the spot when Jax came into view with his camera. This felt like a test.

'Why don't you explain what you've made, Lucy,' Jax asked, just like he did as producer and director of her cooking show.

She'd passed her driving test with Marcus on the deserted outback highway. She'd passed her next set of tests, winning food at each and every stop to win the last barbecue. She's passed lots of little tests all the time.

Her whole life was one big test, that would keep testing her every single day. Wasn't that what life was all about — testing herself to grow? And it was okay to make mistakes by burning the bottom of her scones, because that's how she learned.

And the person who'd taught her to accept that the most was Jax.

He was the one who gave her the confidence to dare face that fear of tests.

Fighting her terror, she took a deep breath and faced her next test, forcing herself to forget about the judges and focus only on Jax and his camera like normal.

She pointed to her dishes set on the table as she explained. 'For entrée, it's a bed of sautéed local warrigal greens tossed with roasted grated pandanus hearts, topped with skewered chilli red claw.' She pointed to the next plate and said, 'For the mains, its Kangaroo and bush pepper skinless sausages with a mash of wild cheeky yam and gravy. It's my version of the pub's favourite bangers and mash, accompanied with a Kakadu plum relish and a wood fire damper. For dessert, I baked a lemon myrtle and wattle seed shortbread as the base for mini fruit pizzas topped with cream, local berries, and barbecued bananas. I then drizzled a caramelised native honeysuckle water from flowering banksias…'

Lucy explained the cooking process of her dishes and the bush foods she'd foraged.

She explained why she chose the menu, even quoting the original dishes that were her inspiration from her CWA cookbook. Sure, she may have changed it a little, but the dish was originally created by other women in an Australian country kitchen who'd dared to share their recipes that she'd made into her own.

Just like she did on her show, it was just a conversation between herself and Jax, that now had over ten thousand followers, and an entire outback town.

Hank had started this, telling her it'd help her get over her shyness by standing before a camera.

Who knew it'd work?

There's no way she'd become some TV star. Lucy was the Station Hand's daughter, who loved to cook using what the land had to offer around her. This country was her home.

THIRTY-ONE

'Lights, camera…action. Now, Hank,' called out Jax with camera in hand as a row of party lights lit up the trailer. 'You can go to work now, cupcake.'

Lucy hugged the man with a wide smile she couldn't wipe away if she tried, the glint of her diamond ring sparkled from the party lights of her spacious coffee van attached to the back of the Tonka Truck. It was parked across the edge of the lawn area of the Elsie Creek Train Station. 'I have a food van.'

'The *Station Hand's Daughter's* pop-up coffee shop is now officially open for business,' said Jax with camera in hand. 'We should have gotten a bottle of champagne or something.'

'I've got one for later, until then we've got a lot to do for our official launch party.'

'We do. I've got our first batch of *Station Hand's Daughter's* bush herbs ready to deliver to Tess at the post office.'

'Do we have to keep saying the name,' she mumbled.

Jax nudged her softly. 'It's the brand, cupcake. It's all about branding these days.'

'Did we fill out all the orders?' Hank asked, approaching them from her van, carrying a round of coffees. He was quite the barista these days.

'All five hundred. With another two hundred orders already for next month,' said Jax, reading from his smartphone. 'Plus, a query from a specialty food chain to supply their stores. My lady is a star.'

'Am not,' she mumbled, feeling the heat curl up her neck to her ears.

'Are those store sales from your visit to Melbourne?' Hank asked.

'No, we just did a food tour, checking out the food vans, pop up restaurants, got engaged,' said Lucy, again admiring the sparkly rock on her finger. 'It's the best idea you ever had, Ironman.'

'I'm a genius, I know,' said the sexy fireman in his uniform. 'Then you can move to the trades area for their morning smoko.'

'Have monthly date-night dinners in romantic locations,' she said.

'The towns football games, the school's sports day, the Rosella Festival, and the Dusty Dingoes softball games.'

'We've got Christmas to get through first, the bookings are huge. Now if you'll excuse me, gentlemen, I'm off to find our friendly water buffalo.'

'I'll come with you,' said Jax.

They strolled the path passing the closed dark Tea House.

She smiled at Hank who gave her a wink as they walked by the platform's empty bench seat that used to be Hank's part-time home.

Along the darkened train tracks, they found the ribbon-wearing buffalo sniffing at the tiny white crosses on the side of the tracks. Lightning flashed beneath thickening thunderheads in the distance as dawn started awakening the alien terrain.

'Come on Cecil, your standard stable booking is just this way, good sir.' She held a bunch of daisies out and the water buffalo sniffed, his eyes widening. 'Remember to write your comments in the visitor's book, any time,' she said, leading the buffalo into his pen and closing him inside with a clang of the rail.

In the distance, children's singing carried on the slight morning breeze. They all peered into the darkness searching for the sound.

'Did you hear that?' Hank asked.

A ute parked on the far side of the cattle yards opened, music escaping from its interior as a stockman stood and stretched.

'Just music,' said Jax.

Lucy brushed down the goose bumps, then grabbed Jax's hand for courage. 'Mum's got the cousins coming to do a traditional smoking ceremony later. It's a good thing, Hank.'

'Hey, if you feel it's too much, mate, you know where I am,' Jax added.

'Thanks, but I said I'd give Miss Lucy a hand.'

'Only until Jenny arrives and then you can finally have that coffee date,' she said, grinning with hope for the guy who'd come a long way.

'Still trying to set me up with your friends, eh? She doesn't learn, does she,' said Hank, wandering back to the light of the station's main platform.

'Only because I want you to be happy like I am.' She smiled up at Jax, who kissed the tip of her nose.

'You two are soppy. Bah, I'll go water your pot plants and open the Tea House.'

'Do you think we scared him off,' Jax asked. Cattle murmurs stirred in the yards, as the outdoor light for the Station Master's house came on, spotlighting the Stock Inspector's vehicle.

'Hope not, Hank's been a great help around the farm, boxing up bush herbs with me and Mum.'

'Well, don't work too hard. Now, if you'll excuse me, I've got to start on my day job,' he said, brushing down his fireman's uniform that fit very well.

Sexiest fireman ever. Her fireman.

'I'll be back for the ceremony.'

'No worries. Can you flash your lights and sirens for me?'

'No,' Jax said with a chuckle, heading for the Fire Chief's truck parked beside the Tonka Truck he rarely drove these days.

'I've snuck a thermos of coffee in the cab for you to share with Marcus. Enjoy watching the planes.' She waved at Jax driving out in his shiny Fire Chief's truck.

Standing before her gleaming new food van with its rows of shining fairy lights, she could just hug herself. From letting go of her snow globes, those sales paid for the new.

She was her own boss.

Not just for the food van, but with lots of side ventures. Jax still managed the online business and her YouTube show as they continued to drag his barbecue with them to explore his property on his days off.

If not cooking, she'd walk the fields with her mother gathering bush herbs like she'd done all her life. Her dad helped her make plans to plant and produce more native herbal varieties on their property, as well as turning one of the many sheds into a small factory where they dried, packaged and sold their bush herbs online.

Jax's house renovations were complete, with the old washing machine and the red hen moved into the dingo-proof chook pen and a new flock of friends to boss around.

Hank, when not playing barista or helping on the farm, lived and created metallic masterpieces in the studio shed.

Her parents lived in the overseer's house a little further on the property with loads of room for dad's horses and the dogs. It was their home base should they ever leave to work another muster. Yet, the way her mum was enjoying Kat's candle making classes and her dad being so involved with the town, Lucy didn't think her parents were leaving anytime soon.

A line of stockmen started for the rainwater tank, as Lucy climbed into her van to greet her first customers. Stockmen mumbled their greetings. They all looked the same with their deeply suntanned faces and collared shirts, stiff with sweat and dust. Wide-brimmed hats shaded their eyes as they wiped away the sleep with work-hardened hands, ready to start the day.

She served them piping hot coffee and warm muffins, fresh from her small oven. She could cook anything on her grill and had a blackboard menu she loved changing so no two weeks were the same.

She loved train days. She loved Jax. And she loved being her own boss.

* * *

With the sun high in the sky, the stationary train overshadowed the Elsie Creek Station as the cattle were loaded. The lawned that ran between the Tea House, the platform and the car park was standing room only with a little space cleared in the middle.

The haunting sounds of an aboriginal man playing the digeridoo was accompanied by the skilled pitch in acoustics from the gumleaf player. The aboriginal women's rhythmic percussion of the hardwood clapping sticks carried the song of aboriginal men, women, and children as they coaxed the many small fires of smouldering ironwood leaves to fill the area with smoke. The traditional smoking ceremony was not only a blessing, but a cleansing to ward off bad spirits, encouraging spirits to move on and to make way for a better future for the people.

Hank stood in the centre as the aboriginal elder approached him with branches of smoking ironwood leaves, she carried in a tin. She was followed by two small children, a girl and boy who weaved around Hank covering him with the smoke. They then widened their circle spreading their smoke to all those who'd gathered in the heart of a town where it had all begun.

The smoking ceremony over, the small controlled fires continued to smoulder and the celebrations were underway. Standing on the platform, Jax watched on with Lucy. The lingering smoke reminded Jax of the steam when he'd first arrived at this station. Back then it was empty.

Today, the place was full.

It was as if the entire town had come to celebrate the re-opening of the Tea House museum. His vintage train had a new home, Lucy was ecstatic over her food van, and Hank could finally put his ghosts to rest.

Hooking his arm around Lucy's shoulders, his hand cupped that curl where the hairline met her slender neck and smiled down at her.

He had a new family. It didn't matter that they weren't flesh and blood, they were a family who put up with each other's faults, shared their fears and faced them together. The poorest man on the planet can be the richest man with the love of a family, that he in turn loved more. He felt like the richer man, every single day.

He'd learned that from his parents, and understood it more through Lucy. She was his family who'd helped him turn his house into a home, that was still an adventure playground for grownups, with the brotherly bucket list he continued to accomplish with Lucy. He'd even wrestled a crocodile, with Marcus and Lucy's dad, rescuing the beast living in his dam. He was living the dream.

'Hey, they tallied the votes, the Pub's pet crocodile will be named Karma,' Jax said to Lucy.

'Who came up with the name Karma the Croc? I like it.'

'Ahem.' A throat cleared behind them and Nancy dropped her bags onto the platform.

'I'll take them for you, ma'am,' said the conductor, collecting the suitcases. 'We leave in two minutes.'

'Have you got everything, Nancy?' Lucy asked her nemesis.

'Yeah,' she said, squinting her grey eyes over the tracks. 'I should have flamin' left this place a long time ago, not that I can stay with your mum around, eh, missy? She already tore strips off me for what I'd done to ya. And, um… I, ah…' Nancy shuffled in her shoes, wincing at the sunshine.

Lucy looked to Jax who shrugged at her. First they'd heard of it.

'Why did you stay so long if you didn't like the place?' She asked Nancy.

'I had nowhere else to go. It's why I pushed you so hard, hoping you'd leave too. All them flamin' snow globes you had, I assumed you wanted to travel.'

Lucy shook her head. 'You were wrong. I'd spent my entire life following Dad as he worked the musters. I was ready to stop and make a home, that's what this town means to me. Home is more than a place with four walls, it's this town.'

'And the people you share it with,' said Jax, giving Lucy a slight squeeze around her shoulders. She reciprocated with that sweet smile of hers.

Nancy held out a piece of paper to Lucy. 'So, um, here, I hope this'll make up for it. You can flamin' add that to your cookbook.'

'Who said anything about a cookbook?'

'Good idea,' said Jax. 'You've got plenty of recipes on the website now for a cookbook for the barbecue.'

Lucy's eyes widened as she read the scrawling handwritten message. 'You gave me your secret recipe for your scones and sponge?'

'I owe you for bein'…' Nancy's lower lip trembled and the sadness softened the lines of misery etched around her eyes.

'And I owe you,' said Lucy, pulling out a small crown from her bag. 'This is yours for teaching me. There's always next year to retain my title as queen of the Billabong Barbie Bake-off.' One of the proudest moments of Lucy's life, crying as she was crowned, while caked in all sorts of crap from the day. She'd stood beside the Caveman who'd retained his crown as king, in front of the entire town. The day her reputation as the kitchenhand who burned everything was buried for good.

Tears welled up in Nancy's grey eyes, as she held the crown to her chest. 'Look after the lil' miss for me, Jax.'

'Absolutely. Just like the lady spoils me,' he said, giving Lucy a squeeze around the shoulders.

Nancy took one last look at the town of Elsie Creek with its mighty pub and row of shops. She gazed past the platform to the Tea House's open bi-fold glass doors where women and men of all ages had gathered to admire the artworks from Hank, Kat, and other local artists.

The stockmen Nancy had once chased away with her broom now drank their coffee at the outdoor tables, shaded by large umbrellas on the lawn area.

The laughter of children carried across the lawn as they safely played within a fenced area containing the large vintage train they'd discovered by a billabong. Their parents sat nearby enjoying coffee and cake from Lucy's food van at the heart of an area that had once stood empty.

'I reckon I'll miss this place, but I doubt they'll ever flamin' miss me.' Nancy nodded and climbed onboard.

The train's horn blared as it slowly pulled away from the station. Many waved their goodbyes to the woman who ran the Elsie Creek Traditional Tea House for over thirty years.

It may have been the end of one tradition, but it was the start of a new one with Lucy's food van, and Jax's first official day as the town's new Fire Chief.

The train chugged towards Darwin like a snake sliding across desert sands, soon disappearing in the endless shimmering heat waves on the horizon.

Cecil, the water buffalo, wandered along the tracks in the opposite direction. His lime-green ribbons wrapped around his horns and tail, fluttered in the breeze. His sides were dressed in matching chalk with the words: *The Tea House Museum Reopens today & we have coffee!!*

He sniffed at the humid air where ash from the smoking ceremony floated like grey snow. Specks landed on fresh new shoots of grass peeking through the cracked soil that rested alongside the tracks.

Puddles of water reflected a monster skyline and the shadowy images of two small children. In shorts and t-shirt, the little boy adjusted his small baseball cap. His cheeky grin showed a tooth missing to the girl in a cotton dress. Her smile crinkled the freckles that scattered across her nose. She swiped at the strands, free from her blonde ponytail that bounced as she skipped up to the metal rail. A loose shoe lace from her tiny sneaker hung over the train rail, both children balancing on either side of the water buffalo. With a giggle, they held onto his horns. *'Come on, Cecil, come play…'*

When they reached across, latching onto each other's hands in front of the buffalo, forcing Cecil to stop as a wave of ironwood ceremony smoke washed over them. Like fine, willowy wisps the children faded to disappear into the clouds lightened from the rain. Their voices whispered on the wind, *'we're gonna be friends, and family forever…'*

Cecil stood in front of the two white crosses spotlighted by the sun peeking through the clouds. His black nose twitched at the slight breeze carrying the scents of dust, cattle, coffee, and the warmth of summer. Happy and excited children's voices filled the air, followed by the laughter of people, young and old. It was the voices of a small town.

As his black ears twitched and with a flick of his tail ribbons, he turned and crossed over the tracks. Beneath the outback sun, the water buffalo followed his shadow that stretched and shifted along a red dirt road that disappeared into the never-wherever of Northern Australia.

And that was the last time Cecil was ever seen wandering those train tracks again.

THE END

For now…

Did you like the story?

If so, *your opinion* matters to me!

I'd love to read your review on
GOODREADS, BOOKBUB.

I'd also be doing my own *dance-in-the-dust* if you shared your cover of this book on social media for me to see how far this story has travelled!

Please add ***#Escape2HEA*** for me to find you.

With much gratitude,

Mel.

MelAROWE.com

Thank you!

Thank you for reading this story of the fictitious town of *Elsie Creek.* She may not exist, yet there is a part of her found in the Northern Territory townships, roadhouses, dusty sports grounds, crocodile-crowded boat ramps, and even in the rural pubs sparsely scattered across northern Australia.

I had a lot of help with this one, so a big *thank you* goes to Tina Holt from Bushfires NT; Snr ACPO Glen Coonan; Aunty; and Tony 'Duwun' Lee of Larrakia Nation.

Thank you to the amazing *Handbrake* for not disowning me, and the rest of the family who have never read a word I've written, so I'm putting this right here in case they do dare to indulge.

Thank you to the writer friends I've met online who've helped me so much when I live in a world where finding decent Wi-Fi is like discovering gold. Thank you to my fabulous first readers team, I'm am truly blessed to have you join me in my writing journey.

Thank you to the quirky, colourful, and exceptionally extraordinary people I've met while working and living throughout northern Australia. The experience has been—and continues to be—priceless.

Thank you, because I can, because I did, and because I continue to do so…

Until next time,

Mel A. Rowe

MelAROWE.com

About the Author

Australian Bestselling Author, Mel A ROWE, creates escapes for you to enjoy from the comfort of home.

Delivered with a dash of drama, witty humour and quirky family units, Mel is known for reinventing romantic versions of *home*, taking her common characters on uncommon journeys that lead from boardrooms to billabongs as they try to find their own HAPPILY EVER AFTER.

Living in Northern Australia, Mel enjoys random outback road trips, fumbling with her camera, annoying her family with her bad singing, and making new friends in the middle of nowhere— except for water buffalos. She's been chased by a few.

Feel free to contact Mel as her word journey continues at…

MelAROWE.com